The Cedar Key

The Cedar Key

Stephenia H. McGee

Books by Stephenia H. McGee

Ironwood Plantation
The Whistle Walk
Heir of Hope
Missing Mercy
*Ironwood Series Set
*Get the entire series at a discounted price

The Accidental Spy Series
*Previously published as The Liberator Series
An Accidental Spy
A Dangerous Performance
A Daring Pursuit
*Accidental Spy Series Set
*Get the entire series at a discounted price

Stand Alone Titles
In His Eyes
Eternity Between Us

Time Travel
Her Place in Time
(Stand alone, but ties to Rosswood from The Accidental Spy Series)
The Hope of Christmas Past
(Stand alone, but ties to Belmont from In His Eyes)

Novellas
The Heart of Home
The Hope of Christmas Past

www.StepheniaMcGee.com
Sign up for my newsletter to be the first to see new cover
reveals and be notified of release dates
New newsletter subscribers receive a free book!
Get yours here
bookhip.com/QCZVKZ

Library Cataloging Data
Names: McGee, Stephenia H. (Stephenia H. McGee) 1983 –
Title: The Cedar Key/ Stephenia H. McGee
358p. 5.5 in. × 8.5 in. (13.97 cm × 21.59 cm)
Description: By The Vine Press digital eBook edition I By The Vine Press Trade paperback edition I Mississippi: By The Vine Press, 2020
Summary: Could the key to Casey's future be hidden in someone else's past?
Identifiers: LCCN: 2020941072I ISBN-13: 978-1-63564-052-6 (trade) I 978-1-63564-053-3 (ebk.)
1. Christian Fiction 2. Women's Fiction 3. Southern Contemporary 4. Small town contemporary 5. Southern Fiction 6. Religious Fiction 7. Family

For Momma
My storykeeper. Thank you for keeping the treasures and
the stories alive.

For Mamaw
For the canning, the quilts, marbles,
and all the laughter in between.
I'll miss you until we get to walk together again on the
streets of gold.

1

Inheritance

All the stories were gone.

Without the stories, I had a house full of other people's memories and no one to decode them.

Wind ruffled my disheveled hair as I stared up at the gingerbread molding on the house the lawyer proclaimed would be mine. The grand Victorian home stood large and stately, built during the era when people took more time and concern with craftsmanship. But this place couldn't be mine. The house was built for people like Ida, and I was still a stranger.

I hesitated on the sidewalk, the balmy spring day out of sorts with the heavy clouds hanging over my heart. I fiddled with the keys. I had to stay here. Like Ida had asked. Like I had promised.

Still, I couldn't move any closer. Stifled by the realization that, if I went in and found the house empty, it would mean Ida's death and funeral weren't a bad dream I could pretend didn't really happen.

Stupid. Ida was gone, and she wasn't coming back.

After thirty-five years, I'd found the grandmother I

would have loved to grow up with, had life been kinder. A woman full of stories, love, and life. A woman I'd been able to open my heart to even in the short time I'd known her.

But Ida's funeral two days before meant the stories that had first lured me to this tiny southern town had all been buried. The will gave me the keys to her house but not the truths I needed. I shoved the thought down and marched up the brick stairs and onto the wide wraparound porch. The key turned easily, and the door swung open.

One step over the threshold. Deep breath. Close the door. Ida had said a person could really only do one thing at a time—and that if I looked at each of my days as one step to take after another, I would find that things weren't as overwhelming as I feared.

How many steps would it take to get through this pain? For now, the entryway would have to do.

Even through the closed front door, sunlight permeated the tempered glass as though light could never fully be shunned here. The rays cast their cheerful amber glow across a foyer Ida had kept filled with fresh flowers on every available surface. The vases now brimmed with wilted roses dropping crumbled petals onto the dusty surfaces of neglected antique tables.

The unfairness fell on me like the blanket of sunlight, only this sensation smothered rather than illuminated. Like something dark and ugly and not at all what Ida said I should feel after she went to Jesus. The cancer took her before we had the opportunity to love one another, and now my one chance to know where I came from—and my identity—was buried in a tiny plot of earth not strong enough to hold the effervescent soul that was Ida Sue Macintyre. All that remained was the shattered remembrance of a beautiful life that God had given me too late and stolen from me too soon.

I took a deep breath. If I couldn't move forward, I should at least go back outside and get my stuff from the car. But I remained frozen. Paralyzed by the anxiety clawing in my veins and insisting this was the one final loss I knew I wouldn't be able to bear. Yet, death came anyway, despite the desperate prayers I'd wielded against it.

Ida had told me not to worry, that He would give us lots of time in heaven for her to teach me the secrets of the older generations, like how to sew and garden and can vegetables. She believed God made time for things like a grandmother and granddaughter stitching a quilt by hand or plucking ripe tomatoes from the vine.

Maybe He did. How would I know? I'd be lucky if I even made it up there to find out. Things hadn't exactly gone my way in life, and I'd made enough terrible choices to find myself in the ditch more than a time or two.

A hollow ache numbed the anxiety as I ran my fingers across an old pedal sewing machine I'd inherited but didn't know anything about. How many times had Ida's fingers caressed this same wood? An old typewriter graced the top, ancient and clunky. Ida had brought the contraption down from the attic during my first visit. The one right after she'd found me and a few weeks before she died. She'd said the machine had a special purpose, and then she'd given me nothing more than a sly wink.

I tapped my fingers on the ancient keys, the click echoing in the wide, sunlight-washed foyer.

A knock pounded at the door, startling me from melancholy thoughts and forcing me to shake off tears.

Keep it down. Hold it together.

I swung open the door. A man stood there, arms at his sides and a smile stretching across a clean-shaven face. Little lines crinkled at the corners of his eyes. He looked somewhat familiar. Maybe from the funeral? He waited patiently, as though his manners required he speak only after first being spoken to. I wasn't in the mood for people to come by and offer their condolences.

And this guy hadn't even brought food. Must not be a Baptist. He ran a hand over his dark hair, cut short on the sides and curling a bit at the top. Eyes warm and inviting roamed my face as if they knew me.

"Yes?" I eyed him warily. Seemed he wouldn't state his business unless asked.

"I'm Ryan." He grinned. "Remember?"

I shook my head. I'd met a lot of people at the funeral home. Didn't remember much about any of them. Under different circumstances, maybe this man with his inviting smile and easygoing manner might have snagged my attention, but my heart bore too many cracks to flutter at the sight of a handsome face.

His grin didn't falter. "That's okay." He extended his hand. "Ryan Watson."

I remained frozen, a testament of rudeness I didn't necessarily mean and inhospitality that maybe I did.

He dropped his hand, not seeming as offended as he should. "It's good to see you again, Casey. I know this must be hard for you."

Casey? No one called me that but Ida.

"Cassandra."

He nodded but continued as if he hadn't heard. "Ida wanted me to give you this." He lifted a manila envelope.

"What is it?"

He shrugged, wide shoulders lifting underneath a red plaid button-up. Ida would probably say I should ask him to step inside, but since I didn't feel like *I* belonged in Ida's house, it didn't seem right to bring in another trespasser.

"Since I'm not in the habit of opening someone else's mail"—did he just wink at me?—"I guess you'll have to find out."

He looked far too chipper to have been close to Ida, so the entire thing felt out of sorts. I took the envelope anyway. "Thanks."

Ryan shoved his hands in his jeans pockets. "Sure. Let me know when you're ready."

"Ready? For what?"

He smiled again, showing straight teeth that were the kind of white you got from good hygiene and not from bleach. "You'll see."

Without another word he spun and bounded down the front steps and jogged across the lawn and to the house next door. A neighbor?

I closed the door and sank to the floor, pressing my back against the oak. Ida left me something? Something she didn't leave with the lawyer? Why give it to the guy next door?

My hand trembled as I slid my finger under the glue and pulled the flap free. Inside, a single sheet of paper contained a letter with thick ink and a blocky font. I glanced at the typewriter. Had Ida typed the letter just before she died?

It took a moment for my vision to clear enough to read the blocky print.

My dear Casey,
    I'd hoped this would be something we could do

together. I started planning this adventure when I found you, but the cancer found me first. Sometimes life works out that way. But I had the opportunity to finish it all, and that is worth more to me than I can explain.

This plan won't be what I'd once thought, but I know God has His reasons for everything. I'm thankful I was able to complete it before He calls me home. I feel in my spirit that I don't have much longer, and the end will probably come sooner than I thought. Much sooner than I told you. I'm writing this now while I still can. I hope you will forgive me. I didn't want to worry you, should the doctors be right.

In her last moments of life, Ida had planned something mysterious. I eyed the typewriter. What kind of unselfishness did that take? I probably would have been planning out my last meals or crossing something off my bucket list.

Ida wrote me a letter. I clutched it to my chest like a childhood teddy bear knighted with the responsibilities of keeping a little girl safe from the dark. *Breathe. Hold it together.* I wiped my eyes with my sleeve.

I could have given you everything when you came to visit. We probably had time to do one or two of the projects together, but I didn't want to start the journey with you knowing I wouldn't be able to finish. I know now that this is the way it was always meant to be. This was my journey, but it will also be yours. Something tells me you'll need the discovery.

Think of this as a way for us to stay connected a little longer. A few more days of stories and tea and laughs. Though I will be gone, know the God who loves me also loves you, and He will be there with the both of us. You are not alone.

Don't rush the process, but don't be afraid to take each step as it comes, either. Sometimes a story has to unfold in its own way, or you miss the meaning.

You have a big heart, my girl, and I know it's filled with a lot of hurt. But every story has trials, and every heroine has to face them to find herself and the truth she is meant to discover. By God's blessing, I had time to finish the letters that will walk you through each step.

Tomorrow you'll get the first piece of the puzzle. Ryan is a good man, and I know he will do everything in his power to honor my final request and walk with you as you discover all I want to share. Try not to push him away. He means well.

My sweet Casey, this isn't the end. Eat something. Get some rest. Tomorrow starts a new adventure. Will you take it with me?

I stared at the letter. No signature. No farewell. But Ida's heart covered the page. I read it three more times, trying to figure out what Ida meant.

A journey? What was she talking about? I couldn't take a trip. I'd lost everything, save one clunker I couldn't even fill with gas.

Maybe the stories were still here after all. She'd written them down. Hope bubbled for a moment and then dashed away.

Apparently, Ida had given all the stories to the too-chipper man next door. Why not leave them for me? Why involve someone else?

Too many questions. Questions I'd have to deal with, but I was too tired to go next door and demand answers.

For now, I figured I'd take Ida's advice. Find some food. Get some sleep. If I could. How long did Ida expect me to stay here? Would I spend the entire summer in backwoods Mississippi? Maryville's claim to fame boasted it was the smallest town with two interstate exits in America.

I rubbed my temples and forced myself to get up. One step at a time.

First thing tomorrow, I'd have a discussion with Ryan about the items that belonged to me.

And then maybe I'd get the stories after all.

2

Fragments of Reality

Mornings had a way of making things feel new. Fresh. But only for a moment or two. Then reality came crashing back down. No sense putting it off. Reality never took rain checks. I tossed off the heavy quilt. Sunlight filtered through the lace curtains covering the wide windows on the second floor of Ida's house.

I swung my feet off the side of the bed and looked around, taking time to admire Ida's loving touch.

The guest room, like everything else at Ida's, cocooned a person in hospitality and Southern charm. Papered walls in a shade of tranquil blue held photographs and paintings of relatives long lost to the annals of history. Nothing like my old apartment back in Atlanta. Funny how the city could be in the same geographic region and seem like another world. Two states over and light-years different.

I wiggled my feet on the thick gray rug and dug my toes around in the softness, in no hurry to start the day. I'd slept fitfully in the four-poster bed, imagining danger in the sounds of the night that were surely nothing more than old pipes and settling wood. I fingered the hand-stitched quilt. Quilting was a winter project, Ida had said.

We never made it that long.

With a sigh, I pushed off the bed and passed by the antique dresser without looking at my reflection in the silvered mirror. The bathroom had been added and remodeled at some later point in the Victorian house's history. And the on-demand hot water heater meant I could let the heat work out the tension in my knotted muscles.

When did I have to start doing things like paying the water bill? Ugh. I shook the thought off. A problem for another day. Today, all I had to do was—

The doorbell rang.

Who in the world would be at the door this early in the morning? I glanced down at my ragged T-shirt and cotton shorts.

The doorbell rang again. Too bad for them. Impatience on the visitor's part didn't mean there had to be any anxiety on mine. They could wait. Or come back later.

It would be fine.

I closed the bathroom door and turned on the shower. Besides, it was probably just Ryan, delivering the next letter from Ida. Since both excitement and apprehension over what the letter might say flooded me in equal measures, a shower would be a better next step than answering the door at—what time was it, anyway? I poked my head out of the bathroom and craned my neck to see the digital clock on the nightstand.

9:45

Oh. Not actually an unreasonably early hour. Ryan would still have to wait. Even better, he could leave the letter or package or whatever it was on the welcome mat.

That way I wouldn't have to talk to him. Avoiding people was becoming my specialty.

Thirty minutes later I trudged down the stairs dressed in baggy sweatpants and a tank top and stepped into the foyer still littered with dead flowers. I really needed to throw those out. Ida liked her house tidy. Another sparkling day spewed sunshine in merry beams over the hardwood floor.

I opened the front door. The welcome mat with a big letter M in scrolling script held nothing more than dust. Great. He'd either come back or would want me to come over to get the package. A conversation that could wait until at least after coffee.

"Good morning!"

I yelped and ducked back inside the doorway, my pulse skittering like a squirrel on a hot sidewalk.

"Casey? You okay?"

The door jerked to a halt mid-slam. Oh. Ryan. Of course. I poked my head out but kept a firm grip on the door. "What are you doing here?"

He unfolded his muscular frame from the swing hanging on the far side of the wraparound porch. "Waiting on you."

I gave him my best cactus stare. The one that warned people of my prickly nature and made it clear they should keep their distance. "Why?"

Ryan closed a book and tucked it under his arm. "Ida sent me."

A good-looking man who enjoyed a book instead of a sports feed on his phone? Interesting. "Ida's gone."

He studied me long enough to jump-start my self-consciousness. I hadn't even dried my hair. It hung in dark strands over my shoulders, dampening my shirt. I crossed my arms.

"But her instructions are not. And I made a promise."

He sounded sincere, his voice deep with emotion. Maybe I'd misjudged him. He'd seemed too chipper yesterday to be grieving Ida, but from the look of his stoic face, this man *had* cared. And he obviously took whatever promises he'd made to Ida seriously.

I glanced at his empty hands and looked past him to the swing. "Did you, uh, bring me something?"

"No."

No? Then what was he doing on the porch?

He kept his gaze disconcertingly steady. Deep brown eyes like liquid chocolate. "May I come in?"

So much for Mr. Manners. What kind of man invited himself into a woman's house? Especially one he didn't know? "No."

"No?" He lifted a dark eyebrow.

I eased the door a little in front of me so I could slam it on him if he made any sudden moves. "Look, Ida may have liked you, but I don't know you. I'm not comfortable letting you in."

He gave a slow nod, and the curls on the top of his head swayed. "She said that might be the case."

Yet he'd still asked. Had Ida told him to? Why?

"So I'll just have to tell you where it is." He rocked back on his heels. Dressed in a blue plaid shirt nearly identical to the red one he'd worn yesterday, he looked like someone who either didn't have much creativity with his wardrobe or who stuck with what he found comfortable.

Uh-oh. He's looking at me funny.

Caught staring like a twittering freshman with a crush. I cleared my throat. "You don't have a letter?"

I inwardly cringed. Duh. I already knew that. Now I

looked stupid as well as hideous.

"Not this time." His voice held a smile, but I refused to look at him. He probably thought I was an idiot. But, Ida had specifically said he would bring me pieces of a puzzle. If he didn't have anything, why come here?

We stared at one another in some kind of weird stalemate that made me feel an entirely new level of awkward. And awkward and I were deeply involved.

Apparently the silence unnerved me much more than him. Would I have to pry information out of him? "So...she hid the letter in the house?" Were they all in the house?

"No." He put one hand in his pocket. "They aren't all letters. Some are. Some aren't."

"And this one is...?"

"Instructions."

Instructions?

"And a story."

Which he didn't have. Was he trying to confuse me on purpose? I waited another few breaths until my frustration bubbled over. "Why don't you tell me? You must have a job or something you need to get to?"

His eyes widened slightly. I'd done it again. Failed politeness 101.

Strangely, he didn't seem offended. "Not today."

Hmm. Looked like it took a little more than the usual to ruffle this rooster's feathers. "You don't work on Tuesdays?"

"Nope."

I waited, forcing myself to keep his gaze. Maybe if I stood here long enough and let the silence suffocate us, he would finally spit out what he'd come to say. Because no matter how long he stood there, seeming perfectly comfortable in this ridiculously awkward situation, I would not let him in the house.

He smiled at me.

"Ugh." I rolled my eyes. "This is stupid."

Ryan cocked an eyebrow, giving his face a cute, curious puppy look. "What is?"

More like *who* rather than *what*. I took a moment to study the blue porch ceiling before retuning my gaze to Ryan. "*This*." I gestured between us. "You rang the doorbell. You're supposed to give me something. But you keep standing there, not telling me anything."

He didn't move. Oh, good grief. Either this man was trying to irritate me on purpose, or he was a certifiable case of ignorant. Or he thought he could trick me.

I closed the door a little more. "I'm still not letting you in the house."

He had the audacity to chuckle. "Sorry." He rubbed the back of his neck. "This is a little weird, I know. But Ida had a specific plan, and I'm trying to fumble my way through it." He looked at me kind of funny. What thoughts churned behind those eyes? "The first story is in the sewing machine. The supplies are upstairs in the trunk."

Trunk? I didn't remember a trunk. No matter. I'd find it. "I thought she was leaving me clues or something." *Supplies* didn't fit.

He shrugged. "Some things are in the house. Others aren't." He must have had enough sense to finally see my irritation, because he hurried on. "Ida's got it all scheduled out. Each day on her schedule I'm supposed to show you something, give you something, or take you somewhere."

Yeah, right. No way I was going anywhere with this stranger.

"I'm sorry for being vague, but all I have is a list of instructions."

What kind of game did Ida want to play? "Fine. I need to find something in the sewing machine and something else in the trunk." Clear as mud.

"That's what it said."

"Thanks." I started to close the door.

"Let me know when you finish. I can't give you the next part until you finish the first."

Unless I dug through the house and found everything on my own. "Okay."

"Well, have a good day." He lifted his hand in a half-wave, still looking reluctant to go.

I offered him a halfhearted good-bye in my best forced friendly voice for Ida's sake and closed the door. What a weird day. Ida left me a string of clues? Why not write down the answers to all my questions?

You have to understand how you got here to understand where to go next.

One of Ida's cryptic answers during our visit surfaced in my memory. Though I'd needed to know more about my parents—why my mother hadn't wanted me and what had happened to my father after I'd been given up for adoption—Ida had instead started with stories from my father's childhood. Painting a picture of his life. She'd said the story had to start at the beginning. A story started in the middle wouldn't make sense.

At the time, I'd enjoyed my newfound grandmother's acceptance and company too much to push. But that was when I'd thought we had more time.

I crossed to the sewing machine. Thick iron legs in a scrolled pattern held a foot pedal at the bottom. The word

Singer hung in worked metal across the back. A heavy wooden tabletop with two tiers held the typewriter and a blue ceramic vase.

If Ida hadn't told me, I probably wouldn't have known this contraption was a sewing machine. Mostly because the actual *sewing machine* part seemed to be missing. This looked like some fancy metal legs with a boxy tabletop. I lifted the vase of wilted roses and set them aside, then wrestled the heavy typewriter off the top.

A slip of paper fell.

I set the clunky typewriter on the floor and plopped down next to it, scooping up the paper. This letter seemed much older than the one from yesterday. I unfolded the yellowed page, careful of the crumbled edges. Tight script flowed over the top of the page.

> *My dearest son,*
>
> *I hope to visit you next month. Mr. Sheppard is going to Jackson and offered me a ride. Your baby sister is doing well enough to travel. The home is good for you, and Miss Steward told me they would be taking all you boys to the zoo once the weather clears. Won't that be nice? Knowing you and your brothers have plenty to eat makes our sacrifice worth it. Stay strong for your brothers. They need you.*
>
> *With love,*
> *Mother*

I turned the letter over. No dates. No names. Who were these people, and where did the mother send her son? Why didn't she keep him?

Why didn't my mother keep me?

More questions without answers. I put the letter on the floor next to the typewriter and glanced back at the sewing machine. I had to be missing something. I leaned closer to examine the top. A smaller piece of wood sat on top of the larger base.

Interesting. I put my fingers on the edge, and the piece lifted up. About two feet long, the wooden top hinged off to the side, revealing a small, black sewing machine hidden inside. It wasn't missing after all. It'd been cleverly folded inside this inner compartment. I just needed to figure out how it unfolded.

I examined the opening. Another flap of wood at the front of the compartment folded back on a set of long hinges, widening the hole. Bits of old wood and dust fell free as I gently lifted the heavy sewing machine on rusty hinges from where it hung in the middle of the opening. Holding the heavy metal contraption upright with one hand, I dropped the front flap back into place, locking the sewing machine into an upright position.

The piece converted from an end table to a functioning piece of machinery with a side wing likely meant for spreading out the fabric. The heavy metal, though a bit rusty in places, was still a smooth black with a gold leaf floral pattern painted around the bottom edge. It had a wheel at the back, and, when I turned it, the needle still moved up and down.

How did the pedal work? I dropped down and looked underneath the wrought-iron bottom. If I turned the big wheel on the right side of the foot pedal, the pedal rocked back and forth.

Sewing machine mystery solved. But still nothing from

17

Ida other than the handwritten letter I couldn't be sure fit into this puzzle. Now what?

I looked closer at the wooden casing, noticing something I hadn't before. Four drawers, missing the knobs and therefore blending in, sat two on each side. Inside the first drawer, a small green box held accessory parts for the machine. Buttons and scraps of material filled the second drawer on the left side. In the right side, the top drawer held more of the same along with some folded scraps of old newspaper from the 1980s, all folded into identical triangles. Weird.

I scoured them for something important, but it didn't seem like anything in particular had been saved. Nothing but random advertisements, local happenings, and a few obituaries. I folded the edges back into the triangle shapes and closed them back inside.

The final drawer contained another letter. I half-expected it wouldn't.

The crisp white page contained the same bold font as Ida's first letter.

My dearest Casey,

This sewing machine is one of our family treasures. It was given to my mother in 1901 as a wedding gift from her parents. This old machine has stitched together countless garments and quilt patterns over the years. Though I started using the electric version in my older days, this Singer is well built and sturdy. It's stood the test of time.

Just like this family.

You may think you are not truly one of us, but you are. Our history is your history. Today, we will start on that quilt. Upstairs you'll find an old cedar chest. Inside are bits of material. In the old days, women would save shirts or dresses and cut them into smaller pieces to turn something that was old and worn out into something new and beautiful.

You may think that your life is in pieces. Maybe it is. But you can take those pieces and stitch them together. In the end, you'll have something even more beautiful.

This first step is going to take time. Let it. Go through my material or find your own. Pick pieces that mean something to you. Then stitch the memories together. One square will become two, and two will become twenty.

With love,
Mamaw

I stared at the letter, tears pricking my eyes. I'd never called my biological grandmother anything but Ida. Mamaw felt much more intimate. I folded the paper and stuffed it in my back pocket. Ida wanted me to make a quilt? With a foot-pedal sewing machine?

Impossible.

3

Stitching Memories

$\mathcal{S}$nooping in a person's private sanctum took the gold in ultimate trespassing. I hovered at the threshold of Ida's room, reluctant to take the final step.

But I was out of options. I'd already searched the parlor, the living room, the library, the kitchen, and the dining room. I'd explored the three other bedrooms, and I knew there wasn't a chest in my room. I stared inside at the perfectly made bed and picked at my ragged cuticles. It had to be in here. I'd looked everywhere else.

Ida's room still smelled like her. Like lavender and gardenias, warm cookies and life. The ache in my chest grew. How much worse would this have been if I'd known Ida since childhood? Or maybe the opposite. If I'd had years of memories to temper the pain, would it ache less?

Grief stole joy either way. Too many memories and loss crippled the heart. Not enough, and the regret laid siege. I gripped the doorframe, letting my eyes roam over the treasures inside. Pictures of Ida and her late husband, Reggie, a war hero and Army Air Corps engine mechanic, sat in matching frames on her mahogany dresser. Trinkets from around the world filled a glass display case in the corner, and, on the far wall, a quilt with little triangles.

Brightly colored, it hung from a long rod near the ceiling like an old tapestry. I leaned in and squinted, trying to get a better look. Small bits of fabric—shaped like the folded pieces of newspaper from the sewing machine—created a larger wreath pattern.

The quilt drew me closer, forcing me to break the barrier and cross into Ida's sanctum. My bare feet squished silently on the thick camel-colored carpet. I edged around Ida's four-poster bed topped with another patchwork quilt and too many pillows to count.

The trunk sat squarely at the bottom of the quilt hanging on the wall as though the two went together. I eyed the trunk, but my gaze returned to the quilt. Most of Ida's creations topped the beds or sat folded in the hall closet. Why had she hung this one on the wall?

I traced the colors around the wreath, now able to make out something very odd. Some of the triangle pieces were cut from various patterned fabric. But others were white.

And covered in writing.

Written in a perfect script, the white triangles contained names and dates. Those connected to other bits of white tattooed with the same perfect script. I lifted up on my toes and started at the top of the wreath. The top contained two names, Elizabeth and Fredrick Macintyre, April 27, 1849. Split down from each side, other names and dates must have followed a family line. I scanned until I found her name near the middle of the wreath on the right side. Ida and Reginald Macintyre, December 22, 1951.

The next line underneath it punched me square in the gut, knocking my breath out just as Billie Ann Warren had in the fourth grade when I'd refused to give her my lunch.

Mike and Haley Macintyre, December 23, 1983. My parents.

They'd been married?

Legs like Jell-O, I melted to the floor, unable to peel my eyes away. My parents had been married. They'd had a child together. Something thick and slimy settled in my stomach, leaving the heavy aftertaste of unwanted truth sour in my mouth. I stared at the quilt, shards of my fragile reality splintering and cutting into me with ragged edges.

I'd been unwanted—not by a mother who was too young or too messed up or too *whatever* to care for a baby like I'd always told myself. I hadn't been saved from a drug-addict or born in prison to a woman who'd done the only thing she could do. I'd forgiven her because I always thought she hadn't had a choice. She'd wanted a better life for me. It wasn't her fault I'd ended up homeless and abused. She'd tried her best.

No, this was worse. Much worse. My mother hadn't been trying to save me from anything. She hadn't been on the run, or in danger. She'd had a home. A husband. A mother-in-law who, up until this moment, I had considered the most wonderful person in the world.

No wonder Ida didn't tell me. It wasn't just my mother who'd abandoned me. It was all of them.

I squeezed my eyes shut, all of my imagined scenarios and fabricated explanations crumbling under one undeniable truth.

No one wanted me.

Had guilt driven Ida to seek me out in her final days? My stomach soured. Lava building, churning, smothering. I stalked out of the room. Before I could gather myself, I stomped down the stairs, out the front door, across the overgrown grass, and up the concrete driveway to the house next door.

Pristine, the Queen Anne boasted sunny yellow fish-scale siding and smiled down from its pedestal of prosperity, proud of the sheltered, healthy relationships stored inside.

I hated it. And all it represented.

A life I should have had. A life that hadn't been stolen from me so much as I'd been deemed unworthy. Seething, I stood there both wanting to berate Ryan for dragging my stupid hopeful heart into this game and wanting to demand he give me everything that belonged to me so I could get out of Maryville, Mississippi, and never look back. I didn't belong here with these close-knit people anyway.

The front door suddenly opened, and the object of my rage stepped out, whistling a tune as cheery as his polished life.

Ryan stopped short when he saw me standing in his yard like a steaming potato. Lumpy, sizzling, and too hot to handle.

His eyes widened. "What's wrong?"

I clenched my fists, digging my nails into my palms until it hurt. "I'm not playing this stupid game."

His dark eyebrows drew together, and he bounded down the brick steps. "What game?"

I tilted my head back to look at him, the concern in his chocolate eyes melting a little of my fury. "You heard me." I pushed loathing into my words, expecting him to shy back. Admit I wasn't worth the trouble. Give me what I needed so he could be rid of me.

Before I could move, Ryan placed his hands on my shoulders, and my breath faltered. I didn't let people touch me. But the weight of his touch felt...strangely comforting.

I shook him off.

He regarded me evenly and waited, though I was pretty sure it was his turn to talk.

That was how conversations worked. One person talked. The other responded. This man waited calmly, his expression nonjudgmental. I both hated how long it took him to respond and oddly, at the same time, found the opportunity to sort through my raging emotions beneficial.

Finally, I groaned. "Look, I don't want to do this. I don't want to go on some convoluted trail of discovery only to end up where I already know I'm headed. It's a waste of time."

He nodded slowly. Weird. I expected argument. Or for him to say I was overreacting. Instead Ryan cocked his head and stared at me, but not in a creepy way. In a way that made my insides turn to slime. No. That was gross. Not slime. More like hot butter or—

"I understand."

His words jarred me out of my weird thoughts. He did? Just like that? "What?"

Ryan lifted his hand like he wanted to comfort me again but thought better of it and ran his fingers through his hair instead. His words came out slow and measured. He spoke like the kind of man who put thought into things before he shared them. "It must be hard, wanting answers when the only way you can get them is to jump through a bunch of hoops. Doesn't seem fair."

Huh. My shoulders slumped, the last of the fire slipping out through my sweaty fingers just like that. I took a step back from him. How had he diffused my emotions so quickly? "Yeah."

His wide mouth tilted up into a smile that further set me off balance. "Can I buy you a cup of coffee?"

How on earth did you argue with a guy like that? I expected a fight. He wanted to buy me coffee. I wrinkled my nose. "You have a coffee shop in this town?"

He laughed, a sound bold and rich like the kind of stew that stuck to your ribs. "Kind of. Really it's a sweets shop, but they make good coffee."

The temptation to go with him surprised me. What was wrong with me? I shook my head. *Get it together.* "Maybe another time. Thanks."

I shifted, unable to meet his probing gaze. Now what?

Ryan wore cowboy boots. Ones with a square toe and plenty of scuff marks. What did this man do for a living? Why had Ida given him the instructions? A more unnerving thought than the usual rambling ones jumped in and strangled my breath.

How much did he know?

I pulled my shields around me and fortified myself, looking up to meet his gaze. "Why do I have to go through all of this?"

His warm gaze held purpose. "Ida wanted it that way." Irritation bit at me, but his sweet smile kept it from lashing out. "And one thing I know about Ida. She always had her reasons. Most of the time, those reasons were pretty soaked in prayer. Do you trust her enough to find out?"

Did I? I loved Ida, even as little as I knew her. She'd been kind to me. Supportive. And she'd found me when she hadn't had to. She'd spent her final days working on something. For me.

I hated being ruled by emotions. They took over, fickle and shifting like a boat with big sails and no anchor. In the course of a few minutes I'd gone from curious to devastated to furious and now to pitiful, feeling guilty that I couldn't trust Ida through the first clue. What a mess.

The wind danced over the swaying grass, ruffling it around Ryan's shoes and my...ugh. Bare feet. I wrapped my arms around my waist and turned away from him, looking back at Ida's house in the glittering sunlight of the late May afternoon.

Maybe she had a reason after all. The truth might not be pretty, but I'd handled plenty of ugly before. I needed to know so I could get past it. So I could move on and figure out a way to have a life.

"I'm too old for treasure hunts," I said, letting my gaze sweep over the manicured lawn and down the oak-lined sidewalk of this quaint little neighborhood. Branches of old trees swept down toward a lazy street, concealing merry birds calling to one another.

Ryan laughed and, strangely, the sound coaxed a smile from my puckered lips and drew my gaze to find his. His eyes danced. What would it be like to have eyes that held that much light? Light untainted by a mean world filled with people who hid pointed teeth behind their varnished smiles?

I shook myself. I didn't know this man. He seemed genuine. He was certainly handsome. But sometimes the ugliest souls hid behind the prettiest faces. I reminded myself never to let down my guard and leveled a prickly stare on this unnervingly confusing man.

"Too old? What are you, ninety?"

I put my hand on my hip and gave him a stern look, which he ignored.

"Nobody's too old to discover something important to

them." He sobered, and those expressive lips mellowed into a solemn line. "I will honor my promise to Ida. I owe her that. But I can't force you to follow her instructions or walk down the road she's led you to."

Conviction dripped from him. So there it was. The reason Ida gave the instructions to Ryan. The reason why he held the power to dole out each piece. Either I got answers the way Ida wanted, or I wouldn't get them at all. Ryan wouldn't let me take any shortcuts, or skip the process, or jump to knowing the answers without slugging through all the things Ida wanted me to do or know first.

"Ha!" I dropped my head back and looked up at the heavens. "I get it now."

Ryan remained silent, probably thinking I was a lunatic. Ida knew me better than I'd realized. And she'd set a formidable gatekeeper squarely in my path.

"Fine." I stalked across the yard, blades of grass poking between my toes.

"Where are you going?" Ryan called after me.

I didn't look back. "To start stitching memories."

4

Forgotten Dreams

ere goes nothing. I popped open the cedar chest, mostly ignoring the decorative molding and hammered metal hinges and clasps. Inside, an old teddy bear wearing a peculiar little wooden charm necklace lay on top of a heap of fabrics. It had been loved well, its black fur faded and worn in several places. Had it belonged to my father?

Probably.

Careful of the fraying seams, I gently carried the worn bear into my room and settled it in a place of honor on my dresser. Had my father loved this bear until it no longer had any fuzz remaining? I gave it a pat and returned to Ida's room, intent on my mission.

I thrust my hand inside and pulled out a fistful of materials. Scraps of floral patterns and other mismatched fragments. It didn't matter. I just had to stick these together into a big rectangle and call it a quilt. Then I'd get answers.

I snatched the materials and bounded down the stairs to the sewing machine. How hard could it be? Stick the pieces together. Make a rectangle. Sew that to a backing with a little cotton inside. Easy.

The machine taunted me. How did I thread the needle? Or get all the thread and the bobbin in the right places? Nothing like trying to do a job without instructions. An ironic laugh bubbled up. How like life in general. Always trying to figure out what to do, never knowing the measuring stick by which you'd be judged, but still hoping you'd be deemed worthy. I'd failed that test enough times to know I lacked whatever basic competence was needed to navigate a world full of people who played games I didn't understand.

A knock on the door pulled me from thoughts I shouldn't entertain. Great. I snatched it open, expecting Ryan, but was met with a prim little woman in her sixties instead.

"Good morning." The lady smiled at me, her lined face warm with welcome. She thrust an object wrapped in aluminum foil at me. "I made this for you."

Dressed in jeans and a simple blouse, she appeared relaxed and friendly. I glanced behind her but didn't see a car in Ida's drive. Had she walked here?

"Thanks." I took the package from her.

"I'm Nancy."

"Cassandra."

The lady grinned. "I know, dear. Met you at the funeral, remember?"

No. I nodded anyway. "Right. Sorry."

Nancy, who couldn't stand more than five feet, waved her hand and managed to make herself appear larger than her stature. "Never you mind that. I know you met too many folks to remember them all." She reached out and patted my arm. "Especially after losing your grandmother like that. I know how excited she was to find you. Hurts my heart, it does, that you two didn't get more time."

I stepped out on the porch and pulled the door closed behind me. "You knew Ida well?"

"Been knowin' her all my life." The smile on her face faltered for an instant, but she pulled it back into place. "I'm glad she had you to leave this place to."

Not that I knew what to do with it.

"Are you planning on staying here long?"

Small town. Nosy neighbors. "I don't know yet."

"I'm sure you have a life back in Atlanta." Nancy's tone held no judgment, at least not that I could tell.

"Not really. At least not until August."

Nancy chuckled. "That's the hand of God, girl. Sure enough."

What? God *wanted* me brokenhearted, kicked out of my apartment, and temporarily stuck living in a town in the middle of nowhere? "Anyway...I'm not sure how long I'll stay." Depended on how long probate took and how many hoops Ida wanted me to jump through. "Thanks for the, uh..." I lifted the bundle in my hand. "This."

"Oh! Silly me. It's a loaf of my famous friendship bread. Ida and I used to make it all the time. I'll bring you some starter, if you'd like."

The thought of baking fresh bread ignited a desire in me long buried and, despite myself, I brightened. "Really? I'd like that."

The lady grinned, bobbing her short curls in enthusiastic agreement. "I'd be happy to. Happy. You like baking?"

I'd once wanted to be a chef. Little girl dreams. "I dabble."

Nancy shifted her purse to the other arm. "So many things like that are lost on the younger generation. Good to see a young thing like you interested."

Young thing? "Thanks."

"I'll bring some tomorrow." She grinned. "We can get started on a new loaf."

Wait. I'd invited a stranger to come cook in Ida's kitchen? With me? When had I done that? "Um, well—"

Nancy clasped her hands. "It'll be lovely teaching someone to carry on my friendship bread. I can hardly wait."

Surprising myself, I returned her enthusiastic smile. "Sounds good." I wished her a nice day and closed myself in Ida's house again. The prospect of baking dredged up a longing so intense I could nearly smell the yeasty goodness. I glanced at the package.

Some melted butter...maybe a little of Ida's fig jam. My mouth watered.

I'd forgotten something important. For the first time, I had access to the kind of kitchen I'd always wanted. Ida had two ovens. *Two.* A farmhouse sink. And a massive pantry. I stepped over the pile of fabric in the foyer and darted into the kitchen.

Why hadn't I thought of it before? With the extra time on my hands, I could take some online classes or something. After all these years, could this be my chance to go to cooking school? Do something I wanted for a change?

No, I'd finally gotten a good job, and cooking school would take longer than my summer in Maryville. Being a library assistant at the high school would get me insurance, set hours, and summers to pick up extra income. Too good of a gig to pass up chasing childhood fantasies. Still. While I was here, spending a little time baking and learning couldn't hurt, could it?

I ran my fingers over the granite countertop. I'd been on

my own since seventeen. When I turned eighteen, I earned
enough to rent a tiny apartment over a nice couple's garage,
supplemented with cutting their grass so I could finish
school. I'd been working and scraping most of my life.

And then Derick had wasted what meager savings I'd
collected and tossed me out, taking my job and my home in
the avalanche of his betrayal. The thought of him left a
bitter taste in my mouth. I shook my head, trying to
dislodge the sensation. His memory didn't belong here at
Ida's house. I swept him and the rest of my past back into a
dark corner of my mind where tear-stained sludge belonged.

This place was meant for sunshine, roses, and painted-
on smiles. For baking and unwinding. Which I intended to
do. Starting with indulging in Nancy's bread. The fragrant
scent of the dough exploded on my senses the moment I
pulled back the foil. I pinched off a piece and popped it in
my mouth, immediately closing my eyes. Still warm, the
fluffy bread coated my taste buds with sweetness and
buttery temptation. So good it didn't even need jam. I cut
off a thick slice, dropped the knife in the sink, and let myself
ponder my new possibilities.

I could live here with minimal expenses for the summer.
Without rent. I'd have to figure out what the bills for a
place like this would cost me. And somehow I'd have to find
a way to buy groceries until I had access to Ida's accounts.
Staying here for a few months would be better than going
back to Atlanta. Give me a chance to get my feet under me
before I needed to find a new apartment.

I could finish Ida's puzzle, sell the house at the end of
the summer, and use the money to pay for a nice place in a
good neighborhood by the school. I paced around the
island, my feet slapping on the cold tile.

As soon as everything cleared probate, I'd have choices. Thanks to Ida. She'd given me more than a house and some old stories. She'd given me a chance for a new life. Hope. But first I had to finish the quilt.

I snatched another hunk of bread, wrapped the rest back in the foil, and scrambled into the foyer. Chewing on carbs I didn't even care would settle on my hips, I plopped down on the hardwood and spread the mismatched fabric across the floor. Ranging from thick flannel to shiny silk and polyester, none of Ida's remnants went together.

The drawers on the sewing machine had contained little triangle pieces that matched the family quilt upstairs. I pulled one out and rubbed it between my fingers, then put it back. I wouldn't be making a family quilt. I didn't have a family.

Simple would be better. I jumped up again, rummaged through the drawers in the kitchen, and finally came back with a set of scissors. I laid the largest pieces of cloth on top of one another, lined them up as best I could, and started cutting.

After some hacking and straining against scissors not sharp enough for the task, I had four big blocks of fabric about a foot square each. Mostly. They weren't exactly square. And the one on the bottom must have slipped while I cut, because it angled sharply on one edge. Oh well. It didn't matter.

I laid them out next to one another, creating a line. There. That would be long enough to make the top of the quilt. I eyed the ancient sewing machine. How would I ever get that thing working enough to tackle this project? Ida hadn't left me any instructions. Ryan might have some, but no way was I asking him. If he doubted my ability to

complete the quilt, he might hold back the next clues. I
needed to get this done as quickly and painlessly as possible.

A knock at the door startled a ragged-edged piece of
flannel out of my fingers. Now what? I brushed off the seat
of my jeans, noting the floor needed sweeping. How had I
let myself tolerate this mess? Ida would be ashamed.

I peeked through the window and onto the front porch
dappled with merry sunshine. Ryan. Who else? Served me
right for thinking about him. Irony, my old friend. I flung
open the door and gestured at the heap behind me. "I'm
doing it. See?"

Ryan tilted his head to look past me at the mess on the
floor, his brown eyes sparking humor. "So I see."

Was he mocking me? "You've got the next letter for
me?"

His eyes darted back to mine, clearly confused. "You're
not finished."

Worth a try. I lifted my shoulders. Waited. He stared at
me. Great. Another round of *who's going to speak first*. I
lost. "So...can I help you with something, or...?"

He rocked back on his heels. "I came to invite you to
church."

"No, thanks." I swung the door inward. "Have a good
day."

"Wait!" He stuck out a calloused hand.

I paused. Here it came. A lecture about how I should go
to church. How it would be good for me. Ida had tried that.
Didn't work for her, and it certainly wouldn't work for him.

"I'll admit. I have an ulterior motive." He offered a
sheepish grin that created soft lines around his eyes.
"Something beyond you enjoying a good sermon."

The honesty stalled me. "What motive?"

He ran his hand across the back of his neck and looked at his boots. "Remember when I said I didn't work on Tuesdays?"

"Yeah?" He looked awkward, which I found strangely charming. It was kind of nice to see a guy fumble for what to say. "Why don't you spit it out? I favor bluntness."

His eyes jumped to mine. Uh oh. Too much honesty. He smiled again, and my nerves settled.

"Oh, good." He pulled his shoulders back, suddenly seeming much more relaxed. "That sure makes life easier."

Easier? Not in my experience.

"I'm the youth pastor at First Baptist. I've been looking for a woman to help me with some of the teen girls."

I gaped at him. "And no one in your church is up for that job?" How bad were those kids?

"I have a few up for it." He quirked his mouth to one side. "But..." He shrugged. "Bluntness, right?"

I nodded, intrigued.

"Most of the help I can get is from the kids' parents, which means the kids won't open up. And parents completely suck the..."—he made air quotes—"'cool factor' out of what I'm trying to do."

I withheld a smile. Pretty sure this dude with his flannel and air quotes did that already. And did kids even call things *cool* anymore?

"Or," he said, "I get offers from blue-haired ladies who want to take the students back to the fifties." His face tightened in a funny way, as though the thought both amused and annoyed him in equal measure.

I laughed. He nailed bluntness. "You don't have any younger women in your church?"

"Only a few who don't have small children they need to

tend. And some of them are more interested in finding a date than connecting with the kids." His earnest eyes searched my face.

Worried he might see something there he didn't like, though not really sure why I cared, I looked away. "And you figure since I won't be here long, and I'm not looking for a date, that I would be a good person to help you babysit?"

Wind stirred up the smells of gardenia and roses, perfuming the air. It ruffled his hair as Ryan watched me. I shifted my feet. Too blunt in return?

"It's not babysitting. They're teens. They want someone who'll take an interest in them, and be real. From what Ida told me, and from what I've gathered in our conversations, you'd be great at that."

Ha. Shows how much either of them knew. No one wanted *real*. People wanted a mask reflecting who they wanted to see. But what did that matter here? I wasn't staying long. Might actually be a good time to test out different versions of myself with teens before starting my job at the school. I picked at my nails, considering. Out of my comfort zone by a mile, but it could have some good test-kitchen-type benefits.

Ryan pushed up the sleeves of his black button-up, which was too hot for this weather. "And coming to church would be a good way for you to meet people."

"I'm not good with people." More honesty. I watched to see how he'd take it.

"Come hang out with some kids." He scratched at his chin, completely missing the reality of what I'd said. "I think you might be able to help me with Emma. She's had a difficult past."

I bristled. How much had Ida shared about me? But his friendly eyes held no judgment, so I relaxed my shoulders. They were getting tight enough to touch my ears. Fine. I had a past. I needed to test out talking to teens. But he didn't need to start thinking I would be some kind of therapist or anything. I couldn't even iron out my own wrinkles.

"*One* Sunday?" His voice coaxed me, as though sensing he'd found a crack in my better judgment. "You can meet the kids, try it out." He turned out his palms. "And if you don't like it, I won't ask again."

"Fine. One Sunday. But that's all."

Ryan grinned again. "That's all I ask."

5

The Pageant Queen

*E*very terrible idea can trace its origins back to a moment in time when someone thought, "Hey, how bad can it be?" Staring at the white steeple of what had to be the largest building in town, I admitted I'd asked myself that very question. How bad could it be to go to a church filled with self-righteous hypocrites who would skewer me with their judgy eyes and turn up their perfectly powdered noses?

They streamed out of a variety of cars wedged into an overflowing parking lot, their heeled shoes clicking across the asphalt. I leaned against the hood of my 1990s-model Toyota and picked at the peeling beige paint. I'd worn jeans. Big no-no. I had chosen a pretty pink blouse with flounced sleeves and a pair of black ballet flats, but I'd missed the memo on pumps, floral dresses, curled hair, and lipstick.

I fingered my long brown hair that never held a curl without the aid of an entire can of hair spray.

"Coming?"

I whirled around to face Ryan. "You know, actually I'm not feeling all that good and—"

"Nope. You're making excuses because you're nervous." He cupped my elbow. "I'll walk with you and introduce you to people."

This man took my invitation to bluntness to heart. Probably shouldn't have opened the door. "I'm not dressed right."

"You're fine." His gaze snapped down my clothing, just now noticing what I wore.

I dragged my feet as he nudged me away from the protection of my Toyota's shadow. "Easy for you to say. Men wear a button-up and shake the dust off their boots and it works. There are way more rules for women."

He stopped and dropped my arm. "Rules? What rules?"

"Seriously? Have you never been in a shoe store? Men have, what, three types of shoes? Work, dress, athletic." I cocked an eyebrow. "How many do women have?"

Ryan glanced at the stream of people filing into the church. "Huh. I guess you have a point."

Score. Had he really never noticed? "Every woman here has on a skirt and heels." I gestured to my jeans. "Clearly, I do not."

"So?" He motioned for the door. "We're going to be late."

Did he really not care that I'd be scorned from the moment I disgraced the doorway? Of course not. Why would he? I was only here to help him wrangle a bunch of disgruntled youths.

I trudged along behind him, averting my eyes from the gawkers. Thankfully, by the time we reached the lobby area, music filled the room. No time for Ryan to introduce me to people. I slipped through a second set of doors into a large room with a vaulted ceiling and bright stained-glass windows that cast shards of colored light across packed pews. Where had all these people come from?

Hoping for a place in the back, I scanned the pew nearest the wall, but apparently I hadn't been the only person with an affinity for keeping a low profile. Ryan put his hand on the small of my back and guided me down the aisle on the left side of the room, past rows and rows of people in their Sunday finest, until we reached a side wing of the large sanctuary. The overpowering onslaught of cologne designated the teen section stuffed full of gum-smacking high schoolers. Several of the boys waved at Ryan, offering him wide smiles and enthusiastic gestures to come sit by them.

These kids clearly loved him. What did he need me for?

A couple of boys scooted over, making room for Ryan at the end of the front pew. He sidled in next to them and gestured for me to join them. Front row. Exactly where I wanted to be.

The people across from me sang from open hymnals or watched the screens on either side of the baptistery for the words to an upbeat worship song. Several churchgoers met my gaze, offering quick smiles before they returned to belting out the hymn. I shifted, uncomfortable, and Ryan nudged me to follow along with the words. I focused on the screen but kept my lips sealed.

An admittedly pleasant service followed the singing, with the pastor giving an interesting talk about how the members of the church were like parts of a body. All different, all useful. I kind of liked that. Made me think. Afterward, the crowd sang a slower song, and then we were dismissed.

No sooner had Ryan ushered me out into the aisle than a perky brunette with a trim figure and *pageant girl* practically stamped on her forehead glided up to us in a shimmering haze of sticky sweet perfume and hair spray.

She turned up perfectly pink lips and placed a manicured hand on Ryan's sleeve. "There you are, sweetie. I missed you at the potluck last night."

Ryan offered her a polite smile before assuring one of his students he'd beat him in something called "flip cup tic-tac-toe" in a minute. He shifted out from under her touch and gestured to me. "Mira Ann, this is my friend, Casey Adams, Ida Macintyre's granddaughter." He nodded toward the woman. "Casey, Mira Ann Middleton."

"Hi." I lifted my hand to shake hers, decided that was awkward, and dropped it back to my side.

She tilted her head, spilling perfectly curled milk chocolate hair over the shoulder of her form-fitting purple dress. "Oh, yes, I remember. Hope you enjoy your little visit with us." Her smile revealed bleached-white teeth.

Dismissing me, Mira Ann swung her attention back to Ryan. And just like that, I went from conspicuous outsider to the invisible woman. "What happened to you last night? Didn't you get my invitation?"

"I told you before, I'm not interested in the singles gatherings."

Mira Ann protruded her lower lip ever so slightly, and I had to catch myself before I rolled my eyes. "Next time we'll go somewhere more quiet."

Ryan checked his watch. "I've got to get to the youth room before somebody breaks something." He gestured toward a door at the back of the sanctuary to the left of an upright piano. "It's right through there."

Mira Ann's honey eyes snapped to me. "She's going with you?"

"She volunteered to help this week."

Only the slightest tightening around the corners of her lined eyes gave away her annoyance. Miss America types

41

never had cause to be jealous of people like me, so however unfounded, a childhood part of me cheered.

Taking my cue, I hurried toward the back door leading out of the main sanctuary and into a hallway in the back part of the building. To my left a large sign announced the youth room with bright colors and bold graphics meant to draw attention. I hesitated. Should I go in or wait in the hallway for Ryan?

A boy poked his head out of the room and spotted me. "Hey! I'm Lamarcus."

"Hey."

He grinned. "You Mr. Ryan's girlfriend?"

"What? No." Kids. Didn't their parents teach them not ask such things?

You did say you liked bluntness. I ignored the little voice in my head.

Lamarcus shrugged. "Okay. You hanging with us today?"

"Yeah."

He grinned again and ducked back into the room. Oh, boy. This would be interesting.

Ryan popped through the sanctuary's double doors and gestured toward the youth room. "Go on in."

I almost pointed out I was waiting on him, but what would be the point? I stood there until he opened the door and then followed him inside. The room housed a TV and couch, several pub-style tables with stools, a refrigerator, and a circle of chairs. A couple of kids lounged on the couches, several ate pizza at the tables, and two boys played a card game. They all turned to look at me.

Ryan raised his hand. "Guys, this is Casey. She's here for the summer and is going to hang out with us while she's in town."

Great. Now everyone would call me Ida's nickname. I eyed him. And so much for *one* Sunday. Talk about taking a mile.

"And me, too, y'all." Mira Ann's animated voice preceded her bouncy curls through the door. She gave Ryan a sweet smile and grabbed my arm as if we were old friends. "Won't this be fun? I'm sure you and I will be great friends."

Did she mean that, or was she playing Ryan somehow? I glanced at him, but his smile never faltered. They'd probably discussed it earlier. "Uh, sure."

Mira Ann gave me a squeeze and sauntered over to a group of teen girls sitting at one of the tables. After a moment, the hum of conversation and laughter filled the room again. Mira Ann laughed with four cute cheerleader types and seemed to have no problem doing what I clearly couldn't. Why did Ryan need me when she obviously connected with the teenagers?

Across the room, two girls about sixteen years old sat across from one another at a pub table. One dressed in jeans and a baggy tee, her blond hair pulled into an unceremonious ponytail. The other, with mousy brown hair and thin features, wore high-top pink shoes, jeans with too many holes, and a Nirvana tank top. Both of them scrolled through social media on their phones and failed to engage with the human population around them. These must be the ones he needed help with. Not the others. They seemed fine with Mira Ann.

I studied the girls, trying to come up with something to say. How did you walk up cold to a teen and start a conversation? "How's school going" seemed lame. While I had empathy for the wallflowers, Ryan failed to grasp one basic foundational issue. It took an extrovert to coax out an

introvert. Awkward people lumped together only festered
more awkwardness.

One of the girls, the one with mousy brown hair and
sweeping bangs, suddenly looked up as though she'd sensed
my gaze. We locked eyes. I gave a stupid little wave.

The girl cocked her eyebrow in that same way I always
did when I gave people my cactus stare.

I smiled.

She didn't. With a roll of her brown eyes, she turned her
attention back to the pink phone in her hand.

That went well.

I stood there uncomfortably, not sure what to do next.
Ryan moved off, engaging a group of boys in a game of
flipping cups over. Once one of them flipped a cup, he got
to place it on a tic-tac-toe board.

I stood there, awkward and mostly ignored, until Ryan
called for everyone to gather around for the lesson. I stood
in the back, watching. Ryan seemed good at this. He
engaged the kids in the Bible story, drew real answers out of
them with thought-provoking questions, and prayed for
them at the end.

As the kids filed out, Mira Ann bustled over. "How
about lunch?"

She wanted me to go to lunch with her? I glanced at
Ryan, but he had his head bent in conversation with one of
the boys.

"Unless you have other plans, of course," she said
sweetly, following my gaze.

She thought I had plans with Ryan? I shook my head.
"No, I don't have any plans."

"Good. You can ride with me. Let's go."

Before I could garner a response, she flounced out the
door.

6

The Magnolia

For the second time this week, I'd inadvertently agreed to a social interaction. How did that keep happening?

The door closed on Mira Ann's swaying form. She expected me to follow her. Just like that. What kind of person invited random strangers out to lunch? And worse, into their car? How did she know I wouldn't hijack her or something? No way I'd ever invite a stranger to hop in and go to lunch. These people were crazy.

Kids cast me weird glances as they skirted me on their way out, revealing that the one social interaction I'd consciously agreed to had been a monumental failure. Ryan clapped boys on the shoulders and reminded teens to do their homework. One set of cheerleaders had a competition this week, and he promised to come support them.

When the last of the kids filed out, Ryan walked up beside me, his goofy grin indicating I hadn't made a total mess of my first day. That, or my stupidity amused him.

"Next time maybe actually talk to the kids, huh?"

Yep. Definitely the latter. I'd blown the one thing he wanted me to do. "I told you I wasn't good at this kind of thing."

He regarded me for a moment, his stare seeking to decode me. Did he think I said stuff like that because I was
trying to play some kind of game for attention?

I huffed and returned his stare. He wouldn't get anything different from me. I was tired of being a chameleon.
Always trying to fit in and be who I needed to be in any
given place. People might not like the real me, but they
didn't like who I tried to be either. Derick's betrayal, the
loss of my home and job, and then Ida's death had stripped
me of the energy it took to try to make people like me.

I ran my fingers through the tangles in my hair. "Mira
Ann said I was going to lunch with her. She took off before
I could say anything."

Ryan glanced at the door. "Yeah, she does that." His
broad shoulders expanded with a deep breath. "Want me to
go with you?"

I didn't want to go at all. "How about you go, and I go
home?"

He laughed as if I'd been joking and gathered up empty
cans and discarded candy wrappers and tossed them in the
trash. I hurried to help. Maybe if I was too busy to meet
Mira Ann, she would go on without me. I dumped pizza
boxes into the trash and pulled the big black bag from the
can.

"That would be rude, Casey." Ryan finally said. His
tone held no judgment, no annoyance. Only simple, clear
fact. He straightened a few chairs and took the trash bag
from me.

I could get used to this man. His honesty was as refresh-
ing as a strawberry slushy on a hundred-degree day. "I don't
mean to be rude, but I'm not—" I struggled to find the right

words.

"Good with people?"

"Yeah. Sorry."

He walked toward the door and held it open, waiting for me to step out. "I'm not good at playing the tuba."

What? What did that have to do with anything? "Um, okay...?"

He gestured for me to pass through and then turned off the lights behind me. "Do you know why I'm not good at the tuba?"

"No musical ability?" I turned toward the sanctuary to go back out the way I'd come in, but Ryan gestured toward a glass door at the other end of the hallway.

"Because I never practice it. You won't be good at getting along with people if you never practice it." He opened the door and stepped out, leaving me to stand in the hallway alone to contemplate the truth of his statement.

I didn't want to be good at getting along with people. It required far too much emotional energy, and, in the end, I always ended up hurt. Ryan came back inside the church after having disposed of the trash. He wiped his hands on his jeans and stepped around me, leaving me to follow him down yet another gray carpeted hallway.

We passed several rooms with chairs set in circles obviously meant for Bible studies and Sunday school classes. "In my experience, people aren't worth the effort."

Ryan paused and glanced at me, his expression thoughtful and somewhat...concerned. "Jesus said the greatest commandment was to love the Lord your God with all of your heart, mind, soul, and strength. The second commandment was equal to that. To love your neighbor as yourself."

I kept walking toward the door. After a few steps, he followed me. I didn't need a lecture. In my experience, love was a one-way street. I'd pour out love to other people until they drained me like a bunch of leeches stuck to a blood sack, all while never gaining much from them in return. And once I was empty, I was just another bit of trash to throw away, no longer useful. "When other people start practicing that, maybe I will too."

Ryan wisely refrained from commenting. Smart man. He quickened his pace and darted around me to hold the door open. I eyed him as I stepped out into the balmy afternoon already thick with Mississippi humidity. Birds sang their merriment, and the lingering voices of a few remaining churchgoers hung in the air. A car sputtered by, spewing out an acrid puff of smoke.

The parking lot stood mostly empty now, save for a few cars near the couples chatting while their children played tag on the asphalt. Looked like my stall tactic worked. Mira Ann must have given up on me. She'd think me horribly rude like Ryan had said, but I didn't care.

Okay, maybe not. I did care. I didn't mean to be obnoxious or anything. Either way, I was on my own for lunch and—I checked my watch—it was already close to one. I hadn't eaten any of the kids' pizza, and I was starving. I had a few tubs of leftovers in the fridge from the gathering after Ida's funeral. They were still good. Probably.

A car horn blared, making me jump. A white SUV sat near an awning I hadn't noticed when we came out of the side door of the church.

"That's Mira Ann." Ryan jogged in her direction, and she rolled down the window.

Maybe I should sprint back to my car and hightail it out

of the lot. This uber-friendly act was getting under my skin. No way had that woman waited fifteen minutes on me without some kind of motive. I was already way out of my comfort zone, completely off my regular schedule, and now—

Ryan waved me toward the vehicle. I'd taken too long. Lost my chance. If I turned away now, it would be the epitome of rudeness, and not even I was that contentious. I stuffed my hands in my pockets and trudged toward them, casting one last glance at my Toyota.

Ryan bounded around the front of the shiny white SUV and popped open the passenger door. Did he plan on opening every door I came to? Odd...but kind of nice. I slipped onto a gray leather seat, and he shut the door. My heart fluttered. Did he plan to trap me in here with Miss America and make a run for it?

The back door behind me opened, and he jumped in. I ignored the surge of relief. I hardly knew this guy. He was still a stranger. Why should his presence make me feel more comfortable?

Mira Ann smiled. "Now, isn't this nice?" She shifted into drive and bounced us out onto a potholed street.

I grabbed the handle in front of me. Mira Ann cranked up the air conditioning, flooding the pristine interior with artic air. We bumped through the middle of town, past the sweets shop, the bank, the school, and the gas station, before she turned the whale of a vehicle onto the main highway.

"So, where are we going?" I scanned the passing pines. I hadn't seen a restaurant in Maryville. And I was fairly certain I hadn't missed anything in the one-stoplight town.

"We're going to The Magnolia. Their potato salad is

divine. You simply have to try it." Mira Ann sped up, passing farmhouses, one small neighborhood, and a large factory I'd had no idea rested outside town.

Mira Ann turned the knob on the radio, and country music filled her car with steel guitars played in minor keys. I'd never cared for country music. The old songs were sad, and the new ones were nothing more than an ode to half-dressed women riding in pickups. Or "good old boys" bragging about picking up short-skirted, boot-wearing girls at a bar. No thanks.

We came into the outskirts of the next town over. Ida'd bought her groceries here, since Forest Hill was big enough to have a Walmart. We pulled into the gravel parking lot at a big metal building. The front looked like something from an Old West town, but it had been decorated with swags and wreaths made from magnolia leaves. Inside, a massive twist of metal rods stretched to the ceiling, forming the shape of a tree in the center of the entryway.

Mira Ann bustled to the desk at the front of what appeared half gift shop, half restaurant, and a young girl with a big bow in her ponytail handed Mira Ann three menus. The left side of the establishment boasted typical gift shop fare: candles, home accessories, monogramed and overly fancy kids clothes, and gaudy jewelry. On the other side, small tables covered a black-and-white checkered floor. Stools lined a long bar with a mirror in the back. The owners must have been going for a 1950s soda shop. Mira Ann swayed past me, wiggling her fingers for me to follow.

We selected a booth against the far wall. Ryan scooted in first, and I chose to sit across from him. Mira Ann settled down next to Ryan. I busied myself with the menu while the two of them talked about the church service and people in town I didn't know.

It was a good thing Ryan had come. He could carry the conversation so I didn't have to. Come to think of it, that made total sense. Mira Ann seemed like the kind of woman who would realize I was socially awkward and had invited me knowing that Ryan, being the chivalrous sort, would offer to come along. Kudos, Miss America.

"So," Mira Ann said, "tell me about how you knew Ida."

The question pulled me from my perusal of a variety of sandwiches and salads. I glanced at Ryan, who seemed to have no interest in answering for me, and then addressed Mira Ann. "She was my grandmother."

She unfolded her napkin and spread it across her lap. "Oh, that's right. I remember now."

Remember what? No doubt small-town gossip had already circulated. Still, the way she said it seemed weird.

"What a blessing you found her right before she passed."

I hesitated. Did she accuse me of something with those sugary words? Or was I just being cynical?

"Absolutely," Ryan said, setting down his laminated menu. "God's timing and all."

"Of course, sweetie." Mira Ann waved her fingers at a tall waitress with bright red glasses. "Such a wonderful convenience can only be divine intervention."

The waitress scribbled our orders on a notepad. I ordered a side salad with ranch. Ryan got a double bacon BLT with a bag of chips and an extra side of hot potato salad.

Mira Ann tapped her finger on her cheek. "I think I'll have the same. And bring us a cup of hot potato salad for Casey, too. She simply has to try it." She smiled at me. "I told you it was heavenly."

I blinked at her. This woman had to be, what, a size two? And she was going to eat the same thing as the bulky man next to her? No way. The other two ordered sweet tea, but I asked for mine without the extra four hundred calories in sugar.

"So Ida left everything to you," Mira Ann said as soon as the waitress scuttled off.

"Uh-huh." At least, I think that was what the lawyer had said at our meeting. I'd get the house and Ida's accounts after some kind of probate period. I was still a little hazy on the details. I needed to meet with him again when I had my head on straight.

Mira Ann's eyelashes fluttered. "I always thought that house would make such a lovely B&B. Don't you think so?"

Ryan laughed. "Who wants to visit Maryville? As far as tourist stops go, I'd say we are at the bottom of the barrel."

A line formed between Mira Ann's perfectly arched eyebrows, but she quickly smoothed it away. "Haven't you heard of Airbnb? People are going all kinds of places these days. Market it as a Southern gem in a quiet little town, and you'll be full in no time."

The thought of a bunch of strangers descending on Ida's house turned my stomach. "I don't think Ida would have wanted that."

"You obviously can't keep it, so I was giving you some options. If you sell the property to someone looking to make some money with it, you may get a better price."

"How do you know she can't keep it?" Ryan leaned back against the red vinyl cushion and laced his calloused fingers on the Formica table.

The sound of Mira Ann's laugh reminded me of one of

those old Hollywood starlets from the 1950s. Put this place in black and white, and Mira Ann would fit in perfectly. "Seriously? You think a city girl wants to stay here?"

"*You* came back."

They stared at one another a moment, tension clearly building.

"I haven't decided yet what I'll do with Ida's house." I straightened and imitated Mira Ann's regal posture. "But I want to honor her wishes as best I can."

"Of course, sweetie." Mira Ann flashed her brilliant white teeth in a smile as dazzling as her sparkling eyes.

Ryan rolled his shoulders. "Weather says we're going to have some nasty storms this week."

Glad for the obvious shift in conversation, I jumped on the chance for predictable small talk. "I hate storms. I hope we don't lose power."

The waitress returned with our tea and asked me if I wanted any Splenda. I thanked her but declined. I stirred the ice around with my straw and grappled for something else to talk about. "So, Ryan, what can you tell me about your youth group?" Stupid. I sounded like a high school kid working on an interview project.

"We've got good kids. Some've had a hard life. Several of them, even though this is the Bible belt, haven't heard any of the Bible stories before. It's a lot of fun seeing God's word hit fresh ears."

I nodded, not sure how to respond to that.

"Did you grow up in church, Casey?" Mira Ann asked, sipping her tea and leaving red lip marks on her straw.

"Not really. My dad didn't care for churches. My mom dropped me off at a few VBS camps, though, so I've heard most of the stories."

The waitress returned with the food, serving my tiny salad alongside Mira Ann's and Ryan's triple-stacked sandwiches. Mira Ann must have noticed my gaze because she giggled and said something slightly snide about how delicious my lettuce pile looked. Her mountain of bacon looked mouth-watering, and much better than what I had, but I knew better than to eat it.

Ryan bowed his head and asked a simple blessing over the day and our meal and then went after his sandwich with gusto. I picked at my salad, answering questions tossed my way as best I could while marveling at how much food Mira Ann packed away. Her appetite almost made me hate her. But she probably spent hours in the gym. Had to, if she could eat that way and look like that.

Mira Ann pointed at my bowl of creamy sliced potatoes. "You haven't tried them."

I poked at the contents of the little bowl. Laden with cheese, this thing probably had at least 600 calories. Per bite. Mira Ann looked at me expectantly. I forked one slice and popped it in my mouth.

Gooey, cheesy temptation erupted on my tongue.

"See? I told you." Mira Ann giggled. "It's not anything like cold potato salad full of mustard. This is the good stuff."

No kidding. Herbs balanced the creamy goodness, and I'd guess the cook had put in a hearty share of cream and butter. I stabbed another bite and paused with it halfway to my mouth. "You're right. This is awesome." I finished off the bowl, ignoring the little voice inside of me that warned I'd lost control and, at this rate, I'd be an oinker by the end of the week.

We finished the meal, which Ryan insisted on paying

for, and returned to Mira Ann's car. Ten minutes later we were back at the church. I grabbed the door handle, then paused and turned to offer Mira Ann a genuine smile. Despite my misgivings, the lunch hadn't been half bad. "That was nice. Thanks for asking."

"Glad to, sweetie. We should do it again."

The door suddenly lurched underneath my fingers. I hung on, and the momentum snatched me from the seat. I screeched and churned my legs beneath me, trying to gain some kind of traction. My ballet slippers slid on the running board but couldn't hang on. I let go of the door, but it was already too late.

"Casey!" Ryan reached for me.

Mira Ann gasped.

I tumbled to the ground in a heap of bruised pride and mortification.

7

Polished Excuses

I hated the smell of blood. It turned my stomach and threatened to expel my hot potato salad all over the church parking lot. Not a good thing. Even the tiny little scrapes from the asphalt were enough to make me tremble.

"Are you okay?" Ryan tugged on my elbow, easing me to my feet.

My ankle hurt, and my good jeans had a giant hole in the knee. Not to mention I'd humiliated myself. No. I wasn't okay. "Yeah, I'm fine. Sorry about that."

Ryan kept his warm hand under my elbow and wrapped his other arm around my shoulders. "Why are you apologizing? I'm the one who sent you tumbling."

Mira Ann rounded the purring SUV and scrutinized me, narrowing her eyes at the foot I held off the ground. "Can you put weight on it?"

I put my shoe down and tested the pressure of my weight, then winced. "I can. But it hurts."

Before I could say anything else, Ryan scooped me into his arms.

I squirmed. "What are you doing?"

"Taking you home."

Mira Ann caught my eye, and a line of worry dipped between her brows.

Ryan offered thanks for both of us for lunch and carried me across the hot asphalt, leaving Mira Ann to whatever thoughts churned behind her eyes.

I'd never been carried by a man, and the strange sensation made me feel both sickeningly helpless and cared for in the same moment. He gently tucked me into the passenger side of his gray pickup. Not nearly as pristine as Mira Ann's vehicle, Ryan's truck hosted hats shoved between the dash and the windshield, stacks of papers on the center console, and three Coke cans.

He bounded around the front of the truck and leapt inside with the grace of one who never stumbled over his own two clumsy feet. I wanted to argue, to say I needed to get my car, but it would be futile. The man who Ida had entrusted as the gatekeeper to all my answers didn't strike me as the type who would cave to puny arguments. The church was less than five minutes from Ida's house. I could get my car later.

Ryan rolled the windows down, and fresh air whipped strands of dark hair over my face. I drew in a deep breath and let the scents of pine and flora cleanse my senses. A few bumpy minutes later, we pulled into the drive at Ida's house.

Knowing better than to grab the handle, I waited as Ryan exited the truck and walked around. He opened my door, but I refused to let him carry me again. Too disconcerting. Instead, I slid down to the concrete driveway and steadied my feet beneath me. It hurt, but not badly enough for me to think I'd torn or broken anything. With a little support, could put most of my weight on my ankle. With his help I made it up the steps, the scrapes on my knee smarting.

Ryan opened the front door. And paused.

"What's wrong?" I leaned to look around him, but his big frame blocked the doorway.

Without answering me, Ryan swung the door the rest of the way open and gripped my elbow again. As I hobbled inside, the reason for his hesitation became painfully clear. The scraps of material—which I'd tried to stitch together by hand—were spread out over the dusty hardwood floor. I'd gathered together ragged edges of the mismatched fabric and looped a threaded needle unevenly through the pieces. The result was a roughly four-foot by six-foot misshapen rectangle sprawling across the floor. It looked terrible.

"Just wanted to be sure you wouldn't mind me coming inside."

Oh. Right. The smile in his voice brought heat up my neck. Crazy lady afraid of strangers.

Ryan stepped around the fabric without a word and steered me toward the kitchen. Sunlight dappled through the lace curtains of the bay window brimming with herbs and lay in speckled patterns across the farmhouse table. Ryan pulled a chair out for me and waited until I'd lowered myself into it before flipping on the light to the pantry. A moment later he returned with a bottle of peroxide and two bandages.

He certainly knew his way around Ida's house. "How often did you come over here?" I looked over the top of his head, too glad someone else was eyeing my cuts to be unnerved by his presence.

The fresh hole in these jeans was too big to pass off as a

fashion choice.

Ryan poured some peroxide onto a cotton ball and dabbed at the scraped flesh on my exposed kneecap. I prided myself on withholding an embarrassing yelp.

"Lots of times. That's why Ida moved the first-aid box from the upstairs bathroom to the pantry." He chuckled. "She knew I'd need it often enough, and the relocation saved her needless treks up the stairs."

"Why?"

After dabbing the wound and pressing on the two adhesive bandages, Ryan rose and tossed the packaging in the trash. "I did maintenance work for her. Nothing big, since I'm not a plumber or carpenter or anything. I cleaned the gutters, cut the grass, and fixed sagging cabinet doors."

I examined my knee. "Thanks." I couldn't even see the scrapes under the two little bandages. They couldn't have been all that bad. I was just a wimp.

Ryan put his hands on the countertop and regarded me across the central island. "It's good for you to let people care about you."

Not the response I'd been expecting. I shifted in my seat.

"Ida wanted you to enjoy making the quilt."

Uh-oh. Another uncomfortable subject switch. I should have known he wouldn't let the mess in the foyer slide.

"She wanted to connect with you because she cared about you." He tapped a finger on the countertop, but his eyes were soft.

I bristled anyway and tilted my chin in defiance. "I *am* doing the quilt. As best I can, anyway. I'm not a quilter. Or a seamstress. I don't even know how to use the machine."

Ryan shrugged. "Google."

I fished my phone out of my back pocket and held it up.

The old-style flip phone with a cracked top barely took calls. I wouldn't be Googling anything with my limited data, which I saved for emergencies, and Ida didn't have a computer. My computer had been lost with the rest of the stuff Derick had bought for me and insisted on keeping when he tossed me out.

"You have a lot of excuses."

His words washed over me, settling into cracks and stinging worse than the peroxide. "Pardon me?"

Ryan drew in a deep breath and blew it out slowly. "In the short time I've known you, you've told me several things you're not good at. I'm starting to wonder if you're using that as an excuse to avoid working or to keep you from getting out of your comfort zone."

I glared at him, his words pricking at my insides in ways I didn't appreciate. "You think me not knowing how to make a quilt is an excuse? For what? I'm doing it. I'm sorry if it's not as pretty as you'd like it to be." I wouldn't have another man pointing out all my flaws. I could see them enough on my own. I didn't need his help.

"That's not what I meant." He stared at me a moment, and this time I lost the battle to hold his gaze.

I looked at my shoes. Great. I'd scuffed the left one. Chalk up ruined shoes to go with my ruined pants. The back of my throat burned. I clenched my teeth. I would *not* cry over scuffed shoes.

"I meant that you say you're not good with people—"

"Because I'm not."

"—and maybe that's true. But you're letting that label you. Define you. You say you're not good with people, so you use that as a reason not to try to get better. People don't need to practice what they're good at as much as they need to practice where they're weak."

Two sermons in one day. Just what I needed.

"You say you don't know how to quilt, but that's exactly the point. Ida knew you didn't know how. But she gave you the project so that you could learn from it. Figure it out."

The truth of his words sank into my middle, and I hung my head. "I'm failing at that, too."

"You're only failing because you're giving up. If you run from every problem, you never solve anything."

"I'm making the quilt, aren't I?" The words sounded childish and petulant even to my own ears, and I hated myself all the more for it. Why could I never sound like a put-together grown woman?

"Did you care for Ida?"

I snapped my gaze to his but didn't see anything condemning in his eyes. "Yes."

"Then why are you avoiding doing this project her way? You're rushing through it using the excuse that you're not already an expert so therefore you can't do it to the best of your ability. Do you think that's what she wanted?"

No. But I'd already messed it up. I'd already hacked at the fabric Ida'd left me. Just like everything else in my life, I'd made a mess of it. Tears I didn't want burned my eyes and slid down my cheeks.

"I'm not trying to berate you, Casey. I'm trying to show you what I see and, well, what I think I'm being led to tell you."

I ignored that last part. This man might be insightful, since that was probably a necessity in his line of work, but that didn't mean God had spoken any specific words meant for me. I swiped the wetness from my lashes. "I've already messed it up."

His smile warmed some cold place deep inside me. "There's nothing too messed up that it can't be fixed. It may take time, patience, and determination, but everything can be fixed."

Even me?

The thought sprang up from nowhere, and I tried to push it down, but it refused to drown. Could this process, this working through my grief for Ida and everything else staining my life make me better in the end? New?

A yearning welled in my heart that I couldn't ignore. I wanted to be different. I didn't want to live in constant fear of failure. Of never being good enough for anyone. I'd been enough for Ida simply because of who I was, not because of anything I'd done or not done. I wanted to learn to be myself without being crushed by other people's rejection.

But how?

Ryan fished something out of his back pocket and handed it to me. "Something tells me you probably need this now."

I took the envelope from him and ran my finger over my name in Ida's shaky script. Why? Why did I have to lose the one person in this world who wanted me?

Ryan placed a heavy hand on my shoulder. "Need me to help you upstairs?"

I shook my head. "I don't think my ankle is that bad. Besides, I'll probably stay down here awhile."

After he gave me another squeeze, he fished a paper out of the junk drawer and scribbled something on it. "This is my number. Call me if you have any problems."

I nodded absently.

Ryan crouched down in front of me and forced me to

meet his gaze. "I mean it. Don't fall down the stairs or anything stupid because you're too stubborn to ask for help when you need it."

Mouth suddenly dry, I swallowed deeply. His words carried more layers than I cared to admit. I offered a weak smile. "Promise."

He probed at my ankle but, not finding any swelling or bruising, declared I'd probably only twisted it. I almost quipped something about that being proof I was fine and obviously didn't need him after all, but I swallowed it down. Score a point for me for not being rude.

After promising to pick me up in the morning to go get my car, Ryan let himself out.

I stared at the letter in my hand, alone again with the silence and the ghosts of Ida's memories.

8

My Father's Friend

rocrastinating wasn't always avoidance. At least that was what I kept telling myself as I hobbled around the kitchen smelling leftovers from Ida's memorial and lamentably throwing most of the remnants in the trash. A shame I hadn't thought ahead and put the containers in the freezer.

Ida's letter sat on the table like the proverbial elephant in the room, simultaneously calling to me and mocking me. Things must be pretty bad if Ryan deviated from Ida's instructions and gave me the letter before I'd finished the quilt. I scraped a few bites of chicken spaghetti in the trash. The sour milk smell couldn't be denied. Pity. It had been pretty good. All of Nancy's bread had already settled around my hips.

The lady's postponement of our baking appointment disappointed me, but she probably had better things to do. I surveyed the fridge. A half-gallon of milk two days past its best-buy date, a carton of eggs, one piece of lasagna I was pretty sure was still safe to eat, and an array of jellies and condiments completed my choices for dinner.

Lasagna it was. Eggs for breakfast and lunch tomorrow, and I could probably scrounge up some canned goods in the pantry. I could survive a bit longer. But first thing tomorrow I had to get to the lawyer's office and figure out what probate and the transfer of Ida's accounts meant. I'd starve waiting around for him to call me with more instructions.

My ankle spurted little flicks of pain up my leg, but I'd felt worse. A lot worse, actually, and still worked a ten-hour shift at Bistro. As long as it held my weight, I could deal with the discomfort. A cup of ice water and lack of reasonable excuses later, I had Ida's letter in hand as I limped toward her overstuffed couch in the parlor.

A crocheted afghan covered the back of the couch and scratched my neck. I gently folded half of it back and sank into the caramel-colored cushions. It still smelled like the lavender fabric spray she used on the furniture. I pulled the lever to pop the recliner on my end of the couch, elevating my injured ankle.

The letter trembled in my hand. What was wrong with me? Why did I fear what the letter contained? Ida wouldn't know how badly I'd botched the quilt even though Ryan did. He might be a man of God, but even he didn't have that kind of access. I wouldn't get a reprimand. Just another piece of this weird puzzle.

The letter slid out of the envelope covered in the same blocky type of the ancient typewriter. Ida's voice filled my mind as I began to read, causing an ache in my chest.

Casey,

I'm so proud of you. You stepped out of your comfort zone and did something new. I know that's not easy for you. Now you have something you can treasure and pass down to future generations, should that be in God's design. The quilt represents the combination of the past and the present. Me and you. You and your parents. It means so much to me that you poured your heart into the project. Stitching those memories isn't always easy, but it takes knowing where we came from to understand our past. And sometimes God can use those memories to heal our hearts in the future. Congratulations on finding old memories and turning them into something you can be proud of.

My heart sank. I hadn't found any memories. I must have missed something. And I hadn't done anything to make Ida proud. That mess I'd barely threaded together couldn't even be counted as half-effort. My heap of mismatched fabric with uneven edges wouldn't hold together for generations. Not that I held out any hope of ever having a family of my own. That idea had died on my thirty-fifth birthday when my gynecologist said my maternal clock was ticking and, if I wanted children, I had better start trying right away. No way would I bring a kid I couldn't provide a good life for into this world. I knew what that was like.

I pushed away melancholy thoughts of spending the remainder of my life alone. How bad could it be? Free to do what I wanted without other people depending on me made things much easier. No one to fail or let down or abandon me. Easier.

No one to pick you up when you fall down, though, either.

Shaking my head against the inner voice, I returned to

the letter.

> *By now I'm sure my good friend Nancy has come by with her friendship bread. She would love to see your quilt, if you wouldn't mind calling on her. I think you will like her. You remind me of her in a lot of ways. And something tells me you two being friends could lead to great things in the future.*

What did she mean by that?

> *I'll have another step in this journey for you soon. For now, I have a story for you.*

I straightened and peered closer, my eyes eager to find answers to my past and my family. When Ida told a story, it was because she wanted me to learn something important.

> *When your father was thirteen, he adopted a scraggly cat. It had to have been surviving out of the dumpster at the middle school, and my boy had a big heart. He couldn't stand to see anyone, not even a mangy cat, suffer. Every day for about a week Mike would crouch down by the dumpster, ignoring other boys' taunts, and coax the skittish creature out from under the dumpster with saved bits of his lunch. Finally, Mike got the cat to let him get his hands on it.*
> *It didn't go well.*
> *That Friday when he came home from school, he was covered in thin scratches from his forehead to his fingertips. That cat had gotten him good, but he was still determined to bring it home. For the cat's*

own good, he said.

Sometimes, Casey, what we think is best won't come easily. It requires ingenuity, fight, and determination. Sometimes, the one we are trying to help resists. They may bite or scratch. But, if we know in our hearts we can help, then the struggle is worth the fight.

I snuggled deeper into the couch, the metaphor not lost on me. Whatever Ida was doing with this game, she meant it for my good. And she was warning me I might not like it.

So, my Mike came home covered in scratches but grinning ear to ear. That year at school had been hard on him. Kids can be cruel at times, and Mike's gentle heart often landed him at the wrong end of some mean boys' hormone-induced bravado. He held the cat close, so proud to show it to me, even though my mind was already racing with fears of cat scratch fever and rabies.

But I hadn't seen that much joy in his eyes in a long while, so I couldn't bring myself to tell Mike he couldn't keep that cat. After a long talk about how God gave cats fur for a reason and assuring Mike that the cat had spent many nights outside and wouldn't freeze, I gave him an old pillow and a couple of old pie tins for food and water to put on the porch.

Mike feared the cat would run away, but I told him the cat knew it had a warm bed and plenty of food on our porch, food that tasted and smelled better than the dumpster. Why would the cat have any cause to leave?

Something twisted in my stomach. At Ida's house I was safe and warm. No predators came for me here. No ex-boyfriends pounding on my door. Despite the scarcity in the fridge, I would have plenty to eat once the accounts cleared probate. I'd been given a new life. Why would I want to return to the dumpster?

The implications too heavy to handle, I buried them to examine later and returned my focus to Ida's story.

> *That cat ate scraps on my porch for one day. One. Want to guess where I found it the next morning? On Mike's pillow. With Mike curled up next to it.*

I laughed, picturing Ida's dismay at finding a flea-infested critter in her pristine house.

> *One expensive vet trip later, Mike's new friend had been properly vaccinated, washed, and checked for mange and fleas. That thing lived with us until after Mike left home. Then somehow, after he was gone, old Scruffy became my friend, too. Almost as though he knew we both missed Mike and that maybe by sticking together we could bear it as a team.*

How hard must it have been for Ida to lose her only child after losing her husband years before? Poor Ida must have felt so alone.

Like me.

9

Pretty as a Picture

The next morning, I was prepared. This time, I'd set an alarm, showered, cooked eggs, made coffee, and even cleaned up the dead flowers in the foyer before nine. I folded—or at least wadded—the heap of material I'd been calling my quilt and promised both Ida and myself I would fix this mess. Even if I got a few scratches—or at least needle pricks—along the way.

The fabric safely stored in the trunk in Ida's room, I gingery made my way back down the stairs in time for Ryan's knock. I swung the door open and smiled.

"You look spry this morning." Dressed in a solid black tee rather than another button-up, Ryan tented his brows and gestured toward me.

Spry? Wasn't that a word people used for elderly folks who could move more than expected? "Uh...thanks?"

His gaze zoomed in on my bare toes. I'd found some of Ida's polish in her bathroom last night and had coated my toenails in *Poison Apple* red. "Looks like your ankle isn't bothering you."

Oh. Right. "An ice pack and elevation, and all's good."

I wiggled my toes for effect.

He still watched me as I stepped down from the porch. Seeming satisfied with how well I hid any signs of discomfort, he bounded past me and scurried to his truck to open the passenger door. Using my left leg to hold my weight, I lifted myself inside. Ryan waited until I settled into the cloth seat and then rounded the pickup and hopped in.

"Don't work on Mondays, either?"

Ryan's eyebrows pinched into confusion—or maybe annoyance—as he shifted into reverse. I'd meant to be funny. Inside joke from that time when I'd been rude and—yeah. Failure.

"Not until after lunch." His tone held none of the annoyance his face portended. He must be good at keeping his voice even. Probably necessary when one worked with unruly teens. Man had to have a good dose of patience.

We rolled out of Ida's drive and past Ryan's house. I tried again for friendly conversation. "So you work Monday afternoon but not Tuesdays?"

He paused for a stray dog to cross the road and then continued at the posted twenty-five mile per hour limit down Ida's street. "Sorta. Monday afternoon is staff meeting. We go over everything from the previous Sunday and plan for the next, but that's all."

The drooping trees parted, and we lingered at the stop sign at the end of Ida's street.

Ryan glanced at me, brown eyes probing. "Oh, I meant to tell you. Mom said she's sorry she had to cancel on you and was hoping you'd be willing to reschedule. Will Wednesday work?"

My brain scrambled to give his words meaning. When had I met his mom? Or planned anything with her?

Ryan turned at the old train depot and headed toward the church. The truck bounced over a major pothole, jarring me hard enough to nearly hit my head on the ceiling. Ryan didn't notice.

"You were going to make bread...?"

Realization hit. "Nancy? She's your mom?"

He grinned and pulled into the church parking lot. "You didn't know?"

Nope. Would I have accepted an invitation to bake if I'd known? A line from Ida's letter surfaced. She wanted me to be friends with Nancy because "good things" could come from it. I scooted a little closer to the window. She was crazy if she thought any of those "good things" meant something with Ryan.

Ryan pulled around the side of the brick building and parked next to my Toyota. "I'll follow you back home."

I popped open my door before he could get out to do it for me. "Thanks, but I'm not going home." Or, rather, to Ida's. That felt weird.

He leaned forward in the seat, one arm propped on the steering wheel. "Where are you headed, if you don't mind my asking?"

I slid out, jarring my still sore ankle on the pavement. I kept the pain from my face. "To the lawyer's office. I have to figure out this whole probate thing."

The corners around his eyes crinkled. "Want me to go with you? I might be able to help."

"No, thanks. I'm good." I shut the door and fished the key out of my pocket. Should have brought my purse with my driver's license. But I probably didn't need it anyway. I'd obey the slow speed limits and avoid any Barney Fife types. Three blocks or so over, the law office shared the same strip of real estate with the bank, the sweet shop, and the library. And I could see those from the church parking lot. If my ankle didn't hurt I'd walk and save the gas.

Ryan rolled down the window. "What do you want me to tell Mom?"

Oh, right. The bread. I stuck the key in the door and turned. "Wednesday's fine."

"Great! I'll let her know." He waved good-bye and churned out of the parking lot.

The interior of my Toyota boiled with heat, and I left the door open for a few seconds before sliding across the cracked vinyl seat. It took three tries, but the engine finally cranked. I checked the gas gauge. Eighth of a tank. It would have to do until I got access to Ida's accounts. I didn't plan on going anywhere until then anyway.

I pulled into the law office designated simply *Norbert Shaw, Esq.*

Too bad Ida didn't still have a car. I could have used one of those, too. But once she went into hospice, she'd given hers to a single mom so the woman could get to work. I couldn't begrudge her that.

I pushed the glass door etched with the lawyer's name open and stepped into a tidy waiting area. The walls were painted a calming turquoise, and plush chairs invited patrons to settle in and wait their turn while flipping through various magazines.

"Well, look who it is!"

The familiar voice drew my attention to a desk nestled into a corner to my left. Mira Ann. Dressed in a white fitted blouse, she'd swept her long hair into a professional twist and brought a new layer of style to the already chic office.

I stuffed my hands into my jeans' pockets and hoped she

didn't notice the stain on the hem of my pink tee. "Hey. You work here?"

Mira Ann rounded her desk, an A-line gray skirt brushing the top of her knees. She crossed her arms and tapped one painted nail on her elbow. "I'm the paralegal."

Pictures covered her desk. The largest photograph, displayed with a heart-studded white frame, depicted Mira Ann and Ryan, both several years younger. He had his arm wrapped around her shoulders, and they both wore goofy smiles.

She followed my gaze. "That's when he took me to Gatlinburg. We had such a great time sightseeing." She wiggled her eyebrows. "And that cabin was *so* cozy."

Preacher Man had shared a cabin with Miss America? I met her gaze. None of my business. "Sounds nice."

Something in her smile appeared predatory, but it disappeared so quickly I told myself I'd imagined it. She probably wanted to stake her claim on Ryan. They looked to be a couple. Or had been at one time. Either way, it wasn't any of my business, and I had no intentions of getting involved with her man. "Derick never took me on any trips like that." I shrugged. "But he was an overbearing jerk to begin with." Why had I spouted that? Stupid nerves always made me say awkward things.

Mira Ann offered a sympathetic smile. "Bad breakups. I get it."

I shifted my weight and circled back to the reason for being here. "I came to check on Ida's estate."

"I figured you would." She sat back down in her chair and laced her long fingers together. "We have to make sure no creditors have any claims on the estate and that all posts are credited prior to releasing the funds. It'll probably be several weeks."

Could I survive on canned green beans that long? Derick would say the diet would be good for my waistline. It seemed terrible of me to ask about getting money any faster, though, so I nodded along as if I had any idea how these things usually went. I could always get a temporary job.

Mira Ann grinned. "But don't worry, sweetie. I'm going to make sure it gets through as quickly as the law allows."

She seemed sincere, and now that the Ryan thing was out of the way, she apparently realized I posed no threat. That, or she'd help me get out of here as quickly as possible to make sure of it. Whatever her misguided motives, that worked for me. "Thanks. I really appreciate your help."

"Of course!" She waved a hand toward my feet. "Oh! How's your ankle?"

"Fine. Just needed ice."

Mira Ann laughed. "I'm not surprised. Ryan is so dramatic. I'm sorry he embarrassed you like that."

"He was being nice. Ida's wishes and all."

She cocked her head. "What wishes?"

"She left me a series of letters, telling me about my family's history and the stories that go along with all the heirlooms in the house. Ryan is supposed to give me one at different points in the process."

Leaning forward, she placed her chin on her laced fingers. "Is he now?"

I shrugged. "That's what Ida said. One letter at each phase. But my first project isn't going so well. I'm supposed to make a quilt, but I'm doing a terrible job."

Mira Ann leaned back in her chair, regarding me with a curious glint in her eyes. "Bless your heart. And you don't get another letter until you're finished?"

Excepting the one Ryan gave me early, but mentioning that seemed unnecessary. "That's what he said."

"Isn't that interesting?" She flashed me another grin. "You need help with any of it, you let me know."

I thanked her and hurried out the door. Nothing I could do about the house or Ida's accounts for now.

All I could do was finish the quilt and wait.

10

The Mighty Oak

Technology could be a wondrous thing. Despite Ida's choice to live without computers and my own lack of a smart phone, a couple of days, a trip to the library, and a few YouTube videos later, and I had the ancient sewing machine threaded and ready.

Grinning at my own ingenuity, I sat at the machine and placed my feet on the wrought-iron pedal the way the lady on the video had demonstrated. Bless people with too much time on their hands. You could find instructions for anything these days, provided for free by people with nothing better to do.

Left foot forward on the grate, right foot back. I started a rocking motion. The wheel on the right hand of the machine spun, and the needle dipped up and down, pulling black thread through the material I had laid across the machine's bed and under the presser foot.

"Yes!" I rocked the pedal again, slowly feeding the material and watching the thread dip in and out of the fabric.

Thunder rumbled outside, followed by a pop of lightning. I jumped, and the needle shuddered to a halt. I clenched my teeth and turned the wheel on the back of the machine to get it spinning in the right direction again.

Good thing I didn't have to sleep in my car tonight. Homeless and staying the night in the back seat of a rundown Toyota was bad enough. Stormy nights could be downright terrifying. I'd never take a big, safe house for granted.

I guided the needle along one small square and connected it to the next. I'd made a pattern from a piece of newspaper, same as Ida had done, and now had a neat stack of congruent squares organized into an alternating color pattern. One by one I connected them together until the last piece in the stack joined its brethren.

Something groaned. The old house's bones creaked with the weight of the fury outside. I leaned closer to the machine. Watched the needle rise and fall. A window rattled, desperately trying to shield me from the tempest wrapping itself around Ida's Victorian like a python.

Twisting the wheel, I lifted the needle from the final piece of fabric and pulled my quilt free. I cut the thread, making sure to leave enough dangling out to start the next time. There.

A bolt of blue fire spit through the sky, washing the foyer in light. Nothing to worry over. Just a little thunderstorm.

Eight neat little rows of squares. Nothing fancy. No intricate patterns or detailed designs, but I'd taken my time and made something I was certain my grandmother would be proud of.

A clap of thunder rattled Ida's china. A tingle shot down my spine, a tiny reflection of the electricity popping outside. The lights flickered. Shadows pounced, then retreated.

Better call it quits before the storm's black maw gobbled up the power. A piercing, high-pitched tone split the air. A siren screeching a death wail.

I jerked out of the chair. It toppled to the floor and bounced on the hardwood. My quilt pooled on the floor.

The wail faded, then swelled again. My pulse thrashed against my veins. The power trembled. Murky shadows wrapped around me, squeezing out my shuttering breath.

Focus. Think.

The lights popped on again, vanquishing the adversary.

I gripped the edge of the sewing machine. In my youth, a tornado siren meant we had to sit in the hallway at school with a notebook over our heads and hope it saved us from falling bricks. In my adult life, it had meant a few moments on break while customers scurried for cover.

My phone rang. I patted my pocket. Not there. The sound came from the kitchen. I sprinted through the house, skidding in the doorway. There. I plucked it off the counter and flipped it open. "Hello?"

"Casey?"

Ryan. I let out a breath hot with relief. "Yeah?" The bay window in the breakfast nook exposed slashing rain and whipping limbs. I turned my back.

"You hear the tornado siren? Get in the hall closet."

The controlled concern in his voice had me scrambling down the hall toward the linen closet in the center of the house. The siren screamed again, warning the people of Maryville a cyclone of death had set its sights on their perfect little town.

"Do you still have power?"

As though to test his words, the lights flicked off and immediately on again like some specter thought it would be fun to toggle the light switch.

"For now." I gripped the phone and forced my voice to sound nonchalant. "Are *you* hiding out in a closet?" Failed. My voice warbled like a child searching under her bed for the bogeyman.

Ryan's taut voice pulsed with a single word. "Yeah."

I yanked open the linen closet. Small. Tight. Safe. I scurried inside and pulled the door closed behind me. Darkness swirled around me, choking out my breath. Pulse thudded in my ears, creating a weird *whooshing* sound. I rubbed slick palms down my thighs.

Nope. Too dark. I reached out into the hall and flicked the switch, flooding the little space with light and solace. I sucked in air, held it, and let it slide out of my nose as slowly as possible.

Shelves wrapped around three sides, stacked with tablecloths, spare sheets, and a few random Christmas decorations. Better. At least with the light I didn't have to add childish fears of the dark to the real terror of impending danger.

I sank to the floor. I hadn't hidden in a closet in years. Not since I was little and trying to escape my parents' fights. The phone grew sweaty in my hand. I held firm. "Are you still there?" I drew my knees into my chest.

"I'm here. I'll stay on the line until it passes."

The siren wailed. I squeezed my eyes tight.

"Don't worry. It'll be gone—"

The lights flickered and went out. I caught my breath. "Ryan?"

A low rumble vibrated through the house. Raw panic surged in my veins, and I jumped to my feet. "What is that?"

The phone crackled, and Ryan's voice came through the other end of the line, firm but calm. "Casey, don't leave that closet."

I paused with my hand on the knob. How did he know I was about to bolt? The house moaned. I held my breath. Suddenly, a sickening crash and the sound of splintering wood tore through the air.

I screamed.

"Casey?"

I dropped to my knees and threw my arm over my head. The house shook. Would it come down on top of me? I threw the door open. I needed to escape. Run.

"Casey! Can you hear me? Don't move."

Gripping the phone like a lifeline, I huddled in the darkness. "The house is coming down!"

I stared out into the hallway but couldn't see anything in the dark. Rain pounded the windows, beating a steady rhythm like a madman trying to break in.

"You're in the safest place in the house." Ryan spoke calmly, and something about his reassurance settled my nerves. "As soon as it passes, I'll come get you."

The siren swelled again, seeming louder than it had before. The smell of rain tickled my nose. Had the storm blown a window out? I pressed my back against the shelves. The line crackled, and I pushed the phone tighter against my ear. What if the tornado had taken out Ryan's house? "You okay?"

He chuckled, and some of the tension drained out of me. "Fine. We're huddled in the pantry, waiting for it to pass."

"We?"

"Mom says hi."

Grasping at the normalcy of the conversation to distract me, I asked, "You live with your mom?"

"Sometimes."

All this time Nancy had been next door? Why hadn't I

noticed? And what did he mean by *sometimes*? "Oh. Hi, Nancy."

The line went quiet, and I stood as still as I could, listening to the pounding rain. At least the weird moaning had stopped.

A rush of relieved breath flowed through the phone line. "I think it's past us. You good?"

I stared out into the dark hallway. No. I was terrified. "Yeah. I'm fine."

"Good. Stay put."

The line went dead before I could answer. Great. Now what? He expected me to stay in a closet until he came to rescue me? What kind of impression would that give? Pitiful.

I gathered my resolve and stepped out. Wind groaned through the house, and my pulse skittered.

Where did Ida keep the flashlights?

Lightning cracked again, and a burst of bluish light illuminated the small hallway. I felt my way with my hands. I'd probably find what I needed in the utility closet in the laundry room. The front door banged open.

I sucked a breath and pressed myself to the wall. I could have sworn I'd locked it.

"Casey?"

A beam of light bounced through the foyer. I peeled myself off the wallpaper. "Here."

Ryan pushed the door closed and clomped through the foyer. "You good?"

I raised my hand to shield my eyes and nodded. I couldn't see him behind the beam of blinding light, but I knew he could see me. He turned the flashlight toward the kitchen. "Come on. Let's go have a look."

He turned and swept the light back toward the foyer. I

followed his broad shoulders, not wanting to admit that his presence made me feel better. I was a grown woman. Why would I be afraid of the dark and a few weird noises?

Still. Maybe I should get a dog. For protection.

The idea brought immediate comfort, and I tucked it away to examine later. We traipsed through the house and rounded the corner into the kitchen. Ryan paused.

"What?" I moved to look around his dripping wet body. "What's wrong?"

Ryan rubbed the back of his neck and pointed the flashlight beam through the kitchen and into the dining room.

My heart sank. A tree had torn a hole through the roof, letting in spitting rain. The trembling branches of an uninvited oak had smashed Ida's dining table. I put my hand to my lips.

Ryan's arm draped over my shoulders and pulled me close, but I hardly noticed the attempt at comfort. Rain poured through the hole in the wall, shimmering off the leaves and pooling on the hardwood.

What was I going to do now?

Ryan took charge, and in a few moments we'd gathered every towel in Ida's house. I pushed a green one across the floor, mopping up rainwater. "It keeps coming inside."

Ryan dropped a stack next to me. "You keep at it. I'll go get a tarp."

I kept myself focused on one section of floor at a time and tried not to look at the gaping hole in the wall. Ida's words repeated in my head with each pass I made with the towel.

One thing at a time.

I hated when things were out of control. It made me feel like a kid again, stuck on the current of other people's whims. Of course in this case, it had been God Himself who'd sent my little sailboat tumbling.

The front door opened and closed a few moments later. Ryan's boots squished across the floor I'd just dried. I kept my focus on mopping up the water at the base of the china cabinet. Thank goodness Ida's grandmother's china hadn't been lost. The table I could replace.

A sudden roar vibrated through the room, and I fell backward. What the—?

Ryan revved a chainsaw. I covered my ears and scrambled out of the way. The least he could have done was warn me. I ducked through the doorway and watched him from the cover of the kitchen.

He pushed branches aside and sent water droplets spraying all over the floor. With each sweep of the saw, tangled limbs shuddered and dropped to the hardwood. Finally, Ryan turned off the loud machine.

"There. Now we can get these pushed out and the hole covered." He jerked his chin toward the front entry. "I left a tarp by the door."

I scrambled to the front of the house and scooped up the heavy blue plastic. It wouldn't keep out intruders, but at least it would help with the water.

We finally pushed all the limbs into the yard and cleared the area. The rain slowed to a trickle, glistening off the jagged edges of what had once been the baseboards.

This was awful.

Ryan's arm eased around my shoulders. "It's okay. We got the limbs out. We'll get the wall covered to protect the house, and we'll deal with the rest in the morning."

I nodded numbly.

The rest would be more than I could handle.

11

Aftermath

Morning light revealed more of what I didn't want to see. Ryan had tried. I had to give him credit for that. The large tarp we'd tacked to the wall blocked my view of Ida's yard. We'd spent most of the night hammering the tarp to the wall, clearing the broken table and chairs into a pile in the corner, and drying up the rest of the water on the floor.

Today, I'd need to wash nearly every towel Ida owned. I'd left them in a sodden heap in the laundry room.

Ida's beautiful dining room was ruined. The entire corner was missing. The tree had taken out a chunk of the roof, nearly all of the wall, and a portion of the floor. At least it had hit here and had taken out only one story instead of two.

I stood frozen in indecision. Who should I call first?

The house was still in probate. Who paid for repairs? Would the house need foundation work? What about insurance? Surely Ida had insurance. Could I file a claim on her behalf? More questions for the lawyer.

Towels. For now, I could wash towels. But what was I

going to do about the gaping hole in the wall, the water damage, the smashed furniture, and—

I took a deep breath. Ida's voice returned, calming my nerves. *One thing at a time.*

After shoving the first load of soggy towels into the washer, I tugged on my sneakers. Better go outside and see what I was dealing with. I plodded down the front porch steps and headed to the side of the house opposite from Ryan's. The soggy ground squished underneath my feet, creating a little sucking sound each time I took a step.

Tree limbs littered the yard and street, evidence that the storm hadn't visited its fury only on Ida's house. Birds twittered in the budding morning sunshine and bounced along the ground to pluck up worms. Early morning dew and leftover rainwater clung to the grass and dampened my shoes. I rounded the side of the house.

The tree, a massive oak that had shaded this entire side of the yard, lay prone across the grass. A giant mud glob churned up the earth at one end. The winds had ripped the oak clean out of the ground. Its roots hadn't been strong enough to hold it.

"I thought I'd find you out here." Ryan rounded the side of the house.

"Looks pretty bad."

He rubbed yesterday's stubble on his chin. "Got the AC, too."

My heart sank. No AC in a Mississippi summer? Not good. Besides, a new one would cost, what? Seven grand? "Roof damage, water damage, and an AC unit. Anything else?"

Ryan rocked back on his heels, oblivious to my bite of sarcasm. "Won't know until I get in there."

Wind shifted through the leaves and sprayed water droplets in the air. I rubbed my hands down my arms.

"Get in there?" I eyed him. Did he plan on cutting the entire tree himself?

"We'll get some guys from the church out here." He glanced at his watch. "I'm headed up there now. We'll see what kind of damage we have around town, then get everyone organized."

I swallowed, not sure what to say. I wasn't used to other people handling my problems. Part of me wanted to protest and say I could take care of it myself, but the more logical portion realized I had no idea how to handle something like this.

"Uh, thanks."

Ryan nodded and trotted off, leaving me to stare at the damage. How hot would it get in there? I would probably have to leave the windows open to circulate a breeze. But that didn't seem safe, at least it wasn't where I came from.

"Hello there!" Nancy rounded the side of the house.

I gestured toward the tree. "I don't think we'll be doing any baking today."

She patted my arm. "No, I didn't reckon we would. I have some cinnamon rolls in the oven. Why don't you come over, and we'll have hot rolls and coffee while the men figure out what to do about the tree?"

The idea both offended my sense of feminism and at the same time filled me with a surge of relief. Still, I hesitated.

"Come on now." Nancy patted my arm again. "You aren't alone. Got folks around here to help you. Don't push their good intentions away."

How much had Ida told her about my life? She walked away without waiting for me to respond, so I hurried along after her. We crossed the yard and up the steps to Ryan's house.

Or maybe it was Nancy's house.

"Ryan lives with you?"

She opened the front door to the cheery Queen Anne and gestured me inside. "No. I live with him. But only during my treatments. He insists."

The foyer contained a bench with coat rack, blue papered walls, and a square iron-and-glass light hanging from the ceiling. Wood floors and wooden trim complete with stained pocket doors complemented the historic design. Ryan had obviously taken care of this place.

"Treatments?"

Nancy led me past a masculine living room with modern furniture to a bright and airy kitchen in the back. Full windows revealed a small but manicured fenced-in yard out back. The kitchen wasn't as updated as Ida's, but he'd kept it clean and made it look homey.

"Breast cancer, dear. But I'll beat it." Nancy gestured toward a breakfast bar as if she'd told me today's weather forecast rather than dropping the cancer bomb. Thoughts of Ida tightened my chest. Would Ryan lose Nancy, too?

"The treatments make me tired," Nancy continued in her matter-of-fact tone. "Ryan likes to dote on me when I have to take them. Insists I stay here with him." She grinned. "I think he just wants to keep an eye on me." She winked. "But I don't mind the attention. He's a good boy, wanting to take care of his old mom."

Would any of the men I'd ever dated do something like that? I pushed the thought aside. I wasn't dating Ryan, nor did I plan to. Even if he vanquished house-demolishing trees and took care of his sick mom like some kind of knight in shining armor.

She plucked an oven mitt from a drawer and pulled delicious-smelling rolls out of the oven. I shoved a stool away from the bar and placed my hands on the gray granite. "I'm sorry to hear that."

Nancy opened a container of icing and smeared it over the hot rolls. "Don't be, dear. It's in God's hands."

I had to admire her faith. At least her outlook seemed to bring her a measure of peace.

Nancy pulled down two white ceramic mugs and poured coffee from a pot on the counter. "Cream and sugar?"

"Both, please." I accepted the cup while she pulled a bottle of creamer from the fridge. "So, where do you live when you're not here?"

"About ten minutes out from town. Not far, but in the middle of the woods."

I could see why Ryan didn't want his mother alone in the woods at night. I stirred a spoonful of sugar into my coffee and watched the dark liquid swirl.

"Don't waste energy worrying," Nancy said. "They'll get that tree cut up in no time. Plenty of folks will be glad to haul it away for firewood."

One problem solved. I watched Nancy bustle around the kitchen. Something about her reminded me of Ida, and my heart clenched. I gripped the hot cup. "But what do I do about the big hole in the side of the house? Talk about a security problem." Someone had broken into my house in the eighth grade after I'd locked all the doors. A missing wall invited trouble.

Nancy chuckled. "Get a dog."

Hadn't I thought the same thing? Must have been some kind of sign. I couldn't stand the thought of staying alone in a big house with no way to lock out intruders. A dog would alert me if anyone tried to sneak into the hole in the house in the middle of the night. Or through the windows, since I'd have to leave them open or suffocate. "Where do I find one?"

Nancy placed a plate with a steaming roll in front of me and stood on the other side of the counter with her own. "I was kidding. You'll be fine. Maryville is safe."

Safe or not, it still made me uncomfortable. And I already had far too many things making me uncomfortable. Not being able to sleep at night wouldn't help. "I think a dog is a good idea. At least while I'm here. People foster dogs, right? Keep them for a bit until the shelter finds them a permanent home? Could be a win-win." And maybe having a dog in the house would keep me from feeling so lonely.

I kept that part to myself.

Nancy assessed me with knowing eyes. Had she read my thoughts? "You looking for a puppy?"

I shook my head. "Too much work." And a puppy wouldn't protect me from prowlers. "I want something that will bark if anyone tries to come in the house."

At least it would give me enough warning to call the cops.

"And will that help you stop worrying?" Nancy raised graying eyebrows and blew on her coffee.

"Sure." I shrugged. "I mean, it can't hurt, right?"

I had no money for groceries, no way to fix Ida's house, and no experience owning a dog. But at least I'd be safe.

What was the worst that could happen?

12

Two of a Kind

I'd become the Grinch. In the scene where he places his hands over his ears and complains about all the *noise, noise, noise.*

After a long call with Mira Ann, in which I'd finally gained a promise she'd look into the insurance claim for me, and nearly a full day of listening to chain saws, I needed to get out of the house. I made it to the animal shelter in Forest Hill an hour before closing. The rows of pens filled with barking dogs made me question the choice. This noise wasn't any better than the chain saws.

"Take a look." A robust lady with a green apron and hair pulled into a ponytail tight enough to create an artificial facelift gestured at the row of caged dogs.

Maybe this wasn't a good idea. Ida didn't have a fence, and a dog would need to be walked and trained. Plus it would slobber everywhere.

The woman left me alone outside with the discarded canines. I checked the big guy in the first cage. Black fur and beady eyes. He growled at me.

I moved on.

The next cage held a stubby-legged fellow with floppy ears. He barked at me too. I walked to the end of the line, none of the yapping creatures drawing my eye. Hole in the wall or not, this was a stupid idea.

Had I really let loneliness drive me to looking for a pound mutt?

I could sleep with a kitchen knife for protection. I didn't need a dog. Still, the ache in me longed for something to love unconditionally, something that wouldn't judge my every move. But who was I kidding? A dog was too much work.

Back inside the animal shelter, I closed the door on the boisterous dogs and shook my head to clear it. The woman who worked there had disappeared.

I made my way down the hallway. A large window in the wall gave me pause, and I looked into a room filled with an entire wall of metal cages filled with cats.

Hmm.

Cats used a litter box. They didn't need training. Of course, they didn't guard anything either. But if I were being real, my loneliness had driven me to furry companionship more than the need for a guard dog. My hating to be alone could be a problem.

Probably why I went from one bad relationship to the next. I could find comfort in something fuzzy instead of the arms of another bad decision. Without considering it further, I pushed open the door and entered the cat room.

The scent of cat litter hit me in the face. The abundance of perfume couldn't diffuse the smells of too many cats with too little bathroom space.

At least it was much quieter in here. One or two let out a soft mew, but for the most part, the cats were calm and quiet. The tension in my shoulders eased.

Cats shared a large play area, where they curled up together taking naps or batted around little stuffed mice. All except for one. A giant gray cat with long hair sat in a cage by itself without a single toy.

Alone.

My heart clenched. I knew the feeling. I stepped to the cage and put my fingers in the holes. The cat stared at me, bright yellow eyes sizing me up. I imagined something passed between us. A kind of understanding. We could be alone together, and maybe it wouldn't be so bad.

The door swung open, and the woman in the green apron entered. "Did you find a dog?"

I kept my eyes on the lonely cat. "I think I've decided on a cat instead."

The woman lifted her eyebrows. "That so?" She shut the door behind her, muffling the incessant barking. She pointed to the fluffy gray cat. "This one doesn't like other cats."

"I don't have any other cats."

"She doesn't like people much either."

Maybe we would be kindred spirits. "That's okay."

The woman lifted her shoulders. "Fine. If you want, you can take her to the visit room. If you like her, you'll need to fill out the forms and pay the adoption fee."

My insides tightened. "What's the fee?"

"Fifty for dogs, twenty for cats."

Lucky for me, yesterday I'd found a washed twenty in the laundry room. I'd planned on using it to buy food, but this cat needed someone. There was enough tuna in the pantry for both of us. At least until I got access to the funds. How much longer could it take?

"Okay."

The woman shook her head as if my wanting this cat was a stupid idea. She lifted the latch on the cage. The cat flattened gray ears against its striped head and growled. "Now come on, you. Be nice, and maybe this lady will take you home."

She reached for the fur ball, and it made a terrible screeching sound but allowed her to pick it up without a fight. "Good thing she doesn't have any claws, or I'd be shredded."

As though to answer the woman's claim, the cat did her best to churn her back feet and scramble out of the woman's grasp.

This one wouldn't be a friend to anyone. But before I could change my mind, the volunteer stepped out of the cat room and turned down the hall, leaving me no choice but to follow.

The woman opened the door to a small cinder block room the size of a tight closet. The smell of bleach and urine burned my nose. I sat on the folding chair in the corner. The woman tried her best to gently place the growling, convulsing ball of fluff on the floor but mostly ended up dropping the cat before she scrambled to get out of the room.

The door shut with a click, leaving me alone with the disgruntled creature. I stared at the cat. It crouched in the corner and stared at me. Apparently, I had as many social skills with cats as I did people.

I stood up and tried to gently step around the agitated creature blocking the door so I could tell the woman I'd changed my mind. The cat tilted her head and meowed. It was a pitiful sound. Nothing at all like the growling. She meowed again, and I swear I imagined pleading in that voice.

"You don't really want to go back in that cage, do you?"

The cat blinked at me with big yellow eyes and settled down on the floor, splaying out her striped gray fur and tucking her paws under her chest. It didn't seem so bad now. Maybe she didn't like that volunteer. I regained my seat and watched the cat. She lifted one paw, and then the other, using her bristled tongue to clean her feet. She didn't seem very social.

Still, I had nothing better to do, so I sat there and watched. When she'd finished both paws and used one to clean behind both ears, she rose and arched her back and yawned. With slow gliding steps, she explored the small space until eventually her little pink nose sought out my toes. Probably shouldn't have worn flip-flops. At least she didn't have claws.

The cat's whiskers tickled my feet as she sniffed my toes, my shoes, and the ragged hem of my jeans. She rubbed her face on my leg. Followed by the rest of her long-haired body.

"Huh."

My voice caught her attention, and she looked up at me, eyes big and searching. I remained still. Her head sunk down into her shoulders, and her tail twitched.

Uh-oh. Instinctively, I leaned back in my chair.

The cat pounced.

I sucked in a breath and gripped the sides of the chair.

The cat landed on me with soft feet, inquisitive eyes staring into my face. We sat there a moment, locked in a staring contest, until the cat spun in a circle and settled down.

Warmth covered my legs, and, after a few breaths, the cat started to vibrate. I laughed. "That's a pretty strong purr you've got there."

The door swung open, and the volunteer woman stepped in with wide eyes. "How'd you get her to do that?"

I shrugged. "I didn't do anything. I guess she figured my lap was more comfortable than the floor."

The cat raised her head, and the purr shifted into a growl. One thing was clear. This cat did not like that woman. My heart constricted. I knew what it was like to be stuck somewhere with people you didn't like. I couldn't leave this cat here to be shoved into a cage all by herself.

Without considering my safety, I reached under the cat and scooped her up. She fit comfortably in my arms, a surprisingly compliant soft ball of fur. She stayed curled there as I walked out of the room as if I had any idea what I was doing and past the baffled volunteer on my way to the front desk.

I fished the twenty out of my pocket. The woman at the desk pushed her glasses up on her nose, her eyes locked on the purring cat in my arms.

"Have you filled out the forms?"

"Not yet."

This was completely irresponsible of me. I knew it, but knowing didn't change anything. Crazy, sure, but I couldn't leave the cat here anymore than my father could have left the cat in the dumpster. Despite reasonable logic, this cat gave me a connection to my father I wasn't willing to give up. I'd figure out a way to feed both of us.

The woman behind the desk handed me a clipboard. "Fill these out. You can come back tomorrow to pick up your new pet."

"Tomorrow?"

She bobbed blonde curls. "Policy."

I sat on a hard chair in the waiting area and settled the fur ball on my lap, awkwardly trying to figure out how to write without squishing her. Finally, after giving enough information to apply for a passport, I cradled my new friend and returned the paperwork. The cat purred contently, which the woman at the desk frowned at.

"Why do I have to wait until tomorrow?"

The receptionist looked at me as if I was two crayons short of a box. "We have to get the papers filed, we have to get the cat ready to leave, and you'll need a proper crate."

Seemed to me they could file papers after I left, and the cat appeared plenty ready to go. Before I could respond, the woman in the green apron stepped through the swinging door that separated the lobby area from where they housed all the animals. The cat in my arms immediately tensed.

I took a step back. The cat growled. The woman exchanged glances with the other one behind the desk.

"But, uh, I suppose you could take it now, if you wanted."

I smiled, a strange sense of victory welling in my middle. "Thanks." I spun toward the door. Behind me, the woman sighed.

"She'll be back."

I pretended I didn't hear her and marched outside. I opened the passenger door on my car and placed the cat on the seat. She curled up and looked at me. I didn't have a crate, but the cat didn't seem like she minded.

"Okay, Kitty. Let's get you home."

Buckled in, I glanced at my new friend and hesitated, but she didn't jump up and start making laps in the car, so it had to be fine. I cranked the car and pulled out of the parking lot.

Yowl.

I cringed. That didn't take long. She flattened her ears and yowled again. Uh-oh. Suddenly, she leapt up and bounded into the back seat. I glanced in the rearview. She circled around and settled on the seat again.

Maybe she liked the back seat better. I went slowly over the bumpy road, trying not to jar the kitty too much and agitate her further. The cat yowled again, and I tensed. But she quieted and seemed to settle.

We crept through Forest Hill, drove past The Magnolia where I'd had lunch with Ryan and Mira Ann, and eased our way down the highway toward Maryville. This would be fine.

I glanced in the rearview. No cat.

My stomach clenched. Probably in the floorboard.

It'll be fine. Maybe Ida even had some old cat stuff lying around somewhere. I passed the Maryville train depot and turned onto Ida's street. Almost there.

Yowl.

Something scrambled up the seat behind me, and I gasped. The cat topped the headrest and balanced herself on the impossibly small space. What in the—?

With another piercing yowl, my new friend used my head to regain her balance to keep her from slipping from the headrest. Soft paws mingled in my hair, and I stiffened. The cat settled, her back half on the headrest, and her front paws dangling on my forehead.

Then she started to purr.

13

Realization

*I*f I didn't know better, I might think Nancy had taken it upon herself to replace Ida as my grandmotherly voice of reason. She lifted her eyebrow and pointed at the ball of fluff purring contently on one of the chairs in Ida's breakfast nook.

"I thought you wanted a dog."

I pushed the button to preheat the oven. Thanks to the tree, our Wednesday bread-baking session had moved to Friday. "Dogs have to be walked. Cats don't."

Chainsaws buzzed outside, filling the kitchen with a low rumble we had to speak over and the permeating scent of sawdust. How long could cutting one tree take? But then, people had jobs, and they came as they could to cut off and haul away chunks. Since they did the work for free, I couldn't complain.

"Hmm." Nancy pulled a kitchen towel off the first of the two loaves that had been left since this morning to rise. "Ida had a cat once. Used to be your father's."

"Yep."

"She told you about old Scruffy?" Nancy leaned her

99

elbows on the counter and regarded me with a knowing gaze. Ida had used the same one. Did the expression come standard on all older women?

"In one of her letters." I poked at the dough.

"Don't do that." Nancy swatted at me. "So, because your dad once had a cat, you got a cat instead of a guard dog?"

The coffee pot gurgled. She pulled down a ceramic coffee mug and helped herself to a cup. The rich aroma filled the air and helped mask a little of the sawdust.

The sentiment sounded stupid spoken out loud. I shrugged and moved away from her dough. "Looks that way."

"Good choice." Nancy winked. "Fluffy there will make good company, and you won't have to take him out at all hours of the night." She took a sip from her coffee. "He have a name?"

My shoulders relaxed, though I didn't know why I cared if Nancy approved. "She. Girl cat. And no, I haven't named her. I keep calling her Kitty."

The oven beeped, and Nancy stuck the fresh loaves inside. She wiped her hands on her floral-print apron. "It's good you aren't alone." She leveled kind eyes on me.

The intensity of her gaze made me uncomfortable, and I looked away. "She's a good cat. And I can take her with me when I go. Cats are easier to keep in an apartment." Assuming I found a decent one. But I didn't have to think about that now.

Nancy caught my gaze. "That's not what I meant. You aren't alone, Casey. Even without the cat."

I brushed the comment aside. "For now, anyway. But I can't stay here forever." Besides, I could be surrounded by people and still be alone.

"Maybe. Maybe not." Nancy wiped the countertop. "If you go back to Atlanta, you still won't be alone. God is always with you." She lifted her eyebrows. "Even if you don't acknowledge Him."

I should have expected a sermon from the preacher man's mother. I simply nodded to avoid a conversation I didn't want to have. I believed in God. I knew He was real. I'd even given my heart to Him as a little girl afraid of the world and unwanted by her parents. But experience had taught me that just because God was out there, and had saved me from eternal torment, didn't mean He would save me from pain.

I had a problem with a God who *could* do things yet chose not to. My parents *could* have loved me. Any of them. They all chose not to. Kind of hard to want to be with someone like that.

Nancy rubbed my shoulder. "I hope you find what's missing."

Sudden tears burned my eyes, and I forced myself to swallow them down. I didn't like insightful people. Gave them too much power over me. I laughed her off. "Thanks. As soon as your son gives me all of Ida's letters, I'll have all those missing pieces."

Nancy's rueful smile plucked a raw nerve. "Maybe. Maybe not."

Great. Another old woman who spoke in riddles.

My phone vibrated, saving me from an awkward answer. I flipped it open without even looking at the number. Probably Ryan with more information about the church men and their plans for the tree in the dining room. "Hello?"

"It's great to hear your voice again."

My breath seized. "Derick?"

Worry clouded Nancy's eyes.

"Hey, babe. I've missed you." Smooth voice, as always. The kind that had slithered over my senses and made me eager to please him. That Italian finesse didn't help either.

Nancy's eyebrows drew together, adding deeper wrinkles to her forehead.

Pulse skittering, I scooted out of the kitchen. "What do you want?" Thankfully, my voice came out as cold and distant as I'd intended.

"Ouch." He sounded almost wounded, but he deserved a lot worse than any bite I could put into my words. "Is that any way to speak to the man you love?"

"Is sleeping with someone else any way to treat the woman *you* love?" I gripped the phone and paced the living room. Why was I even talking to this guy? I'd sworn I'd never speak to him again. Right after he blamed me for him cheating. Claiming that my defying him and taking my long overdue vacation days to visit Ida had pushed him into Vicky's arms.

Pictures of Ida and Reggie watched me from their perch on the mantel. Fire churned in my middle, spiking my veins with a potent cocktail of frustration and humiliation with a twist of betrayal. "Or how about kicking her out with nowhere to go?" With nothing more than a few changes of clothes, a couple of toiletries, and the cash in my purse.

The line went silent. I paused, my heart thudding. I'd never spoken to him like that before. But pain and distance could make a person bold.

"I deserved that."

Was that actually remorse? My throat constricted. Now

what? Would he ask me to come back? I looked around Ida's living room. This house represented all the things I'd always wanted. A fresh life. A family.

The sudden pinch in my heart surprised me. When he'd first kicked me out and kept everything, I'd dreamed of him calling me, saying he was wrong, and begging me to come back.

Now that he'd called, I suddenly realized I didn't want that life. I didn't want to hold his betrayal over him. Make him beg for forgiveness. Make him earn my trust back. Because, even if he did, I didn't know if I wanted to go back to the life he'd given me.

"Look, I'm sorry." His accent quivered with frustration. "I'm a passionate man. You know that. Italian blood and all. You always enjoyed it."

I closed my eyes and tried to push away the dirty feeling that welled up inside me. Did I even like the person I was with him?

"I didn't mean to hurt you, babe. All that, it's over. Out of my system. I want you to come back. I miss you. Let's go back to the way we were."

And what way was that? At first, Derick had doted on me. Showered me with compliments and attention. I'd resisted him, since he owned the restaurant I worked in. But the more I turned him down, the more he pursued me. Truth be told, I'd liked the attention. And, at first, our relationship had been good. He was romantic. Took care of me. Bought me things.

Slowly, I'd made one compromise. And another. Things so small that I didn't even realize how far those little steps had taken me. Soon, I'd moved in with him. His house was better than my little apartment. He asked more and more of me, and I gave it, because he'd already given me so many other things.

Tears pricked my eyes and burned their way out past my lids. I was so easy to use and throw away.

"Are you there?"

I unclenched my fist. "Yeah. I'm here."

Derick's voice took on a pleading tone. "Come home."

Home. That word didn't belong on Derick's lips. He'd invited *her* into our "home." I pulled my resolve up around me. "I can't do that."

He sighed. "I know you're mad. But be reasonable. I can take care of you. You won't even need that job at the school."

He knew about that?

"I'll take care of you, babe. You won't have to work unless you want to. I'll even marry you. Anything you want. Come home, and we'll work it out."

Something within me longed to reach out for his promise. For the comforts he could provide. Was I so desperate for security that I'd be willing to go back to a man who would probably cheat again, just so I wouldn't be alone? A woman who had always told herself she didn't need anyone? The hypocrisy soured my stomach.

"No."

Surprise filled his voice. "No?" His tone turned icy. "Found yourself another man already?"

Anger boiled through me, filling my veins with fire. I looked at Ida's picture on the mantel. She wore a fitted, calf-length dress from the '50s. Her expression held quiet strength and a sense of dignity I longed to emulate. And that started with knowing I was worth more than the way people like Derick treated me. No matter what I had to deal with here, I wouldn't crawl back to him.

I straightened my posture and stared at Ida's determined features, imagining her approval. "I don't need a man. Not you, not anyone else."

He laughed. "Right. Keep telling yourself that. I'll be here when you get this *thing* out of your system."

I clenched my teeth.

"Love you, babe. Call me when you're ready."

The line went dead. I stood in the living room for a long time staring at Ida. What would she do? She'd have something wise to say, no doubt.

"You okay?" Nancy stood in the doorway.

I stuffed the phone into my back pocket. "Yeah. Fine."

She watched me a moment. "If you ever want to talk about it, I'm here."

Ida had said the same thing. And I'd let her gentle probing dig way too deep into my life. Look at all the problems that had come from that.

No, not problems. Opportunities. I'd lost Ida, but her love and acceptance had opened up part of me I'd kept walled off for a long time. Of course, now that meant I had to keep examining parts of myself I didn't like to see. "Thanks. I might take you up on that."

The timer in the kitchen dinged. "We can talk about it over a slice of fresh bread," she said.

Since I wouldn't have Derick watching my waistline, I let myself enjoy the idea. "With some of Ida's fig preserves."

Nancy grinned and led the way back into the kitchen. She sliced the hot bread, and I opened the fridge to find the jam.

"Uh, looks like you need a trip to the store." Nancy peered around me to frown at the empty fridge.

"Oh. Yeah, I'll get around to it."

She didn't comment but busied herself with slicing the bread and putting it on two white plates. "So, who was that on the phone? If you don't mind my asking."

The buzz of the chainsaws started again. As soon as I finished the bread, I'd need to go out there and have a look. "No one. Ex-boyfriend."

Nancy spread the thick preserves on her slice and passed the jar to me. She took a bite. "Mmm. Delicious."

I slathered my own slice and let the sweetness melt on my tongue. Heavenly.

"You know what would go good with that other loaf of bread? Homemade lasagna."

I smiled. "Sure would. Put some garlic and butter on a few slices. Maybe a Caesar salad on the side."

She plucked off a piece and popped it in her mouth. "Problem with lasagna is I always make a giant pan. Too much for two people to eat."

I paused with a piece of bread halfway to my mouth.

"You come on over this evening, and I'll teach you my grandmother's recipe. Then you can help us eat it."

She'd made the offer because of my empty fridge. My pride welled up within me against the thinly veiled charity, and I almost shook my head. But Nancy's invitation was also neighborly friendliness. No harm in accepting a dinner invitation. I could always return the favor later.

"Sounds good. Thanks."

Nancy grinned. "And tomorrow we'll make applesauce and apple pies." She tapped a finger on her chin. "Or maybe a blackberry cobbler." She shook her head. "No, those aren't ripe yet."

Wait a second. Did she plan to—?

"Don't give me that look." She pointed a bony finger at me. "You have to eat. And no one likes eating alone." She glanced at Kitty. "Cats don't count."

I opened my mouth to protest, but Nancy plowed ahead. "I like to cook. Ida said you do too. So we can cook together." She smiled brightly. "Besides, what else do you have to do?"

Clearly, Ryan had come by his bluntness honestly. "I don't want to impose."

"If it were an imposition, I wouldn't have suggested it." She took another bite. "Besides. I like you."

My heart warmed. She didn't really know me, but the sentiment felt nice all the same.

She wiped up crumbs on the counter, put away the preserves, and tidied the kitchen while I ate. The woman reminded me of a hummingbird. Tiny, but always in motion.

Nancy patted my shoulder. "All right. I'll see you in a couple of hours. I'm going to take a nap before we get started."

I started to agree, but she cut me off.

"And when you come over, you're going to tell me all about that man and what he did to put that look in your eyes."

I blinked at her. So much for letting the awkward topic drop. I should have known better.

"We're going to talk it through. Understand?"

Um, what just happened? "Yes, ma'am."

She wrapped her arm around me and squeezed my shoulders. "Good girl. See you soon."

She bustled out the door, leaving me with nothing to do but stare after her.

14

Hidden Memories

*T*he incessant buzzing of chainsaws outside swarmed in my head and frazzled my nerves. With Nancy gone, I had nothing else to distract me. I threw a load of clothes in the dryer and leaned against the machine. Kitty meowed and wove around my legs.

"We need something to do, don't we, girl?" Anything to keep my hands busy and my mind from plucking at problems I couldn't solve.

Meow.

I took the feline response as consent. I couldn't fix the house or cut the tree, but I could work on Ida's project. I'd let too many things distract me from my primary focus. Ida had left me her plans to unravel my past, and so far I'd made little progress. She deserved my attention, and I didn't need to lose any more time.

Gathering the squares I'd cut, Kitty and I headed to the foyer and settled down on the floor. After three tries, I finally got the cat out of the fabric and settled in my lap so I could see. I stroked her soft fur while she purred contently. If I laid out each square I had left into the appropriate rows, there wouldn't be enough. Not good. I set Kitty on the floor and earned an annoyed *meah*.

"Sorry. I need to look at something."

The cat swished her tail and stretched out on my quilt squares, scattering the pattern.

I found one of Ida's quilts in the hall closet and returned to the foyer. It would give me a good indication of the correct size. I needed at least a twin size, preferably a full. Maybe a queen. I spread Ida's blue and yellow star patterned quilt out on the floor next to my partially finished one. Ida's blanketed the floor and bunched up against the wall opposite the sewing machine. Even without the full width, I could still see the truth.

Not enough fabric. What I had would only complete roughly half. I slumped on the floor. Now what? Kitty took the opportunity to return to her perch, preferring my lap to the thin fabric draping the hardwood. I tangled my fingers in her long fur.

Barely started, and already I'd failed. Familiar disgust soured my stomach.

No.

Discouragement wouldn't get the better of me. Not now. I'd gotten a century-plus old sewing machine to work, hadn't I? I placed Kitty on the floor and put my hands on my hips. For once in my life, I wouldn't avoid the problem. I'd face the challenge head on.

One step at a time.

So what was the next step? The continued buzzing from the kitchen clouded my brain. I shook my head, trying to dislodge it. I tried not to fixate on the sound, but the harder I tried, the louder it became.

Focus.

Ida had said something about old clothes or something in her letter. Back in the kitchen, I pulled open the drawer by the fridge. On top, the handwritten letter from the unknown woman to her lost son begged to be decoded, but I had no answers there. I set it aside.

The buzzing outside revved with the addition of at least one other chainsaw, dragging my attention to the shattered dining room. I eyed the blue tarp popping in the breeze. Maybe I should go check on them.

No. I had other things to do. Ryan would handle it. I unfolded the letter I needed and scanned the contents.

> *In the old days, women would save shirts or dresses and cut them into smaller pieces to turn something that was old and worn out into something new and beautiful.*
>
> *Go through my material or find your own. Pick pieces that mean something to you...*

My clothes wouldn't be an option. I had few enough already. I folded the letter and placed it back in the drawer. So what else could I use? I plodded up the stairs and headed into Ida's room. I checked the trunk. Empty. I'd used or ruined every scrap of what she'd kept in there.

I stared at her dresser. A violation.

I traced the top of the wood and rubbed dust between my fingers. She wanted me to take meaningful things and stitch them together into something beautiful. My fingers lingered on the brass handle of the top drawer.

Not that one. Probably too personal. People usually kept their underwear in the top drawer.

I chose the one underneath it, rubbed my palm down my

jeans, and tried again. Taking a deep breath, I pulled the drawer open. Stacks of socks. Nope. The next drawer contained slips and camisoles. I closed that one quickly, too.

The wardrobe. Probably better luck there. I turned to the heavy cedar closet and pulled the door open. Tucking a stray piece of hair behind my ear, I eyed the items inside. Better. What would I do with all her clothes anyway? Give them all to a shelter?

I fingered a soft pink blouse, then trailed my hand across silks, flannels, and cotton. I paused on a purple floral. Ida had worn that shirt the day we met. I'd laughed to myself that the woman shone as bright as the flowers she talked on and on about.

The back of my throat burned. I swallowed down the sticky heat and focused. Ida would want me to remember her with fondness, not tears. The shirt slipped from the hanger, and I pulled it close to my chest. The fabric still smelled of cedar and gardenias.

This was what she'd meant. This shirt would be better in my quilt than on a Goodwill rack. I could keep something of hers close and remember her. I picked out another one, a turquoise short sleeve. My grandmother's favorite color. I tucked them under my arm and closed the wardrobe.

My gaze landed on the family quilt on the wall. Pieces of family. Of history. Of our lives. What else did Ida have stashed away? I laid the two shirts on the bed and crossed to the closet by the bathroom door. Inside, small shelves tucked into the wall. Someone must have added the space when they'd built the modern bathroom. Two shoe boxes and a larger plastic storage box crammed the center shelf. An iron, starch, and neatly folded hand towels took up the bottom. The top shelf held two packages of toilet paper and four boxes of tissues.

I pulled out one of the shoe boxes and raised the lid. Construction paper, drawings, and cards filled the inside. I sank to the floor and crossed my legs. On top, childish script scrawled over an orange piece of paper decorated with tissue paper flowers.

Happi Mothers Day. I love you!

My father. He had to have made this. My shoulders slumped, and I pulled the box closer. Drawings of two parents and a little boy. Happy stick people with big smiles and oversize heads stood close together, facing the world with solidarity.

Traced handprints made to look like a turkey or a baby Jesus manger. I covered the tiny hand with my own. So small. If only I could have known the man he'd become. Had he always been close to his mother? Did he go to college? Get a good job? Think about having children one day?

Regret throwing away his own baby?

The bitter thought soured the precious innocence in my hands. I tried to thrust it away, but still it lingered.

I unpacked one art project after another. All treasures Ida had kept stored away. These memories I didn't need stories to decode. They each painted a picture of a mother who'd loved her child and cherished the imperfect creations of his little hands. Weight settled on my shoulders, pressing me closer to the priceless shards of love in my lap as though nearness to them could somehow infuse their essence into my splintered heart.

Had my adoptive mother kept anything I'd made in

school? If she had, I hadn't found them after she'd died. My adoptive father certainly wouldn't have. He'd tossed the picture I'd drawn of him wearing a "#1 Dad" shirt into the trash. Said once he'd seen it, we didn't need to fill the house with useless clutter. My heart still bore the third-grade scar of rejection.

I put the top back on and gently returned the treasure box to the tomb where it could remain unsullied. Wiping moisture from my nose, I smeared my hand across my jeans and fortified myself. What had I expected, digging through other people's private memories?

But Ida had wanted me to know the stories. Understand my family and our history. These treasured items belonged to me now. If I didn't honor them, who would? Grabbing the next box, I hoped I didn't find anything embarrassing. I flipped open the lid.

Interesting. This box contained several folded t-shirts. I laughed as I pulled out the one on top. Seriously? Metallica? I shook out the black cotton shirt. The purple band name shot lightning bolts into some kind of spark plug or something with the words *Ride the Lightning* across the bottom. Wow. Next I found a Motley Crue 1983 "Shout Tour" shirt, a Harley Davidson Orlando tee, and an acid-washed Led Zeppelin shirt featuring a blimp. Crazy.

My dad had been into Harleys and hair metal? Not at all what I'd expected. At what point did a little boy who made paper flowers and a tender-hearted middle schooler who had rescued a dumpster cat turn into a head-banging biker?

Why had Ida kept all of this? I stacked the shirts neatly on the floor next to me. Wouldn't that make an interesting quilt? Ida's floral fabric next to my birth dad's Harley logo?

What would I find next in this plastic Pandora's Box? Finally, something other than acid wash or black. I unfolded one much smaller than the rock shirts. *Maryville Hornets Band* in peeling white letters slashed across the front of a kelly green shirt Dad must have worn in middle school. I ran my fingers across it. This was a good find. I pictured the little boy from Ida's albums wearing this shirt as he coaxed a stray cat from a dumpster, and the image conjured a smile.

The final shirt at the bottom of the box, in the same green, boasted "Hornet Dad." My chest tightened. Reggie. In my quest to understand Ida and my birth father, I'd all but forgotten my grandfather. Ida had showed me an old pair of Reggie's fatigues. I could probably take a square or two from those as well.

Who knew Ida had been such a packrat?

She'd provided me with all the things I needed to repurpose the past. Each of these fabrics could be incorporated into my quilt. To be displayed, rather than locked away in old boxes. Warmth swelled in my middle and tingled down my veins. I tossed the Zeppelin, Harley, and two school shirts onto the bed with Ida's blouses.

I hefted the box and angled it to go back on the shelf. Wait. What was that? I placed the box on Ida's nightstand and leaned down to look at the back of the center shelf. A bit of some kind of fabric had been wadded up behind the box. I pulled it out.

My grip tightened. Winnie the Pooh and his friends danced across a cheery yellow cotton. Why would Ida have this? I rubbed it between my fingers. Had she bought it to make something for a child? Saved it for her first grandchild? Did she—?

"Casey?"

I yelped and stumbled back, nearly dropping the fabric. I covered my fluttering heart with a shaking hand. "Ryan! You scared the daylights out of me."

He stood in the doorway, faded green shirt covered in bits of sawdust. His deep brown eyes swept an assessing gaze over the shirts on the bed, darted to the open closet, and settled on the fabric in my hand.

I shifted my feet but held his gaze. Even from here, I could smell the sawdust and a faint hint of rain.

He lifted one eyebrow, then a smile pulled up the side of his mouth. "How's the quilt going?"

I lowered the mysterious fabric to my side and shrugged. "She said to find material that means something."

His eyes lit with approval, and the sudden flutter in my stomach made me blink. What was it about this guy that made me want to please him? And not in that pathetic kind of way that yearned to swindle people into liking me. Something about him brimmed with sincerity and goodness. An inner light that drew me closer. I squelched the startling thought. I couldn't end up like a mosquito drawn to the zapper.

Not that Ryan was a zapper, just that I'd end up hurt and—

"That's awesome. I won't keep you." He thumbed over his shoulder. "I wanted to ask what you wanted to do with the wood we cut up. Do you want us to stack it for firewood or…?"

What would Ida do? I rubbed the Pooh fabric between my fingers. "Give it to elderly people in the church. You know, ones that could use the wood in the winter but maybe wouldn't be able to cut any on their own?" I shrugged, feeling stupid. Did people even do things like that

115

anymore? This wasn't the 1800s.

Ryan rocked back on his heels and flashed me a proud smile. "That's an excellent idea. I'll tell Brother Lawrence."

"Brother Lawrence?"

He hooked his thumbs in his belt loops. "The pastor at First Baptist."

Oh. Right. Seemed the pastor had as much say-so in this town as any elected official. "What about your mom? Could she use any?"

Ryan nodded. "I'll split a load for her and take it out there. We'll get some of the other guys helping with the cleanup to do the same for our older members. Lots of limbs and junk all over town, but you're the only one with a hearty oak."

"Lucky me."

"God has a purpose for—" His surprised gaze darted to his feet. "Hello there."

Kitty wrapped herself around Ryan's dusty jeans and smeared her whiskered face on his leg.

"I got a cat."

He tilted his head. "So I see." His questioning eyes searched mine. "Stray?"

He probably thought I'd commandeered one of his neighbor's pets. I jutted my chin. "I went to the shelter."

Ryan's easy nod contradicted my assumed suspicion. "What's his name?"

"Her." I shrugged. "I call her Kitty."

Knowing eyes slammed into mine, and I glanced away, feeling exposed. "What?"

"Plan on keeping her or taking her back to the shelter?"

No way could I take that poor creature back. She'd hated it there. "I don't know yet."

Ryan reached down and stroked the cat's fur. "I best get back to it. We're almost done. Come down and have a look when you get a second."

I watched him leave, broad shoulders swaying with his easy gait. I tossed the cartoon material on the bed with the rest. Maybe Ida had meant it for a friend's baby shower or had planned to make a dress for a girl at church.

Or maybe she'd longed for a grandchild and had bought it after her son's wedding in hopes of making a baby blanket. It didn't really matter. I'd never know. Still, something about the scrap of fabric covered with my favorite childhood cartoon filled in a missing chunk, and so, regardless of Ida's original plan, this piece would be worked into the other mismatched fragments representing my heritage.

I gathered the pieces and closed the door to Ida's room. What other things could I find to put in my memory blanket? I crossed over to my room and opened the wardrobe. Ida must have used it to store quilting materials. Good to know. I'd need the batting and flat sheets to complete the quilt. I put my other finds on the floor.

Past the bags of cotton and rolls of batting, I found a cream-colored sheet that would work well as a backing. At least it wouldn't clash with the hodgepodge of crazy materials.

I glanced at my father's teddy bear sitting on the dresser. "Good finds, huh?" And...I was talking to toys now. Bad enough I talked to the cat. I must be losing shards of my sanity.

All right, Ida. I've found memories.

With one of her dish towels to remind me of Ida's cooking, along with the rest of the things I'd found, I'd have enough material to piece together fragments of the past. Only one thing was missing.

I pulled my suitcase out from under the bed. The jeans I'd ripped the day I'd gone out with Mira Ann and Ryan. They were pretty much ruined anyway. And wasn't that what Ida had said? Take the ruined and transform it into something else?

Feeling satisfied, I gathered the materials, patted the teddy on his faded head, and bounded back down the stairs to check on the progress outside.

15

Food for the Soul

ood has a way of settling the mind and calming the spirit. The scent of garlic bread and tomato sauce smoothed away the wrinkles in my flustered nerves. I inhaled deeply, letting the subtle hints of basil and oregano tingle my senses. Nancy's wooden spoon settled naturally in my palm and glided through the thickening sauce on Ryan's stove.

The men had made a lot of progress dissecting the tree. After the tension of spending an hour fretting over the mess, I preferred the simple joy of the kitchen. Thank goodness for men with chainsaws. I was completely useless out there. In here, however, creation, rather than destruction, ruled.

"You look like you're in your element."

I peeked at the little woman through the corner of my eye. "Yeah?"

She wiped her hands on a yellow dishrag. "You always look stiff. Jumpy." She swatted me playfully. "Except when you're sprinkling herbs or turning dough."

And she knew me well enough to determine what I *always* looked like? I put the lid on the sauce and turned down the heat. Yeasty smells clung to the oven mitt I slid on my hand. "And when have you seen me outside of the kitchen?"

Nancy eyed the slices of bread as I pulled them from the oven perfectly toasted. "Saw you at church. And outside looking at that tree."

"Both stressful situations." I removed the oven mitt and placed it back in the drawer. Feeling oddly at home, I plucked the ricotta cheese out of the fridge and popped the lid.

"Church is stressful?" Nancy leaned around me and reached into the fridge, pulled open a drawer, and handed me a bag of shredded mozzarella.

Globs of ricotta plunked into the glass bowl where I'd cracked two eggs. I added a cup of the shredded mozzarella and stirred before answering. "Anyplace with lots of people, especially new people, is stressful."

Nancy cocked an eyebrow and plopped her hand on her waist. "Ida said you were a waitress. Isn't a restaurant filled with lots of new people?"

Touché. "Probably one of the many reasons I didn't like my job."

Nancy sprinkled basil into my cheese mixture and then cranked the pepper grinder. "What about that man you were talking to earlier? He have anything to do with your job dissatisfaction?"

I darted a sidelong glance in her direction. "Maybe." How much did this woman know about me? I watched her scrape browned hamburger meat into my finished tomato sauce. "Did Ida talk about me?"

She tapped the spoon on the side of the pan and gave the sauce a good stir. Her eyes twinkled. "Of course. After your visit, she hardly stopped talking about you."

My forehead wrinkled. "We didn't know each other long."

"Didn't matter." Nancy wiped her hands on her apron. "You were her granddaughter, and she was proud of you." She patted my shoulder. "That's what old ladies do. Brag on their kids and grandkids. Ida had to make up for lost time."

Something in my middle twisted and skewered me with a strange blend of affection and regret. "She did, huh?" The words mingled with the tantalizing aromas and tainted them with sour disappointment. The one person in this world who wanted to dote on me, and God had taken her.

"Ida loved you. No mistake about that."

But she didn't know me. No one who really got to know me still liked me. Frustration scorched up my throat, but I grabbed my glass of sweet tea and forced it back down. I wouldn't let this evening be ruined by life's unfairness.

"Noodles are ready." I pointed at the pot. "Time to start assembling."

Nancy drained the sheets of pasta while I covered the bottom of a baking dish with a layer of the tomato sauce. We quietly layered noodles, cheese, and sauce. The simple rhythm restored my equilibrium.

"Tell me about the man on the phone."

And just like that, my peace shattered. I shot Nancy one of my cactus stares.

She lifted her eyebrows, disturbingly unaffected. "You don't want to talk about it."

Bingo. I snatched a piece of aluminum foil from the roll on the island and stretched it over the lasagna. Nancy watched me shove the pan in the oven, check the temperature setting, wipe crumbs up from the counter, and head to the sink with the dirty bowls before she spoke again.

"The sore subjects are the ones that most need discussing."

The glass bowls clattered into the sink. I struggled to keep my tone even, but my voice hitched up with annoyance anyway. "He was a jerk. We broke up. He fired me. End of story."

Compassion swarmed in her eyes, and she reminded me so much of Ida that my defenses crumbled. The fire shooting through my chest cooled.

"He fired you because you broke up?"

I shrugged. "He cheated. We had a fight. He fired me and kicked me out. That's what I get for living with my boss."

Nancy wrapped her arm around my waist, and we stared at the dirty dishes crowding the sink.

Her grip tightened. "He ought to be flogged for that."

A laugh bubbled out of my chest with a snort. "Flogged?"

Nancy's chin jerked with indignation. "Or strung up by his toes."

The wrinkles on her face deepened with annoyance, and I couldn't help but sink into her embrace.

"When did that happen?"

My view of the ricotta-smeared bowls blurred. "I walked in on them two days before the lawyer called and told me Ida died. They'd started seeing each other when I came to visit when Ida first found me." I swallowed a lump in my throat. "Pretty awful, huh?" And those few days I'd lived in my car in a box store parking lot made me shiver.

She sniffed. "The worst. I'm glad you told him off."

Had I? At least I'd stood up to him. A tingle of satisfaction scurried through my heart. Maybe talking to Nancy hadn't been a bad idea after all. Like when I'd talked to Ida, talking to her had a way of making me feel better rather than worse.

"He apologized. Wanted me to come back."

Nancy grunted. "And what do you want?"

What did I want? Not Derick. At least I knew that much. But beyond that? Nancy gave me another squeeze, as though sensing her question contained more layers than I could answer at the moment.

"Something sure smells good in here."

Nancy and I whirled in unison at the sound of Ryan's voice.

His gaze darted from his mother to me and back to his mother again. Cords of muscle in his neck tightened. "Everything okay?"

Nancy pushed a perfectly placed strand of gray hair into the clip at the back of her head. "Girl talk, dear."

Ryan's eyes widened. He glanced at me again. "Oh." He rubbed the back of his neck. "Don't let me bother y'all. I'm going to get cleaned up before supper."

"What did you get figured out with the church?" Nancy left me at the sink and rounded the island, effectively shielding me from Ryan's probing gaze.

Bless her. I took a calming breath and gathered myself, somehow feeling a little lighter than when I'd first stepped foot in Ryan's kitchen. A feeling I didn't think would diminish even though I planned to gorge myself on carbs.

They settled into an easy conversation about which church patrons would be taking loads of wood and which younger men would help chop and haul it. The homey scents of the kitchen and the warm conversation stirred a longing in me. Even when I lived with Derick, had our house ever felt like this? An intangible *something* wavered in the air. Something that brought a comforting sense of belonging.

I couldn't put my finger on it, but a desire to grab the sensation and hold on had me bunching the apron at my waist. Man, I must have reached a new level of pathetic. I turned on the water in the sink. Best keep my hands busy with the dishes.

Forty minutes later, the three of us settled around the oval table nestled in Ryan's kitchen, a tray of perfectly golden lasagna, a side of toasted garlic bread, and—just to add the pretense of something healthy—a simple salad before us.

Ryan rubbed his hands together. "Looks fabulous, ladies. Thank you."

Nancy grinned. "You're welcome. Let's eat." But rather than digging into the food as she'd implied, Nancy bowed her head.

Right. Prayers. I followed suit and ducked my head. Waiting. As expected, a breath later Ryan's smooth voice washed over us.

"Father, thank you for good food and good company. Please help Casey with the repairs for the house and help Mom feel better during her treatments. Which we ask to be successful. Please bless this food. In Jesus's name, amen."

I echoed my "amen" and watched Nancy as Ryan cut and served the lasagna. How many treatments would she need? How strong was her chemo? What had the doctor's prognosis been? Each question nicked at my sense of security in this house. Would God strip another good woman away from the people who needed her? I could only imagine what that would do to Ryan.

But I knew one thing for certain. Tragedy, in one form or another, visited everyone. I could only hope cancer stealing his mother wouldn't be on life's agenda for Ryan. Each tired line in her face, each animated wave of her hand as she spoke, I studied. Was she exhausted? Putting on a show to hide it?

Did she lie about how bad the cancer really was, as Ida had?

"Don't you think so, Casey?"

Ryan's words jarred me out of my thoughts. "Uh, sorry. What?"

He leaned back in his chair and eyed me with amusement. I squirmed. Had I missed something important?

Nancy rolled her eyes. "He said you seemed like you were close to finishing your quilt for Ida, and that he thought Ida would like it if you showed it to me."

"Oh." I plucked at my cuticles under the table. Ryan didn't read Ida's letters, did he? I eyed him, but nothing about his relaxed posture and lazy smile said he danced with deception. Not the kind of guy to read someone else's mail. "Yes. Actually, Ida said in one of her letters that she'd like me to show it to you."

Nancy's face lit, and warmth spread over me. I couldn't fathom why these wonderful people seemed to take such an interest in me. But I wouldn't look the proverbial gift horse in the mouth. If it made both Ida and Nancy happy to see my attempt at quilting, I'd oblige.

"Wonderful. Tomorrow?"

"Yeah. Not sure what time, though." I glanced at Ryan. "Did you find out anything?"

He took another bite of salad and chewed thoughtfully.

"Probably won't get Bill out here until Monday. He's knee-deep in the Mosleys' pipe problem." Sensing my question, Ryan smiled. "Bill's our carpenter-slash-handyman-slash-electrician. He'll be the best guy to give us a rundown of the costs."

"Still no word on the insurance." I rubbed a tense muscle in my neck. "How long is it safe to put off repairs?"

Ryan didn't seem concerned. "The tarp is secure, and there's no rain forecasted." He rubbed a napkin over his mouth. "Everything will be fine."

Except me. I was having a terrible time sleeping at night knowing I had a huge hole in my wall. And here I'd gone and gotten a cat instead of a guard dog. What was Kitty going to do? Swat at a burglar with declawed paws?

"This isn't the big city, dear," Nancy said, once again probing my thoughts. "I haven't locked my doors in years."

My eyes widened. She couldn't be serious. "That's not safe."

"I told her the same thing." Ryan pinned his mother with a look that said they'd had this conversation before. "But she's lived out there forty years. There's no convincing her otherwise."

Nancy waved her hand. "You lived out there all your life. You know it's perfectly safe."

I caught her eye. "Please lock your doors. It would make me feel better."

Ryan leaned back in his chair and crossed his arms. "Me too."

Her gaze darted between us, bemused. "Fine. If it sets you two at ease."

At least Nancy would be safe. Ryan would take good care of her as long as she stayed here, and once she went back to her own house, I felt sure she'd keep her promise.

I was the one without a wall. The thought stuck with me all through the rest of dinner and niggled at the back of my mind as I dried the dishes Ryan then put away. By the time I'd promised to have breakfast with Nancy and the evening drew to a close, I realized there was no way I'd be sleeping tonight. My brain had worked itself into overdrive.

Ryan walked me to my door, even though it was only one driveway away. I unlocked the front door and shoved the key back into my pocket.

"Hey, I wanted to thank you for hanging out with my mom. That means a lot to me." Ryan leaned against the side of the house, his relaxed manner always in direct opposition to my own stiffness. I tried to push my shoulders down from where they bunched up to my ears.

"I like her." I glanced toward his house. "She's hanging out with me more than the other way around. I think she feels sorry for me."

Ryan laughed. "Mom's not the type to hang around people out of pity. Cook them a huge meal maybe, but not hang out with them."

She'd done both, actually, so I wasn't sure he'd necessarily made his point. Not that I would call him out on it. I opened the door and hesitated on the threshold. "You didn't have to do everything you've done. The tree, the tarp, all of it. But I appreciate it."

He pushed off the wall. "It's nothing. Any one of the guys at church would have done it."

Right. Nothing special. Just a preacher man helping out people around town. Same as he'd do for anyone else. The idea both needled and relieved me, though I couldn't exactly say why. "Thanks again."

"No worries. You can pay me back on Sunday."

Church. Teens. Ugh. I did owe him that much, even if my helping him didn't make the first lick of sense. "Right. I'll be there."

Ryan grinned. "Good night."

I echoed his words and slipped inside. I turned the lock, though it wouldn't matter with a hole in the wall. Anxiety shifted another gear as soon as the bolt clicked into place. Every breath pulsed with seclusion, every heartbeat a reminder that I occupied this big house alone. My nerves tingled with energy. My mind raced with endless scenarios, none of them pretty.

Letting my mind run rampant wouldn't do me any good. I'd need to keep busy until exhaustion demanded my brain take a break from spinning horrific illusions. Might as well put this energy to good use and have something worth showing Nancy tomorrow.

I gathered my material, thread, and an old plug-in radio from Ida's laundry room. I scanned the channels and finally found one without commercials. Christian music. Not my usual, but I could try something new. Besides, these songs wouldn't taint Ida's house.

The upbeat melody flooded the room, and my nerves unwound.

At least I had something to do to keep me occupied. And if anything rattled that tarp, I knew exactly where Ida kept the chef knife.

16

The Finished Product

Something heavy and—hairy?—pooled across my face. Sleep scattered from my senses. What in the world? I bolted upright and sent the object flying off my head.

Kitty landed in a splash of gray fur on the bed. She pinned her ears at me and swished her tail. Clearly, she'd been jarred awake as well and wasn't thrilled.

"What?" I wrinkled my nose at the offended cat. "You were the one sleeping on *my* face." I brushed cat hair off my eyes. Seriously? She couldn't find anywhere else? Maybe she'd been trying to commandeer my pillow and I hadn't yielded, so she'd settled for stubborn, passive-aggressive tactics.

Or maybe I personified a cat too much.

I rubbed my eyes and swung my feet off the bed. What time was it?

9:07.

Oh no. Nancy would be here soon. I darted to the bathroom, dressed quickly, and scrubbed my teeth. Looked like it would be another no-makeup, ponytail day. When had I let sloppiness become a habit? Derick would be appalled at my lack of primping.

Another reason not to worry with it. There was something almost freeing about not being obsessed over the curl of my eyelashes, the circumference of my waistline, or the style of my hair.

I bounded down the stairs and swept into the kitchen. Coffee. I needed lots of coffee. I measured out the fragrant grounds and dumped them into the filter. I'd stayed up until four this morning, but I'd finished. I hadn't added the hand-stitching that many of Ida's quilts featured, but the fact that I'd sewn the entire thing with a foot-pedaled, century-plus old machine felt like enough old-fashioned success to me.

The bright blue tarp mocked me from the dining room, but I averted my gaze. I couldn't do anything about the hole, the damage, or the repairs right now, so no point fixating on it. The coffee pot gurgled, and soon the uplifting aroma of coffee swept away the lingering sawdust smell.

The doorbell rang. I checked the clock on the stove. Nine-thirty. Right on time. I sauntered into the foyer, slid the deadbolt, and opened the door to Nancy's smiling face.

"Oh, wow." I reached for the huge tray in her hands. "Let me get that."

Nancy relinquished the serving tray topped with an embroidered white hand towel and brushed her hands on her cotton pants.

I closed the door with my foot. "How many people are eating breakfast with us?"

Her tinkling laugh filled the foyer. "None, silly girl."

Did she think the two of us needed a smorgasbord? This thing was heavy. "You should have told me. I would have carried it for you."

"Nonsense. I'm not an invalid." She gestured toward the tray as she bustled toward the kitchen. "And that's not all for breakfast."

I set the wooden tray on the kitchen counter and pulled the towel off the top. Nancy had packed eight different plastic containers with food. I lifted my eyebrows in silent question.

"It's been two weeks since my last treatment. Time for me to head home again." She grabbed three of the containers and headed toward the fridge. "These will tide you over for a few days until I can set up the ladies circle."

"Ladies circle?"

Nancy grabbed four more containers and placed them in the fridge next to the others. "They'll set up a schedule to bring you meals."

I shook my head emphatically. "That's not necessary."

"It's not?" Nancy helped herself to a coffee mug and poured a steaming cup. "So you have a stockpile of food you've been hiding somewhere else in this house?"

Sarcasm?

She laughed, taking the edge off her words. "Don't be prideful, dear. You're going through a rough time. And the ladies practically live for providing meals."

Dubious, I shook my head again. No one "lived for" making meals for other people.

Once again reading my thoughts, Nancy playfully wiggled her eyebrows. "Clearly, you've never met a gaggle of retired Baptist women."

Maybe she had a point. And I did need the food. "That's really kind of them. But I don't want to put anyone out."

"Nonsense." She stirred a spoonful of sugar into her

coffee. "Whenever someone in the church has a baby, goes to the hospital, or has a major life crisis"—she thumbed a gesture toward the blue tarp—"we bring casseroles. It's what we do."

That made me feel a little better. They would take food to anyone who'd had a tree crash through their house. Not just an unemployed freeloader shacking up in her late grandmother's home.

Nancy pulled the top off the final container, and the tantalizing scent of cinnamon rolls mingled with the coffee. We heated a few in the microwave and settled down on the barstools with our coffee.

"So how's that quilt coming along?"

I grinned over the top of my floral-print coffee mug. "I finished."

"Already?"

"Yep. Worked most of the night. It's nothing fancy. No intricate patterns or anything, but I'm happy with it."

Nancy pulled her iPhone from the pocket of her starched blue pants. Her fingers tapped out a quick message before she put it back. Obviously, Nancy didn't share Ida's unfamiliarity with technology. But she was also a good twenty years younger.

"That's fabulous, kiddo. I'm proud of you." She smiled warmly. "Can't wait to see it."

Her praise tingled down my spine. We finished our breakfast, and then, while Nancy waited in the kitchen, I retrieved my prize from the hall closet.

Hopefully, my accomplishment still looked as good after a few hours of sleep. I cradled the thick fabric to my chest and strode back into the kitchen. I paused in the doorway, suddenly self-conscious. I'd done my best, but what if I'd still fallen short?

"Let's see it!" Nancy clasped her hands and scrambled off the barstool. She wiggled her fingers at me.

I handed over my quilt. "I just did squares."

She shook out the folds, and the length dropped to the floor. "Oh, it's lovely." Nancy draped it over the breakfast table and stepped back, placing a hand to her lips.

I shifted my weight while her eyes glided over all the little pieces of fabric.

"Reggie's fatigues?"

I nodded.

"And your father's band shirt." Her voice held wistfulness. She laughed. "Oh, I remember when he went thorough that rock phase." She pointed at the Harley logo. "And when he got that bike…" Her voice trailed off.

My heart skipped. "What do you know?"

She drew a quick breath and waved a hand. "Ida hated that thing." She pointed at the turquoise. "Is that Ida's favorite shirt?"

I wrapped my arms around my waist. "Is that okay?"

Her gentle eyes found mine. "Ida would rather see it on your quilt than sitting in the closet. Or handed off to charity."

Breath fled my nostrils, and a small smile wiggled on my lips. "She said to take memories and stitch them together, so I tried to find things that would remind me of her."

Nancy wrapped her arm around me, her rose-scented perfume clinging to my shirt. "That's exactly what she wanted. She'd be so pleased."

The doorbell rang.

I frowned. Who could that be?

Nancy scuttled to the door as if she lived there. I followed and waited in the middle of the foyer. She swung open the door, revealing her son.

Hair neatly combed and dressed in yet another plaid cotton button-down with the sleeves rolled to his elbows, Ryan greeted his mother with a kiss on her cheek. His eyes traveled over the top of her head and snagged mine.

"I brought you something." He lifted an envelope. "Mom said you were finished."

I plucked the letter from his hand while Nancy closed the door behind him and told him to come get a cinnamon roll with her while I read my letter.

When they'd disappeared into the kitchen, I popped the seal and slid out two sheets of paper. Same blocky font. I glanced at the typewriter I'd placed on the narrow table on the opposite side of the entry space and imagined her fingers pecking at the keys.

My dear Casey,

If I know Ryan, and I do, since I watched that boy grow up, he gave you a letter before you finished the quilt.

I sucked a breath. If I was the kind of person to believe in ghosts, I might think she lingered around and watched what happened around here.

Don't be surprised. I planned for that, too. I made a note that if at any point during the quilt-making process you got overly discouraged, he had my permission to give you an extra letter to encourage you along. Of course, I couldn't know the circumstances. If you finished first, then you got that letter and this one at the same time. Both are important.

I should have known. Ryan hadn't technically broken any of Ida's rules after all.

I bet your quilt is beautiful. I hope you incorporated things that mean something to you. Now that you are finished, it's time I give you the next little piece of our journey. By this point, I'm sure you've gone through the sewing machine drawers. But you may have missed something. Look in the drawer on the right side, bottom. In there, you'll find a small envelope on the back wall of the drawer.

No way. How had I missed that?

After setting the letter on the top of the stored sewing machine, I pulled out the bottom drawer. It was deep. I slid it all the way forward and pushed the box of implements, old buttons, and various other objects out of the way. A small, square envelope had been stuck in the crack of the drawer, keeping it tucked tightly against the back. I gently wiggled the envelope out and opened it.

The same script handwriting I'd seen on the old letter tucked under the typewriter.

Son,

Is it true? You've enlisted? I fear for you, so young and going to war. I pray you will reconsider. Even so, I know you will serve your country well, if you are determined to go. Know that you will always have my most fervent prayers.

Mother

This had to be the same mother and son from the other letter. The one who'd sent her children away. Why had Ida

135

kept this in the back of the sewing machine? What did it mean? I replaced the aged paper in the envelope and picked up Ida's letter.

During the depression, a man owed your great-grandfather money. The man came to the back door one morning during breakfast. Rufus opened the door, his four-year-old son behind him. Rufus had pressed the man for the money he owed. They argued. The man drew a gun and shot him. Reggie was standing right next to him.

My throat went dry.

Times were very hard during the depression, and a widow couldn't take care of four children on her own. She had an infant and was pregnant when she lost her husband. In order to make sure her oldest three didn't starve, she had to send them to the Methodist Home for Boys. Your grandfather spent most of his childhood there. Two days after his seventeenth birthday, he joined the Army Air Corps. He'd go on to be a paratrooper and later a mechanic. During the Vietnam War, they would recover crashed planes in the jungle. Your grandfather's job was to put the planes back together so the soldiers could get home.

Why am I telling you all of this? One, because your grandfather was an incredible man, and I think you should know his story. But also because I want you to see Pamela's story. It tore her heart to send her boys away to the children's home. Sometimes, a parent does what they think is best for their child.

Even if it doesn't seem that way to the child. And even if it tears a mother's heart to shreds.

That gives you another piece of our family history. Your grandfather didn't live with his parents for most of his life. Other people raised him, but that didn't diminish his family ties. The separation didn't cripple him. He accomplished a great many things, married a woman he adored, and had a family of his own. He loved us well. In many ways I wish this weren't a legacy you had to repeat, but having lived on the other end of Reggie's story, I know that you possess the same strength as your grandfather. You are not defined by your past. You are defined by God and the choices you make.

Now, we move on to the next piece of our journey. Go to the living room. Over the mantel, you'll find a picture I want you to see.

With my love,
Mamaw

That was it? What would the picture tell me? Nancy's and Ryan's voices still drifted from the kitchen, followed by Ryan's rumbling laughter. I turned toward the living room. Sunlight drifted through the lace curtains and draped its fingers over the furniture.

The carved mantel contained several pictures. Which one did she want me to see? I started at one end. Ida with several older women standing in front of a dilapidated old house. They all seemed to be in their sixties. Probably her sisters.

Another photo of Ida and Reggie. He in his uniform and her with tight 1950s curls. Two photos of my father, one from elementary and one from high school. My gaze lingered on his face, but I couldn't find any of my features in his.

Hanging on the wall, a large photograph featured a little boy in a wicker chair. His wide eyes reflected the pop of the old box camera he'd probably struggled to stay still for. The sepia tones painted his world in shades of amber and beige. A black-and-white photo on the right side of the large one showed two stiff couples dressed in early 1900s attire sitting on the porch of an old house. Next to them, an old man with a long white beard perched in a chair.

On the other side of the wide-eyed little boy, a man stood in front of what could be the same old house. I glanced at the other photographs. The turn-of-the-century one, this one, and Ida with her sisters.

Had to be a family home. I looked closer at the one with the man. A quilt hung on the line behind him. I narrowed my eyes and lifted onto my toes to get closer. This had to be the one. The patchwork quilt couldn't be a coincidence. But who was the man?

Rufus? My great-grandfather, the one who had been shot. It was the only explanation I could come up with that connected the pieces of the puzzle Ida had given me. But what did it mean?

"Find something?"

Ryan's voice pulled me from my inspection of the photograph. I lowered to the flat of my feet and shook my head.

"I don't get it. She wanted me to look at a photo over the mantel, but I don't see anything about my parents or why they left me." I rubbed the bridge of my nose. "I still don't have any of the answers she promised." I eyed Ryan where he stood in the doorway. "Did she tell you anything?

Give you any clues about that letter?"

A crease formed between his eyebrows. "Sorry. All it said was to give you that letter after you completed the quilt."

I sighed. More questions without answers.

17

Noises in the Night

Nothing good happens after midnight. The words of my father—the man who'd adopted me—pulsed in my head along with each thud of my heart.

It was nothing.

Just a noise. After several days of no burglars creeping through the wall, I'd finally started sleeping better. No sense getting myself worked up now. Old houses made noises. It was nothing.

The thumping sound came again, and I clutched Kitty to my chest. She let out a low growl. Fearing I'd hurt her, I relaxed my death grip. She swished her tail and growled again, then leapt out of my arms.

"No!"

Kitty streaked out the crack in the bedroom door. Why hadn't I shut it? Locked it? I dug my fingers into the blankets. Now what? Did I attempt to save my guard cat from whoever poked around downstairs, or did I huddle under the covers and wait for a madman to trap me upstairs?

I'd seen enough horror movies in my teen years to know

that only idiots tried to hide upstairs.

Rrrrawow

Kitty's fearsome growl-slash-yowl iced through my veins and pushed my pulse into another gear. Someone was definitely down there. Adrenaline laced my blood and flooded my senses.

Think!

I needed a weapon. And I needed to call for help. Weapon first.

I unplugged the lamp and wrapped the electrical cord around the heavy base. Nothing flimsy like porcelain or shaped glass. This thing had a hefty wooden base and a metal pole. It could do some damage, if I needed it to. Thanks, Ida.

Properly armed, I flipped open my phone. I'd never called 911 before. Not even that time when I'd accidentally caught the kitchen on fire during high school while my parents were away in Vegas. Or when that guy had broken our window and stolen a bunch of electronics in middle school. I'd just hidden under my bed until he left. My adoptive dad took the price of that mistake out on my hide when my parents returned to a ransacked house the next morning.

I punched in the digits.

The line clicked, and a female voice came on the phone. "Nine one one, what's your emergency?"

"There's someone in my house." I crept to the door and poked my head out, lamp at the ready. "The tree fell, left a big hole in the wall. Someone's here."

"Stay calm, ma'am," the professional on the other end of the line said. "What's your address?"

"One-twelve Old Mill Road, Maryville."

Something crashed. Kitty screeched. I dropped the phone and sprinted out the door. Before I could even gather my senses, I'd darted down the stairs, through the foyer, and into the kitchen. I flipped on the lights, chest heaving and lamp raised.

Nothing.

I whirled around. Where did she go? "Kitty?" My voice wavered. I cleared my throat and tried again. "Here, Kitty Kitty."

My imagination fired images of a man in all black holding my cat ransom. And like a dimwit, I'd run right into his trap. Stupid. I gripped the doorframe, senses on high alert.

Hey, God, I could use a little help.

Prayer? I shook the oddity away. Desperation had a way of making people search for any kind of lifeline, even ones that had proven they didn't work. I needed to pull myself together. I wouldn't be a victim. If I had to, I could level this lamp right in a guy's face.

The tarp popped against the wall.

My heart nearly exploded. I grabbed at my chest and consciously slowed my breathing. *Get it together. Breathe.*

My self-calming did nothing to ease the tingling shooting over my skin like a thousand fire ants. I pressed myself against the wall by the kitchen doorway and forced myself to focus. The tarp was still nailed to the wall. All the way around. Either the burglar had put the material back to cover his tracks or—

Bam!

I sucked in a breath. Raised the lamp. My eyes darted around the space and tried to locate where the sound had come from. Scraping.

Thump.

It was in the kitchen!

The cabinet in the island quivered. He could grab me! I bolted out of the kitchen, stumbled backward, and landed in the middle of the foyer in a heap. I churned my legs. Had to get up. Had to run.

The front door shook with the force of an erratic pounding.

I screamed.

Shouts. More pounding. I covered my ears with both hands, suddenly the little girl hiding behind the couch again.

The door burst open.

I gulped in air but didn't find enough to fill my aching lungs. A shadow filled the doorway. Reached out a hand.

It flipped the light switch, filling the foyer with light. I blinked. Then blinked again and forced my mind to focus and my eyes to comprehend the scene before me.

Time slowed. A tall man with short-cropped hair filled the doorway. Olive drab uniform. Patches of lighter green. Thick black belt slung around a trim waist. His hand thrust out in front of him. A Glock swept toward me.

Blue lights flashed outside, washing the porch in an eerie glow behind him.

Breath wheezed from my lungs.

His eyes found mine. His gun lowered.

"Are you all right?"

Throat too dry to answer, I nodded and pointed toward the kitchen. He scooted past me, black gun glistening in the revolving light. He cautiously stepped into the kitchen.

"Casey!" Ryan burst through the doorway, wild eyes searching.

I gathered my knees under me and buried my face in my hands. In an instant, his strong arms pulled me to my feet.

He tucked me against his chest. Suddenly enveloped in protection, my limbs trembled. His heart thudded in my ear.

"Are you okay?" Wide palms stoked my tangled hair. "What happened?"

My voice strangled in my throat. I dug my fingers into his shirt and breathed in his clean scent. Something in me stirred. Tears burned the back of my throat, and I buried my face in the shelter of his embrace. His concern blanketed me. I breathed deeply. Steadied.

Safe. I was safe, and no one could get me here.

"All clear." The deputy stalked out of my kitchen, holstering his gun at his waist. Serious jaw and stern eyes. This guy could handle an intruder.

I pushed away from Ryan. "Did you get him?" I hadn't heard a shot or any kind of scuffle. The thief must have immediately surrendered. Smart. I wouldn't want to take on Deputy Beefy, either.

He lifted dark eyebrows. "Didn't figure you wanted me exterminating the vermin. It's not safe to discharge a firearm in a civilian's home."

His words made no sense. I blinked several times to focus on him. "What?" Had he called the intruder *vermin*?

The guy looked at Ryan and jutted his chin toward the kitchen. "City gal here let in a possum. It's scrounging through the trash."

A possum? No way.

He nodded toward the kitchen doorway. "Saw a raccoon scamper out of the dining room window." He gave me a curt nod. "I suggest screens if you plan on leaving the windows open."

"Ryan?" A man in a blue bathrobe stuck his balding head through my front door. "Everything all right?"

"Just a possum, Bill." Ryan's smooth voice filled the space. "Nothing to worry about."

Bill, the handyman who'd quoted an astronomical repair cost I'd never afford without Ida's insurance, snorted. "Y'all woke the whole street up for a possum?"

Heat gathered in my chest and scorched through my cheeks. The entire street? I looked to the deputy. He crossed thick arms over his chest. I hadn't heard a siren. How had my call caused such a stir?

Ryan stepped out on the porch to talk to the handyman and who knew who else.

"Everything's clear, ma'am. Have a good night." The deputy nodded curtly and followed Ryan out, leaving me alone in the foyer.

A possum. I'd called emergency services for a furry vermin. I straightened my spine. At least it hadn't been a murderer. Or a madman. All things considered, a raccoon and a possum weren't all that bad. The town would laugh at me, but I was alive.

I'd take embarrassment over mutilation any day.

"Go on back to bed, folks!" The deputy's booming voice called out to however many neighbors had gathered on the street. "Nothing to see here."

I wrapped my arms around myself. What a mess. They must have freaked out because I'd dropped my phone. Must have thought the guy had me.

A sudden thought slammed into my head. Kitty. Oh, no.

What had happened to her after that terrible noise? Did raccoons fight with cats? I hadn't seen either my cat or the four-legged intruder.

The deputy must have opened every cabinet in the kitchen. If he hadn't killed the possum, then where was it?

I cautiously eased around the island. "Kitty?"

Man, I was an idiot. I'd opened the windows during dinner for airflow and had totally forgotten to close them when I went upstairs. That's the kind of thing that happened when I let illusions of safety lure me into stupidity. I flipped the light switch.

No Kitty. I ducked down to look under the china hutch. Could she even squeeze under there? Nothing but cobwebs.

If the raccoon and the possum had come through the window, it stood to reason Kitty had gone out of it. Had the raccoon hurt her? I didn't know anything about wildlife.

"Casey?" Ryan slipped up behind me. "What's wrong?"

Everything. Obviously. I looked around the dining room. "I don't know what happened to the cat."

Surprise flitted over his face. He smoothed his features into a warm smile. "Don't worry. We'll find her."

All this mess, and he wanted to help me find the shelter cat? The one I'd lost while being idiotic enough to leave the windows open and let in pilfering wildlife? Worse, I'd called in the cops and woken the entire neighborhood. Gold star for failure.

Still, he looked at me with concern and compassion. Did nothing anger this man? Derick would have shouted at me. My dad would have berated me. Ryan had hugged me, soothed me, and offered to find my missing cat.

Moisture stung my eyes. "I feel so stupid! It was just so hot...and...and..."

He wrapped a comforting arm around my shoulder and nestled me against his side. "Easy. I've got you. There's no reason to be upset."

There was every reason to be upset! I'd just made a fool of myself in front of—what?—half of this town? No doubt the rest would hear about the crazy girl who called 911 for a possum by the time they rolled out of bed. And on top of that, I'd also lost the one creature who I was supposed to take care of. So much for being dependable.

"Come on. We'll find that cat." Ryan slipped his fingers into mine and pulled me toward the front door.

Something about my hand in his felt right. Peaceful. Secure. It wasn't anything romantic. Nothing like what books said about passionate tingles when two hands touched. I didn't feel lightheaded, and my heart didn't go pitter-patter. Instead, something more solid radiated through me. He made me feel safe. Protected. And nothing about the way he responded to me said he thought I was as stupid as I thought I was.

He kept hold of my sweaty hand until we reached the front porch and then released me. I wrapped my arms around my waist. The sheriff's deputy had turned off the flashing lights on his sleek black Dodge Charger. The door slammed, and in a moment, the car rolled out of the driveway. Several people still in pajama pants and robes lingered on the sidewalk. Phone flashlights bobbed in the darkness like nosy fireflies.

Ryan stepped in front of me and lifted his voice to the stragglers. "Anybody seen a cat?"

A few people called back, none of them with anything helpful. My heart sank as people returned to their own homes. I'd lost Kitty.

Or maybe she'd taken the opportunity to escape. Either way, she was probably long gone by now.

Ryan grabbed my hand again, and we stepped down from the front porch. He shined his cell phone light over the grass. Droplets of dew hung to the tiny skewers like blood on the end of a thousand blades. I stepped into it.

Despite my morbid mental picture, the grass felt pretty good under my toes. Soft. Cool. I could have told Ryan I didn't have any shoes, but then he probably would have sent me upstairs to put some on. And released my hand.

The moisture under my feet cooled some of the fire clinging to my skin. I trailed along behind Ryan as he poked his phone around under Ida's gardenia bushes.

"I don't see her anywhere." He crouched down to shine the light under the edge of the porch. "Nothing here, either."

Right. I should be helping. "Kitty!"

Crickets chirped a response. We waited. Nothing. Ryan rounded the side of the house, and I stepped carefully behind him. The flashlight beam bounced over the huge sections of the tree trunk in the yard. Limbs had been trimmed and the leafy ends hauled off. Stacks of smaller logs stood in neat little piles, ready to be carted away by church members.

The giant trunk, however, flattened the grass in the yard like a submarine out of water. How long would it take them to cut through all of that?

Ryan bent down and peered around the open windows along the side of the house. I made a face at my own forgetfulness. I wasn't totally incompetent. I'd planned to leave the upstairs windows open for ventilation and close the ones anyone could get into. But I'd forgotten.

"You want to try again?"

Oh, right. Kitty. Man, I really stunk at this. "Kitty!" I cupped my mouth and called louder. "Kitty, kitty, meow, meow."

The light beam swept over me. I shielded my eyes, and it

dropped down to my feet, illuminating my bare toes, unshaved legs and—

Oh, no. What was I wearing? Realization flashed through me in a painful streak of mortification. Threadbare pink tank top. No bra. Very short shorts. Attire for sleeping in a house with no AC.

Completely inappropriate for wandering around the yard with the preacher. Or facing a law officer. Or being scrutinized by neighbors.

Heat raced up my neck. How had I let Ryan hug me?

"Kitty kitty meow meow?" Ryan laughed. "Seriously? How do you call a dog? Puppy puppy woof woof?"

Sweat popped out on my neck. My heartbeat slowed. This wasn't happening. I hadn't had a panic attack in years. Thought I had it beat. I swayed, lightheaded.

"Casey?"

The light washed over me again, and I twisted to angle my shoulder to him in a pitiful attempt to hide my barely clothed body.

"I was only kidding." He took a step closer. "I thought I was being funny to lighten things up." He groaned. "I wasn't trying to be a jerk, I swear. I'm sorry."

I took one step back, and then another. Blood whooshed in my ears and made his words sound like they came from underwater. He took another step closer.

No. I didn't want him to see me like this. He called my name again, but it drifted away on the humid air. Too much.

I ran.

18

Sinking Ships

ho had I become? What had happened to the woman who pulled up her big girl pants and faced the world armed with cynicism and sharpened barbs of defense? These people made a mess out of me. I scurried through the still open front door—another testament to my monumental lack of judgment while in this place—and into the foyer.

I closed it behind me—soundly, for good measure—and clomped up the stairs. Ida's funeral, the letters, probate, all of it left me wading through murky emotions that twisted and turned my senses. The tree, the cat, and the raccoon—not to mention the possum—and I could add terror, humiliation, and stupidity to the list.

Then there was Ryan.

Why had I let people behind my walls? Under my skin? That mistake always turned out the same. I let down my guard, followed the detrimental advice showered on every pretty-pink-sparkle-princess little girl, and showed people the real me by "just being myself." That's when the distancing started. Followed by the sudden "business" and dodging my calls.

Ryan had seen too much. How long until he started avoiding me?

I stomped up the stairs and into my room and leaned against the door. I stared up at the ceiling. Maybe I was being slightly unfair. Neither Ryan nor Nancy had tried to push me away. In fact, they kept trying to pull me closer.

Truth be told, that terrified me.

Get too close and the pain of loss would be unbearable. Wasn't that what had happened with Ida? In too short of a time, I'd let her in. Loved her. And I'd lost her. I dropped my head back against the door and stared up at the ceiling.

Half-formed thoughts and a swarm of disjointed emotions swirled around in my head, none of them making any sense. Almost like two different versions of myself vying for dominance.

A tear snaked its way down my cheek and left a little track of loathing in its place. I didn't want to cry. Hated it. I became snotty, illogical, and always ended up with a headache. I ground my teeth to battle the fire burning in the back of my throat and trying to leak out of my eyes.

The door rattled behind my back with three quick knocks. "What happened? Talk to me."

That voice. So calm and yet concerned at the same time. How did he do it? Walk around with such peace even in the middle of his mom's cancer treatments and dealing with the disaster who'd moved in next door?

"I, uh, realized I needed to change." I twisted a piece of hair around my finger and made no move toward the closet.

Three pounding heartbeats of silence. "Oh."

I'd become completely unraveled. I'd once been an organized, composed, and ordered person. Every bit of that had gone out the window as soon as I'd stepped foot into Maryville.

Or had I really shed a false shell instead? Like a crab. I crossed my arms over my chest. *So* not a good thing. When a crab lost its protective shell, the poor creature was nothing more than a soft meal waiting to be scooped up.

Not good.

"You finished?"

What? Oh. Right. I was supposed to be changing. "Not yet."

I pulled on the baggiest pair of sweatpants I owned—the ones I'd met Ryan in, ironically, but I wasn't going to think about that. My legs immediately felt wrapped in an inferno. Ugh. Why'd I have to lose the AC? Sticky humidity clung to my skin.

Nope. I shimmied out of the sweatpants and into an acceptable-for-being-seen-in pair of shorts and a huge baggy T-shirt a food supply company had once passed out to all the waitresses. Pulling my hair into a somewhat cleaner ponytail, I shuffled out of the closet and stared at the door again. Was he still waiting out there, or had he given up and gone home?

I tiptoed across the carpet and pressed my ear against the door.

Meow.

I jerked my head back. Kitty? I flung the door open, only to be met with my antisocial cat purring contently while snuggled in Ryan's strong arms. Who could blame her? Horrified, I immediately pushed the thought away. Not going there.

"I found your cat." His probing eyes worked their way over me, chipping out hunks of mortar from my protective shell.

Can't be a blue crab.

"Thanks." I stared at him.

He stared back. Suddenly, we were back to that day when we'd reached a stalemate. I was too tired to get caught up in another one.

Ryan, maybe thinking the same, stroked the cat's head and then attempted to thrust her toward me.

She growled. Great. Even my cat liked Ryan better than me.

My head throbbed. "Just put her down."

A second later, Kitty darted between my legs and under my bed. I watched her until I could avoid eye contact with the man in the doorway no longer.

"What happened?" His question, layered with more than the simple words, hung between us.

My ship, the USS Competence, was sinking anyway, so why bother trying to fix leaks in the hull? "Under the duress of the situation, I failed to remember I had dressed in, uh, something cooler. Not okay for everyone to see me like that."

Did his cheeks redden? I leaned a little closer. Strong, tree-cutting, Bible-wielding men blushed? He awkwardly jabbed his fingers through his messy hair. Something in my heart melted. Did he feel as weird about the situation as I did?

His being awkward did more for me than his confidence could. My shoulders relaxed. "Look, I haven't been fair to you. You've gone way above and beyond helping me. You've kept your promise to Ida, and I know she'd be thankful for all you've put up with from me. I'm sorry I can be such a train wreck. I was scared, embarrassed, and frustrated."

I took a breath, and Ryan immediately filled the space.

"And when I made fun of you, that compounded the already high emotions." He reached for pockets he didn't have in his pajama pants and settled for holding his hands in front of him instead. "I'm really sorry for that. I thought I could make you laugh. Hurting you was never my intention."

This new emotional-discussion territory felt strange and uneven beneath me. I took another step across the rocky ground of honesty and vulnerability, checking my balance. "I overreacted. It wasn't what you said. I just suddenly realized I was barely dressed. After already being humiliated in front of a policeman and half the street, I couldn't take the added disgrace of you thinking less of me."

His head pulled back as though an invisible hand had swatted his face. "Think less of you? What are you talking about?"

Here came that moment. The one where I said too much. Maybe I'd already passed that line. I couldn't even tell anymore. But one thing suddenly became glaringly clear.

I didn't want to be who I'd become. And I didn't mean who I'd become since meeting Ida. I didn't want to be the hardened woman from Atlanta. Somewhere along the way a hopeful, imaginative child had turned into a distant, guarded, and lonely woman.

A woman who'd lived with a man not her husband and let him chip away at everything within her that should have been cherished, not scrutinized and found lacking. I didn't want to be the cold woman who maintained her composure by pushing away anything real in her life because she was too afraid to relive the rejection.

Was there a different option? Could I step out of that shell and, instead of walking around like the blue crab, maybe grow a different shell? One that fit a little better?

Maybe that was exactly what Ida had wanted. I owed it to her—and maybe myself—to find out.

Ryan still stared at me. His eyes swam with concern and confusion, but he'd stood there and waited, letting me think through what I wanted to say. I respected him for that.

I hitched up my shoulder. "You're a good guy, Preacher Man. You were kind in my moment of fear and"—heat crept up my neck, and I resisted the urge to scratch it—"you comforted me. I didn't want you compromising your good standing by being too close to a...um..." What was the right word? This wasn't the Victorian era in one of my library books. And I'd been more clothed than most women on the beach. I'd hadn't been naked, and his embrace had been friendly, not inappropriate. I scrubbed my hands down my face.

He crossed his arms over his chest. "I don't understand. You were woken up in the middle of the night. It's hot in here because you don't have air conditioning. No one thinks you should have stopped in the middle of all of that to change clothes." He leaned against the doorframe. "What's this really about?"

The way his eyes probed my face, he seemed to think I had some kind of ulterior motive for my actions. I didn't. My conflicting emotions spun like a hurricane inside me, scooping up any logical reasoning and twisting it around on the winds of confusion. I was acting crazy. I could see that.

"Want to know what I think?" He arched an eyebrow and proceeded to tell me without my answer. "I think you're scared. There's been a lot happening, and a lot of things confuse you. Tonight compounded a lot of emotions, and they became overwhelming."

I could only nod.

"But no one, least of all me, thinks less of you because you got upset." He jabbed his hand through his hair again but held my gaze. "And I don't think anything bad about you because of your pajamas."

I wrapped my arms around my middle and dug my toe into the carpet. I'd made a fool of myself, but he didn't hold it against me. Not even when I tried to hold it against myself.

"You're really upset because you feel like you've lost control. Things are happening that you can't do anything about, and so you're grasping for anything you can have some power over."

The air left my lungs. I blinked. Twice. Tried to focus. My forehead wrinkled so deeply I could feel it crowding my nose.

He was totally right.

How had he been able to decode Hurricane Emotion when I hadn't? Something about that deeply unsettled me, so I shoved it aside to examine later.

Ryan looked at me expectantly.

"Uh, yeah. I think you're right." Great. A gaping hole in the USS Composure, and my entire fleet was about to sink.

A warm smile spread over his face. "It's okay to not be okay. You've been through a lot. Being emotional is natural." He lifted a hand like he wanted to reach for me but used it to rub the back of his neck instead. "But, you know, God can help you through it. Maybe in the middle of all of this, He's using uncertain circumstances to get you to turn to Him."

I pressed my lips together, my desperate little prayer from earlier pushing into my mind. I'd asked God for help. Ryan stood right in front of me. Nancy and her church ladies would make sure I didn't starve. People cared about me.

Maybe this was my chance to finally make some changes in my life. I offered a warbling smile, and his next words washed over me like a summer breeze.

"You're not alone. I've got you."

19

Emma

I am not alone. Remembering Ryan's words helped a little, but not much. Sometimes being in a crowd could make a person feel more alone than ever. But if I chose to be alone because I was too chicken to take any chances to get to know people, that was my own fault.

I sat in my car and watched the church people file into the building. Many were dressed in their finest, but some came in clean, but decidedly humble clothing. The first time I'd come here, everyone seemed to be better off than I was. When I looked a little closer, maybe without my own judgy eyes, I noticed something different. Many of these smiling families looked like hardworking people, not pretentious snobs. Why hadn't I seen that the first time?

Waffling in indecision, I gripped the steering wheel. If I went in now, I could probably get a seat in the back. But I'd have to sit there uncomfortably until the service started and would be expected to introduce myself to every curious person who passed by. I mean, I wanted to take a few risks and put myself out there a little, but maybe not that much. On the other hand, if I stayed here, I could be late. Maybe end up in the front row again. Everyone would look at me when I had to walk past them. Neither option seemed appealing.

Sweat clung to my palms, and I released the steering wheel. The thick humid air filled my car even with the windows down. My jeans stuck to the backs of my knees.

Better get out, or you'll be a stinky, sweaty mess, and that'll be a whole different problem.

The inner voice had a point. I wanted to hear the service. And the teens weren't too bad.

Besides, I'd promised Ryan. I owed him one. Where was he, anyway? I scanned the faces trickling in, and my gaze snagged on a girl. The one from the youth group who'd given me a better version of my cactus stare. She trailed behind her parents, one arm wrapped around her waist, her head hung low. Dressed in black pants, Converse shoes, and a gray T-shirt, she practically screamed *leave me alone* with her body language.

Something in my heart twisted. I knew that look. As they neared the front doors, the girl's mother said something I couldn't hear, and she—I thought her name was Emma—straightened and attempted a smile.

Wonder what's bothering her?

Before I could talk myself out of it, I climbed out, crossed the quiet street, and headed for the front door. A connection I couldn't explain drew me to the girl, and I watched her split from her parents and veer toward the student section. Her parents, a couple I guessed to be in their fifties, were both dressed in cowboy boots, jeans, and ironed shirts. They moved in the other direction and chose a pew in the center section.

I hovered in the doorway, unsure where I should go.

Where was Ryan? Shouldn't he swoop in right about now and rescue me?

Whoa. Not okay. I pushed that disturbingly damsel-in-distress thought away and squared my shoulders. I'd been in plenty of new places before. Lots of schools as my parents moved around. I could totally handle—

"Bless your heart, you look like a lost puppy."

Mira Ann. Why did her sugary voice make me cringe? I hid my discomfort as best I could and turned to smile at her as she joined me in blocking the far left aisle.

"Mira. Good to see you again."

"Mira *Ann*." She batted thick lashes at me as if I were some kind of pageant judge she needed to impress, her silky smile bright.

That wasn't nice.

Not fair of me to dislike someone simply because they reminded me of snotty cheerleaders from high school. Mira Ann had been nothing but kind to me. Mostly. "Right. Sorry."

She gripped my arm. "Come sit with me."

We took three steps before I paused, remembering my primary purpose. "I think I'm supposed to sit with the student group."

Mira Ann arched one eyebrow. "Helping out again this week?"

Yep. Only reason I was here. Probably. Helping Ryan. Returning favors.

"Casey?" Mira Ann waved a hand in my face. "Space out again?"

"I, uh..."

She chuckled as she flipped her long hair over the shoulder of her fitted emerald green dress. "I'm only teasing you.

I'm going to sit with my friends." She nodded toward three young women a few rows up, all primped and styled. "You're welcome to join us."

I glanced back at Emma, who stared at something— probably a phone—in her lap while the other students laughed together. "Thanks. But I promised Ryan I'd help with the kids, so I'll sit over with them."

Mira Ann flashed me a bright smile. "Of course. Another time." She swished off, wiggling her fingers at the gaggle of women who openly stared at me.

No hanging out in the back now. Ignoring the fluttering in my stomach, I purposely marched down the aisle to the youth wing. Emma sat on the last row of the section, nearest the wall. Several of the kids noticed me, and I did my best to counter each curious stare with a friendly smile.

I scooted down the pew—why were these things so long?—in an awkward shuffling motion and plopped down right next to Emma.

Her head jerked up, and her brown eyes widened. "Who are you?"

"Cassandra." I shook my head. "Casey." I was Casey here, thanks to Ida. Should I stick my hand out? No. That'd be weird. "I'm, uh, Ryan's friend. I came before."

Her eyes scraped over me, and she gave a quick nod, then looked back at her phone.

"You're Emma, right?"

"Yeah." She didn't even look up.

Great. Now what? I drummed my fingers on my knees. "So, what grade are you in?"

The child rolled her eyes at me. Like full on, up to the ceiling, rolled her eyes at me. While I should have been annoyed at her rudeness, I could see right through the act.

Exaggerated responses and cactus stares? Yeah. Knew all about that. This kid wasn't a brat. Call the feeling in my gut intuition or whatever, but I knew Emma acted like a cactus to keep herself safe.

Been there. How would I talk to me as a teen?

I'd had a teacher once who took it upon himself to show an interest in me. Physics class. I hated all those equations and theories. Didn't really get why it mattered. But Mr. Mallot, he would kneel down at my desk, look me in the eye, and keep asking me questions until I responded. That year at school had been extra hard, and I'd wanted to give up on everything. But that physics teacher refused to give up on me. Eventually, he got me to understand. The only reason I passed was because Mr. Mallot persistently ignored my teenage rudeness until he got through to me.

Same thing might work on Emma. I tried again. "Sixteen, if I had to guess. So, what, tenth grade?"

"Eleventh."

I smirked. "Right. How's school going?"

A flash of eye contact. "It's school. It's boring."

She had a point. I'd never want to go back to high school. Some people called it the best years of their lives. If I had to guess, Emma probably wasn't that type. "Do any clubs or anything?"

Emma dropped her phone in her lap and stared at me. "Why do you care? Who are you, anyway?"

I held her gaze and kept my voice light. "I'm Casey. Ryan's friend."

"You said that already."

"And you asked already."

She blinked at me and the hardness cracked. She barked out a single laugh. "Yeah, I guess I did."

I liked this kid. Feeling decidedly more comfortable, I leaned back against the pew and faced the front. Easier to talk without the awkwardness of staring at people. "So, clubs?"

Emma followed my example and faced the front of the church as the choir filed into the seats on the stage. "Nope. No clubs."

"Hobbies?"

Her shoulders lifted. "Nope."

Oh, boy. Talking to this girl was like pulling teeth. A pang skittered through my middle. Maybe that was how other people had felt trying to talk to me. I'd take a page from Nancy's book and sweetly and persistently keep trying. Maybe only the persistently part. Sweet might be beyond my reach.

"Eleventh grade. No hobbies, and not all that interested in school." I pointed to myself. "Out-of-work waitress, one hobby I'd forgotten I liked until I came here, also hated school."

Emma actually smiled. "Where are you from?"

"Atlanta." At least, most recently.

"Is it nice?"

"Not the part I come from."

Emma turned to face me, the look on her features saying she was surprised I'd said that. Should I not have? Were there rules I missed somewhere?

Ryan strode in from the side door near the choir's steps to the stage, a smile on his face for his students. Like the last time I'd been here, the boys jostled for his attention, and he clasped several on the shoulder. More kids filed in as the pianist banged out a lively song.

Emma stood, and I followed her lead. Words filled the

screen, and a music director said we could also find the words in the hymn book. I moved my mouth, but I didn't really sing. I noticed something interesting. As stealthily as I could, I edged a little closer to Emma.

Wow. Girl had a good voice. I strained my ear toward her, trying to hear her softly sung words. A little more confidence, and she could be on stage. Though I had the distinct feeling she'd object to standing in the choir.

The service went the same as before, and I once again found myself leaning into the preacher's words. He had a way of taking Bible verses and making them apply to real life. This week, he talked about the fishermen Jesus called to follow Him. Not the priests. Not the educated and had-everything-together people everyone probably expected. He gathered the plain, regular, and unwanted.

The words lingered with me as the service ended. As soon as the final notes of the last song ended, the students erupted into jokes and animated talking. Ryan's eyes found mine over their heads, and he smiled. I offered a nod but then turned my attention back to Emma.

"You've got a pretty singing voice."

She fell into stride next to me as we headed out. "Uh, thanks."

The youth room brimmed with activity and boisterous teens. I lingered in the doorway, not sure where I should go. Emma headed toward one of the pub-style tables. She looked over her shoulder and lifted her eyebrows.

Taking that as an invitation, I followed and sat across from her. She regarded me with interest. "So, out-of-work waitress from Atlanta, what are you doing in Maryville? No one comes here on purpose."

The kids picked up games of flipping cups and grabbed

sodas out of the small fridge in the corner. The room soon filled with the smell of too much cologne, the twitter of girlish giggles, and the whoops of boys trying to best one another.

"My grandmother lived here." I traced a finger along the imitation wood grain on the top of the table. "I met her right before she died."

Emma brushed her long bangs out of her eyes. "You hadn't met her before that?" She had a knowing quality to her question that gave her more depth than a sixteen-year-old should have.

"She was my birth dad's mom. Never met her son."

A thoughtful expression crinkled the corners of her eyes, and she gave me a solemn nod. "Never knew my real dad, either."

I tried probing a little as the other kids crowded around a guy bringing in several boxes of pizza. "So the man you came in with. Stepdad?"

Her shoulders tightened. "Foster parents." She watched me intently, as though my reaction would determine everything.

I simply nodded.

She relaxed and stuffed her phone back in her pocket. "Want to get some pizza?"

Ryan caught my eye and lifted his eyebrows when I took my place in the pizza line. Not sure how to respond to that, I stretched my lips into an awkward smile. Emma stacked three pieces of pizza on her plate. I took one slice of pepperoni. Oh, to eat like a teenager with a Speedy Gonzales metabolism.

We took our places at the table again, and Emma chewed thoughtfully. Her eyebrows flicked up, she gave a small shake of her head, and dropped her gaze back to the table. Curious, I turned to look over my shoulder.

Mira Ann. Interesting. Why had Emma reacted that way? I watched Mira Ann from the corner of my eye as she joined the same girls she'd sat with last week. They immediately started laughing and twittering over something.

The girls seemed to like her. Emma, though...maybe not. I put my elbows onto the table and leaned over my pizza. "You know Mira?"

Emma shrugged. "She comes back here sometimes. I've never really talked to her."

We sat alone while the other kids gathered in clusters around the tables or lounged on the couch. I scanned their faces, remembering something. "Where's that girl you sat with last week?"

"Don't know."

Right. Not overly forthcoming with information. "What's her name?"

"Sarah."

"Y'all friends?"

Another shrug. Okay. We ate in silence. I couldn't think of anything else to talk about. After throwing away our plates, we settled back at the table for Ryan's lesson. I turned in my seat so I could face him.

I'd planned on paying attention, but I kept thinking about the girl behind me. What was her story? How had she ended up in foster care? Did she like it better there, or did she miss her real parents?

My gaze drifted over to the popular table, headed by Mira Ann. She sat with a straight spine and perfect posture. I attempted to iron out my rounded shoulders. The girls at her table all had shiny hair and perfect makeup. Would they turn out just like her?

Yikes. What was wrong with me? Why did this woman irk me when she'd been so nice?

You don't like her because she dated Ryan. Might still be dating him.

I wrinkled my nose at the voice in my head. But what was the point of arguing with myself? I knew the facts. Ryan was a good guy. I wasn't planning on messing up his reputation. Mira Ann didn't have anything to worry about from me. Ryan and I were just friends.

Friends. The word felt good. Not neighbors, not acquaintances. We'd passed that. Through the storm and the possum fiasco, and with our ties to Ida, we'd become fast friends. I smiled to myself. It was nice having a friend. Someone whom I could be comfortable with. Be real with. Someone I didn't have to worry about impressing or maintaining impossible standards for.

Nope. She had nothing at all to worry about from me. I wouldn't do anything to jeopardize having my first real friend since...what? Middle school?

If that counted. I thought I'd had a best friend back then. We were inseparable all sixth grade. Told each other everything. Until she made cheerleader, and I wasn't worth her time. Or good enough to be seen with, wearing my Goodwill clothes. A short skirt and some pom-poms, and my friend entered a new social circle I couldn't breach. When seventh grade started, all of a sudden I didn't exist anymore.

Movement around the room jarred me out of my thoughts. Had I missed the prayer and sat there staring into space while everyone else bowed their heads? Heat clawed up my neck. Mira Ann had been right. I was totally spacy.

The meeting ended, and kids filed out of the room, all erratic movements and pent-up energy. They ranged from gangly freshmen to seniors about to take on the world for themselves. As I watched them mingle and interact, I was struck by the diversity of the group. Several different races and different social groups were represented among the thirty or so kids. I hadn't really noticed it before, but I found it interesting. Maybe I'd expected backwoods Mississippi to be a little more...segregated.

Wow. And there I went being all judgy again. Something twisted in my chest. I should really get a hold on that. Especially if I wanted to keep accusing others of doing the same.

"So, I'll see you again next week?" Emma's voice at my shoulder surprised me.

Seemed like I'd done a decent job connecting with her. "Yeah. I'll be here."

The side of her mouth ticked up. "Cool."

She trailed out behind the other kids, watching her feet as she went through the door. After she'd gone and the room emptied, I picked up leftover soda cans and pizza plates. Mira Ann's laughter filled the nearly empty room. She and Ryan stood together by the door. I did my best to give them some privacy and keep my eyes on the task at hand.

After I'd gathered the trash, I tucked the stools under the pub tables. I was running out of things to do. I flicked a glance toward the door. Mira Ann and Ryan still stood together, talking softly. Her hand rested on his arm, and he nodded along to something she said.

"Casey?" Mira Ann's voice drifted across the space between us. "You want to go to lunch again?"

With her and Ryan? No, thanks. I offered my best smile and an apologetic shrug. "Thanks, but I already ate pizza."

She leaned into Ryan's side and nudged him with her shoulder. "Guess it's just us."

"Sorry." He extracted himself from her grip. "Not today. Promised Mom I'd head out to her house and help her with a leaky sink."

Mira Ann cut me a look, but it wasn't my fault the guy had plans with his mom. She flipped her hair and said something about maybe next week, then glided out the door. Ryan crossed the room, collecting a paper plate I'd missed.

"Saw you talking with Emma," he said. "How'd that go?"

Awkward. A little weird. So, normal. "Fine." He waited as if he wanted me to elaborate. Right. People did that. "She seems like a nice girl. Has a pretty singing voice. Said she's in foster care."

He let out a low whistle. "You learned all that on the first day?"

"I came before." His expression said that didn't exactly count. I turned out my palms. "I like her. Nice kid."

Ryan nodded along. "I'm impressed she talked to you that much. Normally, she hardly says two words to anyone. Her foster parents make her come. She doesn't really want to be here."

I could understand that. Ryan kept looking at me. I searched for a response since it was my turn to talk. "Nice kid," I repeated. "But she's not overly forthcoming. It was hard to keep a conversation going with her."

His eyebrows rose nearly all the way to his neatly combed hair. "I have no idea what that's like." The sarcasm of his words sparked with humor.

Okay, so I totally deserved that. He laughed. I played it off. "You know her better than I do."

Ryan shook his head slowly and chuckled. "I'm glad you two had a chance to talk. She could use a good influence."

That particular descriptor didn't fit me, so I didn't bother with a response. We cleaned up the room and exited the church together. Ryan walked me to my car, always the gentleman.

I fiddled with my key. "Nancy has a leaky pipe?"

"Kitchen sink. I keep telling her she needs a new faucet. I'll probably just run by Mike's and get her one. Then I won't have to keep tightening the rusty one." He leaned against the hood of my car. "Want to go?"

"To the hardware store?" No thanks. I wouldn't know heads from tails in there. I couldn't even use a hammer.

Ryan laughed. "I meant out to Mom's. But I do need to stop by Mike's first."

What would Mira Ann think of that? It didn't matter. We were friends. And I liked Nancy. "I'll run home and change. Can you pick me up after you go to the store?"

"Yep." He spun his keys around his finger. "I'll call Mom. I'm sure she'll come up with some kind of project for the two of you." He winked at me. "That way she won't be looking over my shoulder the entire time."

I laughed. "Win-win for both of us, huh?"

He popped up off my car. "You got it. See you in a few."

After he sauntered off toward his truck parked in the paved lot on the side of the church, I opened my car door and let the heat pour out. Despite the smashed AC unit at home and having to deal with the inability to file an insurance claim with the house in probate, today was a good day.

I'd faced my fear of a new place, met a nice kid, and was heading to hang out with friends. A pain twisted in my chest. How would I ever go back to Atlanta now? Where I had no home, no friends, and no moody teens to hang out with?

I shook the thought away. I had a job waiting on me. A good one. The position came with medical and retirement. State benefits. No way could I give that up to stay in a house I would soon own but couldn't afford. When the summer came to a close, no matter what happened here, I had to go back to Atlanta.

Even if leaving meant losing the few people I'd come to care about.

20

Tattered Truths

*T*he scalding of May boiled over into the raging inferno of June, and I still had a hole in my wall and no air conditioning. Mira Ann kept insisting she was working on the house problem, but until thirty days passed for creditors' claims, I couldn't do anything. Not even file the insurance claim.

Sweat slipped down my forehead. I wiped it out of my eyes and dunked the mop again. I couldn't fix the damage or pay for a new unit, but I could clean the house.

The quote from the repair guy still sat on the kitchen table, mocking me. It would cost thousands for the repairs to the house, and thousands more for the AC. Money I didn't have. Ryan's guy was willing to get started on the repairs, but I'd have to buy supplies first.

Everything hinged on Ida's accounts, the savings and two CDs the lawyer had mentioned when he'd told me Ida had left me an inheritance. My skin crawled with sweat and antsy thoughts. No matter how much the ladies' circle liked making casseroles, they wouldn't feed me forever. Good thing they baked in bulk and I'd remembered to use the freezer this time. I wouldn't starve. Worry myself to sleep most nights over a hole in my wall and sweat through my sheets, but not starve.

The mop plopped on the kitchen floor, and I pushed it back and forth. The past two weeks I'd attended church services, cooked with Nancy, ate other people's food, and watched Ryan and some other guys haul off the last of the oak.

And I'd searched every inch of Ida's house.

More than two weeks since the last clue, and I still didn't understand what it meant or what to do next. I'd looked at her pictures over and over again. Nothing told me what to do next. Whatever Ida had hidden in this house, I wouldn't find it without her help. I dipped the mop again. What would happen if I never figured it out and had to return to Atlanta without any answers?

No way. I'd fallen too deep into this rabbit hole to leave empty-handed. Ryan would give me the rest of Ida's letters. I just had to wait on Ida's schedule. Always waiting. Maybe the next clue would give me something more concrete than simply telling me to look at old pictures. I hoped. While I enjoyed my time with Ryan and Nancy, a clock ticked in the back of my head, counting down the days until the end of the summer.

Thinking of Atlanta brought on another host of issues I needed to sort through. I picked up the mop and moved into the foyer. I had to find an apartment. Which I couldn't do until I had at least a little money for a down payment and a little more to cover rent until I got my first paycheck. A few pieces of furniture to go inside would be nice, too. Some that actually belonged to me, not to my landlord or jerk boyfriend.

My gaze slid over to the living room, and I propped the mop against the wall. I could probably take some of Ida's. A U-Haul couldn't cost more than new, even cheap, furniture. Not that I'd ever rented one to know for sure, and driving the thing through Atlanta traffic would be a challenge. Still, depending on how big of an apartment I could find, I might even be able to take the couch and coffee table. The photos on the mantel drew me, and I stared at them one by one, but no new information jumped out at me.

How did Ida expect me to decode clues to my family's past when I knew so little about them? I could guess who some of these people were, but that didn't tell me anything about my parents, what had happened to them, and why they'd given me up. So far, Ida had given me information too many generations back to soothe the burning in my chest.

Sighing, I returned to the mop so I could keep myself busy. After mopping, I checked the tarp to make sure it was still secure, and I opened the last few windows on the bottom floor to circulate a breeze. Critters probably wouldn't scamper inside in broad daylight.

I hoped.

Ryan had given me the direct number to the sheriff's office in case something more nefarious than vermin slipped inside. I rinsed out the mop and put my hands on my hips as I surveyed the kitchen. Over the past day and a half, I had cleaned every surface, dusted every nook and cranny, and polished every stick of furniture to a shine.

Now what?

The library. How long had it been since I'd sat down and enjoyed a book? A new goal in mind, I rinsed out the mop and headed into the small room filled with decades worth of Ida's books. A little while later, I'd showered, made myself a glass of sweet tea, and selected a historical romance from Ida's collection. I preferred something less sappy, but Ida had very specific tastes.

Stepping out onto the front porch, I nudged the front door closed with my toe and made myself a reading nest on the swing—complete with freshly dusted cushions and a side table stocked with my tea and one of Nancy's peanut butter cookies. The swing moved silently as I pushed my feet against the porch. While still hot, a nice breeze skipped over the lawn and caressed my damp hair. I sank deeper into the cushions, leaned my head back, and closed my eyes.

When was the last time I'd been this relaxed? I tried to think back but couldn't remember. Since I was eighteen, I'd worked nearly every waking hour to make ends meet. I barely scraped out of high school with my diploma, and if it hadn't been for the kindly elderly couple who'd rented me a little room over their garage—and let me work off part of the rent by doing yard work—I probably would have ended up on the street.

After graduation, I'd been able to get better jobs but never really had enough to survive in the expensive city where my parents had abandoned me. Until I'd landed a waitressing job at Derick's swanky restaurant. With the stellar tips, I'd finally started to get ahead. Then I'd started dating Derick.

The thought of that slimeball tightened my stomach, so I purposely pushed the thought of him away. He'd ruined enough in Atlanta. I refused to let him ruin my peaceful moment here.

The breeze carried the scent of Ida's flowers, and birds called to one another in the swaying trees. I breathed deeply.

"Don't you look comfortable."

Mira Ann's voice snapped me from my contemplations. I jumped up, sending the swing flying behind me. It crashed forward into the table and knocked over the glass of tea. Liquid splashed over Ida's book. I yelped. Scooping the book up from the pooling liquid, I tried to fling away the moisture. Tossing the romance on the swing, I righted the little table, and turned to face my visitor.

She smiled brightly at me. "I didn't mean to startle you."

Dressed in pink slacks and a white silk blouse, Mira Ann looked as unbothered by the heat as a sunning alligator. I ran a hand over my damp hair. "Hey. Sorry." I gestured toward the swing. "Want to have a seat?"

Mira Ann took the last step onto the porch. "I won't take long. I've come to buy Ida's house."

Uh, excuse me? "What?"

"I've been thinking, and I've decided this place would make a lovely bed and breakfast."

She'd said the exact same thing that day we went to lunch. "Uh, yeah. We talked about that, remember?"

Her smile faltered. "We did?"

"At lunch. You said it would make a good B&B and would do well on Airbnb. Ryan said he didn't think anyone would come to Maryville."

At the mention of his name, her eyes darted to the house next door. "Yes, well, I said the place would be a good investment for *someone*. Now I've decided that someone should be me. I can give you a good price, and you won't even have to go through the trouble of listing it."

Tempting. Maybe. It would save a bunch of real estate agent fees. "But it's still in probate."

"I'm sure that'll be cleared up soon." She waived an airy hand and pulled something from the designer purse gracefully draped over her arm. "Say you'll at least consider my offer?" She waved an envelope at me.

When I stuffed it in my back pocket, Mira Ann frowned, obviously wanting me to make a decision immediately.

"With all the expenses and repairs"—her gaze roamed over the yard—"I figured you'd want an easy solution to all your problems."

An easy solution would be great. I wasn't sure if selling would be the right answer, though, even if it was the easiest. But I might not have much of a choice. "You'd take over the repairs?"

"Sure!" She flashed me a bright smile. "I'll buy it as-is, and you can head back to your life without having to deal with all of this mess."

All of this mess included Ida's stories, my family history, no apartment back in Atlanta, and no job until school started in August. Even if she bought the house, I couldn't go anywhere. At least, not anytime soon. "I'll think about your offer. But I can't do anything until it's legally mine."

A crease formed between her eyebrows. "Of course." She tucked a curl behind her ear. "I'll leave you to your"— she sniffed toward the swing—"your lounging. Have a good day."

I watched her sashay down the steps, slip into her massive SUV, and pull out of the driveway. Once she was out of sight, I pulled the paper from my pocket and read the offer. Holy cow. I didn't know much about houses, but that seemed like a pretty good price to me. Enough to make a fresh start in Atlanta.

Boots fell on the stairs, followed by Ryan's rich voice.

"Whatcha got there?"

I stuffed the paper back in my pocket. "Mira Ann wants to buy Ida's house. She came by with an offer." I glanced toward the end of the road. "You just missed her."

He nodded, a strange look on his face. The corner of his mouth hitched up, though there was something almost sad about the expression. He held out a manila envelope. "Interesting timing. I've got something for you, too." His mouth twisted to one side. "How about we finish what Ida left before you worry about what Mira Ann brought?"

Taking the letter, I held his gaze. "I didn't learn anything from the last letter. I'm hoping this one gives me something more."

Ryan rocked back on his worn boot heels. "Best open it and see, I guess."

I pressed my lips together, considered, and jerked my chin back toward the swing. "Want to sit with me while I read it?"

His eyebrows shot up, and his eyes widened as if I'd just asked him to run for president or something. Instead of answering, he sauntered across the porch and settled onto the swing like he belonged there. Maybe he did.

The empty glass reminded me of Ida's manners. "Wait here. I'll get us some tea."

A few moments later I returned with two glasses and found Ryan skimming through the book I'd left on the swing.

"Good book?"

I shrugged as I handed him a glass. "Haven't started it."

He handed me the romance, and I set the novel and my tea on the table. Ryan leaned his shoulder into mine, and together we began to read.

Casey,

If Ryan is following my instructions, you should get this letter two weeks after the last one. You're probably wondering why I'm spacing them out instead of giving you everything all at once.

A soft chuckle bubbled out of my throat. Yep.

No reason to drink from a firehose, dear. The biggest lesson I can teach you may be to learn how to slow down and breathe. Take time to enjoy God's creation once in a while. Enjoy a book on the front porch swing. Take a bubble bath.

My gaze darted to Ryan.

He caught my eye and barked a little laugh. "Looks like you figured that part out on your own."

Having him read this with me seemed strangely intimate. Like having someone listen in on a private conversation with your therapist. But at the same time, the comfort of having a friend who could understand pushed away any awkwardness. I raised my eyebrows in response and turned back to the letter.

During this time, I hope you've gotten to know people around town, been listening to Brother Lawrence bring the Word, and found time to rest and rejuvenate your soul. You've worked so hard and been through so much. I pray God uses this time to quiet your heart, and, without so many troubles pressing down on you, you'll see His presence in your life.

My shoulders tensed, and I closed my eyes.

As though sensing the shift, Ryan's hand fell on mine. "You okay?"

I sucked in a long breath of the humid air. "So much for no troubles, huh?" I'd meant for the words to sound ironic, maybe even a bit snarky, but instead they poured out bitter.

"Life is full of trouble no matter where we are."

Comforting. I shot him a look and wiggled the paper in my other hand. "She wanted me to have a time of quiet to see God, but instead, God gave me a tree through the house, no AC, and problems with the insurance." I dropped my head back against the swing and groaned.

"That's true. But in the middle of that, you've had a good time cooking with my mom, you bonded with a teen who needs a friend, and you even brought a book out to the porch." Ryan squeezed my hand until I lifted my head and met his gaze. "The good parts are like water. They flow all around the troubles in our lives. What you really need is to find peace in the midst of troubles and thank God for the good parts that flow around them."

His words made sense, the logic sound. "I get what you're saying, but it's hard to find peace when you're struggling to survive."

He laced his fingers between mine, infusing me with his quiet strength. "You're right. It is. That's why we're promised a peace from God that passes all understanding. He can give peace even when it makes no sense."

Must be why Ryan never seemed riled. I lifted the paper and cleared my throat. "Let's keep reading."

He held my gaze for a moment, brown eyes searching way too deep. Something inside me tightened, splintered...cracked. Did he know his words had knifed through me, cutting into my walls and piercing tender places inside? I wanted peace. But experience had taught me that I'd never find peace when life kept shooting me with barbed circumstances. I swallowed back a burning in my throat. Heat that had nothing to do with the weather crawled over me, making it difficult to breathe.

I broke eye contact before he could do any more damage to my composure. I focused on Ida's letter. First I'd find answers. Then maybe I'd find peace.

What I'm going to share with you next is going to be difficult. But by this time I'm hoping you've learned enough about our family and my heart to know that I never wanted you to be hurt. I wish things could have been different, but there is purpose in everything. God can bring good from all pain, and I thank Him each day that I was able to know you. Even if only for a little while. I do love you so.

I swallowed deeply.

"Would you like to read this privately?" Ryan's tone held gentle compassion.

"I don't want to be alone." Whoa. Not what I meant to say. Truth, but not truth I'd meant to share.

Ryan simply held my hand while I gathered myself and we continued to read.

It's time I tell you what happened to your parents. There's no easy way to go about this, so I'm just going to get everything out on paper. By the end of my story, I can only pray you don't hate me.

Mike loved Haley. He'd have done anything for her smile. Their love was like a tornado, wild and out of control. She made him laugh, brought a spark to his eyes. Everything he did revolved around her. The intensity of his devotion scared me. I didn't like the idea of my son being obsessed with a girl. I feared the power she could hold over him or what a breakup would do to him.

The winter of their senior year, Mike insisted he would marry Haley. I objected. He hadn't even graduated high school. There was so much he needed to do first. Go to college, grow up.

But love has a way of overshadowing everything else. I should have tried to be more understanding. I shouldn't have pushed Mike so hard. By trying to protect him, I hammered a wedge between us.

Mike believed I didn't like Haley. I did. Haley was a sweet girl. Kind, thoughtful. And she doted on Mike. But they were so young. So inexperienced. I kept telling him he wasn't ready. If they were really in love, they could wait a few years. Finish college.

For the first time since his father's death, Mike refused to listen to my advice. I see now how I'd blamed Haley for the rift growing between us. Blinded by love in my own way, I could only see the way she'd completely stolen my son's heart.

In hindsight, I can see how selfish I was. I wasn't ready for him to have a wife, to have another woman in his life. That's terrible. I know. But I promised myself I would be honest, and there's the awful truth of it. I didn't attend my son's wedding because I'd been too stubborn and selfish to support his decision. I should have been there for him no matter what. If the marriage had fallen apart, I could have been there to help him pick up the pieces. Instead, my only child felt he had to escape me to be happy.

In Mississippi, you had to be twenty-one to get married. In Alabama, you only had to be eighteen. They left one morning during Christmas break, and, when he came home, he was a married man.

That moment is seared into my heart and soul. I'd waited by the window for hours, fearing what he'd done. I'll never forget seeing him hop out of his truck, open the door for her, and tug her toward the house. She seemed so hesitant.

Mike had given me a second chance. An opportunity to embrace the young lady he loved and welcome her into our lives. For years I wondered what would have happened if I'd only loved without judgment and put aside my need to be right.

I hope, Casey, you'll learn from me. Love isn't without pain. But nothing in life is without pain. Refusing to love because you fear being hurt is like refusing to breathe because you're afraid something in the air might make you sneeze.

That day, I squandered my second chance. Don't squander yours.

Regret squeezed around my heart. I gulped breaths of humid air.

Ida's pain leaked off the page with every word, dripping like saltwater into my own wounds. A fog settled on my brain, and I couldn't think. Too many thoughts crashed into one another. Something had happened to my parents, and Ida blamed herself. She'd been afraid to tell me.

STEPHENIA H. MCGEE

Ryan's arm slipped around my shoulders and tucked me into the safety of his side. Infused with courage, I blinked away as much of the fog as I could and focused on the letter. The answers I both wanted and dreaded splattered painful truths all over the page in front of me. I couldn't chicken out now.

Mike led her by the hand up my front porch, eyes full of hope and excitement. I met them at the door with nothing more than harsh words. I yelled at him for being stupid. He had no plan, no way of supporting a wife. I watched my son's face harden, and the boy he'd been solidified into a man determined to protect the woman he loved.

Even from his own mother.

Haley cried. I can still see her beautiful face streaked with tears. Blind with anger, I told Haley she'd ruined Mike's life and insisted that if she cared anything at all for him, she would annul this foolish marriage. She buried her face against his chest, and he glared at me. Beneath the anger, I could see how badly I'd hurt him.

Mike took her away. I didn't see him again for two weeks. When he finally came home, I knew I'd lost my sweet boy. A stoic man entered my house. Nothing I said, no apologies I made, could erase the pain and anger flashing in his eyes. He stuffed his clothes in a duffle bag and stomped out of the house. That was the last time we ever spoke.

He wouldn't answer my calls. He and Haley rented a room in a trailer with some of Mike's friends going to community college. I went by twice,

184

but neither of them would see me. I decided to give them space. I'd hoped his anger would cool by graduation.

I should have tried harder.

Rain beat against the house the night Haley called. Her panicked voice crackled on the line, spitting out words I couldn't comprehend.

The bike. A wreck. Mike in ICU.

I dropped the phone. Left it dangling on the wall. How I made it to the hospital in that state, I'll never know.

Hysterical, I assaulted the nurse's desk until she allowed me to see him. He'd been hit by a truck on his motorcycle. Internal bleeding. Too many broken bones. My heart nearly stopped when I saw him. My baby boy, bruised, bandaged, filled with tubes and IVs.

Haley screamed at me, blaming me for everything. She said if I hadn't disowned him, then they wouldn't have had a fight. He wouldn't have left in the rain.

She was right.

Three months after I missed my son's wedding, I stood at his funeral. Haley left soon after. I didn't know she was pregnant.

I can only hope you will forgive me. I ache fearing that whatever affection you had for me will be wiped away under the truth. I probably should tell you all of these things in person while I still can, but I'm a coward. You have your mother's face and your father's eyes. I don't know if my heart can bear to see Mike and Haley reflected in your face when you realize that all the pain in your life is my fault.

I'm selfish, I know. Please forgive me. I want to get to know you. I want to love you just for a little while. Teach you all the things I should have taught your mother. I'm sorry, my sweet Casey. So very sorry.

Now that you know the truth, you may be done with me. I wouldn't blame you. But I pray you can forgive me. I pray that you will keep walking with me a little longer. Even though I don't deserve it, stay with me. And when you're ready, we'll take the next step together.

With all my love,
Mamaw

21

Pains of the Past

*M*y hands trembled and dropped the paper to the porch. Sunlight wrapped warm fingers around Ida's house, but even in the heat, my veins ran cold. I shivered, and Ryan pulled me closer on the porch swing. For a long time, he didn't say anything.

If Ida had accepted Haley, would I have grown up in a loving home? Would life had been different? I dropped my head against Ryan's arm and stared at the ceiling. "Because Ida rejected Haley, Haley rejected me."

The words sounded petulant. I loathed the emotions swarming inside me almost as much as the tears burning in the back of my eyes.

Ryan rubbed his thumb up and down on my shoulder. "I'm not sure Ida rejected Haley so much as she feared they jumped into marriage too soon."

I leaned forward and rubbed my temples, trying to fight off a headache. "She didn't say anything about what happened to Haley or why Haley gave me up for adoption." Though if she'd lost her husband and had no support, maybe she didn't have much of a choice. Besides, she'd only

187

been eighteen. "Ida should have told me."

"Would you have listened?" Ryan cocked an eyebrow at me.

Yes. Maybe. Probably not. I worked my lower lip through my teeth and took an honest look at myself. "I don't know. At that point, I may have agreed with Ida and blamed everything on her. But that's probably because all these years I've been looking for a reason behind why my life turned out so terribly."

If I hadn't taken the time to get to know Ida, even just a little, maybe I'd have found it easy to blame her for my troubles. Not that focusing my anger on anyone ever changed anything in my life. Anger only poisoned. I knew that, yet still found it a hard truth to walk out. Blame and deflection came easily.

"If you don't mind my asking," Ryan said, tugging me from my thoughts, "what happened after, you know—?"

"After my birth mother abandoned me?" At least now I knew it was only my mother who hadn't wanted me. Mike probably hadn't known she was pregnant. Then again, maybe he did, and that's what they fought about that night. Ida didn't say. "I was adopted by Paula and Howard Adams. Though I never figured out why. They didn't even want kids." At least not after they'd already signed for one.

Ryan started the swing again, and we swayed gently as the afternoon dipped toward twilight. He didn't push, and I respected him for his depth of understanding. Pressure built inside me, begging me to open a valve and let the infection spill out. I was tired of holding on to the past. Tired of it poisoning everything I touched.

Ryan needed to know the truth. Better he find out about me now, before I let myself care for him too much. I cleared my throat of the thickness choking off my words.

"For as long as I could remember, my parents fought. They argued about money and not being able to travel. As a little girl, I hid behind the couch and tried to block out the arguments. The older I got, the more I realized a lot of their fights centered around me. My father complained about how much extracurricular activities cost or how they couldn't do anything because they'd have to hire a babysitter. I started to realize my dad wasn't the responsible type—or the fatherly type. He loved my mom but resented things like bills, PTA, and a kid dragging down his freedom.

"I tried my best to be a good daughter, but I always seemed to be in the way. I learned to take care of myself for the most part. And around the age of nine or ten, they started leaving me alone more. First, they went out at night. Then for a whole weekend. It didn't bother me. Much. At least I had a peaceful house when they were gone. And when they came back, they didn't fight as much. Things seemed to get better."

My throat burned, thick with words long left unspoken. I pulled in one slow breath, then another. Tried to keep my mouth from twisting down into the precursor of a sob. Three calming breaths later, I could continue.

"I started to think whatever problems they'd had, they worked them out. I relaxed. Stopped trying to hide out in my room so much. Figured we could be a happy family if I could get them to do things like game night. My friend's parents always seemed to like that."

Ryan rocked the swing beneath us, his gaze strong and steady. Not judging. Not pushing.

How many times had I analyzed my actions? If I hadn't pushed them, would things have turned out differently?

Would I have gone my entire life never knowing I'd been adopted? I'd often wondered why they'd never told me.

I relaxed a fraction as he rubbed a small circle on my back. Strange to have a man's touch in such a sweet way. No expectations. I could probably trust him, and I needed a friend like that. I hadn't realized how desperately I craved meaningful friendships until I'd met Ryan and Nancy. Having people in my life who looked to give, rather than always take, filled me with the courage to face the monsters I'd locked deep inside.

Time to get this over with. I'd told one other person this story, and vowed I'd never share it again. But Ryan wasn't Alison, and he'd never humiliate me.

"One night when I was twelve, I heard them fighting. My dad had lost his job, but he told my mom that all their troubles were her fault. She'd been the one who just had to have a baby and had cost them thousands first in failed fertility treatments and later in astronomical adoption fees. After all of that, they'd ended up with a burden they could never really love as their own."

Tears spilled over and coursed down my cheeks, but I couldn't stop. "That was the day I found out I was adopted. In some ways, learning the truth helped me understand things that hadn't made sense. Like why I didn't look like them, and why in so many ways I seemed to be their opposite. But his next words hurt the most. He laughed bitterly and said they should've gotten a dog. At least you could take those back."

Ryan's arm squeezed around me. I swiped at the tears and tried to maintain my composure. I didn't want to ugly cry. Ugly crying was the worst. Burning eyes, distorted face, and mucus. The snot alone would disgust a pig with a sinus infection. Not the way I wanted anyone to see me.

"My mother, whom I'd hoped would defend me, only sighed and apologized. Said she hadn't known how much time and money a kid cost. How little fun and how much trouble kids actually were. None of her friends had talked about that part. She'd wanted to buy frilly baby clothes, but the fun had quickly worn off. How was she supposed to know they'd end up with such a messy, scatterbrained, and awkward kid?" I shrugged as if the words hadn't cut me to the core. "They'd been popular kids in school. Into sports, that kind of thing. In more ways than I can even say, I was nothing like them."

I sniffled, drew a calming breath, and continued. "Anyway, Dad landed his dream job when I entered ninth grade. My parents had some money again. I don't really know what he did. Something with financial business consulting. We moved to Atlanta, but the company sent him all over the country. Sometimes overseas. My mom didn't have to work anymore, so she went with him. A lot. Often leaving me home alone for weeks at a time."

Ryan tensed.

"But I didn't mind. Those were good times. When they came home, they didn't fight. Sometimes even seemed happy to see me. Asked questions about how school was going. I made sure to always tell them how good things were, no matter what. When they left, they made sure I had plenty to eat." I smeared my sweaty palms down my jeans. "They died in a car crash on their way to Florida the summer after my junior year of high school. Turns out they left a mountain of debt, and the bank took everything. Thankfully for me, I only had to sit in the foster system for three months until I turned eighteen."

I closed my eyes as my shame settled around us, thicker than the humid air.

"I'm sorry that happened to you." Soft words, gentle and laced with pity. But Ryan couldn't know how much I hated pity.

I got up from the swing and moved to lean against the porch rail, putting a little space between us. "Anyway, now you know why I'm a little screwed up."

At least maybe now he'd realize he should keep his distance. I'd given him a glimpse of the mess inside me, and he'd seen a pile of baggage no man wanted to deal with. Even as a friend. I'd done the right thing. Pretending to be better wouldn't be fair to him. He should know that I was such a disappointment my own parents wished they could have returned me.

Ryan stared at me in the fading light. "You're not screwed up. You're a person who had to deal with a lot of pain."

Kind of him. Really. But he didn't get it. "Not every kid gets a great childhood." I shrugged. "Mine wasn't nearly as bad as some." I crossed my arms, uncrossed them, then crossed them again. Working with teens, Ryan had to know about the abuse so many kids endured. I was just a wimp. An emotional basket case who couldn't handle life. I infused steel into my spine and straightened. "My life was pretty good actually, all things considered."

Furrows bunched his forehead and Ryan reached up to rub them.

I took the cue. He needed an exit strategy. "It's getting late. You should probably head home."

"Casey, stop trying to push me away."

My pulse ticked up. "I'm not. You've been a great

friend. But there's no need for you to get bogged down in my crazy."

Eyebrows bunching again, Ryan rose and came to stand next to me at the rail. We stood there, side by side, as darkness swathed the porch in shadows. Crickets came out to begin their nightly chorus, and the temperature lowered a fraction.

"Would you do something for me?" Ryan leaned against a post, his relaxed posture a paradox to my tension.

Heat churned in my center, and I scratched at my throat as the sensation crawled up my neck. "What?"

"I want you to hear me out. Don't interrupt or come up with an argument. Just listen, and try to hear what I'm saying." He pulled on the collar of his customary button-down, either from discomfort or humidity. Probably both.

The heat boiling in my stomach turned into a buzzing in my ears. I braced myself. Now he'd tell me I was pathetic, irrational, and illogical. He'd explain why I shouldn't feel what I did and show me all the ways I was wrong. I'd get a lecture about how I just needed to get over myself. If I didn't owe him so much, I wouldn't have stood there. He didn't need to point out my flaws. I already knew each one.

I hated when people felt the need to point out where my veneer wore thin and the cheap particle board of my true self broke through. Almost like having a volcanic pimple on my nose. I knew it was there, thanks. I'd tried to cover the blemish but had failed. Everyone thought they were doing me a favor by telling me I had something on my nose. As if I didn't know.

"Your feelings are valid," Ryan said, oblivious to my inner ramblings. "You have every right to feel hurt and rejected."

My breath caught. Wait. What? I opened my mouth, but no words found their way out. A renegade tear snaked down my face, but I refused to betray my weakness by swiping it away.

"I understand now." Ryan shifted next to me, his boots scuffing on the porch. "Why you push people away, why you act like you don't care when you do, and why you alternate between trying too hard and not trying at all."

My chest rose and fell with shallow breaths. How? How could he see through me like that? I'd been better before, right? Back in Atlanta, I'd been able to play the part of a put-together woman too tough to be shredded by a few rejections. I blamed this stupid town and the pushy people here for damaging walls that had protected me for years.

Ryan's hand laced through mine. My breathing deepened. I should pull away. Run. Stop whatever happened between us before it ended in more pain than I could take. Because every friendship, every relationship ended badly. Eventually, he'd realize I wasn't worth the trouble, and he'd walk away.

Still, I couldn't pull my hand from the comfort of his. I hated myself for the weakness that needed to cling to him even as I knew the coming pain would obliterate my heart.

"It's a lie, Casey. I want you to know that." His gentle words hung between us, teasing, testing, begging me to see something I couldn't.

"What's a lie?" My voice squeaked out in a lame attempt at forming words.

Ryan squeezed my hand. "You think your worth is wrapped up in what you do. Your value is something you earn by being useful or by acting a certain way."

I tried to swallow, but the lump in my throat refused to

budge.

"Am I right?"

Was he? I shook my head. Paused. Memories flashed before my mind's eye. Bad relationships. Bad choices trying to fit in with friends. Losing friends when I couldn't measure up. Losing relationships because I was too much to handle. "I don't know."

"Do you believe in God?"

The out-of-place question punched me in the gut. Should have seen that coming. He was a preacher, after all. Why hadn't I realized he'd see me as a church project?

Strangely, the idea of a sermon instead of a lecture didn't sour my stomach. Not coming from Ryan. "Yes. Was even saved as a kid, if you can believe that." I shrugged. "Maybe it didn't stick."

Before I could say anything else, Ryan's next words burned like a branding iron. "So you believe *in* Him, you just don't believe Him."

My thoughts sputtered to a halt. "What? That's the same thing."

"It's not. I can believe a chair exists. But if I'm scared to put my weight on the seat, I don't trust the thing will hold me up."

A chair? He compared his faith to a chair? "I don't understand."

His shadow shifted again in the darkness. "You trusted in God for salvation." He bumped my shoulder with his. "And if you believed in earnest and meant your prayer, nothing reverses your salvation. But you can be saved and still live without peace if you don't turn your daily life over to Him. You're not trusting what He says."

I made a sour-lemon face. Seemed like a fine line of

distinction.

"God says you're valuable." Ryan's warm brown eyes lit with conviction in the dusky evening light. He believed what he was saying. "He sent his Son to die for you, but deep down inside, you don't believe you're worth the sacrifice. You don't believe you're worth love or commitment. Yet the God of the universe says you have infinite value. Not because of who you are or were, your parent's decisions, or what you do or don't do. Because He loves you, you're valuable."

Ryan didn't understand. Preachers always painted with flowery words what didn't hold up in the real world. Valuable things were treasured and protected. Not abandoned.

"You think that no matter what you do, you'll never measure up."

Tears escaped with vengeance now. How did he see through me? I'd let myself slip. Had let my problems make me vulnerable.

He released my hand and turned me to face him. "It's a lie." He leaned close, his face only inches from mine. "You are valuable. First, because God says you are. I wish you'd listen to His definition of your value rather than stake all your beliefs on the people who hurt you. Second, you're valuable because of who you are. You're tenacious, smart, creative, and keep me on my toes." He leaned closer. So close I could see the intensity of his eyes even in the scant light. "Do you believe me? Do you believe Him?"

Eyes wide and heart racing, I nodded.

A smile quirked one side of his mouth. "You want to. At least that's a start. I'll keep working until I prove it to you." He released me and once again leaned back against the porch rail.

I blinked. "Why?"

He bumped his shoulder into mine. "Because you're worth it."

No one had ever said anything like that to me. But he didn't know. Had only scratched the surface. Dig any deeper and he'd realize his mistake. Not that I'd tell him. I tried to smile instead.

"Do something for me?" Without waiting for my answer, he looped his fingers around my wrist and tugged me back to the swing. "Pray about it?" He sat and tucked me against his side as though we were lifelong friends and the closeness was as natural as the sound of cicadas buzzing around us.

"Okay." I meant it. I'd try. If only for him.

Ryan pushed the swing, and we rocked back into motion in the dark. He still held my hand. Nothing romantic. Just an infusion of solidarity and friendship. He reached down with his free hand and plucked the letter from the floor. He handed it to me.

Ida thought I'd blame her for what happened to my parents. I didn't. I stared at my scuffed tennis shoes, just two ghostly smudges in the dark. "I wish she'd told me. We could have talked. I wouldn't have blamed her."

Ryan pushed his foot against the porch and kept the swing going. "I can see where she'd be afraid to, knowing how little time she had left and—" His mouth twisted to one side as he searched for words.

"And knowing how things ended with my father." I sighed. "She didn't want to risk me being angry with her when she died like Mike had been angry with her when he died."

He nodded. Yeah, I could see that. Maybe Ida had been wiser than I'd given her credit for. I still had questions. A lot of them. But for tonight, I'd learned enough. All I could handle, really.

I tugged Ryan from the swing. "Come on. Let's get something to eat."

Laughing, he followed me across the porch. "Are you asking me to dinner?"

The playful tone plucked at me and lifted the shadow hanging over my shoulders. "I microwave a mean chicken spaghetti."

He followed me inside. "How convenient. That happens to be one of my favorites."

22

Whispers

*H*ow much could a person's life change in half a year? By my estimation, quite a lot. In the span of a few months, my once ordered—though admittedly not ideal—life had been overturned. I'd found and lost my grandmother, moved into her house in Maryville, and now consistently read a book that at this time last year I'd have considered a waste of time.

Kitty purred contently in my lap as I turned to another Psalm. Sunshine poured through the windows, kissing the kitchen in vibrant tones. The morning breeze, though laden with humidity, stirred the pages in front of me and chased a little of the heat from the room.

I found I enjoyed the Psalms. Many of them talked about finding shelter when life gave you storms. I'd seen plenty of those these past months. Both the kind that raged on the inside and the kind that brought destruction and looming bills. I refused to look at the tarp still hanging on the dining room wall. Nearly a month since the tree had crashed through the corner of the house, and still life hung in limbo.

Strangely, though, the uncertainty didn't claw at me as it once had. Ryan had been right. At first, I'd tried simple prayers because I'd promised Ryan. Soon those had turned to an all-out excuse to vent. I tangled my fingers in Kitty's fur and stared out the window at Ida's flowers.

Those nights turned out to be more cathartic that I'd ever imagined. I blamed God, yelled at Him, questioned Him, and finally stilled long enough to listen to Him. The stirring I'd felt in my heart as a girl returned. Quiet. Gentle. The Maker of the universe wasn't at all intimidated by my rage. To Him, I probably seemed like a toddler throwing a tantrum.

Ryan had been texting me verses. I looked them up and thought about them during the days of tending the house, cooking with Nancy, and keeping Ida's flowerbeds in pristine shape. Before long, I started reading passages Ryan hadn't mentioned. I read all the Gospels. Then started on the Psalms.

I took a sip of iced coffee and glanced at the clock on the stove. Nancy would be here any minute to bake a cake for the church Fourth of July picnic. As much as those people had fed me and taken care of me, I found any way I could to help out. I cleaned up after potlucks, volunteered whenever Ryan asked me, and attended every service.

Not that I'd admit it out loud, but I liked the church. And the people. Helping where I could made me feel like I belonged. Like I was a part of something good.

Besides, I had a little while longer before Ryan would give me the next letter, and I had to find something to keep me busy. All this free time without a job gave me downtime, but it also made me a little antsy. Still nothing on the mystery of the mantel photographs.

Apparently, my current assignment from Ida was to learn to rest and find peace. So far, I'd made pretty good progress on both. I should be close to moving on to finding more answers. But only if I convinced Ryan I was ready.

I closed Ida's giant Bible and ran my fingers through the cat's thick fur. "I'm getting up now."

She lifted her head and regarded me with half-closed eyes. I reached underneath her, earning a rumble. But I no longer feared her threats. Kitty was all growl and no bite, as the saying goes. I plopped her down in the chair and brushed cat hair off my jeans.

Right on time, the doorbell rang. Nancy scooted inside and made a face. "You plan on setting the cake out on the counter? I bet it'll cook just fine in this heat."

I hardly noticed anymore. I shrugged. "Sorry." What more could I say? Nancy knew I had two more days to go. Mira Ann had said they needed thirty days for any creditors to make claims on Ida's accounts. Then probate would be over and all of Ida's assets would be mine. I couldn't file an insurance claim on a house still in probate.

Come Monday, I'd finally be able to move forward. Even if I decided to sell the place to Mira Ann, I had another few weeks in this house, and I planned to spend them with air conditioning.

Nancy blew a huff of air up her face. "No, ma'am. We're not staying here." The basket of supplies on her arm flared out with the force of her spin as she whirled away from the kitchen. "I spent my childhood without air conditioning." She fished her phone from her pocket and pecked at it as she sauntered to the door. "I won't spend my golden years under that torture."

So why had she asked to come over here? I shrugged

and followed her out the door, locking it behind us. Ryan had cut the grass in both our yards yesterday, and the fresh scent still lingered on the air. What would I have done without such caring neighbors?

We plodded up the steps to Ryan's house, and Nancy produced a key from the purse hanging over her shoulder.

"Are you going to tell him we're using his kitchen?" I cocked an eyebrow as the little woman swung the door open.

"No need."

I laughed and made a mental note never to give Nancy a spare key. Of course, she could always use Ryan's if she wanted. He still had one from when he'd helped Ida and had used it the night of the infamous possum, but he didn't seem the type to abuse the trust it signified. Still, I probably should get that back from him.

Nancy hummed as she strode into the kitchen. She flipped on lights and set down her basket, then tapped the buttons to preheat the oven. "Why don't you pour us some tea?"

I glanced around the kitchen, uncomfortable. "You sure this is okay? Why don't I call him? Only seems right."

Tinkling laughter bubbled up from where Nancy dug around in the lower cabinets. "You're a funny girl. Of course I already told him. Texted him from your front porch before I rang your bell. I had a sneaking suspicion that house would be hotter than a blister bug in a pepper patch."

Oh. I put my hands on my hips. "You could have said so."

"And miss the look on your face?" She grinned and pulled a pie pan from a drawer. "He said if we made him supper, we were welcome to use his oven anytime." She winked.

Not sure how to respond to that, I pulled the tea from the fridge and tried not to dwell on the fact that I knew my way around Ryan's kitchen a little too well. Truth be told, it sure beat Ida's right about now.

"Ryan tells me you're a great helper with the youth."

I don't know if I'd go that far, but her compliment warmed me all the same. "They're great kids."

Nancy set a glass bowl on the table and nodded toward the fridge. Taking my cue, I pulled out eggs and milk. She sipped her tea and waited while I stirred the eggs, milk, and oil together, then poured in a couple of teaspoons of vanilla extract.

"He said you're connecting with Emma." Nancy sifted flour and sugar together in a larger glass bowl, then sprinkled in baking powder. Two dashes of nutmeg and she scooted the mixture toward me.

"She's a sweet girl." I poured the liquid ingredients into the dry ones. "She seems to be doing well with her foster family, though I'm worried about that new boyfriend of hers. I think it's a little too serious." Irony slammed me in the gut, and I gulped for air. Choked on nothing.

"You okay?" Nancy moved the bowl and rubbed a hand on my back. "Wrong pipe?"

Eyes watering, I simply nodded. Ida hadn't approved of my parents' young love either. Thought it was too serious too soon just the same as I thought of Emma and her Brady. Thinking of my parents got my mind churning. Ida's letters couldn't be the only place to find answers.

Nancy waited until I could breathe normally again and resumed stirring the batter. I sipped my tea and contemplated how to ask something I probably should have considered earlier.

"How much do you know about my parents?"

Nancy kept her focus on the batter she beat with a whisk instead of using an electric mixer. "I've been wondering how long it'd take for you to ask."

She finished whisking the batter while I buttered three round pans. Finished, I set them neatly in a row in front of her and waited. I resisted the urge to drum my fingers on the counter. Ryan got his way of answering questions from Nancy. Once she considered her response, she'd give it to me. I nibbled on my bottom lip and watched her work, anticipation zipping through my veins like grease popping in a skillet.

Finally Nancy spoke again. "Ida and I were friends at the time, though not close. Neighbors and Bible study pals, I guess. With the twenty-year age difference, we didn't talk about too many personal matters back then." Her eyes sought mine. "Ida loved Mike. I hope you know that."

I nodded. Seeming satisfied, she returned to the batter with vigor.

"Ida didn't think the kids were ready to get married. Can't say I disagreed with her. They were younger than I was." She darted a questioning look my way, but when I didn't say anything, she continued. "For years Ida blamed herself for Mike's death. I tried to be there for her through the pain, but only God can heal wounds like that. Always hurt me, knowing how she lost everyone close to her."

I knew the feeling.

"I don't have much to tell you." Nancy took a break and wiped her hands on a towel. After taking a sip of tea, she resumed whisking. "All I really know is Mike and Haley eloped to Alabama so they could get married. Ida didn't approve. Mike got into a motorcycle accident a few months later. Haley disappeared, and we never saw her again."

All things I already knew. But Nancy had lived in this small town for decades. She could tell me more than just what Ida revealed in her letters. "What about Haley's parents? Did they approve of the marriage?" I plucked at my fingernails, my interest in the cake forgotten.

Nancy tapped the whisk on the side of the bowl and dropped it in the sink. "Her dad died on an oil rig when she was little. Her mom always had one boyfriend or another." Nancy swiped a hand across her brow even though the kitchen was pleasantly cool. "Haley's mother, Lorain, married a real estate agent and moved to Jackson during Haley's senior year. Haley didn't want to go with her and have to change schools." Nancy huffed. "Lorain could have waited a few months and let the girl finish high school."

Might be one reason why Haley and Mike eloped. They hadn't wanted to be separated, even though Jackson was only an hour away from Maryville. In some ways, the story was kind of romantic.

Nancy poured the batter into the three cake pans. Remembering I was supposed to be helping, I took them from her and slid them into the hot oven.

Her eyes met mine. Compassion swam in their chocolate depths, reminding me of Ryan. "That's all I know."

I nodded, believing her. No one seemed to know what had happened to Haley after Mike died. Was she even still alive? "What's Haley's last name?"

Nancy held my gaze. "Last I knew, it was Macintyre."

Right. Same name as Ida. And my dad. "What was it before?"

"Willis. Lorain became a Parker with that last marriage," Nancy said, anticipating my next question. "She died three years ago. I went to the funeral but didn't see Haley."

My chest tightened with sudden concern. "Did Lorain die of cancer?"

Nancy shook her head. "No." She patted my hand. "You don't have cancer on both sides. Least, not that I know of. Lorain lived to be seventy-four. Died of heart complications brought on by type 2 diabetes."

At least I didn't have a double-sided family risk of cancer. Still, it seemed like everyone related to me had died. "Did she have any siblings?"

Nancy shook her head.

No aunts or uncles out there. No cousins. My family tree contained nothing but dead branches. "Guess that just leaves Haley. If she's still alive."

I found a box of strawberries and another of blueberries in the fridge. Had Nancy ever planned on cooking at my house? Why not just ask me to Ryan's in the first place? Shaking my head, I placed the fruit on the counter while Nancy gathered the cutting board and fruit knife.

"Do you want me to help you find her?"

The words, softly spoken, nearly stilled my heart. I stared at the fruit, both palms pressed firmly on the cool counter. Did I? Did I want to find the woman who'd disappeared and given me up for adoption? What good would it do? A closed adoption meant she didn't want to know me, or me to know her.

I'd found Ida. That was enough. Whatever had happened to Haley, whatever choices she'd made, maybe I didn't need to know.

For now, life was pretty good. Sweltering, but pretty good. I'd learned to live with the hole in the wall and fans blowing in the widows. I'd renewed my passion for cooking and spent time learning from Nancy. The church ladies refused to let me starve, and I'd become humble enough to appreciate their kindness. Ryan and I had built a steady friendship, and I enjoyed the kids in his youth group.

I wiped up a smudge of spilled batter and offered Nancy a genuine smile. "Thank you, but I'm good." And for the first time in a long while, I meant it.

The next day, I balanced our completed American flag cake while Nancy opened the door to the church fellowship hall. With the Fourth falling on a Sunday this year, the church planned to make a day of it. We'd have regular service, followed by a church-wide picnic, then the youth would play water games on the lawn for the afternoon. Come evening, men would fire up their grills and attempt to outdo one another with burgers, hot dogs, chicken, and deer sausages. The plan concluded with a small-town fireworks display set off in the cattle field across the tracks.

Infectious excitement hung in the air. Trading their usual Sunday dresses for cropped pants and red, white, and blue tops, women of all ages flowed in and out of the fellowship hall depositing a plethora of tantalizing dishes.

Ladies from Nancy's Bible study group greeted us as I followed her into the blissful cool of the large meeting room and added our cake to the already overflowing dessert table. One thing about Baptists, they knew how to rock a potluck. Several of Nancy's friends asked me how I was doing and about Ida's house. Rather than feel like nosy vultures were pecking at my personal life, I actually believed well-meaning neighbors wanted to coat me in their prayers and provisions.

"Girl here is a natural chef," Nancy said. She thrust her shoulders back, a bright gleam dancing in her eyes. "Can cook anything on sheer intuition alone. Takes every recipe I give her and adds her magic touch, making a creation better than I ever could." Nancy patted my arm like a bragging grandmother. "A true gift, for sure."

Mrs. Henderson, a sweet lady with a puff of white hair and large rimmed glasses, beamed at me. "Is that so?" She bobbed her head, as if answering her own question. "Why, you might just be the solution I've been looking for. If I purchase the ingredients, would you make a few meals for me? Cooking is getting harder on these old arthritic hands."

"Of course." Anything I could do to repay their kindness. "I'd be happy to."

She bobbed her head again. "Good, good. You tell me what you want to make, and I'll have Eddie run to the store."

Nancy snapped her fingers. "How about she makes up a menu of what she cooks, and you can pick out a few things for each week?"

Wait. This would be an ongoing thing? Not that I minded. I could help until I left for Atlanta.

Mrs. Henderson grew excited and waved her hands around as she talked. "You cook, keep half for yourself, and send the other back with Eddie." She pointed a gnarled hand at me. "Think you can do that?"

I tucked a loose piece of hair behind my ear. "Yes, ma'am. I'm happy to cook for you, but you don't have to split the food with me. You ladies have done more than enough already."

Another lady—I thought her name was Lucy Preston— laughed. "Don't be silly. Bible says a man is worth his wages." She winked at me.

"I think that's a fabulous idea, Gurdie," Nancy said to Mrs. Henderson. "And beneficial for everyone." She nodded once, the matter apparently settled. "A good barter."

Mrs. Preston agreed. "I'd like to schedule the same with you, and I'm pretty sure several of the ladies in the church would as well. Even the young ones would be happy to have a night or two off from cooking."

I gaped at her. The idea was brilliant. The women twittered, planning a feasible operation for me. I watched them, wondering if I would be asked for any input on this plan.

"Get a menu together, dear," Mrs. Henderson said. "We'll select what we want and purchase the ingredients."

Nancy shook her head. "What sense does that make? Why doesn't she just go to the store and buy the ingredients? Saves everyone a trip, and she can buy in bulk and split the costs among you."

I stood there, incredulous, as the ladies ironed out the details of what seemed to be my new catering business. By the time we filed into the church service, I had promises for multiple orders. I'd do the shopping, cooking, and packaging, and, in return, I'd keep a portion of everything I made. Not only would I have a job I enjoyed, but I wouldn't continue to siphon off their charity.

After service, I played Frisbee with the teens and sat with them while we stuffed ourselves on a smorgasbord of picnic foods. Soon after, Ryan brought out a bucket of water guns and a hose, and the kids scurried off for a water fight I had no interest in joining.

When it was time for dessert, I crossed the road and slipped into the fellowship hall to grab a plate. Several others had the same idea, and I took a place at the end of the line. Two women ahead of me whispered and shook their heads. Oh boy. Small-town gossip in the picnic line.

One lady cut a glance at me, leaned to her companion, and whispered again. Caught staring. Or maybe they were talking about me. I had looked a little silly out there with all the kids. I withheld an eye roll. But what did I care if a couple of middle-aged women laughed at my less-than-athletic Frisbee skills?

I filled my plate with small slices of three different cakes, a brownie, some kind of pie, and a spiced pear half. I'd have to start working out soon or none of my clothes would fit. But it felt nice not to worry constantly over every bite that went into my mouth. I walked among the circular tables in the fellowship hall. Probably just my imagination, but it seemed more eyes than usual lingered on me, and more than one person leaned to someone close to them to whisper as I passed by.

Skin crawling, I kept going all the way out of the fellowship hall and to the humid day beyond. A large oak similar to the one that had once shaded Ida's yard spread its branches over the lawn on the far side of the church. Most of the people gathered in the shaded field across the road, so I made a beeline for the lone tree and settled down with my back against the bark.

Life in Maryville differed quite a bit from life in Atlanta. I watched people as I tried to decipher the ingredients in each treat on my plate.

Ryan exited the fellowship hall, shoulders back and

head high. Dressed in dark jeans, his usual scuffed boots, and a green Maryville Hornets T-shirt, he looked every bit the rural farmer. Not a preacher. But who was I to say all preachers had to dress in suits?

He tugged off a black ball cap and ran his fingers through his hair before pulling it on again. He scanned the area across the road, clearly looking for something. I watched him as I sampled the pie. Key lime with a toasted meringue on top. Delicious.

Ryan's head turned my direction. Eyes landed on me. He turned sharply and stalked in my direction. Uh-oh. Had I done something wrong? Or not done something I should have? I racked my brain as he came closer but couldn't come up with a single reason for the serious set to his shoulders or the strained look on his face.

He stopped, towering over me. "Casey. We need to talk."

23

Accusations

"What?" This couldn't be happening. The sounds of laughing teens and twittering churchgoers faded into the background. I stared at Ryan, not quite able to understand what he'd said. The words tangled in my brain.

I emphasized each word, holding Ryan's intense gaze. "I don't have a criminal record."

The already firm lines around his mouth tightened. "They were on the pastor's desk."

Sweat gathered along the base of my hairline and slithered down my neck. "I don't know what you're talking about."

One heartbeat. Three more. His eyes bore into mine. Testing. Probing.

"Ryan." I barked out his name, fire zipping along my nerves. How dare he assume I was lying about being some kind of felon! "I've *never* been arrested. Got a speeding ticket once and two parking tickets, but that's the extent of my run-ins with the law." I tried for a bit of humor to defuse the tension smothering us, but it fell flat. Having

Ryan look at me like a liar diced my insides.

The air hung heavily around us, thick with humidity and accusations. Clenching my teeth, I took a step back but came up too hard against the giant tree that only moments ago I'd been sitting under to enjoy dessert. Until Ryan dropped a bomb on me that the church had discovered my "criminal record."

Ryan closed his eyes and rubbed the middle of his forehead. When he looked at me again, his expression held disappointment. "Brother Lawrence didn't show me the specifics. Someone left a note on his desk along with what he called 'fairly convincing paperwork.'" Ryan scrubbed his hand down his face. "We have to be careful about who we have working with kids."

His words hit me squarely in the chest. They thought I was a criminal. Didn't want me around the kids because I was trouble. Bits of uneaten cake dropped to the ground as my fist tightened around my plate. "You don't believe me, do you? Nothing I say even matters."

Ryan's stiff shoulders said everything. Whatever papers they had, whatever story someone told, my defense against it meant nothing.

"This has already gotten out of hand. Apparently several people knew about it even before someone took the paperwork to the pastor."

Explained the looks I'd gotten. Gossip spread like wildfire, and I was nothing more than tinder to be gobbled up. Had the same person who had left the "evidence" on the pastor's desk told everyone in the fellowship hall? Or had the pastor started the rumor?

Ryan waited a moment, but I had no response as to why the entire church knew. He sighed. "Brother Lawrence says that until we get this cleared up, you can't work with the youth." His disappointment in me hung on every word.

"So that's it?" My shoulders strained, and I rolled them back as I took a deep breath that did nothing to soothe the scalding in my chest.

Ryan reached for me, stopped, and dropped his hand. "We can run a background check, if you sign for it."

What for? From the look on his face and the whispers and cutting glances, they'd already made their decision. "Guilty until proven innocent, huh?"

I flung the paper plate on the ground and pushed past him. He called after me, but I ignored him. Criminal record? Of all the asinine things. Why on earth would someone say I had a criminal record? And what "proof" could they have if none existed?

People watched me as I marched across the church lawn. Their judgmental eyes devoured every detail of my disgrace, but I kept my head held high. Vultures. All of them. Looking for any bit of rotten gossip they could peck, peck, peck. I pressed my lips into a stubborn line and ignored a lady calling my name.

When I flung the door of my Toyota open, it boiled with heat, but I didn't wait for it to air out. I slid inside my rolling oven. Keys. Where were those stupid keys? Fingers trembling, I dug them out of my pocket, found the key, shoved it into the ignition, and wrenched it sideways.

The engine ground. *Come on!* I tried again. A small sputter. I slammed my fist on the steering wheel. Sweat poured down my neck. I wiped moisture from my face, gulped fiery air, and turned the key again.

Please, God, help me escape.

The engine whirred, caught, and gurgled to life. Tears

streaked down my cheeks as I thrust the car into reverse. The tires caught on the gravel and churned it up as I rocketed backward. I shifted into drive and glanced through the windshield. Nancy stood on the open lawn, her hand pressed to her throat. Several ladies around her stared at me. Kids stopped playing. The weight of their eyes pressed down on me, robbing me of oxygen.

So much for feeling welcome in this place.

I pulled out of the church parking lot and bounced onto the road. My blue sleeveless top did nothing to help with the heat, and my tennis shoes may as well have melted onto my feet. Once home, I stomped into the house and made my rounds on the lower floor, flinging open windows and turning on fans.

Still too hot. Heat bubbled inside me, adding to the inferno already roasting the air. Kitty greeted me on the stairs with a friendly meow, but I didn't even stop to pet her. I peeled off sticky clothes and discarded them on the floor in my room.

Cold water poured from the shower, and I stepped inside. I dropped my head and let the liquid relief cool the back of my neck. Why in the world would anyone want to pin a criminal record on me? To get me away from kids at a church? Why?

Mira Ann. Her face flickered into my mind's eye. Was she so jealous of me working with Ryan and the youth that she'd try something like this? She did work at a law office.

But that didn't add up, either. First, she was only a secretary. I doubt she had any way of fabricating police records. Because she'd have to forge them, since none existed for her to dig up. Second, I'd been working with those kids for weeks. So had she. We'd all been having fun

215

together.

I shook off the ridiculous thought. Mira Ann had been nice to me, even if she wanted to make sure I knew she had dibs on Ryan. I couldn't let my old childish hang-ups over "her type" make me pin devious deeds on someone for no reason. She'd given me no evidence of being cruel. A little snotty, maybe, but still sweet. No way she'd go to those kind of lengths just to separate me from a guy I wasn't dating and a bunch of youth not many people wanted to work with.

Who else? I wracked my brain. Someone wanting Ida's house? What for? I would sell the place soon, and who would want a house so badly they'd try to frame the almost-owner? Maybe make the situation so I *couldn't* sell it somehow? No, what difference would that make? Convicted felons could still inherit and sell property, right? I shivered and adjusted the temperature to lukewarm.

Another twenty minutes in the shower, and I still didn't have any answers. Maybe I'd talk to Nancy. But would she look at me like her son had? I toweled off and dressed in comfy shorts and my dad's old Van Halen shirt. The design on the front had been too big for a square on my quilt, and I was kinda glad I hadn't cut this one up.

Damp hair hanging over my shoulders, I made my way to the kitchen and busied myself scrubbing a stove that didn't need cleaning. While the rest of the town smoked meats and celebrated, I emptied, cleaned, and reloaded the refrigerator.

By the time darkness crept in, my shoulders ached and the house gleamed, but my mind still hadn't settled. I made a glass of iced tea, grabbed Ida's Bible and my ornery cat, and settled down in front of a fan in the living room.

Kitty turned circles on me but decided she'd rather perch on the back of the couch behind my head. Her purr added to the hum of the fan as I opened the Bible. In middle school, my friend—the one who later abandoned me when she made cheerleader—had taken me to a youth weekend. She'd wanted to go to see cute boys, but the minister's message had seeped into me.

I'd meant what I'd said when I'd asked for salvation way back when. But after camp, I didn't have anyone to teach me. A well-meaning lady at the event had given me a Bible, but most of what I'd tried to read didn't make a lot of sense. I gave up after a while. I tried praying, but when nothing I asked for ever seemed to happen, I gave up on that too.

Ida's Bible spread open in my lap, and I turned back to my place in the Psalms. Maybe I'd find some comradery with the poor guy who always seemed to have so many enemies after him but kept turning to God anyway. Unfortunately, no matter how I tried, I could hardly focus. It seemed like every time things started to go well in my life, the breath got knocked out of me.

I doubted the ladies would bring me food now or take orders for my new cooking business. Should have known better than to let myself get excited about the idea. Or get so comfortable here. Not that it really mattered anyway. Maryville was a temporary stop. I had a job in Atlanta. Plans. I didn't need these people and their rumors.

The pop of fireworks announced the grand finale of the day-long celebration. Kitty flattened herself against the back of the couch and growled. I shut the Bible and scooped her up. "Come on. Let's go to bed."

Mind still buzzing with annoyance, disappointment, and

the stench of betrayal, I marched up the stairs, Kitty in my arms. I shut the door, locking her inside with me for the night, and got ready for bed. As I lay on top of the sheets and stared at the ceiling, Kitty curled up on my pillow, her soft fur tickling my face.

You should have known not to get involved with these people.

The inner voice plucked at me. True. Why had I let my guard down? As if this town, these people, would be any different than the people I'd known all my life. No matter the state or town or stage of life, people were all the same. So quick to make judgments.

Ryan hates you, too, now. Thinks you lied to him.

I grabbed the other pillow and smacked it over my face. Kitty startled and scrambled off the bed. Another mistake.

I shouldn't care what people thought. But I did. I cared a lot about what Ryan thought of me. The way he'd looked at me.

Stop. Go to sleep.

Arguing with my inner self never did any good. My subconscious—or whatever you called that voice that stings you with unwanted truths—continued to point out each and every one of my flaws until my head pounded.

I glanced at the clock on my nightstand. Quarter 'til twelve.

Go to sleep!

I stared at the ceiling in the darkness, seeing nothing but shadows. Kitty growled. The sound was so out of place that thoughts rushed out of my head, and I focused on the silence.

She growled again, a little gremlin under the bed. I sat up. Oh, no.

Stupid, stupid, stupid!

I'd been so upset when I came upstairs that I hadn't closed the windows. Again! Groaning, I grabbed my phone and wrenched open the bedroom door. Great. Now I'd have to deal with those raccoons again. Or worse, that beady-eyed little possum with his wicked teeth. I stepped out into the hallway and reached for a light switch. Maybe if I turned on all the lights and made a lot of noise, the vermin would scamper out on their own.

"Ouch!" A startled voice bounced up the stairs.

The breath left my chest. That wasn't a possum. Or a raccoon. Someone was in the house! I flipped open my phone and started to dial Ryan's number, then paused. No. I didn't need him. I'd memorized the number to the sheriff's office for this very reason. I'd get Detective Beefy over here. I punched in the number and held the phone to my ear, breathing slowly and straining to listen to any noises below.

The phone rang twice, and a woman's clear voice came over the line. "Scott County Sheriff's Department."

"Someone broke into my house." Where was that lamp? "And it's not an animal. Animals don't talk." The words left me in a rush. I hovered in the doorway of my bedroom, eyes searching the darkness. My mind scrambled. How long until they came? Five minutes? What if he left by then? Stole Ida's things or planted something else to use against me? I gave my address and hung up the phone.

If someone had it out for me, would they break into my house and leave damaging evidence to go along with whatever they were trying to do at the church? My lip curled. What kind of person did things like that?

More scuffling downstairs.

My heart hammered out a cowardly rhythm in my chest.

Only idiots confronted a robber. He could be armed. But if I didn't go down there, he might get away with whatever nefarious plan brought him in my house in the middle of the night.

If I could just get eyes on the guy. At least see what he was doing so I could tell the deputy if he got here too late to catch the criminal red-handed. I grabbed the lamp from my nightstand and crept into the hallway. I closed the door behind me to lock Kitty inside.

Stupid probably. But I wouldn't get close or let him see me. I just had to make sure I had a description. And I needed to know what he wanted to steal in Ida's house. Or whatever else he intended to do. I eased down the hallway, mind racing.

Could this guy be the same one who planted a false record at the church? That sounded pretty far-fetched. Why would a thief do something like that? I eased down the stairs, placing my bare feet carefully. Thoughts skittered through my head, none of them making much sense.

But nothing today made sense.

My stomach clenched. The voice in my head warned I should find somewhere to hide. I ignored the rapid pounding of my heart. Not this time. I wouldn't cower in a corner. The lamp slid in my sweaty palms. I tightened my grip.

I reached the bottom of the stairs. Gulped air. Held it. Let it out slowly. Lightning raced along my nerves, heightening every sensation. But all I could hear was the pounding in my ears as my heart pushed blood and adrenalin through my veins.

A noise came from the kitchen.

I held my breath. Listened. Feet scooted across the floor. Blue light flicked on and spilled faint rays across the doorframe.

What? I paused in the foyer. The perp had opened the fridge? Scenes from scary movies I never should have watched pounced on my brain. What terrible things would he put in my fridge?

I crept closer, easing to the kitchen doorway and peeking one eye over the doorframe. I blinked, willing my eyes to focus. Ugh. Why didn't I have a smart phone so I could take pictures?

The refrigerator door stood open. Someone poked around inside. I tightened my grip on the lamp. Deputy should be here any second. Sweat beaded and slid down my forehead, but I couldn't wipe it away.

The fridge door started to close. Light washed over a small figure holding a backpack before it disappeared behind the closed door.

Was that...?

I gulped in a breath and flicked on the kitchen light, weapon lamp held out in front of me.

The intruder yelped. I dropped the lamp to my side.

"Emma?"

24

Just My Luck

I sagged against the kitchen wall, my knees weaken-
ing. "Emma." I cleared my throat and tried to get my
dry mouth to function properly. "What are you
doing?"

The lanky teen rubbed her hands down her black jeans.
"I'm sorry." She darted a glance at her backpack on the
floor. "I didn't think—" She took a deep breath, clearly
rattled. "I, uh, didn't think you'd mind."

What in the world? I crossed into the kitchen and rested
a hand on the center island. "You didn't think I'd mind you
scaring me half out of my wits by digging around in my
kitchen in the middle of the night?"

The way her eyes widened reminded me of Kitty staring
up at me that day at the pound. Poor kid. Something must
have happened. Yelling at her wouldn't do any good. She
took a small step back from me and my heart clenched. I
softened my tone. "Why not knock on the door?"

Emma fished in her pocket and pulled out a rumpled
piece of paper. "I was going to leave you a note."

Leave me a note after she'd broken into my house? I

rubbed my temples. "Are you okay?"

"Yeah." She blinked at me.

Right. Because kids who were perfectly fine stole food in the middle of the night. "Can you start from the beginning, please?"

Emma pulled the sleeves of her black shirt down over the backs of her hands. Outfit for robbery? No one wore long sleeves in a Mississippi July. Not even at midnight. I watched her, waiting.

Finally, she let out a long breath and a rush of words tumbled out. "The window was open. I came through. Figured I'd grab a few supplies and duck out. Didn't think you'd mind helping me."

Oh boy. Runaway. I kept my voice calm and even. "I don't mind helping you." Her shoulders relaxed a little as she studied my face. I took another step closer. "But I need you to tell me exactly what I'm helping you do."

"I—"

A knock pounded on the door, and we both jumped.

Emma yelped.

I put a hand to my throat. The deputy.

If he saw her dressed like a robber with a pack draped over her shoulder, it wouldn't be good. I'd been in the system. DHS would be all over her come morning. "Quick. Get in the pantry."

Emma's eyes rounded and then filled with understanding.

I hurried her to the door as another knock rattled the house. "Don't come out."

Emma slipped into the walk-in storage area and closed the door. Great. Now what? I hustled through the kitchen as a muffled voice penetrated the front door.

"Sheriff's department. Open up!"

Ugh. He was going to wake the neighbors. One in particular. How was I going to explain this? Foster kid charged with breaking and entering would mean a lot of trouble for Emma. I didn't want that for her. Could get her shuffled around in the system again.

Thinking quickly, I scurried to the front door and pulled it open. The tall deputy in his olive drab uniform assessed me in a single glance and then looked over my head, eyes darting around the foyer.

"Everything all right here, ma'am?"

I swallowed hard and gripped the door. "Uh, yeah. Sorry I called. Everything is fine."

His eyes narrowed. "You said someone was in your house." His voice lowered. "If you are under duress, give me a sign."

Stepping back from the door I tried to look calm. "No, really. It was a mistake." I flicked a glance toward the kitchen. "I was wrong. No one is here."

The deputy stared at me, eyes assessing every line of my face. "You're certain?"

Only one way out of this. I hung my head. "I'm sorry. Turns out it was a possum again after all."

The deputy stared at me for a long moment, then dipped his square jaw in a single nod. "Maybe start closing your windows at night?"

"Yes, sir. I'm sorry."

He cast one final look over my head and then mumbled good night before clomping down the stairs. At least he hadn't turned on his squad car lights and disturbed the entire street this time. I stuck my head out the door and glanced down the darkened road. No one gathered on the sidewalks.

After closing the door softly, I scurried back to the kitchen and yanked open the pantry door.

Emma stood there, arms wrapped around her middle.

"You can come out now."

She followed me into the kitchen, face scrunched in disbelief. "You called the law on me?"

I crossed my arms. "I called the police when I heard someone in my house. People do that."

Emma narrowed her eyes. "But you sent him away. Did he know I was here?"

I shook my head. "Don't worry." I let out a breath in a huff. "I told him it was just a possum digging around in the kitchen."

"And he believed you?"

I barked an ironic laugh. "Let's just say he had probable cause to believe I'd be frightened enough by a few invading vermin to call in the cavalry."

Emma looked dubious, but she kept quiet. We stood there in the sweltering kitchen staring at one another. What could this kid be thinking? I hadn't reported her, but that didn't mean I'd approve of whatever she'd gotten into. We teetered there, my own lack of trust in humanity flickering on her face.

"You're not in trouble, Emma. I won't tell anyone you were here."

Her eyes shimmered, but she blinked the tears away and gave me a strong nod instead.

Poor kid. Trying to look tough when your insides quivered wasn't easy. "Maybe it's time you tell me what's going on. Why do you need food in the middle of the night?" I pointed at her bag. "And what's with the supply pack?"

Her thin shoulders drew back. "I'm leaving."

As I suspected. I kept my reaction in check. Instead of an outburst, which she probably expected from an adult, I simply nodded. "Okay."

Emma's shoulders deflated.

I took a step closer and rested my hand on her arm. "Mind telling me why?"

She pulled away and wrapped her arms around herself. "Things are just getting...complicated. Time to move on."

Spoken like someone who'd bounced around more than a time or two. I leaned against the counter. "I get that. I always found it easier to move on when life got too sticky." *Like when an entire town thinks I'm a criminal.* I pushed the thought away. "Problems with your foster parents?"

Mouth puckering, Emma looked conflicted. "No, not really. They're pretty good people. Kind." She shrugged. "Even when I give them trouble. Don't want to cause them problems, you know?"

So not the parents. A suspicion wiggled. "This have anything to do with Brady?"

The way the color drained from her already pale face was all the answer I needed. Emma pulled her head back and stiffened her shoulders. Yep. This kid stood on the edge of jumping behind thick walls I might never get past.

Before she could come up with some kind of story, I turned my shoulder to her and leaned against the counter. Less eye contact, less threatening. "Did I ever tell why I'm staying in Maryville?"

She hesitated, then turned to lean against the counter next to me. She was quiet for several moments before curiosity got the better of her. "Yeah." She drew the one syllable word out into several. "You got this house from your grandma when she died."

"But if it wasn't for what happened with Derick, I probably wouldn't have ever come to see her at all." The truth of the words settled on my heart, squeezing me like a sheet of pasta through the press.

Emma shifted beside me, scuffing her Converse on the tile floor. "What happened?"

Maybe this wasn't the best story to tell her. But I got the feeling this kid had seen enough of life to handle it. I probably wouldn't even come close to shocking her, and she needed to know she wasn't alone. "He became possessive. Started telling me where I could go, who I could see, keeping an eye on me all the time. I didn't mind at first because I liked the attention. I thought he was being protective." I looked at her tense profile. "But protective and possessive are not the same thing."

She nodded along, thoughtful.

"It's never okay for someone to hurt you." I turned to look at her profile. "In any way. For any reason."

Emma tightened her arms around her middle. Something was definitely going on with her and that boyfriend. If he'd hurt her—I shook the thought off. No jumping to conclusions. I'd seen the boy around church. Didn't look like a bad kid. I'd promised myself not to heap judgments on people. Still, looks meant nothing. Emma stared at her feet.

"Anyway," I continued, "the situation became more and more suffocating, but I didn't know what to do. He paid for our apartment, everything. I didn't want to go back to scraping to make ends meet. So I told myself everything was fine. But when he got really ugly with me one night, I decided to cash in a little vacation time and take a chance on Ida's claim as my grandmother. I stayed several days with her, but I went right back to him, knowing nothing would change. A few weeks later, I found him with a waitress from work."

She sucked in a breath, and I knew she'd gotten my meaning without me having to spell it out. "I was so mad in that moment that I finally left for good."

Emma turned to me, contemplative. "So, if you hadn't left him, you wouldn't be living here."

Uh-oh. This was backfiring. Would she take my story as encouragement for her to run away? "Maybe. I see God's timing in it now. Derick was the push I needed because I would've been too afraid to come here and face my past if I didn't also have something pushing me away from the life I had." I squeezed my eyes shut and ran a hand down my face. "Does that make any sense?"

"I think so." She picked at her fingernails. "You wouldn't have wanted to face your birth family if things were good at home."

"Yeah. Like that." I smiled at her. She didn't return it. Ida's letter had come at just the right time, under just the right circumstances. Maybe, even though I hadn't noticed, God had stuck with me after all. What might have happened if I'd stayed with Derick? Became too dependent and lost myself completely? Maybe such a painful moment had actually kept me from a life that could have gotten so much worse.

I faced Emma and put a hand on her shoulder. "Ida taught me a lot. One thing I learned is your problems will go with you no matter where you run to. But if you have people in your life who'll stick with you and fight with you, you can face those problems together." I leaned closer, willing her to see every ounce of conviction I hoped shone through my eyes. "Doing life alone is too hard. If you have good people in your life, let them help you."

Her eyes welled with tears, and she nodded. "I don't know what to do! Brady is sweet. He is. But he follows me everywhere now. It makes me nervous." She sniffled and wiped her hand over her face. "He hasn't done anything bad, but..."—her voice cracked—"but I've seen things happen to other girls in the system. I just don't want—"

I pulled her into a hug and held her as her shoulders shook. "It's okay. There's nothing wrong with being cautious. But you're not alone. You've got people in this town, right?"

She nodded against my shoulder.

I needed to make sure of something important. "Your foster parents are good to you, right?"

Emma sniffled and pulled back from me. "Better than any others I've had. At first I thought all the church stuff made them super weird, but it doesn't. They're actually really good people."

"Are you sure you want to leave them just because of some creep?"

Her nose wrinkled, and tears leaked out and skimmed her cheeks. She slowly wagged her head from side to side, sending her mousy brown bangs swishing over her forehead. "No."

"Then don't run. Have you told them about this?"

Another head shake.

"Stay, Emma." I swallowed hard. How could I help her? Me, the one who probably would have done exactly the same thing in her shoes? How did I convince someone to stay and fight for good relationships when I'd never faced a battle that way myself? I really could only take the lessons

Ida, Nancy, and Ryan had tried to teach me and use them with Emma.

"If you're not truly in danger," I said, leaning close to judge her every reaction, "and no one has physically, emotionally, verbally, or in any other way abused you..." I let the sentence dangle, waiting.

Emma shook her head. Good.

"Don't let how you feel right now make you run and give up all the good things in your life. Tell your foster parents what's happening. Talk to Ryan or the pastor's wife at church. Talk to me. There are a lot of people here who can help you. If you don't think you can work this out with Brady—or you're afraid of him, or you don't think he'll leave you alone if you want to break up—then talk to the adults in your life who are there to help you. Don't think you're alone and your only choice is to run. It's not."

Funny how words directed at someone else can fillet you with irony. As we stood there in Ida's kitchen together, my words to Emma soaked into me. Sometimes it took seeing something in someone else to recognize the same problem in yourself. So what if some people thought I had a criminal record when I didn't? Was that worth losing the friendships I'd gained? Would I roll over and cower, or would I stand up and fight for the relationships I had?

"I guess you're right."

I squeezed her shoulders. Thank goodness. Maybe I wasn't a complete screwup after all. What would I have done if she'd run and her foster parents had blamed me? I let out a relieved breath. "Let's get you home."

Fifteen minutes later, I puttered into the driveway of a brick ranch-style house nestled a half mile outside of town. The front porch lights washed the area in yellow light.

Maybe her parents were waiting on her. Would they come running out? I glanced at Emma, who sat staring at the porch. "Want me to go to the door with you?"

She shook her head and cut a glance at me. "I was kinda hoping to sneak back in so they wouldn't know I left." Emma ducked her head like she expected me to protest.

Sticky situation. They needed to know she'd slipped out in the middle of the night and planned to run away. And they needed to know about Brady. How would her relationship with them grow if she didn't confide in them? But from the pleading look on her face, if I marched her to the door, I'd lose her trust. "Promise me you'll talk to them?"

Emma nodded solemnly, her eyes locked on mine. I'd just have to pray she kept her promise. And maybe confide in Ryan. He'd know how to best approach her parents if Emma didn't.

"You have my number. Call me if you need anything." I grabbed her arm as she reached for the door handle. "I mean it."

A slow smile spread over her sweet face. "I know you do. I will."

Emma slipped out of the car, shouldered her pack, and walked quietly toward the house. I watched her unlock the front door and slip inside before putting the car in reverse and rolling away.

Please, God, don't let her run out again tonight. How awful would that be?

I drove back through town, contemplating Emma, other girls like her, and my own years as a teen. What if girls like that had a safe place to go? Somewhere to escape to, get help, or just be a haven for them to take some time to think

231

through their emotions? A place of refuge for bad home situations. Or even a layover to give the social workers time to connect the girls to the right foster family rather than just an available one?

My mind whirled, and a strange heat bubbled up in my chest. What so many young girls had to face wasn't right.

Not many foster families wanted to take in teens. Teens had too many issues. My heart twisted. If things were different, I would take them. As many as I could. Show them they mattered. They had somewhere safe.

You're not qualified for that.

I pushed the inner voice away. Maybe not. I didn't have any kind of social work degrees or psychology experience. But I could empathize. And I would love on them. And that should be qualification enough. If things were different.

Back at Ida's, I closed all the windows and turned off the downstairs fans. Obviously, leaving windows open invited trouble in one way or another. Well, maybe. At least Emma had come to me. Kinda. She hadn't exactly expected me to find her. Still. Better she came here and got caught than if she'd slipped off without anyone knowing. I shivered as I opened the door to my room. That would have been much, much worse than the two of us suffering a fright.

And another call to the sheriff's department to label me crazy.

Kitty curled up on my pillow. She opened her eyes and flattened her ears. I laughed. "Don't worry. I won't take your spot."

I lay down on the other side of the mattress on top of the covers and stared at the ceiling. What a weird night. I glanced at the clock. 3:47. This time sleep came easier.

The next morning, armed with an optimistic expectancy that air conditioning was in my near future, I showered and dressed quickly. A cup of iced coffee in hand to bolster my three hours of sleep, and I bounded out the door.

The scent of pine hung on the air, and birds twittered to one another from the treetops. I paused in the driveway to pull in the intoxicatingly sweet scent of gardenias. I rolled the windows down in my car and let the wind play in my hair. The car radio didn't work, but I hummed a tune I'd learned at church.

I lurched over a few dozen potholes and rolled into the center of town. The church's white steeple caught the morning light as I drove past, and I tried not to think about the fake papers someone had left on the pastor's desk.

Today, the house and Ida's accounts passed the thirty-day holding period. No more waiting. I turned into a space outside of the lawyer's office. Not open yet. I checked the clock on my dashboard. 8:55. If I had any cash, I'd try out the sweet shop a few stores down past the bank, but it didn't seem right to poke around in there and not buy anything.

I settled back against the seat and waited. A few people meandered in and out of the sweet shop with coffee and little bags of goodies. What would it be like to open a small restaurant here? Maybe serve lunch on the weekdays, and dinners on the weekends? Nothing big. The hours wouldn't be bad. The idea tingled like a burst of cinnamon on my lips, so exciting I could nearly taste it.

Small town, quiet life, the joy of running a restaurant without the overwhelming work hours? Almost sounded like a dream. Living in Ida's picturesque house, working just up the road. Independent, self-sufficient, and satisfied.

Maybe I didn't need the library job in Atlanta after all. Sure, I wouldn't have insurance without it, but I'd never had insurance. Maryville had a clinic with a nurse practitioner. Had to be cheaper than the big hospitals in the city.

If only the entire town didn't hate me now.

Mira Ann swayed up to the door at the law office with a giant coffee cup and turned a key. She disappeared inside, lights flickering to life through the window. I got out of the car and ran a hand over my nicest blouse. Usually, I'd save this for rotation with my only other decent outfit for church. But today was special.

The door dinged when I stepped inside. A candle on her desk spouted citrusy brightness throughout the cheery waiting area.

Mira Ann turned from where she stirred her coffee on her desk and greeted me with a warm smile. "Casey! I figured I'd see you today." Her pink glossy smile faltered, and she gestured toward a chair near her desk. "Why don't you have a seat?"

I sat on one of the plush chairs she indicated nestled in the corner opposite her desk. Situated like a cozy living room, I suspected the arrangement lured people into feeling at ease. Mira Ann came to sit in a matching chair across a small wooden table from me. She crossed her long legs and regarded me through her lashes.

"I'm afraid I have some troubling news."

Her words hung on the air, sucking the hope out of me. Of course. Why would I think anything different? I gripped the arm of the chair. "What's wrong?"

She placed her coffee on the table and brushed a lock of shiny brown hair from her face. "Nothing's wrong, exactly." Another bright smile, flashing perfect white teeth. "We'll get it worked out. I promise."

The optimism of her words did little more than pluck my already fraying nerves. "Explain, please. Get *what* worked out?"

Mira Ann let out a huff of air. "The will states that the house and Ida's remaining assets are to go to her grand-daughter."

I nodded along. Yes, I knew that already. So what was the problem?

"The issue is, we don't have any proof of relation." Her eyebrows pulled together in concern. "Mr. Shaw insists we prove you're actually the biological granddaughter she left everything to. Have to make sure it's legal. You under-stand."

No, I didn't understand. "I sat across a desk from him when he opened that will and read it to me. He didn't say anything about any paperwork I needed to show him."

I searched my memories. I'd been pretty torn up. He'd said something about probate, executors, and paperwork. Somewhere in the middle of his legal ramblings, all I'd heard was lawyers and titles and beneficiaries. Oh, my.

What exactly had he told me? I'd barely registered any-thing he'd said past Ida wanted to give me her house and she had some pretty decent savings. Now I wished I'd asked more questions. Paid better attention.

I glanced toward the door that led to his office. Maybe Mira Ann didn't know what she was talking about. Why had I kept going through her instead of just talking with

Mr. Shaw? "I'll speak with him about it."

"Of course." Another pageant smile. "As soon as he gets back from vacation."

Withholding a groan, I forced myself not to slump into the chair. "When will he be back?"

"He has his annual two-week Continuing Legal Education Conference, and his family adds their yearly vacation onto the end of that since they are at the beach." She turned out a palm. "He won't be back for another two weeks."

Great. Just great. My lawyer took a three-week hiatus in the middle of my life crisis.

"What paperwork do you need?" My brain scrambled for anything I could use to prove my identity. "I have my driver's license in the car."

Mira Ann nodded. "I think he needs more than just your license. That may prove you are who you say you are, but not that you're related to Ida. Do you have a birth certificate or social security card?"

My stomach twisted. "Both back in Atlanta." With Derick.

Mira Ann cocked an eyebrow. "Unfortunately, until we have proof, the house and accounts will sit in holding. Good news is, all the creditors have been paid."

"What about things like the water and light bill? Those things are being paid somehow." Frustration gurgled in my chest. This flouncy girl didn't know anything useful.

She tapped her nail again, pretty face contorting in thought. "I'll have to look into that." She puckered her mouth to one side. "Maybe, since she had several of her bills on automatic payments, they'll continue to draw on her account." She lifted one shoulder of her creamy blouse. "I'll have to see."

Great. Mira Ann wasn't exactly a fountain of information. Was she withholding things on purpose? Or just too vapid to be of any use? I glanced at the lawyer's door again. Must be nice to go on vacation and leave your problems behind. "What about the repairs? And the new AC unit I have on hold? Can those come out of Ida's accounts as well? They are necessary for the house, the same as paying the electricity. And now that the thirty days are up, I can file an insurance claim on her behalf, right? The house needs repairs."

"When Mr. Shaw calls to check in, I'll be sure to ask him." She tilted her head to the side. "I'm so sorry. I wish I could be more help."

Not her fault she couldn't do anything about it. Crummy luck the lawyer was away. But why hadn't he told me before that I'd need those papers? I would've had a month to get things together. I rubbed my temples. "Let me know as soon as you talk to him, would you?"

She smiled sweetly. "Of course. Bless your heart, you're just having a time." She lowered her voice to a conspirator's whisper. "Especially with your record coming out."

Of course, she'd know about that. The entire town probably did. "I do *not* have a criminal record."

Her eyes swam with sympathy, but below the compassion, doubt sparked. Why should she believe me? Why would anyone believe that the stranger dropping into town claiming to be the lost granddaughter of a dying woman was who she said? Never mind that Ida had believed it.

Maybe they thought a woman with a criminal record had made the whole thing up to swindle an old woman. Really, what proof did I even have? Ida told me some stories, talked about my dad, but how did she know I was

237

Mike's daughter? We'd never done a blood test. Or run any kind of DNA.

My blood ran cold. What if Ida was wrong?

Doubt clawed through my stomach, and my head throbbed. When Ida had told me, I'd believed her. Maybe because I'd wanted to.

Mira Ann watched me and took a sip of coffee from her insulated cup. How could she drink that in this heat? I waved my hand in front of my face, my blood firing up from ice to lava. Why hadn't I even considered the possibility?

What if I wasn't Ida's granddaughter?

Mira Ann patted my hand. "I'll let you know as soon as I talk to Mr. Shaw."

She rose, and I took my cue. In a daze, I walked out of the lawyer's office and into the hot sun. I stood there, staring at the white steeple of Maryville Baptist pointing toward heaven. What if Ida had been wrong? What if I'd come here, upturned my life, and she had the wrong person? What were the odds?

With my luck, probably pretty high.

I lingered on the sidewalk, Ida's words swimming in my head.

One step at a time.

"Miss Adams?" A nicely dressed woman in her mid-fifties approached in a pressed gray pants suit.

I lifted a hand in greeting. Pretty sure I'd met her at the funeral, but hers was yet another face I couldn't pair with a name.

"I'm Lesa. Lesa with an E." She smiled and held out her hand.

I grasped it and gave it a good shake. Bless her for repeating her name and not assuming I'd remember it like the rest of the town seemed to think me capable of. "Hi."

"I won't keep you, but the statements are about to go out, and I wanted to know if you wanted yours sent to the address on file or to a different one?"

What? "I'm sorry. Statement?"

"Yes. Your bank statement." She gestured to the bank behind her. "Ida left an Atlanta address on the POD account, but since you're here, do you want us to send everything to her Maryville address instead?"

Whoa. "What POD account? What does that mean?"

Lesa frowned. "Payable upon death. Ida put you on her small checking account. Didn't you know?"

An account? I had a bank account no one had told me about? "I thought all of Ida's accounts were in probate."

She patted her salt-and-pepper hair. "Why don't you come in?"

I followed the lady into the bank, a shot of crisp air-conditioned air rejuvenating my senses. She gestured to a chair in front of a simple wooden desk at the front of the bank to the side of the tellers.

"Before her death, Ida came in and put your name on her personal checking account. It's payable upon death, which means that, after her passing, the account immediately passed to you."

I gaped at her. "No probate?"

She smiled. "You are the beneficiary. It doesn't need to go through probate. In fact, that's precisely why she wanted you on the account. She said you'd need access to funds while you waited on the savings and her CDs to go through processing." She clicked away on her computer. "The utilities are on automatic draft from this account."

239

So *that* was why the power company hadn't cut off the electricity. I knew payments had to have been coming from somewhere.

"All I need from you is proof of identity, and I can give you some temporary checks."

Didn't everyone. "What kind of proof? I have my driver's license."

"That will work." She flashed a grin. "If this address I have for you in Atlanta matches and you know your Social Security number, I can have some checks for you in a few moments. I wondered why you hadn't come by to get a new debit card. Bless your heart."

She typed away again as I pulled my license from my purse and handed it over. All this time, I'd had an account? I could have bought my own food and paid for gas. Why hadn't someone told me?

A thought struck me, and I leaned forward. "You said she named me as a beneficiary. If she did that with, say, the property insurance, would I be able to file a claim?"

Lesa nodded. "Certainly. Mr. Shaw should have that paperwork and contact information."

Which I wouldn't get until he got back from vacation. Great. Maybe Mira Ann would at least give me the name of the insurance company and I could call. Figure something out.

At least I had access to cash. I'd struggled these past weeks for nothing. That's what I got for being so scatter-brained. I should have paid better attention to Mr. Shaw when he read me the will.

Fifteen minutes later I had a few temporary checks, a hundred dollars in my purse, and an order for a new debit card. I thanked Lesa for her help and walked out feeling like a new person.

What were the chances I'd run into Lesa on the sidewalk, and she'd be the one to tell me I'd had a bank account all along? Pretty slim. And just when I'd been about to lose my mind.

Maybe God was looking out for me after all.

25

Complicated Confrontation

Don't let how you feel right now make you run and give up all the good things in your life.

My own words to Emma pulsed through my head as I stared at the Maryville First Baptist church. I drummed my fingers on the steering wheel. Wednesday night service. Would she come?

I'd parked in the lot across the sleepy street thirty minutes early so I could watch people as they entered the church, hoping to find Emma. I hadn't heard anything from her, and I itched with worry over her safety. If she didn't come to church tonight, I'd go to her house first thing tomorrow.

Nancy had called me twice, and I hadn't answered. Ryan hadn't called at all. I'd have to face them tonight if I went into service. The thought of confrontation made my skin crawl, but I'd read in Joshua to be strong and courageous because God went with me. I still wasn't sure if the verse first jumped out and stuck to me like melted taffy because I wanted the words to mean something or because God actually directed them at me.

Either way, my sweaty palms could be blamed on my nerves as well as the Mississippi summer. So far, I hadn't scored well on the strong and courageous test.

People began to file in for the midweek service, talking and greeting one another as they entered through the double doors. Should I go in and watch for Emma or wait here and risk losing a seat in the back?

How many times would I contemplate the same problem? Disgusted with myself for perpetual indecisiveness, I stepped out of my car. Held my head high.

Strong and courageous.

I kept my eyes straight forward, avoiding looking at anyone but also refusing to hang my head. I had nothing to be ashamed of. At least, not for what they thought. Let them gossip. Lies could only defeat me if I let them.

The back pew still stood empty with the thinner Wednesday evening crowd. No youth services tonight. Not that I was allowed in the youth section now anyway. I scooted into the back pew, settled against the armrest on the far end, and covertly watched people filter through the door. If anyone noticed me, they didn't let on.

Nancy strode in, her eyes scanning the people in the crowd. Her gaze landed on me. Eyebrows reaching nearly to her hairline, she made a sharp turn and marched my way. Uh-oh. I sank deeper into the thin seat cushion as if a bit of flattened foam would save me from the coming wrath.

A pair of black cropped pants and silver sandals sidled up next to me. "Good. I almost thought you wouldn't show up." Nancy plopped down beside me and patted the twist of hair at the back of her head. "I'm glad to see you show a little gumption."

What?

Nancy stuffed her oversized purse under the pew in front of her and met my gaze with a no-nonsense stare. "You do what they said you did?"

The muscles in my neck tightened. Here came the lecture. "No."

"Good girl." She gave my arm a squeeze. "Didn't think so." She plucked a hymnal from the pew in front of us and settled it in her lap. "We'll get this mess straightened out." She stated the words with such confidence I almost believed her.

I cut a glance at her smiling profile and twisted on the pew to face her. "Why is this happening? I don't have a criminal record, and I don't know how anyone would have one to show the pastor. And why even do that? If I had a record—which I don't—why on earth would anyone want to bring it to a church?"

Nancy squared her thin shoulders. "I don't know. But I intend to find out."

A wave of gratitude swelled inside me, rising and churning with such force that the only release was to put my arm around the woman and pull her into a hug. Someone believed me. Believed *in* me. Even if she had no proof of my innocence beyond my word.

Tears burned my eyes, but I blinked them away. "Thank you." I removed my arm from around her shoulders and settled back in my seat.

"I told you. You're not alone." The gentle warmth of Nancy's voice bolstered my confidence. Her sitting proudly by my side soothed my anxiety.

But all of that comfort cracked the moment Ryan walked through the door. He glanced at his mother and me, offered a half-smile and a nod of greeting, and kept walking.

My heart wrenched, but I tried not to let any discomfort show. He obviously didn't share his mother's confidence in me.

Not that I could blame him. I'd known from day one that Ryan followed the rules. Church rules clearly stated felons didn't work with minors. He had to be careful. Especially when it came to other people's kids. I knew the logic. Reasoning still didn't uproot the hurt that he hadn't believed me.

Service would start soon. Two older couples entered. I shifted in my seat, trying to keep my eye on the door without straining my neck.

Finally!

Emma's foster parents, Hal and Mary Hammond, walked in. Hal wore the faded jeans and scuffed boots of a farmer, dressed up with a crisp western-style collared shirt. His wife glided forward in a wispy gray skirt that skimmed the top of her feet, and she had styled her dark blond hair into a thick braid that fell down her back. Their smiles didn't depict people having trouble with their teen.

Had Emma told them?

I watched the doorway. Where was Emma? My nerves skittered like fire ants. Had she run away? Had her social worker moved her? What if—

Emma walked in the door, a tall boy wearing a Maryville Hornets shirt close on her heels. Brady. I narrowed my eyes at him. The kid wore an easy smile and waved at some other boys across the sanctuary. He flipped long bangs out of his eyes with a cocky toss of his head.

I focused on the girl he ushered along in front of him. She kept her eyes downcast, brown hair spilling over her shoulders.

Before I could stop myself, I jumped to my feet. "Emma!"

The girl and half the church turned to look at me. Burning with the weight of their stares, heat erupted in my chest and flooded my face. But the way Emma's eyes lit up was worth every prodding gaze and lifted eyebrow. I waved to her, and she darted into our pew.

She slid past Nancy, and I scooted toward the center of the aisle to make room for her on the end. Emma plopped down next to me with a huff.

Brady swiveled on his heel, scanning the pews. When his eyes landed on the hunched girl next to me, he cocked his head and turned out his palms. Emma only shook her head. He did the hair-flip thing again. Frowned. Gestured for Emma to come back. She shook her head again. Finally, he turned to the boys calling to him, confusion tightening his face.

Nancy glanced between the two teens. "Hmm." She pinned Emma with a knowing look. "That boy giving you trouble?"

Intuitive woman. I gave a slight shake of my head to warn Nancy, but she ignored me. Instead, she leaned around me and looked at Emma expectantly.

Emma shifted in her seat and darted a worried glance at me.

The woman wouldn't give up. I leaned to Emma's ear. "Nancy's a good friend. We can trust her."

Crossing her arms over an uncustomary bright blue sleeveless top, Emma hunched her shoulders and stared at the hymnal tucked into the pew in front of her. "He's not trouble. He's just..."

"Infatuated?" Nancy supplied.

Emma's eyes widened, and she regarded Nancy with the same look I'd often given the woman myself—a mixture of shock at Nancy's boldness tempered with awe at her insightfulness. "Uh, yeah. I guess."

"Teenage boys." Nancy laughed and rolled her eyes. "At that age they're all hormones and nervous energy. They don't know what to do with themselves most of the time. Especially when they like a pretty girl. End up coming on stronger than all that cologne they douse themselves in." Nancy chuckled at her own joke. "Sometimes a lady has to give it to a guy straight. Speak clearly and directly. They don't take hints very well."

The teen in question shoved his hands in his pockets and lumbered toward some other boys who appeared to poke fun at him as he sat in the back pew on the other side of the church. Probably ribbing him because his girl had ditched him.

Emma tilted her head, thoughts churning behind her eyes. I wanted to ask her if she'd talked to her foster parents and what had happened after the night of the Fourth, but the music started, and I didn't get the chance. I hardly paid attention to the service, my mind whirling with all the uncertainties I couldn't quite get a hold on.

Where was Mira Ann? I scanned the backs of people's heads but didn't see her. She still hadn't called. I had tried her twice without an answer, and I didn't know anyone else who would be able to give me the name of Ida's insurance agent. I pushed thoughts of Ida's house out of my mind and tried to focus on the preacher's message.

What did Brother Lawrence think about the charges against me? Did he believe them? Why wouldn't he? How many other people wondered if I was actually Ida's granddaughter? Did I look like my parents? Ida had said I did, but what if she'd seen only what she wanted to?

Another song started, and I realized I'd missed the entire message. Great. I'd been hoping God would have some wisdom to sprinkle on me through the service tonight, but I'd been too distracted to even listen.

Emma's pretty voice sang next to me, and after the hymn finished, people filed toward the fellowship hall for Wednesday supper.

Nancy patted my arm. "You're staying to eat, right?"

Hadn't planned on it. "Not sure."

She tented one eyebrow, an expression she shared with her son, and pointed a finger at me. "No cowering, young lady. Besides, you're supposed to have a menu to show Gurdie. Did you bring a list?"

I drew my head back in surprise. "They still want me to do that?"

"Why wouldn't they?" Without waiting for my answer, Nancy scooted toward the end of the pew. "Best think quickly."

We watched Nancy make her way to the rear of the church with the crowd. I turned to Emma. "What happened?"

Knowing exactly what I meant, Emma darted a glance at her foster parents, who waited to make their way through the doorway. "I told them I snuck out. Planned to run away but came back instead."

Tension in my shoulders uncoiled. "Good. That's good. What did they say?"

She brushed the bangs from her eyes and offered a sheepish smile. "They thanked me for being honest and for deciding to stay. They said they'd have been very sad if I'd left."

I draped my arm around her shoulder and squeezed. "Proud of you."

"Thanks."

Stepping away from her, I scooted out of the pew and into the center aisle. Most of the people had cleared out now, except the teen boys. I nodded my head toward them. "What about him?"

Emma stared at her sandaled feet. "Didn't say anything about him."

"Why not?"

She shrugged. "I don't know."

Leaving the conversation for another time, I followed Emma into the fellowship hall. Families signed up each week to provide food, serve, and clean. Usually, I signed up each Sunday for Wednesday night cleanup crew. Given the events of this past Sunday, I doubted anyone would ask why I wasn't volunteering tonight. The fellowship hall buzzed with conversation and swelled with the aroma of two dozen different casseroles.

My skin crawled with the stares of people sitting at round tables or waiting in the potluck line. Some darted quick glances my way. Others openly stared. A few talked low to one another, leaning close. How many stories had people concocted the past few days? Rumors left to fester decomposed into something uglier each day that passed. By the end of the week, I'd likely be touted as a member of America's Most Wanted.

In an act of defiance, I lifted my chin and met several gazes. As soon as I did, their eyes dropped. I straightened my shoulders. I had nothing to hide and nothing to be ashamed of. I wouldn't let lies destroy me. And I wouldn't teach the girl beside me to let other people's opinions of her make her shrink under their judgmental stares.

"Emma."

We both turned at the sound of the male voice. Emma paused near the back of the room as Brady approached. I could leave them to have this conversation privately, but unless Emma asked me to go, I'd offer support by standing at her side. My confidence seemed to bolster hers, so I infused more into my posture than I really felt.

Brady darted a glance at me, and then leveled his eyes on Emma. "What happened? Why didn't you sit with me?"

Emma plucked at her fingernail, her eyes locked on her hands. Her soft voice held a spark of annoyance. "I wanted to sit with Casey."

His head tilted. "Without telling me?"

When her thin shoulders drooped, a strange surge of protectiveness overwhelmed me. I crossed my arms and glared at the boy, stepping slightly in front of Emma. "Does she need your permission to sit somewhere else at church?"

Brady's bright blue eyes widened at the venom in my tone. "No, ma'am. I didn't say that."

I narrowed my eyes. "What are you saying, exactly?"

He blinked at me, then looked at Emma, who still wouldn't raise her head. "I just wondered, you know." He gripped the back of his neck. "She's been avoiding me." He shuffled his feet. "Did I do something wrong, Emma? Are you trying to break up with me?"

Now, we both stared at Emma. I willed her to speak up for herself. She didn't move. Wouldn't look up. Pain filled the boy's eyes, and I almost felt sorry for him. Maybe the poor kid held on too tight because he sensed her pulling away. Wrong response, but understandable in a way.

"Emma?" She looked up at me. I nodded toward Brady. "Do you want to break up?"

She flung her arms out wide, suddenly erupting in emotion that made my pulse jump. "I don't know! I like you, but you're freaking me out!"

Her outburst sent a hush over the room. I put a protective arm over her shoulder, but Emma shook me off. "You're always asking me where I'm going. What I'm doing. You're making plans for us for next year's prom. Prom! That's like ten months away. I'm not ready for that."

Brady held up both hands. "Whoa. Okay. I'm sorry."

Oh boy. Maybe we had less of a stalker case and more of a love-sick puppy with a commitment-phobic girlfriend. Two middle-aged couples hurried over to us. Emma's foster parents and another couple, whom I suspected to be Brady's parents. They squared off beside their respective teens. Tension bubbled around both the kids and their parents. My heart fluttered, but I kept my posture relaxed. Emma breathed heavily beside me.

"What's going on here?" Hal, Emma's foster dad, directed the question right at me.

Right. Felon lady had to be the problem. I lifted my chin. "Brady's attentions were making Emma nervous, but she didn't know how to talk to him."

Brady paled, and his parents both looked taken aback. For a moment, no one moved. Emma's foster mom broke the stunned silence.

"What happened?" Mary pointed a finger at Brady. "Did you do something to her?"

"No." Emma stepped between her foster parents and Brady. Her eyes flicked to me. She straightened and took a long breath. She looked up at Brady, who stood several inches taller. "I'm sorry." Her mouth puckered. "You just...well, you just made me nervous with all that attention." She flicked a glance to her foster dad, then to Brady's parents, understanding about how such a statement could be taken flashing in a bolt of worry in her eyes. She quickly continued. "He didn't do anything wrong. I promise." Her cheeks flushed. "I just got nervous. It was silly. Instead of talking to him, I pulled away. So he tried harder. I see that now."

Brady hung his head, wide shoulders lifting in a sigh. His fingers flexed at his sides. His mother rubbed his shoulder, but her eyes stayed trained on me.

Emma followed her gaze. "Casey helped me. Talked me through some stuff."

Hal stepped forward, his large size and frame making him an impressive figure. He nodded to Brady and his parents and gestured to a nearby empty table. "Maybe the six of us should have a little chat."

Emma gave me a reassuring smile, and a few moments later, both the teens and their parents sat down to talk. A strange sense of satisfaction settled on me. Emma didn't run away, Brady wasn't actually a creep, and all the parents seemed to really care about the kids. Communication was a good thing. Whether or not the relationship lasted, Emma taking steps to communicate and to include her foster parents in her struggles showed growth.

"Saw what you did there."

The sound of Ryan's voice washed over me, dislodging all the warm and fuzzies. Right. Wasn't supposed to be working with kids.

I jutted my chin out and stabbed a defiant gaze into him. "Look, I know what you're going to say. But I had to help

Emma."

The corner of his mouth quirked up. "I know." He took my elbow and led me out the door at the rear of the fellowship hall.

I resisted the urge to pull away from him. Confrontation. I could handle complicated confrontations. Communication. Communication was a good thing. The lessons I'd tried to instill in Emma tapped a staccato rhythm in my head. Friendship worth fighting for. Stay.

Outside, the humid air clung to my skin. I twisted my long hair around and pulled the heavy locks off the back of my neck. I watched Ryan. Waited.

He stared out over the parking lot. "Thank you for helping Emma. Hal told me about how she's been opening up to them." He scrubbed a hand through his hair and glanced at me. "I'm guessing you had something to do with that?"

I cocked an eyebrow in an imitation of Nancy. "Possibly."

A breath of air expanded his broad shoulders and left him in a rush. "I'm sorry about what happened at the picnic. I believed the papers and not you."

Mouth dry, I stared at him. "No problem."

He barked out a humorless laugh. "Why do I get the feeling that when you say it's not a problem, it's a problem?"

Insightful. "I get it. You have a job. Rules." I shrugged off feelings of betrayal. I had no right. Still, knowing I shouldn't feel something and forcing myself not to were two very different things.

"I made assumptions. Quick judgments." The muscle in the side of his jaw flexed. "I try not to do that."

What did he want me to say? That I'd wanted him to believe in me? Not think the worst of me? To care enough to take my side no matter what evidence seemed to point against me? Too late for that now. I couldn't tell him that I desperately wished he'd reacted differently, so I said nothing. Telling him revealed too much. Made me too vulnerable. Might even give him ideas that I wanted more than friendship.

Which I didn't.

This guy had already slipped past too many of my fortifications, and that always led to pain. Case in point.

"I want you to keep helping me with the kids." His voice thickened with conviction. "You're good with them."

The words rocked me off guard. Spoken from guilt? Or true sentiment? Not sure if that mattered now. I dropped my hair and rolled my shoulders back. "No can do. Against policy." Even I wanted to cringe at the bite in my tone. But distance was for the best. And I wouldn't put his position in jeopardy by allowing him to break the rules. That wasn't fair to him.

Regardless of my personal feelings, he'd still need a job when I left this town behind. He'd been Ida's friend, and I owed him that much.

"I understand." He reached for me, but wisely dropped his hand. "I hope you'll forgive me for jumping to conclusions."

Forgiving him was the right thing to do. I couldn't hold a grudge against the guy for not thinking the best of me. Especially when someone went out of his—or her—way to smear my reputation.

Shoot, I rarely thought the best about myself. I don't know why I'd expected—or at least hoped—others would do anything different.

"Let us run the background check?" He leaned closer. "All we need is your signature to clear everything up."

"Maybe." But until I figured out why someone wanted to sabotage me, proof didn't matter. "But at this point, why bother?" These people had probably already made up their minds about me.

His mouth opened, then closed in a tight line of disapproval. I hated the way he looked at me. Hated that every time things started going well in my life, my feet got knocked out from under me.

Emma didn't need me anymore. And Ryan would be better off without me making a mess in his life.

"Casey, I—"

"It's okay." I cut him off and held up a hand to stop any words that might shatter the cracking shield I struggled to hold between us. "Really."

My chin started to quiver, so I dipped it in a hasty goodbye and left him looking after me as I darted to my car.

26

Options

I dangled a string and watched Kitty bat it around on the floor, her fuzzy paws flying over the carpet. The two of us made a pair.

Kitty didn't care about my past, my parents, or the rumors. Not like everyone else.

I dropped the string and went to stare out the window. Maryville had wiggled under my walls, set up a tent of hope, and laughed when the winds of life came to rip my flimsy plans to shreds. Turning my face up to the ceiling, I looked for God in the textured white paint.

Would He ever let me have anything good? Did He enjoy dangling hope in front of me like a carrot only to rip it away?

Even as I thought it, I pushed the idea away. No. God wasn't cruel. I'd sensed His love. Seen it radiating in Ryan's compassion and patience. God probably kept trying to give me good things, and I just kept screwing them up.

Help me to figure out how to stop making a mess of my life.

Feeling no immediate answers, I drew a long breath. I

needed a plan. Sitting around waiting and doing nothing hadn't panned out. Time to wrestle this disaster into my own hands and get something done.

I hadn't seen Ryan in days. With Emma safe, I'd skipped church on Sunday. Her parents would take care of her. No matter what happened with her boyfriend, she had them. That would be enough.

Outside the open window, a lady walked down the street, a tiny dog on the end of a pink leash. Sunlight glistened on her blond hair. A little boy in a bike helmet peddled furiously past Ryan's house, his little feet churning. My body shifted, rotating so my eyes could linger on Ryan's mailbox.

He hadn't followed me when I left him at the church. Or called since. Why had I let myself hope he'd keep coming after me no matter how many times I pushed him away? Even a man like that could have only so much patience.

Restless energy pricked through my veins. I reached to scratch Kitty's head, but her mood leaned more toward biting, so I left her on the floor with the string. Twisting my damp hair into a braid, I wandered downstairs and into the dining room. The ugly blue tarp shivered with a slight breeze, mocking me.

The next people to live in this house would have to deal with the repairs. I had only two and a half weeks left before I had to be back in Atlanta to prepare for my new job. Having insurance and a steady paycheck were more important than the rush of excitement I'd felt over the thought of my own catering business. I turned away from the tarp.

Reality beckoned. I'd forever be grateful for Ida's gift of this reprieve. Rest. An opportunity to realize I deserved better than Derick. Now that I had the checking account, I could afford gas again. Stay in a cheap hotel in Atlanta for a few days and look for an apartment. I needed to get my head on straight and plow forward.

With or without the answers I'd hoped for. More stories from the past wouldn't change anything anyway.

I trailed my fingers along the kitchen counter. Going back to a studio apartment with a microwave and a countertop burner would stink.

But I'd manage. I always did.

Wandering out of the kitchen and into the foyer, I ran a fond hand over the sewing machine. Where would I put this thing? Or Ida's quilts? Or my great grandmother's china? Tears burned the back of my throat. Maybe I wouldn't even have to decide. Maybe these things had never been mine after all.

Walking through the house, I studied each photograph, every heirloom. The old teddy bear I'd found in Ida's chest with his faded patches of fuzz and heart-shaped wooden necklace. I pulled my quilt from the little cedar closet and held it against me.

Even if I didn't share blood with the people represented here, they'd found a way to burrow into my heart. I could thank Ida and her stories for the peace I'd found here. Maybe Mike and Haley's story belonged to me. Maybe it didn't. I might never know what happened to my birth mother or why she gave me up, but I knew enough to guess.

If Mike and Haley weren't my parents, maybe mine had suffered something similar. Either way, it didn't matter. I wasn't someone else's past. Just me, and I had to forge my own future.

On my own.

A tear trickled down my cheek, and I swiped it away. I put the quilt on the dresser next to the teddy bear and slid my phone from my back pocket. Kitty purred and rubbed on my legs. I glanced down at her. "Decided to be sweet again?"

She blinked up at me. Meowed.

"Just me and you, fuzzy. Hope you like Atlanta."

Time to move on.

After making a necessary call, I thrust my phone back in my pocket and marched downstairs to prepare lunch. I lost myself in the chopping, mixing. In the beauty of food. Creating something cohesive from disjoined components gave me a sense of accomplishment. I tasted my chicken salad, added a little salt, and placed it back in the fridge to let the flavors combine.

By the time the doorbell rang, I'd set the small breakfast nook table with Ida's white porcelain plates and two frosted glasses I'd filled with ice. I tucked my hair behind my ear and drew a breath. Maybe I should have worn something better than cutoff jean shorts I'd made from the pants I'd ruined and Mike's Van Halen T-shirt. But what did it matter?

Even if I'd taken the time to dress up, I'd still look like a grilled cheese next to filet mignon and lobster in comparison to my guest.

I swung open the front door and plastered on an Emmy-worthy smile. "Mira Ann. Thanks for coming."

Sunshine smile lighting her face, she followed my gesture to enter. "It's so sweet of you to invite me." Her eyes roamed over the entryway, no doubt checking every detail and analyzing the house's B&B potential. "Beautiful home."

Just a vase missing the vibrant flower that had been Ida

Sue Macintyre. "Have you ever been in here before?"

Mira Ann flipped curled ends of glossy hair over her shoulder. "No."

I led her into the kitchen and motioned for her to take a seat while I poured sweet tea into the glasses of ice on the table.

"Have you thought more about my offer?" Mira Ann asked as she draped her graceful frame over the chair and crossed her long legs. Dressed in a knee-length purple skirt and black pumps, her outfit showed off her perfectly toned and tanned calves.

I took my time topping off her glass and set the pitcher on the table. "There's more than just the house."

A light flickered in her eyes. Excitement? Curiosity? Suspicion? Not an easy woman to read. "Like what?"

I meandered to the fridge and opened the door. "If I sell the house, I don't know what I'd do with Ida's treasures." If I did get the house and furniture, then I'd also get Ida's savings account. The one still going through processing. I'd be able to rent a storage unit. Maybe even be able to afford a nice enough apartment to keep a few of Ida's things.

But with all the uncertainty, I needed backup plans. Options.

Mira Ann remained silent while I pulled the salad I'd made from a rotisserie chicken from the fridge and a loaf of Nancy's bread from the counter. When I turned back around, I found her watching me.

"What kind of treasures, exactly?" She hitched an eyebrow and glanced around the kitchen as though wondering if Ida had stashed pirate gold somewhere in the house.

Laughing, I slid the bread knife through the loaf to create four even slices. "Just family heirlooms. Ida's personal treasures. Like that old sewing machine that's been in the family for over a century." I smeared generous portions of the chicken salad between the bread. A tomato slice would go well. Maybe a piece of crisp lettuce. I added both.

Appearing dubious, Mira Ann tapped a finger on her glass, the pink nail making a clinking sound. "What about...well, you know...the other?"

I paused with the sandwich platter in hand and tilted my head. Other? "What do you mean?"

"Didn't her husband leave her a bunch of stocks or something that she hid away?" Mira Ann's already large eyes widened farther.

"Uh, not that I know of."

Her lids narrowed for a split second, and she laughed. "Of course. Silly old rumors."

I placed the sandwiches on the table, along with what remained of some broccoli salad Gurtie had made, and took a seat. "Want to say the blessing?"

As though taken by surprise, Mira Ann gawked at me for a second then regained her poise. "Sure." She flashed me a smile and ducked her head. "Lord, thank you for good company and friendship. Please bless this food. Amen."

"Amen." I scooped a large spoonful of broccoli salad and deposited it on my plate. "So, I had an idea. Wanted to see what you thought."

Mira Ann dabbed her napkin on her mouth and swallowed a bite of sandwich. "About Ryan or the house?"

Ryan? Why would I be asking her anything about him? "Uh, the stuff inside the house, actually. Ida's heirlooms."

"You want me to buy the items as well?" She hitched up one shoulder. "Sure."

Uh, no. Why was she acting so weird? I pushed my

barely touched plate aside. "What I mean is maybe I could rent you the house instead. You can run the B&B like you wanted, I would go back to my life in Atlanta, and the house and all of Ida's things would still be mine." Option one. Option two would be to sell the house, buy my own, and set aside which parts of my family heritage I wanted to keep.

Option three meant I didn't get the house or its contents at all, but I'd had a safe place to stay until my job started. And a little money to function until then. All in all, I couldn't complain.

Mira Ann set her fork down and regarded me for a moment. "Interesting. But I'd still rather buy it." She said the words with thinly veiled eagerness, almost to the point of determination.

Also interesting. "Why?"

The woman blinked rapidly, as though I'd asked her the secret of the universe and not her motivation behind wanting to buy a house. "Because I think it would make a good business."

Not an answer. I offered for her to run a B&B here even without buying the house. Seemed like a good idea to me. A way to test it out. If Ryan was right and no one wanted to come to Maryville, then she had an easy out. "Buying the house makes you all in. Renting gives you a chance to try the position out." Another thought occurred. "What about your job at the lawyer's office?"

A muscle in her cheek flexed. "Temporary."

Okay... "So why a B&B?" I gestured around the kitchen. "Why here?"'

Mira Ann leaned back in her chair, something dark filling her bright eyes. "You ask a lot of questions."

All logical questions, in my opinion. I lifted my eye-brows and waited.

Her countenance shifted, and the sweet smile I'd come to expect settled back on her lips. "Sorry. It's just that, well, I want to run a business of my own, but no one in this town is interested in selling me the kind of place I need. Small-town people can be petty, as I'm sure you've discovered."

Touché. I focused on the other part of her statement. "Why won't anyone sell you property?" Maybe no one ever moved, and houses not passed from one family member to another were hard to come by. What did I know of small-town property sales?

"My dad." The way she said the word *dad* had me lean-ing forward. "He was wrongfully convicted. Sent to jail." She flung a hand toward the wall, apparently gesturing toward the town. "They all think he ran some kind of scheme back in Arkansas that conned people out of their money." Her shoulders tightened. "He didn't. Anyway, he was arrested here my senior year. I finished high school alone."

My chest constricted, and my compassion welled. I knew what that felt like. Maybe we had more in common than I'd thought. "That had to be hard."

"Ryan got me through it." A wistful smile edged her shiny lips. "If he hadn't loved me so deeply, so passionately, I wouldn't have held myself together."

The breath caught in my lungs, and I grabbed my tea to take a long gulp. I'd known they were together. Why would her words take me by surprise? I took my time setting my glass back down, studying the woodgrain pattern in the table. But Mira Ann couldn't be much younger than I was. If they'd been so in love in high school, why hadn't they gotten married? I forced down my curiosity. None of my business.

"Anyway." Her voice hardened, and I looked up at her. "I left. But when I finally realized everything I wanted had stayed in this Podunk town, I came back. And nothing is going to stop me from achieving my dreams."

Dreams of running a B&B in a nowhere town? But then, who was I to judge? "I'm sorry. About your dad."

She flipped her hair over her shoulder. Large honey-brown eyes measured me. "Thanks."

If she thought the people of this town wouldn't sell her anything and would judge her by something her dad *didn't do,* then why stay here? The truth wrapped a fist around my stomach and squeezed. Ryan. Of course. I couldn't keep my gaze from flicking toward his house.

Everything I wanted stayed...

Not everything she wanted *was* here. But had *stayed* here. I could put the pieces together. She'd run away. Left him. But then she'd realized life without him could never satisfy her heart, so she'd come back.

I cleared my throat. Time to get this conversation back on track. "I'm not able to sell everything outright. I'm sorry."

She waved a hand. "I get it. You want family connections." She offered a gentle smile. "Hoping that maybe by keeping some old junk that belonged to someone of good standing in this town, you'll get them to forget about your record." She reached out and patted my hand. "But trust me, they won't. If I were you, I'd get away from here. Take the money and enjoy a good life back in the city." Her eyes filled with sincerity, and my pulse skittered.

"Maybe you're right." Admitting it hurt. Truthfully,

even if I only admitted it to myself, I'd wanted Ida's house. A quiet life in a small town of friends. I'd let myself hope for life to be like those few blissful moments at the church picnic before the sabotage. But when had wishing things could be different ever made them that way? "Once I get the house out of probate, it's yours."

Her smile widened.

"Assuming, of course, I actually get the house at all."

The smile vanished, replaced by a sudden scowl. "What?"

"It's like you said. Mr. Shaw needs proof I'm actually Ida's granddaughter. What if I'm not? What if she got the wrong woman?"

Mira Ann's eyes widened. She slumped back in her chair as if I'd delivered a blow. Maybe I had. If I didn't get the house, I couldn't sell it to her. "You can always bid on everything at an auction, I guess."

"Auction?" She sat forward and braced her hands on the table. "What auction?"

I turned out my palms. "You'd know the law better than I do, but if another person isn't named and there are no other relatives, then I assume the house and contents would become property of the state and be auctioned off."

The thought sent a hot knife through my center, but what could I do? The news seemed shocking to Mira Ann, however, and she scowled.

"I suppose we'd better get your paperwork finalized."

Something odd flicked in her voice. Resignation? Annoyance? I couldn't quite place the tone, because as soon as I caught a glimpse of anything slightly unpleasant in Mira Ann, she immediately shifted into the perfect pageant queen again. Hiding emotions. I got that, too. She and I definitely had more in common than I'd first thought.

We both picked at our sandwiches and finished the meal with awkward conversations about church and the weather.

Finally, I walked her to the door. "Thanks again for coming. We'll get the details settled once I get the house out of probate." I opened the door and followed her onto the porch.

Mira Ann paused on the doormat, her eyes swinging toward Ryan's house.

Curiosity brimmed, and words I probably shouldn't ask jumped out of my mouth. "What happened with you two, if you don't mind my asking?"

She laughed, but it sounded forced. "Oh, you know. The usual. We had a fight. I left. He didn't chase me. When I finally came back, things had...changed." Her fingers entwined in the ends of her long hair. "We'll get back to that place again. These things just take time."

The passion in her voice said she'd love him to the moon and back. Ryan deserved that. Someone who would take good care of him. "He's a great guy."

Her shoulders suddenly stiffened. "He is." She pinned me with a scathing glare. "Too good to be run through the mud."

What? I leaned away from her. The usual sweetness on her face had been devoured by a snarling lioness. And I was the gazelle. No, those were elegant. I'd be more like the meerkat. Or maybe the wart—

"Don't think you can swoop in here and get all involved in the church and wrap him around your finger." Mira Ann pointed a long fingernail at me, breaking off my bizarre thought. "He's just being nice. That's what he does. He cares about everyone." Her lip curled. "But he doesn't care about you like you think. He just can't resist trying to fix screwed-up people."

Mouth dry, I stared at her. I'd never tried to wrap him around my finger. I knew he didn't think of me as anything but a church project. And maybe a friend. I wanted to tell her. But the words stuck in my mouth like a heaping spoonful of peanut butter.

"That little stunt you pulled the other night cost him. The entire church is talking about why he let you around the kids when it's clearly against policy." She shook her head. "After as nice as he's been to you, why are you making trouble for him?"

My heart pounded. I didn't want to make trouble for him. I'd only wanted to help Emma. I shook my head, my throat burning.

Mira Ann's eyes softened. "I know you probably mean well. But sometimes good intentions lead to bad outcomes, you know?"

I wrapped an arm around my stomach as bile rose into my throat. She was right. "I don't mean to cause any issues for him."

She rested a hand on my shoulder. "I'll help you with the probate stuff as best I can. Let you get back to your normal life."

Right. The sooner she got rid of me the better. "Thanks."

She gave me a friendly squeeze and swayed off the porch, the picture of physical perfection I'd never be.

27

The Last Letter

Hope deferred makes the heart sick.

Proverbs something or other. And I could add hope planted, watered, tended, and then yanked up by the roots made a person wonder why she'd ever succumbed to such stupidity in the first place.

July heat clung to my skin, and even Kitty found it hard to move around in the stifling air the box fan in my room couldn't dispel. She lay on the bed and watched me out of one yellow eye, too hot to bother swishing her tail. Poor creature. Wearing a fur coat in this heat had to be torture.

I stuffed my clothes into my ratty suitcase. Ida had better ones, but until I knew if I'd inherited any of this, I wouldn't take anything. Just what I'd come with and a lot of memories. And a quilt that I'd spread over the bed in my new apartment.

No more sitting around in this house waiting. I had to get out. Take charge. Control what I could until the lawyer gave me some answers.

The doorbell rang, the merry chime echoing through the house.

My fingers stilled. One heartbeat. Two more. Should I answer it?

Nope. I tugged on the zipper, which stuck halfway around the side of the suitcase. Kitty found the energy—probably fueled by insatiable feline curiosity—to hop up and rub the side of her face on the edge. I really should have gotten a cat carrier, too. No way I'd survive Atlanta traffic if she wanted to perch on my head again. But where would I find—?

The doorbell rang again. Twice.

Huh. I left the half-zipped suitcase and plodded down the stairs. A fourth chime. "I'm coming!" Geez. Talk about impatient.

Ryan stood on the porch dressed in his customary jeans, envelope in hand and eyes intense. Uh-oh. "What's wrong?"

He glanced behind me into the house. "Is Mira Ann here?"

Oh. I leaned against the doorframe. "She came for lunch but left hours ago." I scrubbed my bare toe along the floor. "How'd you know she was here?"

"She called and told me. What did she say to you?" Ryan's eyes bore into mine, clearly riled. About what? Me knowing about their past?

"We talked about the house." I shrugged. "She wants it for a B&B." And other things, mainly him, but I didn't see how bringing that up would help.

He cupped the back of his neck. Kneaded a muscle there. "Did she intimidate you? Make you want to leave?"

Not exactly. "She pointed out a couple of things I already knew, but I wouldn't say she intimidated me." At least, not any more than most regular women were intimidated by the Miss America types.

Ryan took a step closer, and I had to tilt my head back to look at him. "Pointed out what things?"

I'd never seen Ryan this intense. "Just that the church is unhappy with me, and that me getting in the middle of the conflict with Emma caused you problems because I went against the rules." A heavy breath left my chest. "I'm sorry. I didn't mean to cause you any trouble." I tried for a wry smile. "Just seems to be my default."

The muscle in the side of his jaw jumped, and his hand landed on my shoulder. "Stop that. Stop putting yourself down."

I glanced away.

"And you didn't cause me trouble. If anything, your helping Emma made me realize the mistake I'd made in not believing you in the first place. And beyond that, even if you did have a record, the past doesn't matter. I want you working with the kids." His voice deepened. "With me."

Oh, Ryan. Such a sweet guy. Loyal. Compassionate. But naïve. "I have to go home." The words slipped out, tinged with regret. Sorrow.

His brows lowered. "Why?"

I barked out a laugh and slipped around him to plop down on the swing. The late afternoon sunshine painted the porch, and the scent of freshly cut grass lingered in the air. I tucked my fingers under my legs on the swing and kept my focus on the way the boards fit together underneath my toes. "I have an apartment to find before I have to report to the school and my new job."

"And?" Ryan joined me on the swing without invitation. Sat too close. The masculine scent of his aftershave tingled my senses, and the heady aroma of...*him* lingered on his Hornets T-shirt. "You've always had those reasons.

Planned on leaving the first week of August. I sense you've moved that time up. Right after a visit from Mira Ann. What changed?"

Ugh. Why did this man have the ability to read me? How could he possibly know I'd been upstairs packing? Had thought about hitting the road today? Even if only to do *something*. "I've got to have time to find an apartment. Especially since I don't even know if I'll get the inheritance. If I can't prove who I am."

He tapped the envelope on his knee. In the intensity of the moment, I'd forgotten all about it. "Today is the final letter. One month from the last one."

I reached for the envelope, but he held it away from me. I frowned.

"First, I want to talk to you about Mira Ann."

Oh boy. "Look, I don't want to cause you problems in your personal life, either. We're friends. You comforted me like you would anyone else. She has nothing to worry about. End of story. I totally understand."

Those chocolate eyes found mine. Held on. Constricted my chest. "No, I don't think you do."

Why was it so hard to breathe? I rocketed up from the swing, away from him. I leaned against the porch rail and waited for whatever he had to say.

"We dated in high school. Two years."

Yeah. I knew that.

He cleared his throat. "And for another year after. Her first year of college. She went through some hard times. So did I. Lost my dad, hers went to prison. We found...comfort with one another."

I sought his eyes, hoping he saw there was no judgment in mine. Sure, he was a minister. But that didn't mean I expected him to be perfect. "I understand."

Ryan laced his fingers together and broke eye contact. "I stayed here, and she went off to college. Things became difficult. Especially with her…sorority activities."

Ouch. Probably code for parties and other guys. Not that I should make assumptions. Maybe the difference had only been the strain of long distances and busy schedules. I held up my hand. "You don't need to explain anything to me. Your dating life is your business."

He continued as if I hadn't said anything at all. "Around that same time, I surrendered my pride and insecurities to Jesus. Found salvation." He ran a hand through his hair, and his face radiated with the wholehearted assurance of a man who deeply believed in his faith. My heart twisted. Strained toward the light in him. "She didn't care for the changes my salvation brought into my life. We broke up."

Yet, she'd come back here. Wanted to make changes in her own life. Get closer to the light that filled Ryan. I completely understood. I squeezed my eyes shut. Longing I couldn't afford to acknowledge sucked the air from my lungs.

Hope deferred makes the heart sick.

I couldn't let myself hope for any kind of future with this man. Not even friendship. Because my traitorous heart would want more. And I couldn't do that to him. Because I'd eventually disappoint him, and that was a failure I couldn't live with.

"Anyway." His voice hardened. Probably because I didn't respond. Couldn't even look at him. "Two years ago she came back here out of the blue. Got a job with her paralegal degree. I…haven't handled it well."

The strain in his voice brought my eyes to his bowed

head. His defeated posture drew me back to his side. The little voice in me screamed to stay away. But Ryan had comforted me when I needed him. I would do the same.

Even if it scorched my heart.

I wrapped an arm around his shoulders. "Sometimes relationships are hard. But that doesn't mean you two can't work it out."

He turned his head, his face only inches from mine. "What? I mean I've avoided her and haven't had the hard conversation I clearly need to have with her. I don't want a relationship with her again. She's not the woman God has for me."

Huh...

What did I do with that? God had been that specific with him on who to date? "She's not? Why?"

Ryan jabbed his fingers through his hair. "First, she doesn't share my faith. That's a major deal. Second, we never really fit. She didn't stir me. Challenge me. Make me desperately want to be everything she needed. Protect her at all costs."

My mouth went dry. I tried to swallow. Couldn't. Did he know what his words did to me? Know that my heart flooded with the painful desire to find someone who thought those things about me? Wanted it so much that I couldn't speak? Could barely breathe?

Escape.

I pushed off the swing. The separation from the heat of his side, the strength of him, immediately opened a loss in my chest.

No! This feeling burned worse than hope deferred. The gnawing in my middle stemmed from something more powerful than hope.

Longing to be wrapped in his arms had me hugging my own around my stomach and turning my back to him.

Breathe. One step at a time. Air in. Out. Relax your shoulders. Lift your head. Control your expression. Don't let him see. Hold it in, and hold yourself together.

Following the instructions of my inner voice, I straightened myself, turned around, and pushed as much unconcern into my voice as I could muster. "Like I said, you don't have to explain anything to me. Your personal life is your business."

He stared at me, assessing. His eyes darkened, probing down so deep into me that, if I didn't do something, I'd drown in his intensity.

I scrambled for anything I could to change the subject. Escape his scrutiny before he saw the truth. "Can I have my letter?"

Ryan held the envelope out without a word, and I plucked it from his fingers and settled back against the rail. I ran a finger over Ida's shaky writing on the front.

For Casey.

He sat quietly, probably knowing exactly what he did to me. But he didn't push. Didn't force me to face feelings I couldn't comprehend. Didn't tear me apart by explaining he hadn't been talking about me. That I wasn't the one God had for him either.

No wonder Mira Ann loved this man. I wouldn't make him have the conversation with me that he'd hesitated to have with her. I understood. No need to make him say the words.

At least I'd reached the end of Ida's journey before leaving. I could find a little closure before heading out for Atlanta in the morning.

I slid my finger under the seal and opened the letter, pulling out a single page. I drew a deep breath, steeling myself for the end. Maybe the truth of what happened to my mother. Why she'd given me up.

My sweet Casey,

I pray this past month has taught you what only time and Jesus can. To rest. To renew. I pray that the Lord uses this time to draw you close to Him and that you've learned that no matter what turmoil life brings, He will walk you through it.

Hurts come with or without faith. But your faith will save you from experiencing pain alone. The love of God in your heart will keep you from being overwhelmed.

Faith won't save you from pain. But faith will save you from desperation, depression, and over-whelming fear.

I pulled a slow breath into my lungs. Held it. I found Ryan's eyes. "Ida says faith doesn't save people from pain. Everyone suffers, I guess. But she said holding on to God saves you from desperation. Overwhelming fear." I dropped my gaze. Dug my toe into the rough wood of the porch. "Do you believe that?"

"I do." His gentle voice coaxed my gaze to his. Snagged me in their depths. "I know from experience. My faith has been the only thing that has kept me sane some days."

I swam in the assurance in his eyes for another second and then returned to Ida's letter.

I pray you believe that truth. You may falter, but you can never fail as long as you keep turning back to Jesus. Keep asking Him to hold your hand.

Tears blurred my vision, and I had to take a second to blink them away. My life had never been easy. Might never be easy. But I didn't have to be alone. No matter what happened with the house or where I lived, as long as I held on to Jesus, I wouldn't be overtaken by fear and desperation. Like a crab shedding its shell, I stepped out of a weight that had hung around my neck for years.

I might be that blue crab, weak and vulnerable. But even I knew God had all the strength I'd need.

This will be my last letter. By this point, your summer here is coming to an end. If you landed the library job you were hoping for, then I suspect you have a decision to make. Stay here in the house and start a new life in Maryville, or sell it all and build something for yourself in Atlanta. Or anywhere else you choose to go.

That is up to you. Know that whatever decision you make, you have my blessing. Don't stay here because you think it's what I want. Things are merely that. Things. You matter more than all of them. Sell them all if you need to. I only want what will make you happy. The Lord has given me the chance to provide you with a fresh start. Pray about your decision, and make your choice with the Lord's prompting.

I've gathered everything you will need to take the next step in your journey without me. But you don't go alone. I pray by now you have a few friends to walk by your side. I hope you've realized that the greatest friend you will ever need is the Lord you trusted with your tender heart.

The answers you seek and the key to the next chapter are waiting. Poppa holds the key.

I love you.

Until we meet again in the radiance of our precious Lord's presence.

Mamaw

I took my time and folded the letter, then put it back into the envelope. Another chapter? More clues and questions and impossible projects?

"Anything you want to share?" Ryan's smooth voice tugged me from my contemplation.

"She said Poppa holds the key." I met his eyes. "But I have no idea what she's talking about."

He stroked his chin, face tight in thought. Finally, he pushed his hands against his knees and stood. "Maybe I can help." A hesitation. "If you want me to."

Yes. No. I both yearned for his presence and, at the same time, feared his nearness. Ryan wasn't Derick. Not by the farthest stretch of the imagination.

He watched me. Patient. Could he see the turmoil inside me? Guess why I hesitated?

"Maybe I'll see something you didn't." He crammed his hands into his pockets. "Or understand something Ida wrote you may have missed."

He had a good point. Logical. Like usual. He shared none of my emotional waywardness. If I had only one night left here, I could deal with the heartache tomorrow. "Right.

Sure. Thanks."

Awkward. And here I'd thought I'd gotten better in that arena.

With a smile, Ryan laced his fingers through mine, undid my heart, and tugged me through the door.

28

Revelations

The answer had to be in there somewhere. Ryan and I stared at Ida's letters spread out on the kitchen island, searching for clues. Hot night air swirled with the rotation of the box fan positioned near our feet. I tugged my hair into a high ponytail as Ryan scanned each personal letter from Ida. He'd already read them all. We'd been at it for hours. Minus the short break to eat dinner and discuss minute details.

I took a moment to escape the kitchen by using the excuse of checking the tarp. The dining room looked the same as it had for weeks. Broken. Damaged. Caught in limbo like everything else in my life these days. Who knew a person could despise a piece of blue material so much? It hung there, a giant Band-Aid on a wound I couldn't fix. Especially not on my own. The irony struck me.

Hey, God, I've got some pretty ugly Band-Aids of my own covering some deep wounds I can't fix.

My heart stirred. Admitting my failures, even to the God who already knew them, stung. Something in me pinched. Right. Letting go of control. I could do that. I could learn to trust.

Would You be willing to fix them for me? Stay with me when I walk through pain, and show me how to find Your peace?

The tingle of agitated nerves abated as I drew one long breath and then another. Ida was right. Life would hurt. But I didn't have to walk through the pain or bear the scars alone. When my time here ended and I said goodbye to Ryan and Nancy and Maryville, God would still be with me. Guiding me through every step as I put my life—and my heart—back together.

A scuffling noise came from outside the open window in the dining room. Ugh. Not again. I marched to the opening and put my hands on my hips. "Go away, possum!"

Another scuffling noise.

I leaned closer to the window. The light from a streetlamp at the front of the house cast just enough of a glow on the yard for me to catch a glimpse of something darting around the corner. Huh. It worked. Feeling satisfied, I tugged the window closed and hooked the latch. The critter seemed fond of this particular window. I'd leave the others open until I went upstairs, but maybe if the vermin couldn't get in here, it would just give up.

"Hey, Casey?"

Ryan's voice tugged me back into the kitchen. He had one arm propped on the counter as he leaned over the letters spread out in front of him. His gaze darted back to the dining room. "Everything okay?"

"Just that possum. I think I scared it off." I flashed a grin. "And I shut that window, so maybe it won't try to snoop around in here again."

Ryan held up one of the letters. "In this one she wanted

you to look at the pictures on the mantel. Do you think one of them could be the Poppa in the last letter?"

Like I hadn't thought of that. I'd looked at those pictures a thousand times. "Maybe. But he wasn't holding any kind of key." His eyes held onto mine. "I guess we can look again." He was here to help me search for things I missed, after all.

He waited for me to take the lead even though he knew his way around Ida's house as well as I did. We crossed into the living room, and I flipped the light switch. Ryan looked around, and I sensed a shift in him. His shoulders tightened.

"You miss her, don't you?" I stood by him and placed my fingers on his arm.

That gentle smile I'd come to know turned up his lips. He leaned closer and rubbed a thumb down my cheek. My heart nearly stilled and then lurched into a fierce rhythm.

He dropped his hand as though he hadn't just shredded all my defenses and turned toward Ida and Reggie's picture. "They had the kind of love that would have lasted seventy-five years." He winked at me. "At least, that's what Ida always said." He stepped away and left me standing breathless in the center of the room.

Ryan picked up the picture of the gray bearded man standing in front of a quilt hanging on a line by an old cabin. "I think this is Ida's grandfather." He squinted and held the picture to his face. "He's holding something, but I can't tell what it is."

Huh. Not Rufus, Reggie's father like I'd thought. I joined him. "Looks like he was carving something. See that little pocketknife in his other hand?"

He squinted hard. "I think you're right. Do you think that's the key?"

"Metaphorically, maybe. But why would an old pocket-knife be the key to my past?"

Ryan rubbed a hand on the back of his neck. "I don't know. Maybe we need a closer look." Something sparked in his eyes. "I have a magnifying glass. Once we can see what he's holding better, maybe we can figure it out."

Excitement bubbled in my chest, and I squeezed his arm. "Perfect. Let's go get it."

He checked the watch on his wrist. "It's getting pretty late. How about we start fresh in the morning?"

And further delay me leaving? He watched me carefully, and I had the feeling this man knew exactly what he was doing. But maybe I didn't really care. What would one more day matter? "Sure."

The grin that split his face was worth every painful tear the concession would cost me later. I took in his features. The scruff on his jaw, the way his dark hair framed his handsome face. Tried to burn every detail into my memory.

His eyes darkened. Uh-oh. I'd been staring. Probably with way too much emotion betraying me. I spun around and headed into the foyer. "Well, good night." I tugged the knob on the front door and opened the house to the sounds of cicadas.

Ryan paused in the entryway, his gaze roaming my heated face. Finally, a lopsided smile tugged one side of his mouth in an expression I couldn't quite read. It hinted at satisfaction. "I'll take the day off. Breakfast at eight, and then we resume the hunt?"

Mouth dry, I merely nodded.

"I'll bring some of Mom's cinnamon rolls." He dipped his chin like an old-fashioned cowboy tipping his Stetson and bounded down the steps.

I watched him until he disappeared into the darkness before retreating back into the house. Making the rounds, I put away Ida's letters and latched every window on the lower floor. No way would Mr. Possum visit tonight.

Kitty wound around my legs as I got ready for bed, even following me into the bathroom when I brushed my teeth. I rinsed and scooped her up. "You won't judge me for giving into just one more day, will you?"

She meowed, but who knew if that meant consent or condemnation. I snuggled her to my chest and put her on the bed. She immediately bounded onto my pillow and curled her little paws underneath her, purring.

I laughed. "Should I start calling you pillow thief instead of Kitty?" Probably should give the cat a more permanent name than Kitty anyway. I stroked her head. "How about Eeyore? You're grumpy like that."

She purred softly, wide eyes watching me.

"What about Spaz? That fits." I laughed and scratched her ears. "Maybe Mousse? Like the fluffy gray stuff?" I shook my head. "No. Sounds too much like Moose."

She rubbed her face on my fingers. "Luna. Like a big gray moon. Would you like that?" Kitty purred against my fingers, and I yawned. I'd keep thinking on it. I turned the lights off and settled on the other pillow, staring at the ceiling. Immediately, the image I'd decided to burn into my memory filled my mind's eye. His gentle assurance. Easy manner.

Bad idea, letting that man under your skin.

Ugh. Not again. I forced the inner voice to be quiet.

You know he would never want you. You're too screwed up.

I could let the voice of insecurity pit my heart like an

avocado, or I could focus my self-destructive brain in a different direction. Rather than let the lies rule me, I worked on praying. I talked about life, the past, and things that bothered me. An hour later, the nagging little voice in my head quieted.

Show me when to go, God. Guide my next step. Help me figure this mess out.

Finally, feeling at ease, I rolled to my side and drifted to sleep.

I startled awake and sucked in a deep breath of hot air. Sitting up, I scanned the dark room. Had it been a dream that jarred me from sleep?

Something bumped downstairs.

My pulse quickened. *Not again!*

I swung the sheet off my legs and headed for the door. No way had that possum gotten in. I'd shut all the windows. I eased my bedroom door open and hesitated in the hall, another thought worming into my sleepy brain. Someone must have broken in. Even Emma had come through the open widow. And I was certain I'd closed them all.

Emma wouldn't break in, would she? Surely, if she planned to run away again, she'd call. Or ring the doorbell.

Pocketing my phone, I crept down the stairs and into the foyer. Moonlight seeped through the front window and painted silver across the floor. Keeping close to the wall, I stepped quietly up to the kitchen doorway.

A lean figure—much too tall to be Emma—rifled through a drawer in the kitchen. Dressed in all black with a hood drawn over his head, this guy hadn't come to beg food. I backed away slowly and hurried down the hall to the linen closet where I'd hidden from the storm.

The room squeezed around me, stifling. Fingers trembling, I fumbled my phone open and punched in the number to the sheriff's department. The same female voice I'd spoken to before answered.

"There's someone in my house," I squeaked out. "One-twelve Old Mill Road."

A pause. "Miss Adams?"

"Yes?" My racing heart echoed in my ears. The dark wrapped around me and pulled the air from my lungs, making me breathless.

"Miss Adams, Deputy Miller said if you called again to ask you to call animal control."

What? "No, it's not—"

Something thumped in the hallway.

He was coming! I snapped the phone shut and held my breath. The deputy wouldn't get here in time anyway. I opened it again and dialed Ryan's number.

The phone rang four times before his sleepy voice came over the line. "Casey?"

"Ryan!" I cupped my hand around the phone and turned toward the back of the closet. "Someone's in the house."

"What?" He barked the word, life surging into his voice.

I squeezed my eyes shut, trying to ignore the suffocating darkness. "It's not a possum. I swear. I saw him."

"I'm coming." Things rattled in the background as Ryan scrambled around. "Stay on the phone with me."

Nodding, I squeezed the mobile to my ear.

Light. I needed light. But I didn't dare flip the switch and let the intruder know where I hid. "I'm scared."

"I've got you." The protectiveness in his voice poured through me, filling in cracks and soothing a little of the trembling in my nerves. "Where are you?"

"In the closet in the hall."

"Good. Stay there." His breathing, steady and even, gave me something to focus on as the seconds ticked by. "I'm on the porch. Coming in."

Swallowing hard, I listened with one ear to the door, but I couldn't make out more than my own pulse thudding in my ears.

A sudden shout. Scuffling. I threw the door wide and lurched into the hallway. Had the robber attacked Ryan? I fumbled my way down the dark hall.

Light poured through the kitchen. Footsteps pounded. A ripping sound. I blinked rapidly, trying to get my eyes to adjust to the brightness. I skidded into the kitchen on bare feet, heart pounding.

Ida's letters lay scattered across the island. Two on the floor. No sign of Ryan.

A grunt. I bolted toward the dining room. I couldn't live with myself if I'd gotten Ryan hurt or—

The tarp in the dining room flapped on the wall, one side ripped free. I'd been so worried about the windows I'd completely forgotten how easily someone could cut through the tarp. Stupid. Ryan must have chased the guy into the yard.

Without thinking it through, I hurdled through the open hole and landed hard on the ground outside. Pain flared through my hip, but I ignored it and gained my footing.

Where did he go?

I scanned the yard in the darkness. Nothing. Then a beam of light swept across the grass, held by a large figure in athletic pants. I let out a breath of relief.

Ryan.

His bare feet hustled across the yard. "Casey. Are you okay?"

"Yeah." I shuddered as adrenaline coursed through my system. Ryan wasn't hurt. Everything would be fine.

"Man, that guy was fast." His shoulders expanded with a deep breath. "He got away." Ryan wrapped an arm around my shoulder and drew me into the warmth of his side. "I'll call the sheriff."

I barked out an ironic laugh. "No need. I called them before you." At his silence, I continued. "The operator told me to call animal control. Guess I called in for a possum one too many times."

"Once is too many?" The confusion in his voice pricked my conscious. Right. I'd lied about Emma.

"Uh, well, and one other time." I hunched my shoulders. His grip tightened, refusing to let me slip away. "I thought Emma was a burglar. When I discovered her in my kitchen—to keep her out of trouble—I told Deputy Beefy she was a possum when he came to the door. Or maybe a raccoon. I can't remember."

Ryan shifted to face me. "Wait. Emma broke into your house?"

"She was planning on running away. Came here for supplies."

"And you talked her out of it." His voice thickened. "I should have known."

Should have known what? "I just reminded her that she liked it here. That she had good foster parents and people who cared about her. She shouldn't let her problems make

287

her run away."

Ryan chuckled and laced his fingers through mine. "Sounds like really good advice." He tugged me toward the front door. "Come on. Let's get you inside."

We went back into the house, and, while Ryan called the sheriff's office to report the break-in, I looked at the items in the kitchen. Knowing better than to touch anything before the cops arrived, I stayed in the doorway. Why would a robber pull out Ida's letters?

Ryan clicked off his phone and stood by my side. "So...*Officer Beefy* should be here soon."

Uh-oh. "Deputy Beefy." A nervous laugh bubbled out. "I couldn't remember his name."

He laughed and wrapped an arm around me. This was becoming a habit. I stepped out from under his touch and pointed to the letters. "Why would a robber pull out all of Ida's letters?"

Ryan frowned. "Weird."

Totally weird. Unless... Mira Ann. Who else would want to see Ida's letters? "Maybe it was Mira Ann."

The look on his face twisted my heart. Right. He had no problem believing *I* was a criminal. But plenty of issues believing Mira Ann could be the one who broke in and dug through Ida's letters. Why should I be surprised?

His shoulders deflated, and he rubbed the back of his neck. "You're probably—"

The doorbell rang, cutting off whatever accusation he was about to throw my way. I clenched my teeth and pushed past him out of the living room. Deputy Beefy aka Deputy Miller stood in my doorway not looking at all sheepish for not believing me.

I crossed my arms. "I *told you* someone broke in. Cut through the tarp."

He gave a curt nod. I gestured him inside.

"I chased the intruder through the tarp and back outside," Ryan said. "But I lost him."

The deputy pulled a small book from his pocket. "Anything missing?"

"Not that I've noticed. Just a bunch of letters taken out and thrown around on the counter." I threw a thumb back over my shoulder toward the kitchen.

Deputy Miller turned to Ryan, even though this was my house, and started asking him about the chase. Lean perp. Fast. No way to tell if the intruder was male or female. Their words bounced around in my head and churned my gut. Without any proof, spouting my suspicions about Mira Ann wouldn't do any good. Ryan hadn't believed me. Why would the deputy?

I left the men to go over the details. They seemed like old chums. By-product of a tiny town. They'd probably gone to high school together. Besides, Ryan seemed to be handling it just fine. If they needed to ask me anything, they'd speak up. I turned into the living room and picked up my favorite picture of Ida.

"What a mess, huh?" I whispered to her. Her confident features shined out from the black-and-white photograph. "Why'd you have to make things so complicated?"

I put the picture down and took the one of Poppa off the coffee table. I looked closely at it. I focused on his other hand, the one not holding the pocketknife. I angled the photo toward the light.

Wait.

Poppa held a stick of wood. On one end, just above his hand, was a familiar shape. I squinted. A little wooden heart.

One I'd seen before.

29

The Key

After the deputy finished jotting down my statement, I locked the door behind him. Every light in the bottom floor of the house burned brightly. We'd searched, but nothing seemed to be missing. Only Ida's letters thrown on the counter and the cut tarp. Ryan watched me, a strange look on his face.

"What?" I tugged the ponytail holder out of my hair and pulled the strands into a bun coiled on the back of my neck. Even at four in the morning, the house felt like an oven.

Ryan, bare feet spread wide on the hardwood, rubbed his hands together. Nervous? Why? He cleared his throat. "I'm sorry."

For what? I cocked an eyebrow.

"What you said about Mira Ann." He shook his head, looking conflicted. "Anybody coming after valuables wouldn't have gone through Ida's letters. But what motive could she possibly have?"

Huh. Seemed Ryan hadn't been about to tell me how ridiculous my suggestion sounded. Old flame or not, Mira

Ann was our best suspect. So why hadn't he said something? "Other than you and your mom, no one else knew about the letters."

The look on his face told me he'd realized that as well.

"Unless you told someone?"

He turned his palms out. "Why would I?" Ryan's voice hardened. "Mira Ann wants to buy the house and start a B&B. It's not a great idea, but it's what she wants. So why break in here?"

Apparently he'd never heard that old saying about a woman scorned. "I don't know. If she wanted anything in here, she could have just waited. I agreed sell the place to her."

That strange look tightened Ryan's face again. Concern? "You're going to sell this house? It's been in the Macintyre family since the 1800s."

Talk about the guilt trip. "Maybe. Probably." I didn't want to argue. Not this close to figuring out Ida's clues. I'd waited too long. Before anything else went wrong, I would discover what Ida had left for me. "I found something you need to see."

I led him into the living room and picked up the picture of Poppa. "See this?" I pointed to the thing in his hand. "I know what he's holding."

Ryan squinted and turned the photograph. "Want me to get the magnifying glass?"

"No need. Look." I traced the tiny fuzzy image. "We were focusing on the knife, but in his other hand he has a tiny little heart he was carving."

His eyes lit with excitement. "That must be the key." He grabbed me into a hug. "You figured it out." I enjoyed the moment for only a second and then pulled away.

"And I know exactly where it is." I hurried up the stairs, Ryan close on my heels. The oddness of the moment struck me as we reached the second floor. The two of us, in our pajamas, hunting for a treasure before dawn.

Kitty, curled on her usual perch on my pillow, lifted her head as we stepped inside my room. She meowed and jumped down, her long gray fur swishing. Bypassing me, she headed straight for Ryan and rubbed around his legs. She blinked up at him, meowing.

Even the cat liked having Ryan around. I was glad he was here. Helping me with Ida's puzzles. Making discoveries together.

Is this what it feels like to have a partner in life?

He scooped Kitty up and settled her in his toned arms.

My gut twisted as I watched such a masculine man melt over the affections of a cat. "Traitor." I laughed and scratched Kitty's head. "Don't make me jealous." The words popped out before I had the chance to catch them. Heat expanded in my middle like bread with too much yeast. That sounded bad. "You're supposed to be my cat, remember?" Couldn't have Ryan think I meant I was jealous of the cat snuggling in his arms.

Ryan's laugh rumbled from his muscled chest and soothed the awkwardness hanging on the air. Even if he laughed at me, the sound still settled my nerves and made me feel strangely at ease. Kitty seemed rather content snuggled against him. Who could blame her? The thought warmed my face, so I turned away. We had a mission.

Get your head together!

The lack of sleep had to be making me lose focus.

"Did you ever name her?" Ryan scratched behind her ears, and Kitty leaned her head into his fingers, her purr growing louder.

"I call her Kitty."

One eyebrow quirked up in that signature look of his. "Right. So if you had a dog, you'd just name it"—he made air quotes with one hand—"doggy?" Kitty looked at him and meowed, clearly protesting that he'd stopped scratching.

I rolled my eyes. "Funny, just last night I was trying out different names for her." I crossed to the dresser and plucked the old teddy from where he sat against the mirror.

Stay focused. Quit looking at him and the cat before you let yourself wish you could see him every morning in his pajamas with mussed hair and a tender look on his face.

"Like what?" Ryan wasn't letting this name thing go.

Didn't he know we had more important things to discuss right now? "Eeyore. Luna." I waved a hand for him to come over. "Other ideas that didn't quite fit." Nimbus, Glacier, Fuzzy, Spaz, Whiskers, Mop, Swiffer. Not that he needed to know. I'd pick one. Eventually.

I pulled the little necklace over the teddy's head. "Look familiar?"

Still holding my cat, Ryan leaned over my shoulder. "That's the carving from the picture."

And it had been sitting on my dresser this entire time. Poppa had carved a piece of cedar into the outline of a heart. Smooth and rounded, the small hollow shape must have been difficult to whittle with a pocketknife. At the bottom, the point of the heart extended down into a little cross. At the top, a delicate loop held a clasp for the chain.

"Looks like a heart sitting on top of a cross." Ryan set Kitty on the floor, which she protested with a meow. "Maybe it means Jesus is the key to love?"

Interesting. "I think there's more to it." I turned the smooth wood over in my hand. "While, yes, Ida wanted me to learn things like that, I think the answer is less metaphorical."

"If it's an actual key, then where's the lock?"

Exactly. I sighed. "I have no idea." I handed the key to Ryan and rubbed my temples. "You knew Ida well. Did she have any kind of safe?"

"Not that I know of." He held the little heart up to the light. "Especially not one that would take a wooden key. We're probably looking for something wooden as well. Made out of cedar like the heart."

Of course!

I bolted out the door. Ryan called after me, but I hurried on. He'd follow. I burst into Ida's room and turned on the light. Why hadn't I realized that a cedar key would go with a cedar trunk? I dropped to my knees next to the family tree quilt and opened the top. No lock here.

Ryan came in behind me. "Find anything?"

I pulled out the last scraps of fabric I hadn't used on my quilt and sat back. "I don't get it. There's no lock on the front, and I opened this weeks ago. I don't see anything in here." I ran my fingers along the bottom of the trunk. "Not unless there's some kind of secret compartment."

Heart hammering, I probed along the inner edges. Nothing. Just planks with knotholes and—

"Look!" I pointed to a knothole in the corner. "This one has a hole." I stuck my hand out. "Give me the key."

Ryan placed the wooden key in my hand. The bottom of the cross fit perfectly into the little hole. I glanced up at him.

His face shone with excitement.

Pulse racing, I pushed the key down until it reached the

bottom of the heart.

It turned.

Something clicked. I gasped. "It worked!" But where—

"Look! The molding at the bottom. It's a drawer."

I swung my head over to look at the side of the trunk. The edge of the molding around the bottom had opened a crack. Cramming my fingers into the hole, I pulled.

A drawer pulled out. As wide as the bottom of the trunk, but only a few inches deep.

And the space was filled with papers. Pictures. I sat on the carpet and pressed my fingers to my lips. Had I finally found all of Ida's secrets? With shaky fingers I started pulling items out of the drawer.

First, a small hardbound book with a ribbon tied around its cover. I opened the pages to find Ida's script, though less shaky than what I'd seen previously. "Must be her diary. This first entry is from twenty years ago." I set it on the carpet next to me. I'd read that later.

Ryan settled down on the floor, his shoulder brushing mine. Behind us, purring announced Kitty's arrival. She promptly leapt into Ryan's lap and began kneading his leg.

I lifted a folded document with heavy paper and some kind of embossing. I carefully opened it. As I read, I grabbed Ryan's knee and sucked in a quick breath. "It's my birth certificate!"

"Cassandra Macintyre. Six pounds four ounces," Ryan read over my shoulder. "Your adoptive parents kept your name."

The one my mother had given me. Tears welled in my eyes. She must have kept me for at least a little while, or the adoption service would have taken me at birth and my adoptive parents would have filled out the birth certificate. I swiped my eyes and reached in for the next item.

"This is my parents' marriage certificate." I handed it to Ryan. I opened two pages folded together and my heart pinched. "These are Reggie's and Mike's death certificates."

Ryan gently placed each item aside on the floor.

One final thick paper contained embossed designs. "Huh." Maybe Mira Ann's rumors were true after all.

"What is it?"

Though probably nothing like she thought. "Looks like old stock for Standard Oil Company." I scanned the certificate made out to Reginald Macintyre. "For a whopping twenty-five dollars."

Ryan took the certificate and frowned.

"Maybe that's what Mira Ann was after. But it's pretty worthless."

"I wouldn't be so sure about that. Let me make a few phone calls." He squinted at the paper. "This is from 1950. It could be worth a lot more now."

Maybe. Wouldn't that be something? I pulled out stacks of pictures, mostly of my father as a boy. I'd linger over those later. One envelope remained, my name scrawled across the front in Ida's handwriting. I opened the clasp only to find another envelope inside.

This one had Ida's address on the front. Postmarked six months ago. Weird. I unfolded the letter and quickly scanned the page.

Ida,

I pray this letter finds you well. I'm sure you don't want to hear from me, but there's something very important I need to tell you. Several things, actually. First, I want to ask your forgiveness for all

I put you through. I should have stayed with you, and we could have mourned Mike together. The past still haunts me, knowing how much different life could have been if I'd made better choices.

Now that I've found Jesus, I'm trying to make a few things right. Most of them I'm just going to have to rely on His grace for. I don't expect you to be able to forgive me for hiding this from you for so many years, but you should know. You have a granddaughter. I was pregnant when Mike died.

I gave her up for adoption because I couldn't care for her. I know you would have. I'm so sorry. I never should have been so spiteful. I've included her birth certificate and all the information I have on her. She lives in Atlanta and works as a waitress at Bistro.

Finding her now won't make up for lost time, but I pray the two of you can have a relationship. You still have family out there.

Haley

My heart pounded, pressing against my ribs in a painful attempt to comprehend the truth. I squeezed Ryan's knee. Hot tears broke free and coursed down my cheeks.

Ryan put his arm around my shoulders and pulled me close. "Are you okay?"

No.

My mother was alive. And she'd known exactly where to find me.

297

30

Proof

I marched into the lawyer's office, Ryan on my heels. I'd had little sleep and bore a heart full of frustrations. Heaven help anyone who wanted to tangle with me today.

Mira Ann leapt up from her chair, dropping her phone on her desk. "Hey!"

I ignored her and strode directly to Mr. Shaw's door. He was back from vacation. He'd parked his car outside.

Mira Ann sputtered behind me, but I left Ryan to deal with her.

The middle-aged man sat behind a large desk, phone wedged between his wide shoulder and head of thick mahogany hair. He glanced up as I strode in.

I slapped the papers down on the desk. "I have your proof."

His brown eyes widened, and he shifted the phone to his hand. "Charles, I'll have to call you back." He settled the phone into the cradle and leaned back in his chair. "What's this about?"

"You wanted proof I'm related to Ida." I picked up the

first page and flicked it toward him. "Here's my birth certificate listing both my parents, Mike and Haley Macintyre." I pushed the second toward him. "Here's Mike's death certificate."

The lines around Mr. Shaw's mouth deepened. "I'm not following you. Why bring this to me?"

What? The flutter in my stomach stilled. "Because you said you needed proof of relation."

"No, I didn't." He leaned forward in his chair. "You and I never discussed anything of the sort."

My lungs tried to pull in more clarifying air than they could handle, and I choked on my breath. "You...you didn't say I needed proof of relation to Ida in order to get the house out of probate?"

Mr. Shaw rubbed his chin. "The house isn't in probate. Remember, we discussed this when we went over the will."

No. I didn't remember. Clearly. "What do you mean, the house isn't in probate?" I shook my head, but only disjointed memories clattered inside.

"Miss Adams, probate simply means that the will is being validated. A process of verification for the will itself." He spread his fingers, speaking slowly. "I've already taken the will to the judge and received the judgment papers. The transfer of the remaining accounts and assets are in process."

I plopped down in the chair across from him. "But...what about the house?"

His keen eyes assessed me as I ran my hand through my hair. Mr. Shaw spoke calmly, slowly, as though trying to talk a jumper off the rail of a bridge. "Ida put you on the deed to her house before her death. I drew up the paper-work for the new deed. We had the property surveyed and applied for the necessary title searches." A line creased between his eyebrows. "I had Mira Ann process the account before I left for my conference. She should have filed the final paperwork with the records department at the courthouse by now."

The air left my lungs. I struggled to find it again. "You're saying the house has been mine this entire time?"

"Of course. You were joint tenants with rights of survivorship. So that means that upon Ida's passing, full ownership passed to you as a matter of law. No probate needed." Concern etched his features. "Has something happened?"

I launched into the entire story about the tree coming through the house, Mira Ann telling me the house would be in probate for thirty days, and then her telling me Mr. Shaw required proof of kinship. The more words I spilled out, the redder his face became.

"I believe I need to have a little talk with my paralegal." Mr. Shaw pushed up out of his chair and rounded his desk.

I scrambled after him. We found Ryan and Mira Ann standing outside on the sidewalk engaged in an intense conversation. As soon as I stepped out, her eyes shot skewers at me.

"Mira Ann." Mr. Shaw's clipped tone widened Mira Ann's eyes. "I need you to clear something up for me." Mr. Shaw tugged on the lapels of his black suit jacket. "Please step back inside with us."

I watched Mira Ann follow the attorney inside and gestured for Ryan to join us. I needed him by my side. And maybe I needed him to understand what had happened. Better for him to hear the lawyer accuse her than to hear it from me.

The air conditioning in the office did little to cool the heat stirring in my veins. I clenched my jaw tight to keep myself from flinging accusations.

Let her boss do all the talking.

Ryan crossed his arms and planted his feet, looking every bit as aggravated as I felt. Mira Ann darted a glance between us and turned up her nose. "Is there a problem, Mr. Shaw?"

"Did you tell Miss Adams the Macintyre estate was in probate?"

A vein in her neck pulsed. "I told her there was still paperwork that had to be processed before she could take possession of the house."

Liar.

The stout man stood tall, like a pillar of justice. "I told you to take that paperwork to the courthouse before I left."

Mira Ann swallowed. "Yes, you did."

Unable to contain myself, I pointed a finger in her face. "You told me I had to wait thirty days for the house to come out of probate. Then, when that time ended, you told me I had to bring proof of relationship with Ida." I glanced at Mr. Shaw for confirmation. "But neither of those things is true."

She shook her head and spoke slowly. "No, sweetie. You didn't understand. I said we still had some paperwork to process and some items were in probate. Which, if I remember correctly, is Ida's savings account and some CDs at the bank." She batted her eyelashes at Mr. Shaw. "Correct?"

Unfazed by her display, the lawyer pinned her with a scathing look. "Did you file the deed with the chancery clerk?"

She glanced at Ryan, but only suspicion colored his eyes. She straightened. "Not yet."

Mr. Shaw huffed. "And why not?"

"I was waiting until all the paperwork was ready so I could finalize everything at once and—"

He held up a large hand. "Enough. You and I will discuss this later."

Mira Ann opened her mouth. Closed it. She shot me a look and flipped her hair over her shoulder.

Apparently noticing his assistant and his client sizing one another up like two lionesses preparing to pounce, Mr. Shaw cleared his throat. "Take the rest of the day, Miss Middleton." His stern voice filled the room.

She might look like a pageant queen, but underneath, this woman was an ogre. Like a liver-and-worm cake topped with vanilla cream cheese frosting.

"Wait." I took a step closer and blocked the door. "Did you plant that false criminal record on the preacher's desk?"

Mr. Shaw scowled.

Ryan pressed his lips into a tight line of disapproval.

But I had to know. I narrowed my gaze on Mira Ann, watching her for any indication of guilt.

She rolled her eyes. "What a thing to say. Of course not."

"And why should I believe you? You lied about the house."

Her lip curled back, transforming her beautiful face into an ugly snarl. "Maybe you should talk to your Atlanta boyfriend."

I drew my head back in surprise, and her smug smile blended into her menacing sneer. "Derick said something about how he wanted you back and would do anything to make you come home. Maybe he let the truth out so you'd realize you didn't belong here and would go back to the apartment you share with him." She flicked her eyes toward Ryan and straightened herself. "Now, if you'll excuse me."

Unable to gather myself enough to stop her, I watched Mira Ann glide out the door with grace and poise no villain should possess. When had she spoken to Derick? Had he really found me here? Planted a record to get me to come back to him?

Did he think something like that would work?

Mr. Shaw cleared his throat. "I'm very sorry, Casey. We will get this all settled. Just let me find your file."

I struggled to find the mask of cold calm I used to be so good at wearing. "Thank you."

Mr. Shaw walked to Mira Ann's desk and shuffled through papers, apparently looking for the deed Mira Ann hadn't filed.

I flicked a glance at Ryan, surprised to see nothing uglier than confusion on his face. I offered an explanation he hadn't asked for. "Maybe Mira Ann thought that if she delayed paperwork or something, I wouldn't get the property."

"But why?" Ryan's eyebrows lowered. "She knew that wasn't what Ida wanted. She knew how excited Ida had been to find her lost granddaughter. For nearly a year, Mira Ann had been visiting with Ida, helping her out with things."

My mouth fell open. *What?*

"I didn't think their friendship mattered." Ryan pursed his lips. "Maybe I should have told you, but I really didn't think it was important. Lots of people visited Ida."

"You didn't think it was important to mention that the

woman who desperately wanted to buy Ida's house had been weaseling her way into Ida's life?"

Ryan's face pinched. Of course he would still be protecting her.

My insides churned, rolling and bubbling like burning caramel. "She lied to me! Multiple times. I specifically asked her if she'd ever been in Ida's house, and she said no."

Ryan shoved his hands into his pockets, but his eyes stayed riveted to mine. Filled with regret.

"Hmmm." Mr. Shaw frowned over something he pulled from the bottom drawer of Mira Ann's desk.

I rubbed my temples, a headache forming from the blood pounding in my ears. I breathed slowly, trying to cool the fire pulsing through me.

None of this made any sense at all. Derick coming all the way to Maryville. Mira Ann purposely not filing paperwork. The break-in. *Think!* "We have to be missing something."

"Maybe this will help." Mr. Shaw cleared his throat, his shoulders stiff. "Looks like she drew up a draft for a power of attorney for Ida Macintyre. The paperwork was never signed, but it designates Mira Ann to handle her affairs."

I locked eyes with Ryan. His widened in disbelief. Would Ida have left the house to Mira Ann if she hadn't found me first? Why? "Mr. Shaw, may I ask what my grandmother planned to do with her house before finding me?"

He regarded me a moment. "She planned on having it sold and all the proceeds, along with the rest of her assets, donated to the Batson Children's Hospital."

Ryan's jaw tightened. "May I ask when that paper's dated?"

"February second."

Ryan's nostrils flared. "The week Ida found out her cancer had returned and they could no longer treat it."

Silence hung on the room. Things clicked into place. Mira Ann would know about Ida's assets. She had access to everything in Mr. Shaw's office. "If she found out Ida was ill, with no family to care for her and her property intended for charity, did she think to swoop in to Ida's rescue? Become the sweet, attentive neighbor that Ida would need to help with her affairs? And maybe gain control of Ida's property and assets in the process?"

Ryan looked sick.

"But then," I said, continuing to think out loud, "if she thought that possible, why not consider that Ida would have left everything to Ryan, her actual friend."

"I don't need anything. Mira Ann on the other hand..." Ryan shook his head, leaving the sentence to dangle.

"Obviously"—Mr. Shaw cleared his throat—"I have several issues to tackle." He dropped the paper on Mira Ann's desk. "I'll file the deed with the clerk myself. Today."

One monumental weight off my shoulders. I found a genuine smile. "Thank you."

"The house is yours, as well as everything inside." Mr. Shaw gestured toward the door. "We'll still need to process out her savings account and CD's, however."

Ida had thought of that, too. Must be why she'd put me on her checking account. To make sure I had money to function until the larger accounts went through processing.

Oh, Ida. What would I have done without her? I closed my eyes against the welling tears.

"I apologize for not calling in to check on you," Mr. Shaw said. "I considered the matter settled, as the deed should have been filed weeks ago."

We walked toward the door. A thought struck me, and I turned back around. "Ida had insurance on the house, right?"

He nodded.

"Can I file a claim in order to start repairs? Mira Ann told me I couldn't do any of that until the house went through processing." Served me right for trusting her.

"Certainly." Mr. Shaw tugged on his jacket again. "I believe I have a copy of the policy. If you'd like, I'll make a few calls on your behalf and see when we can have an insurance adjuster come out."

Relief bubbled up and overflowed. I owned the house. And soon, I'd have air conditioning.

I thanked the lawyer and, a few moments later, Ryan and I stepped out into the July heat. He put his hands in his pockets and looked at me, but I had no idea what to say. Where to start.

He cleared his throat. "Want to get some ice cream?"

What?

He nodded toward the end of the line of buildings, past the bank. "Sweet shop's right there. We can talk over rocky road?"

"I hate rocky road." I crossed my arms. He'd left out some pretty pertinent info on his ex. Not sure I wanted to chat over ice cream pretending the shared details in the lawyer's office hadn't just exploded everywhere like spaghetti sauce in the microwave.

His face fell. A curt nod. "I understand."

Maybe I could try. I relaxed my shoulders. Tried for one of Ryan's understanding smiles. I hadn't been upfront about Derick, either. But that was before I knew he might have something to do with all the weird things going on. "But I love mint chocolate chip."

His steady smile tingled through me, and I followed him down the sidewalk. Why couldn't I stay mad at this man? How did he always manage to diffuse my anger with his gentle eyes and steady presence? No matter what storm tried to sweep me away, he remained firm—my own concrete bunker.

After he ordered two scoops for each of us at The Sugar Hub, we sat on quaint little iron chairs at a tiny round tabletop. The adorable little shop wore a checkered black-and-white floor and red accents like a 1950s lady out for a day on the town. The counter at the back held confections of every kind, including some red velvet cupcakes that I'd have to come back and get acquainted with.

I dipped my plastic spoon into the vibrant green goodness and let the perfection of frozen mint and chocolate melt on my tongue. No matter how badly a day went, it could always improve with ice cream.

"I can't believe I didn't see the truth. I thought we were friends." Ryan's brow creased.

I dropped my spoon into my paper bowl. That didn't sound good. We *were* friends.

Ryan kept his eyes on the mound of ice cream stuffed with marshmallows. "I suppose I just wanted to think the best of her."

Oh, right. Mira Ann.

"I had no idea she'd planned on trying to take advantage of Ida." Only the clench and release of Ryan's jaw indicated his anger. "She just wanted her house and her money."

"And then I came into town, taking the house and uprooting all of her plans."

"Including assisting with the youth." His words dripped with meaning. "With me." He shook his head. "I saw the photos of us on her desk. From Gatlinburg. That was *years* ago. Her first year in college."

Apparently, he hadn't understood how much Mira Ann had wanted him back. Ryan must have thought all her flirting and working with the teens had been innocent. For such a smart man, he'd been rather oblivious. "But Mira Ann still did well with the girls." Why was I defending her? Just to see some of the betrayal erased from his face?

He grunted. "Probably an act. Just like with Ida." His mouth twisted. "I feel like an idiot."

Sweet Ryan. Always looking for the best in people. I could say maybe she did care for the kids and that her involvement wasn't just a way to get to Ryan, but that felt like a lie. One I couldn't bring myself to utter even to comfort him. Especially since she might have been trying to scam my grandmother. "Seems like she fooled a lot of people."

"I don't understand why she would have broken into your house." He stirred melting ice cream he hadn't tasted. "Maybe Derick is the one who broke in."

My stomach clenched in response to that jerk's name coming from Ryan's mouth. The very idea he'd found me in Maryville sent bile into my throat. "I don't see why. He wouldn't have known about Ida's letters." I stoked my courage and held his gaze. "About Derick—"

"Your business." He offered a rueful smile.

Ouch. Same thing I'd said to him about Mira Ann. But Ryan deserved to know. "Bad relationship. He cheated. We broke up right before Ida passed. He called a few weeks ago, but I have no intentions of ever going back to him. Which I made perfectly clear." I lifted my chin, confidence filling me in a way I never expected. "I deserve better than the way he treated me. Small compromises at a time, I ended up in a situation I never should have gotten into."

Ryan's eyes held no judgment. "I understand. Things happen."

No sermon. No condemnation. How had this man remained single so long? "Recently, I realized God was looking out for me even when I'd gotten myself in a bad situation. Ida's call proclaiming to be my biological grandmother pulled me out of a mess that could have become much worse. At exactly the right time, He provided me with a new future."

Light filled Ryan's eyes. "I love how He does that."

The side of my mouth pulled up. "Me too." I took a bite of ice cream, mostly to buy myself a second to think. "Derick's a controlling jerk. And he's also extremely selfish. But I don't think he would have come to Maryville for me, not even to cause trouble. He's not the type to think up a scheme like faking a criminal record."

Ryan sighed. "Looks like we both have someone in our lives who may have done some things we didn't expect."

"What did you and Mira Ann talk about today?" I rolled my spoon between my fingers. "Looked heated."

"I explained, in no uncertain terms, that our past relationship would never be revived." He jabbed his fingers through his hair. "She didn't take it well. Blamed you, actually."

I lifted an eyebrow. "Seems like she's made up all kinds of things to pin on me. Losing a place in Ida's will, not having a future with you. Neither of which is my fault."

Something flickered across Ryan's face but quickly disappeared. "So, what are you going to do about your mom?"

Whoa. Curveball. Guess he wanted to leave the Mira Ann thing alone for a while. I pushed aside my bowl. "Nothing." I didn't plan to do anything about Haley. The woman had abandoned me. Had even known where to find me and still chose to stay away.

"You don't want to talk to her?" Ryan pressed. "Find closure?" He leaned back in his chair, intense eyes digging into me.

The women working at the counter jabbered in the background, but the rest of the store remained empty on a weekday afternoon. I picked up my trash and stood, nervous energy spiking too much to remain seated even to enjoy the luxury of air conditioning.

Confronting my mother meant facing my past. The pains she'd caused. Ryan joined me, and we walked outside and entered the inferno of a Mississippi summer.

He took my hand and squeezed my fingers. His dark hair glistened in the bright sunlight, and his features nearly glowed with sincerity. "No matter what choices other people made, no matter your past or your mistakes, remember that you're valuable. Loved by God."

I blinked back tears and offered a sad smile.

"Ida wanted you to finish the journey, and I believe that means talking to your mother. Maybe someday forgiving her." His expressive lips curved into a hopeful smile that wormed through my excuses. "So you can finally find peace."

Something inside me shifted. Ryan had offered me so much grace. Maybe he was right. Maybe it was time I tried practicing a little grace of my own. I needed closure. I'd started this crazy plan to find out what happened to my parents. One of them held all the answers. I just had to face her one time.

And then I could finally put everything behind me.

31

Grace House

"**A**re you sure you don't want to wait for us to go with you?" Nancy's eyes filled with concern as she stood in my driveway, hand on the hood of my car.

How like her to worry over someone else on a day like this. "This is something I have to do myself." I pulled her into a hug. "But thank you." I held her back at arm's length. "You call me the second you hear something from the doctor." Her sweet smile caused an ache in my heart. "Promise?"

"I promise, dear." Nancy patted my cheek and stepped away.

Birds called to one another in the freshness of the morning, filling the muggy air with their songs. My gaze drifted over to Ryan, who watched me with his mother. Nancy stepped next to him, lifted on her toes to whisper something in his ear and then headed back across the lawn to Ryan's.

"What time is her appointment?" I watched Nancy until she closed herself inside Ryan's sunny yellow house before turning to look at him.

"Nine-thirty." Dressed in dark jeans, clean boots, and a button-down too hot for the weather, Ryan looked the part of country man heading to the city. Not that one could call Jackson any kind of booming metropolis.

I leaned back against my car. "Please call me as soon as you get the results."

Ryan leaned beside me, our shoulders touching. "No matter what happens, Mom's going to be okay."

Unless the treatments hadn't worked. Unless the cancer had only grown instead of subsiding. I couldn't bear the thought of losing Nancy in the same way I'd just lost Ida. A long breath shuddered through me, and my throat thickened.

"Mom is solid in her faith. And resilient. She's taken chemo like a champ. Most people wouldn't have ever guessed what she's been going through." Ryan comforted me as if I were the one with a parent about to find out if cancer would rob her of a vibrant life. "Whatever the outcome, she's ready."

Please, God. Let me have her a little longer.

The prayer surprised me. Not the part about wanting Nancy to be better. That made perfect sense. More the selfish part of wanting her to stay here with me.

In that instant, I knew. I didn't want to go back to Atlanta. I didn't want to find an apartment and work as a library assistant, coming home each night to a cat without a name and a home without loving neighbors.

Even if the majority of this town thought me a criminal. Even if Mira Ann always caused trouble. I didn't want to leave Maryville. Ida's house. The teens—especially Emma. What if she tried to run away again?

Before I could stop myself, words I'd mulled to myself

popped out of my mouth. "Girls like Emma. They need a place sometimes, right? A safe space?" I threw my hand toward Ida's massive Victorian. "I have plenty of it. There are so many at-risk girls and…"

Ryan stepped away from the car and faced me straight-on, eyebrows lifting. My words cut short. I stared at him. Right. Not qualified. What a crazy thing to say. Now he'd tell me how hard that would be. How emotionally draining.

I knew that. But I also…didn't care. The idea burned in me. I could do so much with the second chance Ida had given me. More than just snuggle into my own comforts.

"That's amazing." His soft words brushed over me, and his face lit into a huge grin. "There's a lot of paperwork with the state, of course. And we'd have to make plenty of preparations. There are safety regulations we'd need to consider. Certifications…"

Ryan kept talking, but I lost the rest of what he said. My brain snagged on "we." The excitement animating his face warmed me all the way to the bottom of my feet, and a sense of purpose swelled in me.

Is that what You'd like me to do, God? Stay here and help girls? Cook meals for ladies in town? Put down some roots?

The wave of both peace and excitement that washed over me had me bouncing on my toes.

"I think it could work." Ryan paused in his excited outpouring. "And with what I found out about that stock certificate…" He left the sentence to dangle and wiggled his eyebrows.

In the commotion about the house and the repairs, I'd forgotten about the twenty-five-dollar stock certificate. "What are you talking about?"

"Seems that after a few divisions and a bunch of other stuff my financially savvy friend said and that I didn't totally understand, the stock has had a dramatic increase."

Dramatic? "Like by how much?"

A goofy grin split his face. "Oh, only by about a factor of ten thousand."

My mouth dried. I'd never been good at math, but— "You mean that piece of paper is worth a quarter million?"

"Give or take. And as the sole heir, it's all yours." He glanced up at the house. "I'd say that's enough to start your catering business and a home for girls."

Wow.

"Do you think you'd be up for something like that?" He glanced toward the house. "Teen ministry takes a lot of commitment."

With the means and the motivation? Yeah. I took his fingers in mine. "I've seen firsthand how, when someone puts in a little commitment toward helping someone else, it can make a huge difference in a life."

The smile that slid over his features stirred something in me that had nothing to do with the talk of the girl's home.

Nancy bustled out of Ryan's house, a large black purse slung over her shoulder. She lifted a hand to shield her eyes from the sun. She hurried our way.

"Enough flirting, boy. We need to go."

Did his cheeks just redden? I withheld my laugh and draped Nancy in another hug. "I know. Y'all better get going or you'll be late."

Ryan checked his watch. "Late for being thirty minutes early."

Nancy cut him a reproving look. "You have to allow for traffic. I-55 can be awful this time of the morning."

After another round of promises to call me as soon as they heard something from the doctors, Nancy and Ryan pulled out of the driveway. I gave them a little wave and opened my car door.

I could do this.

Nothing like a three-hour drive to work my nerves into a lather before I got there. I eyed the envelope on my passenger seat. The back of the envelope contained a logo with a magnolia and the words "Grace House." One Google search on Ryan's phone, and I found a rehabilitation house by that name in Biloxi. Same location as the postmark.

I'd called down there. Ironically, today was the first day in my mother's program she'd be allowed visitors. Wouldn't I be a surprise?

Shaking off my own sarcasm, I slid into the car and cranked up the air conditioning. A smartphone with GPS would have been nice, but I'd written down directions from an old-fashioned map. If I could find my way around Atlanta, surely I could navigate my way through the backwoods of Mississippi to get to the Gulf Coast.

By the time I pulled into Grace House three hours later, my stomach had twisted itself into a series of knots that I'd need a surgeon to untangle. I checked in at a front gate and pulled around the paved driveway to a massive mansion.

Whoa. Fancy place.

White columns held up a wide front balcony, where residents sat in rocking chairs eye level with the hanging moss of giant live oaks. Grace House looked like something right out of the antebellum period. How had Haley afforded a place like this?

But what did I know? She could be some rich housewife.

No wonder she hadn't cared to meet me. I pulled around to the parking area designated for guests and settled my ratty Toyota into a marked spot.

The salty breeze hit me as soon as I stepped out of the car. I breathed deeply. Said a quick little prayer for strength and marched up to the house. Along with the rocking chairs, the front porch held tables with chess boards and even a folding table covered with a yellow plastic tablecloth and two jugs of lemonade.

An A-frame sign by the open front door said, "Welcome, visitors!" in cheery blue chalk. I stepped inside, my knotted stomach clenching. Sweat broke out along my collarbone despite the AC. This was probably a very bad idea.

I should go. Wait until she got out or—

"Ma'am?" A blonde woman with a clipboard and a white oxford shirt with the words *Grace House* embroidered on the chest stepped in front of me. "Who are you here to see today?"

I opened my mouth. Closed it. Swallowed. Tried again. "Haley...Macintyre." Assuming she still carried my father's name.

The pert woman frowned as she scanned her list. "She's not expecting a visitor today." Her blue eyes flicked back up to me.

"She didn't know I was coming. It's a surprise."

A professional smile tilted her glossed lips. She pulled the clipboard to her chest. "I'm sorry, we only allow—"

"I'm her daughter."

The woman's blue eyes widened. "Oh."

"You can tell her, if you want. I'm Casey." I shoved my hands in my pockets. "If she doesn't want to see me, I'll go."

And that would be the end of it. No one could say I didn't try.

The woman nodded and hurried off, leaving me in the entryway as more people filed in around me. I moved to stand by a large potted plant near the cream-colored wall. Wooden floors topped with colorful rugs filled a reception area just off the side of the main check-in counter. Families sat on overstuffed chairs and couches, their stiff postures indicating this was no joyful summer visit.

The patients were mostly easy to spot. Women with tired eyes. Some with rueful smiles. Many with tears on their cheeks as they pulled children to them. I watched one dark-haired woman kneel on the floor as three little ones clung to her.

Leaving children, even to get help in a place like this, couldn't be easy. Good for her. That woman showed a lot of courage to get her life cleaned up. And by the looks of the man watching over the huddle, she had someone who still believed in her.

"Ma'am?" The blond woman's voice found me again, and I pried my eyes away from the family in the room across from me.

"Follow me, please."

She turned and hurried off before I could say anything. Haley wanted to see me? I glanced toward the open door. Still time to bolt.

The blonde woman skirted around the receiving desk. Forcing my feet into motion, I followed. We walked down a wide hallway covered in framed landscape paintings and through a screen door to another giant porch on the back of the mansion. Beyond the railing, a small grassy yard boasted two more massive trees dripping with airy moss.

"Haley? Your visitor's here." The woman spun around and smiled at me. "Visiting hours end at two."

She stepped aside, giving me my first look at the woman who had abandoned me. Despite all the pain writhing in my chest, I drank her in. Shoulder-length hair the same deep brown as my own. Thin shoulders. Hands that twisted together. Dressed in simple khaki pants and a plain blue tee, she reached a shaking hand to push her hair behind her ear. Brown eyes roamed my face. She took one step. Then another.

I stayed rooted to the spot.

"Cassandra?" Tears filled Haley's eyes and spilled down her cheeks. "You look so much like your father."

At the sound of her voice, something in me cracked. I took a step away from her. My chest heaved. Why had I come here? This would only lead to more hurt.

Haley watched me, so much sadness in her eyes that, though I wanted to run, I couldn't move. She gestured toward a pair of rocking chairs. "I bet you have a lot of questions."

Questions. Right. That's why I'd come. I scrambled for footing. Anything to anchor myself and dispel the fear trying to keep my lungs from filling.

Hold it in. Hold yourself together.

I drew sticky air in through my nose and let it out through my mouth. All I had to do was sit down for a couple of minutes and get this woman to explain to me why she'd put me up for adoption. Then I could go home. To Ida's house. To Nancy and Ryan.

Start a new life.

We sat in two rocking chairs angled toward one another

yet still facing the yard. No one else sat on the back porch.

I watched the moss in the trees a moment and asked my first question without looking at her. "What happened the night my father died?"

The quick intake of air indicated Haley hadn't expected that. But it seemed like the best place to start.

She spoke slowly, her voice filled with enough sorrow to lacerate the shield I tried to hold over my trembling heart. "We'd had a fight. There'd been several." She clenched her hands. "I yelled at him. Blamed him for not taking a job at the chicken plant I knew he would have hated, just so we could afford a place of our own." Tears leaked down her cheeks, and she closed her eyes.

Without her seeing me, I turned my head to watch her fully. Her cheeks seemed hollow. Skin dull. What vice had landed her here?

"He got upset. Wanted to go for a ride to clear his head. But it started raining. The roads were slick." Her voice cracked, and she drew her arms up around herself. "A truck driver didn't see him on his motorcycle."

I knew the rest, thanks to Ida. No need to make her say more. "What happened...after?"

Haley kept her head leaned back against the white rocking chair but opened her eyes. More tears flooded down her cheeks, but she didn't wipe them away.

I settled back against my own chair and waited. This couldn't be easy for her.

"I ran." Her voice gathered strength but still sounded hollow. "Found out I was pregnant about a month after the funeral. I'd been so distraught I hadn't even noticed I'd missed my cycle. I worked two jobs. But in the end, I knew I couldn't care for you like I should. My head wasn't right.

I'd started drinking. Just to be able to sleep. But when I woke up one morning to realize you'd been screaming all night..." Haley pressed her fist into her mouth. "That's when I knew. Something bad would happen if I kept you."

Her words settled around us. Haley put her head in her hands, shoulders shaking quietly. Not a huge revelation. Not really all that different from what I'd figured must have happened. Still, hearing the truth from her, seeing how giving up her child had torn her up, dissolved a chunk of my anger.

What would Ryan do here? Comfort her. Show some of the grace God kept showing me. I reached out hesitantly and placed my hand on her back. Felt bones. She stilled. I rubbed small circles. My attempt at consoling her wasn't much, but I couldn't muster anything more.

Haley turned to me, eyes shimmering. "I kept up with you over the years. Saw a nice couple adopted you. Many years later, when I found you again, you had a fancy apartment and a husband."

My heart pinched as hope filled her eyes.

"You had a better life than I could have given you. I thank God each day for watching out for my little girl."

And He had. Just maybe not in the way she thought. I removed my hand and laced my fingers together in my lap. Haley didn't need to know all the details of the mess in between. At least, not right now. I stared at my hands. "So, why did you contact Ida after all this time?"

Haley brushed her cheeks and tucked her hair behind her ears. "Jesus."

I cut a glance at her.

A sheepish smile turned her thin lips, and a light bounced into her eyes. "When I came here, they kept talking about Jesus. His grace." She sat a little taller. "I found it difficult to believe them at first. But eventually, I broke. When I had nothing at all left, I turned to Him. Everything changed."

Haley looked at me, eyes earnest. "I can't fix the past. But I knew Ida would want to know about you. I should have told her years ago." The light in her eyes dimmed again. "I held on to bitterness for way too long. Blamed Ida when I should have made things right with her." She pulled her lip through her teeth, the same awkward habit I had when I got nervous. "She would have loved to know you growing up, and I wanted to hurt her by taking that away from her."

The pain in Haley's eyes knifed through my stomach, loosening knots.

"After coming here, learning to trust God, I wanted to try to make things right the only way I could. I'm guessing she found you." Haley swallowed hard. "How's she doing?"

I pressed my lips together, and Haley frowned.

"Ida passed away in May."

Tears gathered in her eyes again and coursed down her cheeks. "Oh, no. I was too late."

"Not entirely." I leaned back in my chair and closed my eyes, just as she had done. I told her all about my life in Atlanta, Derick, and getting Ida's call. Our visit, and how good it had been. I told her about Ida's passing and about how she'd left the house to me, leaving out the details about Mira Ann and false criminal records. When I opened my eyes again, I found Haley watching me. "If Ida hadn't found me at that exact time, I don't know what would have happened to me."

Haley placed a hand to her throat. "God's provision."

Yeah.

She rocked back in her chair, gliding in a smooth rhythm. "Tell me about your childhood."

So much for saving her from that. I gave a brief account of the truth. No need to hurt her with more details than necessary, but I wouldn't hide anything either.

Haley shook her head. "I'm so sorry. I wanted to give you something better…"

Surprising myself, I took her hand. "We all have regrets. Made mistakes. All we can do is move forward and not let the past consume us." Wow. Where had that come from? Maybe Ida had been right. Spending time with Jesus did things to people.

I cleared my throat and dropped her hand. "Anyway, I live in Ida's house now. I have a job waiting on me in Atlanta, but I think I'm going to call in my resignation."

Her eyebrows lifted. "You're staying in Maryville?" She barked out an ironic laugh. "How in the world did my child end up right back in the town I tried to escape?"

Awkward laughter bubbled out of me. Funny how things worked out. I set my rocker into motion again. "How'd you end up here?"

"A very persistent preacher's wife."

I cocked an eyebrow.

"She found me in a soup kitchen her husband runs downtown here in Biloxi. Wouldn't let go until she convinced me to come here." She looked up at the blue porch roof with fondness. "Church paid for everything. Best thing that ever happened to me."

We rocked a while longer. "When do you get out?"

"Next week, actually."

I nodded. Wanted to ask what she planned to do next, but part of me didn't want to know. She'd probably disappear again. Somehow, I was okay with that. All the anger and loathing I'd held on to for years slid off me and puddled on the floor of the Grace House porch. I couldn't hold my hurts against this broken woman any longer.

I didn't know how, but I wanted to forgive her. To let go. Nothing would really change, but I sensed my wounds would finally close. I checked my watch. Almost two. I rose, and Haley stood with me.

"I..." She bit her lower lip. "Thank you for coming here. I never thought I'd get to see you again." She shrugged awkwardly. "At least, not up close."

Feeling scrubbed raw, I offered her an uncomfortable farewell and left her on the porch. I held myself together until I made it to my car.

Inside the Toyota's protective shell, I let all the pain I'd allowed to fester come out in a cleansing flood of gut-wrenching sobs.

32

Loose Ends

hree missed calls from Ryan. Not good. I punched in his number and pulled out of the parking lot at Grace House. After two rings, the line connected.

"How'd it go?"

"How's your mom?"

We spoke at the same time. My question seemed far more important. I merged into traffic and pulled onto Highway 90. The Gulf of Mexico lapped against the white sand just on the other side of the pavement. Someday, maybe I'd get a chance to see what a relaxing day on the beach felt like.

"Great news. Scans are clean." The smile in Ryan's voice brought more tears to my eyes. I blinked them away and focused on the traffic in front of me.

Thank you, Lord.

"She'll go back for follow-ups in three months, but it looks like the surgery and chemo put her into remission. At least, the scans looked clear."

"Oh, Ryan." My voice cracked. "I'm so glad to hear that."

I merged onto I-110 and headed north. To Maryville. To, finally, some good news.

"Mom wants us to go out to celebrate when you get home. Are you up for that?"

"Of course." Why would I want to miss celebrating with my two favorite people? The idea warmed my insides. "I should be back around five. Dinner?"

A smile filled his voice. "It's a date."

Unexpected laughter bubbled out of my core, spreading soothing fingers over my aching heart. "How romantic. You, me, and your mom."

The line grew quiet. Uh-oh. I sat a little straighter in my seat. I opened my mouth to tell him I was only kidding, but his chuckle cut me off.

"Maybe we could call it old-fashioned courting. Chaperone and all."

Whoa. Ryan had thoughts about dating me? Or was he only poking fun at me because it sounded like I'd asked him out? Breathing deep, I laughed again and parroted his words. "It's a date."

"So how about Friday we go out on a modern one?" He chuckled. "Without the chaperone."

Ryan wanted to go out with me? "Like, as friends, right?"

"Uh—"

Great. I'd made monumental mess out of—

"Man, I must be bad at this. Let me try again. Casey Adams, would you like to go out on a real date with me? Not as friends, but as an I-want-to-be-a-couple date. Where I take you to dinner. Hold your hand. Get to know you with every intention of this leading to a romantic future down the road."

Air stuck to my lungs like peanut butter. Heat scorched up my neck, and my stomach did a weird little flop and flutter thing. "Can't think of anything I'd like more."

He laughed. "Oh good. Finally figured out how to ask bluntly enough."

Laughter released some of the tension lingering in my chest. After promising to tell him everything about what happened with Haley when we were face-to-face, we said our good-byes, and I closed my phone, conflicting emotions swirling around within me. Elation over a possible future with Ryan, a good man who would treat me well. Excitement over the possibilities waiting in Maryville.

And soul-wrenching pain over meeting my birth mother.

Sometimes I hated how I felt so much. Wouldn't life be easier if every emotion didn't seem like its depths could drown me? But maybe if I was the kind of person to hurt deeply, I could also be the kind to love deeply.

The thought of Emma and girls like her, like the child I'd been, filled my mind again, infusing me with a sense of purpose. Loving kids with messed-up lives might hurt, but they would be worth the effort.

About an hour later, I exited in Hattiesburg and followed the signs to a Chick-fil-A. In the parking lot, I dug through my purse until I found the tiny little notebook where I'd written down the information I needed. It was definitely time to splurge on a modern phone. One that saved names and numbers, dialed for me, and found restaurants wherever I asked.

I checked the clock. 3:21. The office might still be open. With a quick prayer for courage, I dialed the number to Mid Atlanta High School and asked the receptionist to put me through to Principal Grady. One very awkward conversation later, I'd explained my situation with my new inheritance and resigned from my position.

Thankfully, even with only one week before teachers reported to school, he didn't seem overly upset with my withdrawal. Probably because I was only an assistant librarian. Not exactly a difficult position to fill. A weight lifted off my chest, and I hurried inside for a bathroom break and a quick snack before hitting the road again.

After popping the last chicken nugget in my mouth and wiping my fingers, I pulled out my phone for one last call. The one I dreaded the most.

Derick's confident voice filled my ear. "I knew you'd come to your senses. Finally figured out it's time to come home?"

Anger uprooted any discomfort at having to call him. Maybe Mira Ann had been right. Derick might do anything to stay in control. "You have a lot of nerve, you know that?"

"What?" His voice filled with annoyed confusion. "You called me, remember?"

"And *you* created a fake criminal record and broke into my house! What for? To try to find more ways to sabotage me? Figured if I wouldn't snivel at your feet, you'd try to ruin my new life?"

I'd never yelled at Derick before. The line was quiet for a few seconds. "I have no idea what you're talking about. You're crazy." His cruel chuckle made my skin crawl. "What makes you think you're worth all that trouble, babe?" When I didn't answer, he said, "Where are you, anyway? Living in your car? Offer still stands for you to come back to—"

I snapped the phone closed. Derick wanted me to come

crawling back to him, tail between my legs and without any other options than to depend on him. If he *had* come to Maryville, he wouldn't have done so in secret.

At least now I knew for sure. No one else could have planted the file or broken into the house. Problem was, I still didn't have any evidence on Mira Ann. No security cameras in the church. No proof she'd rifled through Ida's letters in my kitchen in the middle of the night.

The exit for Maryville beckoned, and a weird sense of comfort settled over me as I turned into the tiny town. Who would have ever thought I'd feel so at ease in a town that boasted a population of four hundred?

I turned into my driveway and put the car in park. Stepping out, I gazed up at Ida's Victorian. Filled with stories. My stories. Those of my family. They weren't all good, but they were mine. I finally had all the answers I'd wanted, only to realize that the truth of the past never had the power to define me.

"Hey, neighbor!" Ryan's voice tugged me from my musings. "Ready for supper?"

Still dressed in the nice clothes he'd worn earlier, Ryan sauntered over like he'd been waiting on me to return.

I popped the door closed with my hip. "Give me five to freshen up?"

"Sure. Mom's getting ready too." He lifted his broad shoulders, goofy smile plastered on his lips. "Waiting on women. It's what men do."

I rolled my eyes. Fifteen minutes later, I'd found a little mascara for my neglected lashes, put on a swath of lip gloss, and paired my best jeans with my favorite pink church blouse. I bounded down the stairs to find both Ryan and Nancy swinging on my front porch.

Nancy jumped up from the swing and, before I could even offer a greeting or congratulations, dropped a bomb. "I invited Mira Ann."

My stomach plunged. "You did *what*?"

Nancy lifted her chin and rose to her full five-two height. "We're going to get this little squabble between you girls cleared up."

Little squabble? That *girl* had tried to rob me and ruin my life. I crossed my arms. "She started it."

The look on Nancy's face told me I sounded like a bratty child, but I didn't particularly care. Truth was truth. Mira Ann had started this mess. And I intended to see she got all the punishment she deserved.

The seething thought immediately caused a pinch in my chest I wanted to ignore.

If you don't forgive men their trespasses, neither will your Father forgive your trespasses.

The verse popped into my mind unbidden. Right. Forgive as you have been forgiven. And I had been forgiven plenty. But still.

This is what happens when you spend too much time reading the Bible.

I tried to shush my inner voice, but it continued to argue with my convictions.

"Besides," Nancy continued, giving me a no-nonsense look. "I want to see what she has to say for herself."

Ryan glanced between me and his mother, clearly as uncomfortable as I felt. Had he known about this plan? From the shock written on his face, probably not. But neither of us would dare tell her she couldn't invite whomever she wished on her own remission celebration dinner.

Thirty unpleasant seconds later, a giant white SUV pulled into the driveway; a white whale next to my rusted goldfish. I watched Mira Ann step out, all pomp and circumstance. Something ugly churned within me. Who did she think she was? What made her think she could just crush people who got in the way of what she wanted?

Love your enemies.

Aw, man. How was a girl supposed to seethe in justified anger when Bible verses kept telling her to douse the flames?

Mira Ann waltzed up to us, confidence in every clip of her sparkly wedge sandals. Clad in an airy summer dress that fell much too high on her thighs, she showed off every asset I'd never possess. Perfectly toned legs. Sculpted arms. Tiny waist.

I inwardly groaned. How would I ever compete with that? Sure, Ryan had asked me out. But this literal girl-next-door was far too plain compared to the kind he'd been with before.

No. I pushed the self-doubt away. I was worth more than my figure.

"Mira Ann." Nancy stepped forward, taking the place of greeter since neither I nor Ryan were inclined to do so. "Thanks for coming."

She flicked a glance at me. "Sure. Thanks for asking."

We stood in awkward silence a moment. No way would I be the one to say anything. This was Nancy's idea.

"Mira Ann, I'd like for us to clear up a few things." Nancy patted her coifed hair and presented herself as kind, yet firm. The quintessential Nancy. "Would that be all right with you?"

Mira Ann flicked her hair over her shoulder. "Yes, ma'am."

"First, why did you tell Casey you'd never been in Ida's house when you had?"

That apparently surprised her. Mira Ann's features tightened. "I didn't want her thinking I was after the house."

What? Everyone knew she was after my house. Why would saying she'd been here to visit Ida before change that? Thankfully, Ryan spoke so I didn't have to.

"You mean the B&B you talked about the day you met Casey?" His eyebrows drew low over his nose. "She already knew you wanted the house weeks before you told her you'd never been here before. And besides that, why would you want to buy a house you'd never seen? That wouldn't make much sense at all."

"Well, yes, but—"

"And is that also why you refused to file the deed on the house?" Unable to help myself, I jumped on Ryan's reprimanding tone and threw in a dash of my own scathing accusation. "Because you somehow thought if I didn't know I already owned the house then I would...what? Just hand the place over to you?"

Her lip curled, but then the look of contempt vanished and a patronizing smile returned. "As I said before when you stormed into my office, I'm sorry I misplaced your papers. Things like that happen."

When had she ever said she was sorry?

"You're the one who said the house was in probate." Mira Ann's placating smile stoked the inferno already blazing inside me. "Bless your heart, I suppose you just got that confused with me telling you we had some things still in probate and that there was paperwork that still needed to be filed."

The evening air wrapped us in sweltering heat, amping up the already hot atmosphere. I clenched my teeth. I may have misunderstood what all the legal terms meant, but I had *not* mistaken the fact that Mira Ann had purposely tried to stall the process.

Ryan sighed. "Come on Mi, why are you doing this?"

The timbre of his voice and the use of a pet name for her felt like a hot knife straight through my stomach. My insides roiled in response.

Mira Ann reached for Ryan, but he held up a hand and shook his head.

Her eyes flashed fire. The rejection seemed to finally rip the mask right off her face.

"She ruined everything!" Mira Ann threw up her hands. "I had plans for us. For me." Tears shimmered in her eyes like lightning sparking in storm clouds. "And then *she* shows up out of nowhere and steals my dreams. Everything I worked for!"

The venom in Mira Ann's tone prickled along my skin. I hadn't intended to take anything from this woman. I'd had no nefarious plans. No premeditated coups. I hadn't moved to Maryville homeless and grieving with the intent of dethroning the local beauty queen and snatching any ruby slippers off her feet.

Nancy's eyes softened, and she wrapped a comforting arm around Mira Ann. Great. Chalk up another point for Mira Ann's acting skills.

"And the files at the church?" Nancy asked softly. "Was that you, too?"

Mira Ann hung her head, suddenly deflated, as though releasing the scalding words had punctured holes in her persona she knew she couldn't repair. "I thought if she couldn't work with the kids..."

My mouth fell open. How had Nancy done that? Gotten Mira Ann to confess with nothing more than a gentle touch and a direct question?

Ryan pulled in a long breath, the muscles in his neck taut. "You used your legal knowledge to make a fake record just so Casey couldn't work with teens?" He shook his head. "What's gotten into you?"

"I wanted to work with you. We belong together." Her eyes sparkled with tears before they slid down her cheeks, trailing black mascara. "Don't you see that?"

Nancy removed her arm from around Mira Ann's waist. "Didn't you still help out with the youth? I saw you and Casey both back there."

Her eyes shot sparks again. "I'm not sharing anything with *her*."

Yikes. Suddenly I saw Mira Ann not as a perfect pageant queen but as an insecure woman who'd let desperation make her pin her hurts on someone else. I'd made an easy target. I'd inherited the house she wanted. Was invited into the ministry of the man she longed for. He wanted a future with me when all she held was his past. Something in me twisted.

Did I feel *sorry* for her now?

Wow. I really had been spending too much time in that Bible. I brushed the sarcastic thought aside. No, letting God reshape my jaded, judgmental, and bitter heart was a good thing. Even if it meant learning how to keep forgiving people who'd wronged me.

Look at that. You're growing.

I smiled to myself, knowing the inner voice was right for once. I gentled my tone as best I could, hovering somewhere on the line of detached and kind. "I never tried to take anything from you, Mira Ann. Ida found me. Brought me here. Leaving me the house was her choice."

She wrapped her arms around herself. "She never even mentioned me. I didn't mean anything to her at all."

Ryan, Nancy, and I shared a glance.

"What do you mean, dear?" Nancy asked.

"The letters. She wrote all that stuff to Casey, telling stories. I wasn't in any of them." She wiped a hand over her cheek, smearing mascara. "She never taught me any of those things, no matter how many Saturday afternoons I spent out here."

Time most likely spent trying to be near Ryan rather than visiting with Ida. I rubbed my temples. "You broke into the house just to read Ida's letters?"

Mira Ann ignored me, her imploring eyes searching Ryan's face. "I saw you with her on the porch. How you looked at her. Held her hand." Her chin quivered. "You stayed over. The two of you talking about some kind of treasure together, and I just...I just had to know what was in those letters. If Ida had said anything about me. Wanted me to have something that"—Mira Ann cut her eyes at me again—"*she* wouldn't have wanted me to see. Ida wouldn't have just left me out like that. I know it. Casey's hiding things from us."

Wow. Mira Ann had mentioned something about old rumors that Ida had more assets than she'd let on, and true enough, Ida did have an old stock worth a hefty sum. But did Mira Ann really think Ida would have left letters that passed secret treasures to her outside of the will and think I tried to hide them? The woman had a screw loose. Maybe an entire box's worth.

"Hold on." I fisted a hand on my hip and demanded Mira Ann's attention. "So you committed a felony just so you could read my letters from my grandmother? The ones meant to tell me about what happened to my parents and why my mother deserted me?" I tilted my head. "Just to see if *you* were in them?"

She glared at me. "You just get everything, don't you? The grandmother, the perfect house..." Her lips quivered. "A good man." She stepped away from us, eyes wide. "And what do I get? A con-man dad no one will forgive, more debt than I can ever hope to repay, no family, and the now the contempt of...of..." Her wild gaze landed on Ryan.

"I feel no contempt for you, Mi." Ryan reached for her, but she backed away.

"Fine." She threw her hands up. "I give up." She pointed a finger at me. "Take it. You can have it all." She whirled around, green dress flaring, and stomped toward her massive vehicle that surely had to contribute to that debt she'd mentioned.

We watched her peel out of the driveway. Ryan's fingers flexed and relaxed at his sides. Nancy clicked her tongue. The three of us stood in awkward silence on the porch, no one having much to say about the crazy that had just splattered everywhere. At least now everyone knew the truth. In another life, I probably would have proudly spouted that I'd told them all along Mira Ann was the villain of this story, but right now I just felt exhausted. All I really wanted was an escape from the drama.

"Well," Nancy finally said. "I guess it'll be just the three of us for dinner."

33

All the Stories Are Here

*W*eek one of my new life passed by in a blur. Hammers pounded outside as the repairs hit full swing. Mr. Shaw had pulled a lot of strings, and the insurance company had processed the claim in record time. The next day, men in work boots began to suture the wound in the dining room. The pounding had become a welcome addition to my day, a reminder that both healing and rebuilding required a lot of work.

I'd slept peacefully the night before, cool air allowing me the comfort of snuggling under the quilt for the first time in weeks. I hummed to myself as I dusted in the living room, my fingers trailing along Ida's photograph. If she hadn't reached out to me, believed in me, cared for me when she didn't even know me, I never would have gotten this second chance.

"I promise I'll do my best with what you've given me." I kissed my finger and placed it on Ida's face, then wiped the smudge away and put the frame back on the mantel.

Meow.

Where had that cat gotten to now? I leaned down to

peek under the couch. "You're like Schrödinger's cat. Never know if you are here or not." I laughed to myself. "Maybe that's what I should call you. Schrödinger."

Kitty wiggled out from under the recliner, her furry body as flat as a pancake. I gaped at her. "How in the world did you do that?"

She swished her giant tail and licked a paw as if she dared me to accomplish such a feat. The oven timer dinged, and I hurried into the kitchen to check my lasagna. Cheese bubbled on the perfectly browned top, and the concoction filled the kitchen with the scent of Italian goodness. I tugged two large trays and one small pan from the oven and placed them on the stove top. They'd need to cool before I packaged everything and made my first catering delivery.

Turned out small-town gossip ran both ways. As soon as everyone found out I wasn't really a felon, I'd taken my place with the youth group again and filled three catering orders for this week. A good start.

The hammering in the other room pounded out an uneven rhythm. Kitty growled at the noise and darted through the kitchen like a crazed streak of gray lightning. Maybe I could name her Speedy. Another knocking came from the front of the house. Had someone started hammering out there, too?

Throwing a dish towel over my shoulder, I headed toward the foyer. Kitty scurried between my feet, tripping me. I grabbed the doorframe, barely keeping my balance.

"Crazy cat! What's gotten into you?"

Kitty scooted under the sewing machine, tail swishing. At least she hadn't jumped on top of it again and broken a second vase. Another knocking came. Not a hammer. Someone was knocking on the door. Probably one of the workers with another question. Being a homeowner came with lots of questions.

Or maybe Ryan was coming to ask for a second date. A grin pulled my lips up. Maybe I'd beat him to it. Offer a romantic homemade dinner by candlelight and try to taste a little of my tiramisu on those perfect lips—

I opened the front door and lost my breath. How in the—?

Haley?

We stared at one another. Dressed in the same outfit I'd seen her in at Grace House, my birth mother stood on my porch, twisting her hands. What was she doing here?

She shoved her stringy hair behind both ears. "I...uh, hi."

After a few tries, I found my voice. "What are you doing here?"

Hurt flashed in her eyes, and she dropped her head. "Sorry. I shouldn't have come. But I didn't have a number to call so—" She cut herself off and bit her bottom lip. "I'll go." She turned on her heel.

Suddenly, that moment from Ida's letter leapt into my mind's eye. Mike bringing Haley to this very door. Ida standing in this exact spot and turning her away. "Wait!"

Haley looked over her shoulder, eyes filled with so many emotions that I felt them reach out and pull me into their riptide.

"You just startled me." I offered a half smile. "Never expected you on the doorstep." Glancing behind her, I didn't see a car. How had she gotten here? "Time at Grace House over?"

She nodded. "You'd said you inherited Ida's house." She shrugged and stared at her feet. "Just thought I'd come by and check on you."

The first thing she did after getting out of rehab was to come check on me? I opened the door a little wider. "Want to come in? We could have lunch."

Haley's eyes brightened. "Really?"

The hope in her voice twisted my insides. For years, I'd blamed my parents for abandoning me. For all the pains and hurts and disappointments I'd faced. Yet the broken woman before me had shoulders too thin to carry that weight. Jesus said something about letting Him shoulder burdens.

One step at a time. Just like Ida had said. I might not be ready to let everything go, but I could shift my hurt off of Haley and hand my disappointments to Someone more equipped to handle them.

"Of course. You're welcome here any time." A genuine smile curved my lips. Ida's house was all about second chances. She'd want to give Haley one, too.

Tears shimmered in her eyes. "Thank you."

Kitty suddenly bolted around my legs and onto the porch. Haley yelped as the cat darted past her and made a flying leap into the grass.

Not again.

I hurried past Haley and into the yard. Which way had she gone? "Kitty! Here, Kitty!" I peered under the gardenia at the edge of the porch. "Kitty, kitty, meow, meow."

I fisted my hands on my hips and looked up at Haley, who stood on the porch wringing her hands. "Did you see which way she went?"

Haley shook her head. "I'll help you look."

We made our way around the house to where the men had apparently taken a lunch break. The massive truck topped with ladders had pulled out, taking the four-man crew with it. Likely up to the Hornet Hive in town for some chicken gizzards. Sawhorses, circular saws, and piles of discarded lumber littered the yard. No sign of the cat.

"Wooda wooda wooda wooda!"

I turned toward the weird noise. Haley puckered her mouth and made the strange call again, her gaze scanning the yard.

I cocked my head. "What are you doing?"

Haley lifted her eyebrows. "Calling for the cat." She puckered her mouth again as if she were about to whistle. "Wooda wooda wooda."

Meow.

No way. I turned toward the sound and motioned to Haley. "Do it again."

Haley made the weird noise, and a second later Kitty poked her head out from underneath a mangled bush. The one struggling to survive after being squished by the big tree. I crossed my arms. Crazy cat.

She wiggled out, fuzz skimming the grass, and stretched, arching her back like her maddening dash out of the house had been nothing but a fun game. Kitty swayed past me. I reached for her, but she arched out of my grasp. She swished her tail and sidled up to Haley. She sniffed her leg and rubbed her whiskered face against her khakis.

"Huh. She never came to kitty, kitty."

Haley reached down to rub the cat's ears. "My dad always made that noise for cats. Guess I just fell back on what my dad always did."

Another family story. The first good one I'd shared with my mother. I grinned, a crazy thought dawning. I tried out the weird name. "Woo-duh."

Haley scooped the cat up and nuzzled her. As she buried

her face in the soft fur, the tension in her shoulders dissolved. Kitty had that effect. I watched Haley with the cat. She'd make a good house pet when I got the teen ministry house running.

"That's what he always did," Haley said, catching me watching her. "But I don't know why. I just remember being young and him calling the barn cats like that." A wistful smile turned up her lips just before she kissed the cat's fuzzy head.

"That's her name. Wooda."

Haley stared at me in confusion. "It's not a name. It's just…" She tilted her head. "A noise."

And a story. I grinned. "And now it's her name. Besides, she needs one. I've been calling her Kitty." I shrugged. "And I don't think she liked any of the other names I tried."

"Like what?"

I named off a few. "Loco, Spaz, Rascal, Pinball."

Haley watched me, amusement lighting her brown eyes. "Up to you. They all sound good to me."

She cradled the cat and followed me into the house. Over lunch I asked Haley all about her childhood. The stories came slowly at first, but little by little I pulled treasured memories out of her. Later, after time and getting to know one another, I'd ask her more about what happened to her after my father's death. For now, happy memories would be enough. Ida had used the same tactic on me. So far, the plan had a pretty good track record.

I poured sweet tea, and we sat in the living room, the awkwardness of one another's company slowly fading. Haley's eyes traveled over the pictures, lingering on ones of Mike. She slipped her worn sneakers off her feet and pulled her legs underneath her on the couch. "Looks just like I remember."

"Is it hard for you, coming back here?"

Kitty—Wooda—jumped into Haley's lap, made a few turns, and started kneading her soft paws against Haley's leg.

"In some ways, yes." Her eyes found mine and filled with something I couldn't quite place. An emotion I sensed held a lot of meaning. "In other ways, coming here is one of the best decisions I ever made."

We chatted for the rest of the afternoon, and I told her about the storm and the repairs. About Nancy and Ryan. We talked about my dream of running a catering business and maybe one day a small restaurant, and I told her about my idea of a house for teen girls. A spark of excitement lit her eyes at that, reminding me Haley had also fit into that "at-risk teen girl" category at one point in her life. Maybe she could stay here. Help me with the ministry.

But I'd start with asking her to stay the night.

I checked my watch. "I have to go. I need to make some deliveries. But I'll be back in a little while, and we can make supper together."

Her eyes glistened. "I'd like that."

I hurried through my trip around Maryville, thanking ladies for placing their orders and handing out next week's menu. Gurdie promised to pass my list around to the other ladies in her Bible study group and predicted I'd have plenty of orders come Sunday.

About an hour later, I returned home. I lingered a moment in the driveway, looking up at the house filled with stories. My stories. They'd never really been gone. Only hidden. Ida's journey had taught me a lot. Given me a fresh start and a new sense of purpose.

A house of new beginnings.

Before going inside, I stepped around the side of the house to check on the repairs. The new AC hummed merrily. The work crew had left for the day but had made a lot of progress. A solid wall now stood where there'd been only a gaping hole. The blue tarp now draped the roof—a project for another day—and the exterior woodwork still needed to be finished. Bright pink insulation coated the new wall with a protective blanket to keep in that wonderful new air conditioning.

Feeling lighter than I had in years, I bounded up the front porch stairs and through the front door. I dropped my keys on the top of the sewing machine. "Haley?"

No answer.

My stomach dropped. Had she left me again? I stepped into the living room, heart clenching.

On the couch, Haley had curled onto her side, her fist tucked under her chin. Her chest rose and fell evenly with peaceful sleep. Wooda had welcomed my mother into our makeshift family by pushing her right off the couch pillow. The fuzzy cat's long gray hair draped over Haley's forehead. I chuckled to myself.

I'd let her sleep while I made supper. Upstairs, I pulled my quilt off my bed. I ran my finger over the squares. Each one represented a memory. One where I'd pulled together the fragmented pieces of my past and made something beautiful.

Kind of like what God kept doing with my heart.

I tiptoed down to the living room and draped my quilt over Haley. She snuggled deeper, a contented sigh escaping from her parted lips. I watched her for a moment, then leaned down and whispered a kiss on her temple.

"Sweet dreams, Mom."

Acknowledgments

While Casey's story is entirely her own, in many ways Casey dealing with the loss of Ida mirrored my own heart in losing my grandmother. After her passing, I took some time off from writing. Then suddenly one day this entire story bloomed in my heart, and in a matter of a couple of months, I had it on paper. Ida's love for quilts, canning tomatoes, the old sewing machine, and the cedar trunk (minus the secret compartment!) all came from my own Mamaw. I'm thankful for all she taught me. As I'm writing this, jars of fig jelly made from her recipe are cooling on my kitchen counter.

The cedar key on the cover was actually carved by my own grandfather and we were able to use it for the cover art. It's a fun treasure I get to keep to go along with the book.

Thank you, Momma, for all you did to help me plan, plot, and execute this book. You found old pictures, family stories, and other things that made the story work. I couldn't have done it without you! I enjoyed our mornings spent plotting over coffee. I'm thankful to have a mother who is also my friend.

Thank you to my critique partners and my editors Robin and Linda. Y'all are awesome! I'd also like to thank Ms. Nancy Fredrick, who not only let me borrow her name for my character, but who also graciously allowed me to use her recipes for the companion recipe booklet.

I'm grateful to have been able to pepper Mr. Brad Ellis with questions about the Scott County Sheriff's department in order to write about Deputy Miller. Thank you for answering my questions, and thank you, Mr. Ellis, and all the men and women at the Scott County Sheriff's Department for everything you do each day protecting citizens. Any errors in my characters' mannerisms, clothing, or procedures are entirely my fault.

A huge thanks to my readers. I love you all. No story I create is complete without you. Your imagination is what brings words on a page to life. Thank you for your reviews (they mean so much!), your emails, and your company on social media. It's amazing to have so many great friends out there.

Finally, and most importantly, I'm thankful for the gracious God who has gifted me with the love of story. I pray that somehow He uses my books to bring you closer to Him. He writes the most beautiful stories of all.

Discussion Questions

1) Casey struggles with her identity and believes her worth is found in what she does or who her family is. Have you ever struggled with this same issue?

2) Ida wanted Casey to learn from her past, but not be defined by it. Do you think Casey ever learned Ida's lesson?

3) Casey tries to put on a mask to hide her insecurities and keep people at a distance. Do you think that eventually made things more difficult for her?

4) The more life got out of control, the more stressed Casey became. Has your life ever felt out of control? What do you do to de-stress?

5) Casey eventually realizes that God has her best interest at heart. Have you ever struggled with trust? Either trusting people or God?

6) Forgiveness is often very difficult. Do you think Casey and Haley will ever be able to build a relationship?

7) Ryan's quiet example of faith makes a big impression on Casey. When have you seen someone's example make a difference in your own life?

8) Casey's cat caused some trouble. Do you have any crazy pet stories?

9) Casey discovers her love of cooking and enjoys relaxing with sweet tea and a good book. What are some of your favorite dishes and how do you like to unwind?

10) Your turn! Where do you think Casey, Haley, Ryan, and Nancy end up after the end of the book?

*Book club bonus! Everyone make a dish to share and be sure to bring the recipe for your group! Send me pictures of your event to Stephenia@StepheniaMcGee.com and you might see your group on my website or in an upcoming newsletter!

About the Author

Award winning author of Christian historical novels, Stephenia H. McGee writes stories of faith, hope, and healing set in the Deep South. She's a homeschool mom of two boys, writer, dreamer, and husband spoiler. Stephenia lives in Mississippi with her sons, handsome hubby, two dogs, and one antisocial cat. Visit her at www.Stephenia McGee.com for books and updates.

Visit her website at www.StepheniaMcGee.com and be sure to sign up for the newsletter to get sneak peeks, behind the scenes fun, the occasional recipe, and special giveaways.
Facebook: Stephenia H. McGee, Christian Fiction Author
Twitter: @StepheniaHMcGee
Instagram: stepheniahmcgee
Pinterest: Stephenia H. McGee

Made in the USA
Monee, IL
26 February 2021